Susan,

Enjoy!

Mok

10/22/22

BURNT TO A CRISP
A Detective Paddy Durr novel
Book 3

By Michael O'Keefe

Copyright © 2021 Michael O'Keefe

All rights reserved. No part of this book may be reproduced, stored, or transmitted by any means—whether auditory, graphic, mechanical, or electronic—without written permission of the author, except in the case of brief excerpts used in critical articles and reviews. Unauthorized reproduction of any part of this work is illegal and is punishable by law.

ISBN: 9798724215084 (sc)

BURNT TO A CRISP is a work of fiction. Any similarities to real places, events, or persons—living or dead, are entirely coincidental.

Then I heard the voice of the Lord say, "Whom shall I send? Who will go forward for us?" And I said, "Here am I, Lord. Send me."
Isaiah 6:8

In loving memory of the men and women who were the 9/11 first responders who fell on that day and the many days to follow; The police, firefighters, EMT's, and civilian volunteers from all walks of life discarded concerns for their own safety to search amid the rubble for survivors, and then continue to search for the dead, to bring them home. While many have forgotten their brave service and sacrifice, many have not. Even as the afflicted continue to fall around us, knowing what they now know, they would still venture in and have no regrets for having done so. This is the definition of heroism.

DEDICATION

*As ever and always,
For my beloved,
Janet*

Burnt to a Crisp

CHAPTER ONE

March 12, 2017
Plainedge, Long Island
14:00 hours

Paddy listened as the last soft strains of "She Moved Through the Fair" by Sinead O'Connor receded quietly on the radio. Playing on the end-table in the living room of the Durr house, the song became a mournful lullaby expressing the pallor of angst descending so heavily over the Durr family this past year. The haunting effect of the music on Paddy was fitting. He was already seeing ghosts.

Mairead had grown fond of listening to the Irish music program on the Fordham University radio station. Broadcast on Sunday mornings, *Thistle and Shamrocks* had been indulging their Irish listeners yearning for the melancholy songs of their homeland since the 1950s. She had been raised listening to the program every week after attending morning mass at Sacred Heart with her family. Her parents—both born in County Kerry—were raised in New York, but they listened dutifully for years as a way to stay in touch with their Irish heritage. Mairead had rediscovered the station accidentally. When she first became ill, she related to her daughter how she missed the soothing, soulful music. Katelyn was presently attending Fordham University.

"When I was growing up," Mairead related. "Every Sunday, Irish music was playing from the college radio station at your school. No matter what else was going on, those songs made me feel, if not better, at least calm. I wish it was still on."

"It is, Mom. It's still the most popular show on WFUV."

Katelyn tuned the station in for her ailing mother on the Bose radio next to her bed. Mairead had been listening to the show every Sunday since.

Paddy had also been raised by Irish-born parents who listened to the program. As he regarded them as the filthy, white-Irish-trash kind of parents, he developed an acute resentment for the music, regarding it as a soundtrack, playing incessantly in the background of a miserable childhood comprised almost exclusively of neglect and abuse. He never considered the melancholy melodies and doleful lyrics as anything else—until Mairead got sick.

Now he listened with her in the living room of their home in Plainedge. The sofa, coffee table, and loveseat were piled on top of each other in the garage, replaced by the hospital bed provided by the Detective's Endowment Association when Mairead had gotten too ill to make it up and down the stairs of their split-level home. She now spent all of her time propped uncomfortably in the bed. Stage four cancer will do that.

Paddy held Mairead's emaciated and mottled hand ever so gently for fear he would cause her more pain than the excruciating agony the cancer had already forced upon her. Bony, liver-spotted, and brittle, her once well-toned limbs were a horrific caricature of their former selves. Paddy feared he would shatter her with the slightest pressure. Still, he held on as firmly as he dared. Despite his efforts not to let her go, he could feel his wife slipping ineluctably away from him.

As Sinead O'Connor finished the song, which seemed like a dirge to him, Paddy felt a solitary tear escape from the corner of his eye and run slowly down his careworn face. He thought his heart would break if it hadn't already been shattered to pieces. His sense of loss was total. He knew it would take a miracle to save Mairead now, and Detective Durr was a man who didn't believe in miracles.

Mairead, as she always had, sensed his despair and brought him back from the precipice. She had been the source of all of Paddy's strength—his only source—since they first met. Even in her enfeebled condition, she summoned some of her remaining strength for them both.

"I'm not gone yet, Paddy. You'll have to wait a while to mourn me."

"I know," he said, but she knew he was lying.

He had already surrendered to the impending tragedy of it. Even if Mairead still had some fight left in her, Paddy did not. So, in addition to his crushing sense of loss, he piled on guilt. He wanted so badly to be strong for her, but he lacked the necessary tools. Mairead had a resolute faith Paddy could never muster. He had spent his entire life either victimized by or combatting the depraved awfulness of human nature until the worst-case scenario was the only one he ever saw. He tried to joke about his entrenched pessimism. Mairead didn't see the humor.

She understood it was more than just conditioning forced on by his profession. She knew if she left Paddy to his own devices, he would turn insular and succumb to his own despair. So, she kept a vigilant watch on his state of mind, never allowing him to surrender to his basest emotional instincts.

"I try and see the good in people, Mairead—I do, but I'm too familiar with the horrors they're capable of. I expect to be disappointed, and humanity never seems to disappoint me," he said, with a weak smile that was almost a grovel.

"That's only because you're a grim asshole who can't appreciate the beauty in his own life," Mairead observed. "You're obsessed with your own imperfections, to the point where you can't see yours or anyone else's potential for decency. People are basically good, Paddy. Most are flawed—like you—but they try and do the right thing by and large. Realize that before you judge us all as irredeemable—yourself included."

"You're right, of course," Paddy admitted. "I'm trying."

"Not hard enough," she chided. "You can't waste your time mistrusting everybody. Take a break once in a while. You don't have to be a morose prick all the time. Just don't be *that* guy," she admonished him.

Paddy grunted and nodded, conceding the point.

"I love *you,* though," he said, smiling for once. "I'm never *that* guy when I'm with you."

"And I am the luckiest girl—ever!" she said, making them both laugh.

Paddy's inability to get past the gloom, for Mairead's sake if for nothing else, was forcing on him a sense of self-loathing, which was all too familiar. Mairead was acutely aware of this. She knew Paddy better than he knew himself. She also knew she was wasting her time trying to drag him out of the abyss. He would remain there, irrespective of any effort on her part to draw him out. She knew where her power ended. At the very least, she thought, she could force him to focus on priorities, working on getting him back on point. He needed a mission. So, she gave him one.

"Aren't you going to work this afternoon?" Mairead asked, distracting him from his misery for at least a moment.

"You know I'm not. The palliative nurses are off Sundays. They'll be back tomorrow morning. Then I'll go in for my first day-tour."

"You're up for the next homicide, aren't you?"

"Yeah, but I was thinking about taking a leave of absence to take care of you. There's plenty of time for work. People aren't going to stop getting themselves killed. There will always be more murder."

"I can't let you do that, Paddy. You *need* a case, even if it's just to distract you. I hate having to wish harm on anyone—even in the abstract—but you need a body to drop now more than you ever have. I hope you catch one tomorrow."

Paddy nodded his assent, knowing it was pointless to argue with his wife. In the first place, she was intractable in an argument. In the second, she was almost always right. Neither left him much wiggle room.

"I need you to do something else for me, Paddy."

"Anything, Mairead."

"I need you to get your head out of your ass."

"What?" Paddy chuckled.

"No matter how this ends—and we both know it's probably going to end badly—I need you to keep your shit together for the kids. You're not crawling into the hole with me. They need their father now, especially with Patrick and Katelyn deciding to follow you onto that miserable job you treat like a religious calling. And Casey wants to be a doctor. That means a lot more school for her. She can't do that without you. You don't have the luxury of being able to fall to pieces. Now promise me you'll do this."

"I promise," he said, lifting her hand to brush her knuckles with his lips.

Mairead had long been Paddy's focus and reason to be. Before her, the entirety of his life's purpose had been motivated by spite. He had achieved the things he had precisely because he had spent a lifetime being told by everyone he couldn't. While succeeding in the face of such disdain did nothing to alleviate his formidable sense of worthlessness, at least he got essential things done. He allowed his capability to take the place of his non-existent self-esteem.

After meeting Mairead, the spite turned into an unquenchable need to find favor with her. He wasn't just trying to show up an uncaring world anymore. He wanted to make her proud of him. While he didn't find any sense of self-worth in the endeavor, he at least found a positive purpose. Mairead understood Paddy was losing his grip. It's why she made him promise.

She also knew he would keep his word. In all of their years together, he had only broken one promise to her. The destruction of that one betrayal almost cost

Burnt to a Crisp

him everything—even his life. They both knew he would never violate her trust again.

CHAPTER TWO

March 13, 2017
Plainedge, Long Island
06:30 hours

Monday morning, as one of Mairead's palliative care nurses squared away her medications, Paddy kissed his wife but stopped short of actually leaving for work.

"I think I'm gonna bang in today and just hang around here," Durr said.

"You will do no such thing, Paddy," she declared. "Now, get out of here and go to work. Or, I will be forced to get out of this bed and break my foot off in your ass."

"Yes, ma'am," he relented.

***

In his truck on the way to Brooklyn, Durr tried to get his mind around something other than his ailing wife. He tuned into 1010 WINS News Radio and tried to focus on the reporting. He was only incrementally successful.

The lead story was about the murder of a Polish construction worker the night before. It was being investigated as a possible hate crime. The second story was about another murder, also in Brooklyn, occurring a few hours later. This one was being described as a gang-related reprisal-killing.

Burnt to a Crisp

The stories were only vaguely of interest to Durr because the reports weren't specific about where they happened. Recently, Paddy discovered the media had developed the annoying habit of neglecting to identify the street or even the neighborhood where crimes occurred. It was as if they were afraid of offending the people who lived there by suggesting crime could exist in their proximity. Durr viewed this trend as another example of the political correctness and over-sensitivity of this age, serving no other purpose than to obscure inconvenient and unpleasant truths. He knew all the denial in the world couldn't change the fact that a growing percentage of people were vicious, predatory monsters with no regard for human life. In some neighborhoods, the percentage was greater than in others.

Durr had no way of knowing the two murders were both committed in Bushwick. He tuned them out of his consciousness. The third item was about a residential fire, resulting in some severe injuries to the tenants of the apartment house. Three of the victims were in critical condition at the Cornell Burn Center. As this had not been reported as a crime, the reporter identified the location as Wilson Avenue in Bushwick. According to WINS, the cause of the fire was yet to be determined.

As Wilson Avenue was only slightly out of the way on his trip to the 83rd Precinct, Paddy adjusted his route to swing by the scene and have a look for himself. His longstanding mistrust of the media informed him they didn't know anything and would report whatever seemed remotely plausible. There wasn't much promise of veracity with such a meager concern for facts, but he knew he had a better chance of changing the tides than changing the ways of the press. If he wanted to know the truth of a matter, Durr knew he would just have to investigate it himself.

As he made the turn onto Wilson Avenue, he found himself in slow-moving traffic. He could smell the unmistakable aroma of burnt timbers mixed with the sickly-sweet smell of melted rubber, plastic, and wire insulation found only in the aftermath of a structure fire. It would hang like a shroud over the neighborhood for weeks. He could see the crime scene tape cordoning off the building and sidewalk a block ahead of him. Even from here, he could see the building was a charred shell.

Durr pulled into the spot right in front of the two rookie police officers guarding the scene. He threw his parking placard on the dash and jumped out of the truck. One of the cops came over to the curb to intercept him and tell him to move it. Durr rolled his eyes and dolefully shook his head.

"Easy, Ryan," the other police officer told his partner. "This is Detective Durr. He gets to park wherever he wants."

Paddy scooted under the crime scene tape at the curb and approached the cops. After receiving a warm embrace from Carmine Demiri, he introduced himself to Officer Ryan.

"I'm Paddy Durr. I work up in the squad. If you don't know me yet, I'm guessing it's because you're brandy-new, like *Fuzz-nuts* over here," he said, thrusting his chin in Demiri's direction.

Paddy stuck out his hand to the nervous cop. Durr sensed his unease.

"Relax, Officer. I'm not a boss—just a detective. What's your first name?"

"Um—Matt," he said, returning the handshake.

"Well, *Um-Matt*, take my business card," Durr said, handing one over. "You need anything—even advice—you can call me. Anybody up in the squad gives you any shit; you tell them you're one of *my* guys. You'll be taken care of."

"Thanks," Ryan said. "What about one for my partner?"

"This ass-clown?" Paddy said, laughing. "If I'm not already number one on his speed dial, I'm going to have to rethink telling everyone he's my nephew."

"Paddy was my football coach in high school," Carmine clarified for his partner. "He's the one who dragged me down to take the test for the job, and he's the reason I'm in the *eight-three*."

"Oh, cool," Ryan said.

"So, what gives here?" Durr asked.

"Just a fire," Carmine said. "The Fire Marshalls deemed it non-suspicious. Three people are in the burn unit at Cornell. We're here to prevent looters from getting hurt when the rest of the building collapses; fucking waste of time and resources, if you ask me."

"Yeah, but nobody is asking you," Paddy reminded the rookie cop with a sarcastic glare. "You're going to have to get eligible for a pension loan before anybody gives a rat's ass what you think. Do your job, Carmine. Learn it and be patient. They'll let you play with all the big-boy toys soon enough. Well, I'm here; I might as well have a look around."

Durr walked into the hallway through the shattered glass and metal front door frame with the two rookie cops in tow. As was his habit with young cops, Paddy started making his observations out loud.

"The front lobby is approximately fifteen by eight feet—until you get to the open stairwell on the right. You'll notice no debris or smoke damage till you get to the stairs," Durr said, pointing. "The fire never got to the front door. It looks like it shot up that stairwell and burned everything on its way up to the roof," he said, looking up. "You see the debris on the floor in the left corner and along the back wall leading up the stairs? The super must have stored the garbage there until he could put it out for pick-up. It makes for good kindling, plenty of fuel for the fire to spread up the stairwell," Durr said, pointing toward the burned-out roof.

"The skylight must have been open. You can tell from the smoke delineation and the damage up that way, the fire had a substantial oxygen source. It looks like it got sucked right up those stairs. It had to be hot. Look at the metal staircase. It's the only newish thing in the building. The risers and treads are all warped and bent. I don't know how hot a fire has to be to melt steel, but I'm guessing pretty hot."

"How did the fire start?" Carmine asked.

"That's the rub, isn't it?" Durr said, scratching his chin. "I don't know how it started yet, but *that* was the point of origin," he said, pointing in the left rear corner of the hallway.

"How can you tell?" Ryan wanted to know.

"You see the distinct V-shaped pattern in the corner?" Durr indicated. "That's where it started. Look at the sheetrock walls. They're all crinkled and warped. It's called *spalling*. It comes from the moisture in the gypsum getting leeched out of the plaster from the heat. It evaporates, leaving this kind of damage."

"You're a homicide detective," Carmine reminded Paddy. "How do you know all this?"

"I took an Arson and Explosion course the Detective Bureau was offering a few years ago. The detective giving the lecture knew his shit. Some of the science stuck with me. The V-pattern is troubling."

"Why?" Carmine asked.

"Because somewhere in the center of it was the source and ignition of the fire. You can see there is no electric service in the lobby other than the overhead light, and the tubing running up the wall means the wiring originates above the ground floor. There are no electrical outlets or heating ducts and no other innocuous heat sources in the lobby. Somebody had to set this fire."

"But the fire marshals said it wasn't suspicious," Ryan reminded him.

"Well, they were wrong then, weren't they?" Durr said.

"Why didn't they see what you saw?" Carmine wondered.

"There is no guarantee they even got out of their car and went into the building."

"Why would they do that?" Ryan asked.

"The fire marshals just determine if a fire was arson or not," Paddy clarified. "Then investigate it if it's arson. The fire is out before they get here. The cops secure the scene for them. If they don't want to take a case, they don't have to. If they really wanted to screw the pooch, they could make the *no arson* call from their cots back at the base. Nobody checks their work."

"How do they get away with that?" Ryan wondered.

"How long have you been out of the academy?" Paddy asked.

"About a year," Ryan offered.

"In your short time, have you ever noticed there are some cops who would cut their own throats rather than do any police work? Every time they collect their paychecks, they're stealing. Losers like that are permitted to survive in a bureaucracy like the police department," Durr said, frowning sourly. "Because the rest of us are so willing to pick up the slack for them. Well, the fire department is a bureaucracy too. Whoever showed up here last night was just mailing it in. This is a crime scene. I don't care what those fire marshals had to say. Make sure nobody goes into the hallway. I've gotta find someone to come in and collect the evidence before it gets trashed."

"Okay, Paddy," Carmine said. "Can you let the Desk Officer know?"

"I will as soon as I get into the station house," he said, jumping back into his truck to speed off to the precinct.

CHAPTER THREE

March 13, 2017
Bushwick, Brooklyn
08:00 hours

When Paddy got into the precinct; he went right to the desk. Lieutenant Dan Dailey was making entries in the command log. Paddy approached and offered the boss a quick salute.

"What's up, Paddy?" the lieutenant asked.

"Do you have a copy of the unusual occurrence report for the arson this morning on Wilson Avenue?"

"It's not arson," Dan corrected. "The fire marshals deemed it non-suspicious."

"I was just over there with your rookies, Demiri and Ryan. Trust me, Lou," Paddy said, using the diminutive for the rank of lieutenant. "The fire was set by someone. I'm taking a case on it."

Lieutenant Dailey's eyebrows shot up. He trusted Durr's well-honed instincts—Paddy had never steered him wrong—but at this moment, he seemed to be stepping outside some long-established protocols.

"Not really a call you're allowed to make, is it, Paddy?"

"Yeah, I know. It's the *smoke-eaters* bailiwick. But this time, they're wrong. I need the unusual to find out which morons I have to make come out to change their bullshit conclusions."

"So, I take it I have to make this a crime scene. I can do it, but I'm gonna need a criminal complaint sometime today," Dan said, handing Paddy a copy of the report.

"I'll have a complaint and a reclassification for you by the end of the day tour."

"Do I need to tell my rookies what they're supposed to be doing out there, or did you take care of that for me already?" Dan asked, grinning.

"I squared them away. They seem like sharp kids. They asked me to notify *you*. They're not too happy to be on a fixer post, but they'll do their jobs."

"Yeah. They want to be crime-fighters," Dan said. "I told them they'd get their chance, but as rookies, they have to eat their fair share of the shit sandwich first. I think they get it, but they're anxious to get their careers started. Kind of reminds me of us, back in the stone age."

"Don't remind me how old we're getting," Paddy said, rolling his eyes. "Some days, it feels like an eternity since I was swearing-in. Other days, it feels like only yesterday. I finished my thirtieth year in July. How many years you got in now?"

"Thirty-six and a wake-up," the lou said.

"Thinking of making a career of this, or are you still looking for a better deal?"

"I think I'll give this a shot for a while," Dan said, laughing. Then he got serious. "How is Mairead feeling?"

"Not too good. The radiation and chemo really kicked her ass this round. I think it's killing her faster than the cancer. She's tough, though. She's fighting hard."

"Hang in there, Paddy. Jill and I are praying for you two, and my wife takes communion every day. Between that and having to look at my ugly mug day in and day out, I figure God owes it to her to answer her prayers."

"From your lips to God's ear," Paddy said as he headed upstairs to the squad.

When Paddy got up to his office, he found it a hive of frenetic activity. His teammates were busy at their desks, either typing into their computers or conferring with other detectives or supervisors. He recognized two separate teams from Brooklyn North Homicide. One group was huddled around Joe Furio's desk, along with some other detectives he didn't know. The other group from Homicide was working in the corner with Giancarlo Fernandez. Armando Gigante was on the phone and banging away at his computer. A sergeant was observing him Paddy had never seen before. With all the outside assistance, Paddy surmised the shit had hit the fan with a purpose during his night off. He signed in and went looking for his boss.

Paddy found Lieutenant Mariano Martino just getting off the phone in his office. Martino waved him in and told him to sit down.

"How is Mairead?"

"Better than yesterday, but not good," Paddy said, frowning. "No offense, boss—I know everyone is genuinely concerned—but I'm getting tired of having this same conversation. What the hell happened *here* last night?"

"Armageddon," Martino deadpanned. "You want to work on Joe's hate crime or Gio's gang shooting? The game is murder, and it's dealer's choice for you."

"Thanks, Lou, but I thought I might work on the arson from Wilson Avenue."

"Not an arson—the fire marshals found no criminality."

"Those fire marshals couldn't find their asses with an icepick and a GPS. Sorry to have to piss in your Cheerios, but someone set this fire. I just came from the scene, and the patrol unusual says we got a whole family in the burn unit who are likely to die. We've probably got three more murders coming down the pike."

The lieutenant looked up with heavy-lidded and weary eyes. When his gaze was met and held by the unwavering gaze of Durr, Martino sighed and threw his hands up in submission.

"You're fucking killing me, Paddy. How are we going to square this with the fire department? They're the only ones who can change the call to arson."

"I got the fire marshal's name. He works at Brooklyn Fire Command. I'll call him and get him to come back out to the scene and reconsider his classification."

"Just so long as you sweet-talk him. You can't beat the stupidity out of everyone. Sometimes you have to ease them into doing their jobs."

"True enough, Lou, but I always found I could get more with a kind word and a punch in the face than I could with just a kind word."

"Please, Paddy. The last thing I need right now is an interagency pissing contest."

"I promise to be diplomatic."

Paddy checked in with his partners just to let them know what he was working on. Joe Furio had some insight for him.

"We swung by the fire this morning. I thought it was suspicious, but that jerk-off fire marshal, Appodano, was there. He never even went into the building. I think he was afraid to ruin his Ferragamo loafers. He insisted it wasn't criminal. I hate that guy, but I was busy. So, I didn't argue the point. He's gonna tell you to go fuck yourself, you know?"

"Still, I gotta give him a chance to see the light before I crush him."

"Let me know if I can help."

"Thanks, Joe, but you have enough to deal with. How's it going, by the way?"

"It's coming together. We already got an ID, and I got another witness coming in to view the photo array."

"Who is the doer?" Paddy asked.

"The fat kid who steers on Starr Street—Carmelo Boreo. The man-hunt should begin this afternoon. I'd get him now, but the Hate Crimes Task Force wants to make a dog-and-pony show out of everything. They're a nuisance. What the fuck are they even doing here, Paddy? It's a homicide. I don't need their help—bullshit politics is what it is."

"What makes it a hate crime, Joe?"

"The victim was a Polish construction worker. He was as drunk as Rasputin and passed out on the steps of the dope spot at 220 Starr Street. Carmelo tried to shoo him away. He thought the white boy looked too much like a cop and was chasing away his customers. Spiegnew Zeppodowski was his name. When Carmelo was trying to push him off the stoop, Ziggy got up and shoved him on his fat ass. Carmelo went inside and came back with a baseball bat. Witnesses distinctly heard him call the victim a 'white, Polack, motherfucker,' right before caving in his skull."

"Ah—a magic word," Paddy said. "Not much of a slur, though."

"Enough to make the stuffed shirts from headquarters magically appear."

"Lock up Carmelo, and they'll be gone right after the press conference," he predicted.

Paddy approached his desk to find a well-dressed detective he did not know comfortably ensconced in his chair. Ordinarily, Durr wouldn't have become annoyed so quickly if not for the fact the detective was quite clearly doing nothing. He was looking down at his phone, watching what appeared to be YouTube videos. Paddy cleared his throat to get his attention.

"Who are you?" Durr asked.

"Eddie Lebron, from Hate Crimes," the detective said, awkwardly extending his hand. Paddy ignored it.

"Any chance some police work is going to happen while you're watching YouTube?" Paddy asked.

"I was waiting for someone to give me an assignment," he said.

"You're waiting is over," Paddy said, smiling broadly. "Get the fuck out of my desk and make yourself scarce."

Burnt to a Crisp

Lebron jumped out of the chair with a look of frightened confusion. He had never been spoken to like that on the job before. He did not know Paddy. He had no idea if he was a boss or just another detective. But he recognized the unwavering and resolute glare. He instinctively understood he would either have to move or be physically compelled to do so. He started to walk away.

"One other thing, Lebron," Paddy said. "Tell the rest of the headquarters douche-bags, when I am in the building, my ass is the only one authorized to be in this seat."

Eddie Lebron nodded and made a quick left out of the squad.

Paddy sat at his desk and called Brooklyn Fire Command. It took five minutes for Fire Marshal Appodano to come to the phone. When he got there, he sounded like he had been asleep. Paddy apologized for having disturbed him and got right down to business.

"I know the fire on Wilson Avenue must have been crazy. You had to work under difficult conditions. It had to be hot and dark in the hallway. It would have been easy to miss something. I was by there this morning—in the daylight. I have reason to believe it was arson. I was hoping you might do me a favor and take a second look at it. I can meet you there."

Appodano didn't say anything for a moment. Paddy thought he could feel a wall of indignation building on the other end of the line. He braced himself for the fire marshal's retort.

"You don't get to tell me what to do, Detective. The city charter specifically gives the Fire Marshals Service the responsibility to determine whether or not a fire was arson. Why don't you mind your own business?"

"There are three people in the burn unit who are going to die," Paddy told him. "Somebody set the fire. That makes it murder. Murder *is* my business. I just need you to change the classification. I'll take it from there. Then you can go fuck up the next fire, and forget you ever met me."

"Fuck you!" Appodano said.

"Not today, Sparky. I didn't want to have to do this, but I'm going over your head. I'll expose you as an idiot to your bosses—if they don't already know. I know you think you're a big deal and have the final word on this, but you don't. You keep telling everyone you were a cop, and you know all about how the police department works. It sounded like bullshit when I heard it. So, I checked out your story. You spent three years in the one-eleven. Bayside, you could have spent fifty years there and not have a clue about what I do. I'm trying to do you a favor here. Come out and straighten out your fuck-up, and you'll never hear from me again."

"*Not* arson! And that's my final answer."

"Wrong answer," Paddy said, hanging up the phone.

Lieutenant Martino had been listening in to Durr's side of the conversation from the doorway of his office. While he wasn't surprised the situation fell apart so quickly, he was astonished Paddy hadn't rushed out the door to get his hands around the throat of whoever it was he had been speaking to. Martino wasn't sure whether to be thankful for Paddy's uncharacteristic restraint or worried he had stopped caring. He knew Mairead's illness was taking as hard a toll on him as it was on her—at least psychologically. It would be easy to understand if it had been the case. The Lieutenant was grateful to discover the only reason Paddy wasn't on his way to kicking the fire marshal's ass sideways was he had another ace up his sleeve.

"What now, *Kemosabe*?" the lou asked.

"Now I reach out to my friend in Arson and Explosion to ask for a favor," Paddy said.

"Aren't they a little busy with that failed terrorist bombing from last week?"

"Yeah, but Adam Kirwan owes me a solid. He's got hooks in the Fire Marshals Service. We may be able to backdoor that nitwit, Appodano."

"Kirwan is the guy who teaches the A and E-course in the Detective Bureau training, right? To what do we owe his esteemed grace and intervention?"

"Last year, his neighbor's daughter got nabbed in the *nine-oh* for driving impaired. I got the car released and got the girl rushed through arraignment and ROR'd. She was home three hours after the arrest. He told me if I ever needed anything, I should just call. I need this."

CHAPTER FOUR

March 13, 2017
Bushwick, Brooklyn
09:00 hours

Paddy had first met Detective Adam Kirwan in 2008 when they both were lecturing at the Detective Bureau Homicide Course. Durr was delivering a section on interrogation techniques. Kirwan, already regarded as the top dog in Arson and Explosion, gave a primer on the recognition and action protocol for detectives, should they discover an improvised explosive device. Basically stated: run away, evacuate the area, and call the Bomb Squad and A and E forthwith. Sometimes, just realizing you are underqualified to handle a situation and having the good sense to call people who have the needed expertise will save lives. For detectives, recognizing what you don't know can be as important as what you do.

Having hit it off immediately, the two realized they were both the delegates for their respective squads with the Detectives Endowment Association. So they remained in touch, seeing each other at the delegate meetings every month. It was understood they were at each other's disposal if one of them needed assistance with the other's area of expertise.

In 2010, Adam had caught the case of the failed car bomb in Times Square. When Faizal Shahzad, a Pakistani national, was arrested by the Joint Terrorist Taskforce, Adam was the A and E technical expert for the investigation. Along with his analysis of the failed bomb, he was asked to participate in the questioning of Shahzad with respect to his construction of the explosive device. While he knew the science and recognized what the bomb was intended to do and why it failed to do it, he wanted Paddy's advice on how to motivate the suspect into detailing where he got his chemistry and technical information and how he executed the construction of the car-bomb.

"How do I make this guy want to tell me what he knows and how he knows it?" Kirwan asked.

"I would pretend to be an admirer," Paddy said.

"What do you mean?"

"I mean, act like a science nerd. Pretend to be impressed with his knowledge and bomb-making skill. If you blow enough smoke up his ass, he'll puff out his chest and want to brag about his exploits."

"That's going to have to be some acting job on my part because from what I can see, he's an idiot."

"Really?" Paddy asked, laughing.

"Yeah," Adam said. "He obviously has no rudimentary understanding of the simplest electronics and not a clue what an explosive compound is."

"How so?"

"He had four different timing mechanisms supposed to go off simultaneously. He wired these unnecessarily through a nexus in a pressure cooker. It was a tangled mess, and his timing devices weren't properly synchronized. The idiot used alarm clocks to set off firecrackers. These were designed to ignite two five-gallon cans of gasoline. He wrapped those around a twenty-ounce metal can full of M-80 fireworks. But he didn't cap the top of the can. So even if he managed to get the fireworks to go off, the impact would have been mitigated. It would never have been able to ignite the gunpowder, three propane tanks, and the gun locker full of fertilizer."

"Fertilizer?" Paddy asked, confused.

"Yeah. Timothy McVey used ammonium nitrate—basically horse shit—to blow up the Federal Building in Oklahoma City. This guy used urea-based fertilizer—potassium nitrate—essentially animal urine in soil. It's not explosive. It just smells bad."

"He doesn't know that, though, I would guess," Paddy surmised.

"Evidently not. It looks like he threw all of this stuff together from the Anarchist's Cookbook."

"Lie to him anyway," Paddy suggested. "Let him think he's your hero. But make sure the guys in JTTF know you're going to do that. You don't want to step on each other's game plan. They're likely going to press him hard about his contacts, training, and how he got radicalized. If you keep your questioning confined to the technical stuff, you shouldn't have a problem."

As Paddy had predicted, Adam didn't have a problem. After fawning over the suspect as if he were Robert Oppenheimer, Shahzad couldn't give up his information fast enough. He even threw in a few *As-salamu alaykums* to further suggest they were simpatico.

Just this last week, another self-radicalized extremist attempted to do what Shahzad had failed to. But Abu Muhammed Bashir evidently hadn't learned anything from Shahzad's mistakes.

Bashir was a Yemeni refugee who hated his nation of refuge. He also had no understanding of chemistry because he used the same urea-based fertilizer as Shahzad. This time, to alleviate the confusion of the multiple timing devices, Bashir used a hand-held pressure trigger. Intending to be a suicide bomber, he stayed in the car. As a result, all he managed to do was set himself on fire. He was now under guard at the Cornell Burn Unit—waiting to die. He had third-degree burns over eighty percent of his body. So, Adam Kirwan wasn't going to have an interrogation issue with this case, but he was still responsible for documenting all the technical evidence. While he and his unit might be too busy to take a case on the Wilson Avenue fire, Paddy just needed him to make a phone call to prod the fire department to change their classification.

"What can I do for you, Paddy?" Adam asked.

"I'm having a problem with the fire marshals. I got a residential fire in an apartment house. Three people are likely to die. Brooklyn Fire Command mailed it in and called it accidental. I checked out the scene. It looks like arson to me, but the dick-head won't change his finding. I know you're busy, but I was hoping you could use your contacts in the FD to get them to send somebody down to have a second look."

"What's the address?"

"407 Wilson Avenue."

"Meet me there in a half-hour. I'll take a look at the scene. If I see what you see, I'll get you some fire marshals you can work with."

***

A half-hour later, Paddy met Adam in front of the building on Wilson Avenue. He introduced Adam to Officers Demiri and Ryan. Then the two detectives walked into the building together. Kirwan said nothing as he observed the hallway and looked up the staircase. He took a closer look at the spalling on the sheetrock walls and finally focused on the left rear corner Paddy believed was the point of origin for the fire. Adam finally let out a low whistle.

"Whoever called this accidental couldn't have set foot in this hallway," Adam said.

"Well, in his defense, it was dark last night."

"You know we have this new invention called the flashlight, right? You can't miss the fact there is no other innocuous ignition source at the point of origin. This was arson—plain and simple."

Kirwan pulled out his cell phone and called a number from his contacts. As it was ringing, he turned toward Paddy.

"What did you say the fire marshal's name was?"

"I didn't, but it's Appodano."

"Of course it is."

"So, you know him?"

"Everyone does. He's a legendary fuck-up, and militant about it. He probably won't be a fire marshal for long after this."

"I wasn't trying to get him in trouble," Paddy said.

"You didn't. His persistent incompetence did."

Adam diverted his attention to the just answered phone call. Kirwan spoke to someone named Danny. He told him where he was, what he was looking at, and what he needed. He also made a point of mentioning how Fire Marshal Appodano tried to kick this case to the curb. Kirwan thanked whoever Danny was and ended the call.

"That was Fire Marshal Danny Capparzo from the fire department's Special Investigation Unit. He's coming with his partner, Tommy Kennealy. These guys are the big swinging dicks of the Fire Marshal's Service. They'll be at the 83 Squad within the hour. They'll change the finding for you, collect all your evidence, and follow up and assist with your investigation. They'll be your technical experts. They're good guys. They'll give you everything you need, and they work and play well with others. They both rolled over to the FD from our job, and I think they're sorry they did. They're great detectives, even if they are technically firemen."

"I knew I could count on you, Adam," Paddy said.

"What else are friends for?" Kirwan said. "Now, if you'll excuse me, Paddy, I have to get back to Manhattan."

CHAPTER FIVE

March 13, 2017
Bushwick, Brooklyn
11:00 hours

Paddy was conducting computer checks at his desk back at the squad, trying to compile a list of all the displaced tenants from 407 Wilson Avenue. He had copies of the Aided cards, which corresponded to everyone medically treated after the fire. He was cross-referencing this information against the complaint and aided indexes for the address. Also, running the building for arrests and warrants, he discovered one item of interest.

One of the tenants from the third floor, a Jessica Santiago, had a Sergio Palmiero, listed as her boyfriend, arrested for assault several months earlier. Palmiero lived at the address when he had been arrested. He was not listed on the tenant list for the fire this morning. When Paddy found out where the tenants had been placed in temporary shelter, he would have to explore what the dynamic was between them presently.

He had a call into the Red Cross, who had placed the victims. He was waiting for the assigned aid worker to call him back when the squad Police Administrative Assistant called over from her reception desk at the front of the squad.

"Paddy, there are two fire marshals here to see you."

"Thanks, Ms. Lena," Paddy said.

He looked around the squadroom, trying to find some clear space to sit down and have a conference. Seeing every desk and interview room crowded with detectives and the lunchroom filled with witnesses, Paddy realized the only open space was the hallway outside the office.

"I'll come out to them," he said.

When he came out into the hall, he saw two people he would never have imagined were fire marshals. If anything, they looked more like detectives than many detectives do. The fire marshals wore expensive-looking, well-fitting suits and stylish imported loafers—certainly nothing you would walk into a fire scene wearing. In addition, they both had high-end designer wrist watches and diamond pinky rings. Paddy had become accustomed to dealing with fire marshals wearing smelly, smoke-infused fire department windbreakers and debris encrusted black work boots. The difference was refreshing but wholly unexpected. The shorter of the two evidently recognized Paddy because he smiled and extended his hand.

"Paddy Durr, it's an honor to finally meet you. I was at your interrogation lecture at the homicide course—very impressive and helpful. I'm Danny Capparzo. This is my partner, Tommy Kennealy. We're from SIU, so you won't have to deal with that asshole, Appodano."

"Ever again," Kennealy added, shaking Paddy's hand. "By this time tomorrow, Appodano will be back on an engine company in the Bronx—if the scene looks anything like Kirwan described."

"I didn't want to get him in trouble. I just wanted to see the right thing done. In the next day or two, this case is probably going to be a triple-homicide," Paddy explained.

"Don't worry about him," Kennealy went on. "He bought his own trouble. This is not his first issue. I'm tired of him making the rest of us look bad. So, it's back to the firehouse for him."

"We're here to help you with your case," Capparzo said. "We're going to photograph the scene for you, collect all your evidence, bring it to the lab, and see it's tested the right way. Anything else you need for the case, be it canvasses, witness interviews, and anything you need from the firefighters and officers who fought the fire, we are at your disposal."

"I can't thank you guys enough," Paddy said. "I would love to have you come into the squad, but it's a zoo in there. We had two other homicides last night—one of them a bias crime. We've got lots of outside interference right now and absolutely no room to even change your mind in there. How about I come with you? We'll stop at Starbucks on the way to the scene. I'll buy you coffee and tell you what I have so far."

"Starbucks…in Bushwick? When did that happen?" Capparzo laughed.

Burnt to a Crisp

"This neighborhood has changed," Paddy said. "We've got more hipsters than homicides these days—despite what last night might suggest."

"Well then, let's go get a couple of latte's and go look at a fire scene," Kennealy said.

The three investigators left the precinct and got in Capparzo's unmarked blue Chevy Blazer, which looked like someone's family SUV—if not for all the fire gear, evidence collection equipment, and supplies in the rear of the vehicle. The fire department parking placard was also a dead giveaway. This was an official car.

After getting their coffees on Knickerbocker Avenue, they made their way up to 407 Wilson, parking right in front. Officers Demiri and Ryan were still out there, looking bored and miserable after only being on the post for three hours. Paddy felt for them and understood their impatience, but this was the nature of the job. Rookies get the short end of the stick, and fixer posts were as short end as there was. Although guarding DOA's might have been worse, he thought, what with the unpleasant odor.

Paddy introduced the cops to the fire marshals, who went to the rear of the vehicle, took their jackets off, and hung them on hangers in the backseat. Then they took their shoes off and put them in the backseat as well. They donned fire department coveralls, fire boots, turnout coats, and fire helmets. They grabbed a dozen or so of what looked like aluminum paint cans without labels, two spade shovels, and two garden hoes, which looked new, but actually had been cleaned and sterilized since their last use. Along with these, they grabbed tool belts holding a variety of hammers, hatchets, spatulas, putty spreaders, and sheetrock knives. Thus outfitted, they went into the building.

The fire marshals walked through the first floor of the building. Dan Capparzo walked up the melted stairs, stopping to closely observe the warped metal treads beneath his feet. He continued up the staircase until he was out of Paddy's view. Meanwhile, Tommy Kennealy focused on the v-shaped pattern in the corner of the hallway.

"This was the spot, Paddy," Kennealy said. "The fire started here and ran up the stairs. If you look at the debris on the floor, you'll notice the plastics melted and pooled into little droplets. It indicates the use of an accelerant, but I don't smell gasoline. The vapors from gas never completely burn off. Even in a fire this hot, you'd still smell it. The firebug must have used an alcohol-based fluid."

"Where would he get that?" Paddy asked.

"Anywhere; lighter fluid is mostly alcohol. You can get a can of it in every corner bodega in Bushwick. But I'm thinking it may have been kerosene."

"Why is that?"

"It smells a little sweet, and do you see where the wall is shiny down at the bottom of the vee? The residue is almost greasy. That's a common artifact from burnt kerosene. It's a mineral spirit and leaves just that kind of effect."

"So, we just have to figure out where you can buy kerosene around here," Paddy said.

"It's not that easy. Kerosene is an ingredient in paint thinner. That puts anywhere you can buy paint in play. Besides, you can get kerosene in any hardware store. As we already know, almost anything that can be bought and sold can be found in a Bushwick bodega."

"So, we're back to square one with the canvass. We can deal with that," Paddy said.

"Now for the really bad news," Kennealy said. "People throw shit like kerosene and paint thinner out for the garbage every day. It's possible our arsonist picked up his accelerant simultaneous with his motivation—right off the curbside. It would make it very difficult to put the accelerant in his hands—even when we catch him."

"So, we can't prove it's arson?"

"Oh, it's arson. There is enough visual evidence to determine that. The lab will verify from the vapors present in the debris and structural timbers an accelerant was used. It's just that we may not be able to determine where or when the perp got his hands on it. It's the equivalent of the smoking gun in a shooting."

"I don't need the smoking gun right now," Paddy said. "What I need is motive. I got a feeling the secret lies with one of the displaced tenants."

Capparzo came back down to the lobby with a digital camera in his hand. He showed the camera to Kennealy.

"Most of the roof is burnt out, but I don't think we ventilated it. It looks like the fire used the open skylight to ride the oxygen source straight up, like a stovepipe. We'll ask the firefighters, but I'm sure the skylight was open. It's the only explanation for the fire spreading so fast."

"All right, Paddy," Kennealy said. "We're going to need about an hour or two to properly photograph the scene and collect the evidence and comparison samples. We'll bring it all into the squad to voucher it and bring it to the lab. If you wanted to head back now to try and find the tenants, we'll catch up with you there."

"I would love to, Tommy. But, you guys are my ride."

"Have the uniforms bring you back," Danny suggested.

"They're stuck here until the building is secured. There's still a risk of collapse."

"Not an issue. I'll call our Salvage Unit. They'll have this bitch boarded up in fifteen minutes," Tommy assured him.

"Well, all right then. I will see you after."

CHAPTER SIX

March 13, 2017
Bushwick, Brooklyn
13:30 hours

When Paddy got back to the 83rd Precinct with Officers Demiri and Ryan, the three of them stopped in front of the desk. Lieutenant Daily spied them over the top of his reading glasses. He looked up from the blotter to address Paddy.

"The building better have collapsed, or these young officers are in deep shit. They're still on probation. Abandoning a fixer-post is liable to get them fired," Daily said, feigning consternation.

Matt Ryan looked like he was about to vomit. Demiri, to his credit, looked at Paddy and silently seethed. Lieutenant Daily enjoyed his rookies' discomfort for a bit longer before having a good belly laugh.

"If Paddy brought you in here, I'm sure there's a good explanation. So, what-a-ya-got for me, Detective?"

"The fire marshals are processing the scene as we speak. It's officially an arson, as per Supervising Fire Marshal Kennealy. FD's Salvage Unit was just pulling up when we left. When the fire marshals are done with the scene, they'll board the building up tight—no further need for police presence."

"Bravo, Paddy. You got it done even quicker than you predicted. You'll get me a copy of the reclassified complaint and your unusual?"

"I'll knock it out right now and bring it down to you," Paddy assured him.

"You two!" Daily barked at his rookies. The two young cops snapped to attention. "I know fixer posts are a drag, but somebody has to man them. You did a good job today, and you didn't complain. At least, not so I had to hear it. Tomorrow I'm gonna throw you a bone. You two get to run sector Adam/Charlie for the whole tour. There are a few mutts left on Schaeffer Street. Let's see if you can't make a nuisance of yourselves."

The young cops nodded with excitement.

"Go hang out in the lounge till I send someone for you," Daily ordered. "You're gonna do meal reliefs for the sectors the rest of the tour. Now, beat it."

Demiri and Ryan saluted the lieutenant and made a beeline for the door to the basement. They would watch TV in the cop's lounge until summoned to relieve a sector team coming in for their hour meal. After they left, Daily spoke to Paddy.

"You got anything on this yet?"

"It's early. I need to interview the displaced tenants, find out who had a beef that might have prompted some sick twist to burn a building full of sleeping people. Something's gotta stand out. That's a special kind of evil."

"Where did they put the tenants?"

"I don't know yet. I've got a call into the Red Cross. They should have gotten back to me by now. I'm gonna have to rattle someone's cage."

"Don't let me detain you, Paddy. Let me know if you need anything else from us."

"Thanks, Lou," Durr said as he headed upstairs.

"Go with God," Paddy heard as he turned away.

He could visualize the big lieutenant blessing him, as was Dan Daily's custom. *He would have made a great priest*, Paddy thought.

***

When Paddy got to his desk, he went through his steno pad to call the number of the Red Cross in Brooklyn. He had gotten it, and the name of the assigned caseworker from the patrol unusual. Her name, Millicent Wainwright, gave

Paddy no sense of confidence. For some reason, it inspired a feeling of sad weariness and a suspicion that the fact she had not returned his phone call was no accident. Needing to interview the former tenants of the burnt building, he suppressed his reticence and called the Red Cross.

"Red Cross, this is Allison Jenkins. How may I help you?" asked an exuberant and earnest-sounding young woman.

"This is Detective Durr from the eighty-third precinct. May I please speak with Millicent Wainwright?" Paddy asked.

"Certainly," Allison said before shouting across the room.

"Millicent, you have a call."

Paddy thought it ominous the previously friendly Allison shouted the announcement with impatience and a cold, matter-of-fact tone, invoking none of the warmth with which she had answered the phone. He also thought it was telling she had called her co-worker Millicent, and not Millie, or Miley, or some other less formal and endearing name.

"Who is it?" he heard an impatient voice demand in the background.

Paddy thought he detected a clipped waspy northeastern accent, exclusive to the very wealthy, old-money, New England snob set. He knew from experience, people with an accent like that usually thought of themselves as the American aristocracy and would prove to be difficult at best and impossible the rest of the time. His weary sadness was now accompanied by an acidic churning in his stomach.

"It's a Detective Durr from the 83rd precinct," Allison shouted back. "He asked for you. Next time the phone rings on your desk, pick it up. I'm not your secretary."

"I'm far too busy with my fire victims to waste time speaking with some cop."

Paddy could almost feel the sneer that probably accompanied it.

"I assume you heard all of that," Allison said, returning to the phone.

"Yeah. She sounds like a treasure."

"Actually, she's an entitled brat. But her shift ends at five, and she never stays late—no matter what we have going on here. I'm guessing you're calling about the fire on Wilson Avenue. If you come after five, I can go through her notes and give you whatever you need."

"Thanks, but I'm afraid I need it sooner."

"Then you're going to have to come here and pry it out of her. There's no way she's coming to the phone."

"I planned on coming anyway. Just answer a few general questions for me. How old is *the princess*, approximately?"

"No approximation necessary. Her birthday was last month. She brought in a cake for herself and gave everybody a gift—the same obnoxious leather pencil cup embossed with *her* name. She's twenty-six."

"Does she live in Brooklyn?"

"On the Promenade in Brooklyn Heights."

"Where in *Yankeeland* is she originally from?"

"Bennington, Vermont. Her family founded the city. They still own most of it. We thought she believed she was a Kennedy. It turns out; she grew up with them."

"College?"

"Columbia, and she'll never let you forget it."

Paddy laughed. Having graduated from the school, he knew a degree wasn't as impressive an accomplishment as some people believed. It was his experience the people most impressed with themselves were the academic lesser-lights who barely graduated. He also knew that while the criteria for being accepted to Columbia was as stringent as other Ivy League schools, if your family donated a wing to the library or funded the construction of a building on campus, it didn't matter what your GPA was or what you scored on the SATs. As long as you could spell cat without being spotted the C and the T, you were getting in. Once you were in, you could collect a steady stream of Ds. Even at Columbia, D stands for Degree.

"What does she drive?" he asked.

"Really? Could it be anything but a Prius hybrid?"

"Of course it is. The scumbag sense of superiority comes standard with that model."

"You're funny, Detective. It's like you already know her."

"Unfortunately, I know the type. It's unfair to generalize, but I'm never off the mark when I do," Durr lamented.

"All right," he continued. "I need to check a few things and stop off at the DA's office. I can be by you in an hour. Don't leave. You won't want to miss when I turn her world upside down."

"I can't wait."

After hanging up with Allison, Paddy got to work on his computer doing a full background check on Millicent Wainwright. She made it easy by disclosing her whole life on the internet and social media. She even had her own Wikipedia page. He particularly enjoyed the photo of their "summer cottage" in Hyannis Port. Only royalty could refer to a ten-bedroom mansion on the beach as a cottage. She thought she was bragging. What she was doing was providing Paddy with the tools and material to deconstruct her to her pampered and spoiled rotten core. Durr was looking forward to meeting the self-styled *Duchess of Bennington*.

CHAPTER SEVEN

March 13, 2017
Downtown Brooklyn
14:30 hours

Paddy arrived at the Kings County District Attorney's Office a short while later. He rode the elevator up to the 16th floor, where the offices of the Homicide Bureau were located. Not having an appointment with a specific Assistant District Attorney, he stopped at the reception desk to speak with Ms. Tolliver.

"Hello, Paddy," she said, smiling. "Who are you here to see?"

"Nobody in particular, Ms. T. I just need someone to write a subpoena for me. Anybody available?"

"Dan Bibb is in his office. I'm sure he'll be happy to help you."

Paddy thanked Ms. Tolliver as she buzzed him through the door into the inner sanctum of the Homicide Bureau, just a room with the DA's offices along the walls and a cubicle farm in the middle for the support staff. Durr made the right past the conference room and down to Dan Bibb's corner office with the window view overlooking the Brooklyn and Manhattan Bridges and the majestic skyline of lower Manhattan.

Michael O'Keefe

Bibb must have finished his court business for the day, Paddy observed, because he appeared to be the most relaxed giant man in a tiny box Durr had ever seen. The corner office was bigger by half than the offices along the walls. Even still, the room had trouble containing the larger-than-life prosecutor. Bibb had his huge size sixteen stockinged feet crossed and hanging off the corner of his desk. He was reclined back in his office chair, which looked like it could have been in another zip code; it was so far away from his feet. Dan was absently working the New York Times crossword puzzle and listening to the Grateful Dead on a CD player on the shelf behind him. He looked out over his reading glasses to see Paddy poke his head in the door. Bibb's face lit up, the corners of his gunslinger mustache lifting to reveal a smile so broad and genuine, it warmed Paddy's fractured heart.

Dan pulled his enormous feet from the desk and slowly rose to unfurl his six-foot, nine-inch frame. He came around the desk to hug his friend.

"Paddy, my boy, what brings you down to see me?" the former college basketball player asked. Paddy disappeared in the wingspan of Dan's embrace. When they had first met twenty years before, Durr asked Dan why he wasn't playing in the NBA. The prosecutor was refreshingly candid.

"I had the whole package, save one thing," he admitted. "My first step off the dribble was so slow; it was positively glacial. I'm an athlete, but the NBA is another class entirely."

They got along very well, sharing the status of former college athletes who hit the ceilings of their potential abruptly, stumbling haphazardly into what they were meant to do. They now occupied opposite sides of the same coin. But, what they most had in common was a religious zeal to bring murderers to justice. They had worked more than a dozen homicides together, and Paddy thought if he managed to solve this arson, Dan Bibb would be the exact prosecutor he would want to bring the case.

"Getting a little beefy there, *Dan-o*," Paddy joked.

"Fuck you very much!" Bibb said, feigning offense.

Despite the fake chagrin, Paddy knew his weight was Bibb's sore-spot—which was ludicrous. Dan was long, lean, and covered with tight wiry muscle. He hadn't put on so much as an ounce of body fat since his college playing days. But, a Daily News reporter once referred to him in print as *beefy*. His weight had been an obsession ever since.

"Just messing with you, boyo," Paddy laughed.

"So, what's the rumpus?" Bibb asked.

"I got an arson that's probably going to be a triple homicide in a day or two. I need to find the tenants of the building. The aid worker from the Red Cross is a delusional millennial. She doesn't think she has to cooperate with the police. She won't even come to the phone. I need a subpoena for her paperwork."

"That's easy," Bibb said, turning to his computer screen to write the document. "Gimme a victim's name."

"Mom looks like she might go first. Lucinda Santapadre is her name. Specify on the subpoena I want the originals."

"This millennial really pissed you off, huh?"

"You have no idea."

"Okay then. You have an order for the immediate surrender of all documents, photos, recordings, or any other records pertaining to the displaced residents of…I need the address."

"407 Wilson Avenue."

He typed the address and hit enter.

"What's the deal with this case?" Bibb asked as he printed two copies of the subpoena.

"Somebody torched the building. The three victims are an eighty-year-old sickly couple and their thirty-five-year-old son with Down Syndrome. They could not have been the intended targets and are probably the most innocent victims I've ever had."

Bibb looked into Paddy's face and saw the raw fury there. It stirred a similar ire in the veteran prosecutor.

"When they go out of the picture, I'm your first call. I want this case," Dan insisted.

"I was counting on that," he said.

***

When Paddy got down to 200 Schermerhorn Street, he saw the hive of activity on the second floor through the windows. He checked the building directory to be sure. He took the stairs one floor, eschewing the elevator, which looked suspect in the old and decrepit building. At the landing, he found himself in front of a double glass portico door that no longer sat correctly within the metal door frame. The glass, or what he could see of it around the numerous strips of duct tape holding the cracked panes together, was filthy and smudged with what looked like thousands of sweaty handprints. The gold leaf lettering across the top was chipped and flaking away. Paddy could just make out what it said; *American Red Cross, Brooklyn*. He was impressed with the ramshackle state of the office so far. Knowing the Red Cross was one of the best-funded charities in history, he was pleased to see none of the money wasted on amenities. It appeared the building would fall apart before the aid workers bothered even to slow down enough to notice their place of work crumbling around them. He was heartened to see that kind of single-minded devotion to duty.

Walking through the broken doors, he came to the reception desk. It was as harried as the rest of the office. Behind it, Paddy could see a cubicle farm of desks; the people behind the low partitions were many and all talking at once. Other aides were sprinting around the room from one workstation to another, carrying reams of paperwork. The receptionist was maintaining two phone calls at once. She had separate receivers pressed to each ear while scanning something or other on her computer screen. She looked up from the desk to see Paddy waiting patiently to speak with her. She silently mouthed the words; *how may I help you?* Paddy gestured he would wait for her to finish.

While the young lady continued with her otherworldly demonstration of multi-tasking, Paddy took the opportunity to observe her. She was very young, maybe eighteen or nineteen—probably an intern. Despite the frenetic pace of life within this hive, she didn't seem to be bothered by it. She looked like she was in the zone. Her indomitable spirit was confirmed for Paddy when she finished her two phone calls. No sooner did she put the phones back on their cradles when they both started ringing again. She ignored them for a moment, looked up at him with a pleasant smile.

"Whoo! Busy today. How may I help you, sir?"

Paddy smiled back and produced his shield from his belt where he wore it.

"I'm Detective Durr," he said pleasantly. "Ms. Allison Jenkins is expecting me."

"Oh, easy peasy," she said. "Allison's desk is in the first cubicle on the right. She's nice."

"She was very helpful on the phone. So are you. What's your name?"

"Heather, but I don't really work here. I'm doing a volunteer internship for my major in college."

"Don't sell yourself short, Heather. You're working very hard to help other people, and you're doing it for free. That's called God's work. You're good at it, too."

"It's easy here," she said, blushing. "Everyone is so nice."

"Not everyone," Paddy corrected her. "I'm here to give someone a hard time. She was decidedly not nice—or helpful."

"You're the detective Millicent wouldn't talk to," she said knowingly.

"It might get a little ugly," he warned her. "Please don't think harshly of me when it does."

"Oh, not at all. You were right. She's *not* nice—to anyone."

Paddy gave her a conspiratorial wink as he made his way to Allison Jenkin's cubicle. When he got there, he looked in to discover an attractive brunette wearing glasses, working on her computer. She appeared to be in her early thirties. The intensity with which she was interfacing with the machine gave him the impression she was in equal parts intelligent and feisty. Still, he realized he might have gotten the feisty vibe from when he overheard her scolding Millicent earlier. He took the opportunity to look around her little office. His attention was drawn to a framed photo on the shelf beside her. It was a picture of Allison, a set of apparent twins—a boy and a girl—who looked to be about three years old. Standing behind them proudly was a handsome policeman. The young cop was wearing his class-A dress uniform and had an NYPD Medal of Valor draped around his neck. In the background, Paddy recognized the courtyard in front of One Police Plaza. This was a Medal Day photo.

Allison finally looked up from her computer and saw him there. She inspected him with a critical eye, then smiled.

"Hello, Detective Durr," she said.

"Good guess. How'd you know?" Paddy asked.

"I Googled you," she admitted. "You're famous."

He knew a Google search of his name produced a myriad of results. Depending upon who wrote the item, he was either a hero or a villain. There were also some interesting photos of him online and some articles and links to his novel, *A Thing of No Particular Worth*. But Paddy knew most people were drawn to the more spectacular and salacious items, beginning with the Washington Heights Riots in 1992.

"More like notorious," he said.

"Not hardly," Allison disagreed. "Once you sift out all the bullshit hit-pieces, the image that emerges is very impressive."

"Nice-looking family," Durr said, thrusting his chin in the direction of the Medal Day photo, anxious to change the subject. "Who's the *flat foot*?"

"My husband, Peter," she said, seeming to swell with pride. "He's in anti-crime in the *seven-nine*. I asked him about you. He said you were a legend. You're the guy all the young cops want to be when they grow up."

"For their sake, I hope not," he said, laughing.

"You're too modest. It really is an honor to meet you."

He reached into his inside jacket pocket and came out with two business cards, the ones with his cell phone number reserved only for friends. He handed them to Allison.

"Hold onto one of those. If you need anything in Bushwick, I better be your first call. Give the other one to Peter. If he needs anything job-wise, like a Detective Bureau interview or a recommendation, I can get it for him."

"That's very kind of you. Now, what can I do for *you*, Detective?"

"If you're not too busy, please take me to meet Ms. Wainwright. I need to serve her with this."

He handed Allison the subpoena. She scanned it and looked up, grinning.

"And if she fails to comply?"

"I brought handcuffs. I've never been shy about using them."

"Oh, she's going to lose her shit. This will be delicious. Come with me," she said, leading Paddy down the aisle to Millicent Wainwright's cubicle.

Once there, Paddy was brought up short. He felt like he was looking at an apparition from his past. Millicent Wainwright was seated at her desk talking on the phone with someone named Buffy. He couldn't miss the presence of her clipped, nasally, New England accent. She seemed to be making plans for the coming weekend. They involved a private jet to Aspen. She looked to be in her mid-twenties and was wearing designer clothing Paddy thought cost more than his bi-weekly salary. *The Devil does wear Prada*, he thought. Her flawless hair and skin lent her a certain attractiveness, but perversely, he found it somehow dull. She projected a waspy perfection that once awed him but now brought on vague feelings of disappointment and resentment. When Allison cleared her throat to get her attention, Millicent turned and regarded them both with an annoyed look of haughty disdain. She hurried Buffy off the phone and turned back to them.

"What do you want *now*?" she asked, her words dripping with condescension.

"There is a man here to see you," Allison began. "He's going to need some things. Now, I'm not your supervisor, so I can't order you to do it, but as your senior, I strongly advise you to comply."

"I don't have to comply with anything," Millicent said, jutting her chin out in defiance.

"I had hoped you would say that," Allison said. "She's all yours, Detective."

"Detective?" she spat. "I'm far too busy to waste my time with something as meaningless as police business."

Paddy chuckled to himself, smiled obsequiously, and produced his shield and identification.

"I'm Detective Durr," he said. "The guy you wouldn't deign to speak with on the phone, remember? Perhaps you were too busy setting up your little ski trip. You're going to make time for me now, though."

"I don't have to do anything for you," she spat. "I learned at Columbia; no one has to cooperate with the police. It's my right to resist."

"I'm not surprised you think so," he said. "But that's because you earned a bullshit degree in social work. It's hard to know how many other lies the professors foisted upon you. You might as well have majored in basket weaving for all the practical knowledge they provided. I graduated from Columbia, too, class of '84. I earned a real degree—Bachelor of Arts in comparative literature. It hasn't been of any use to me in my chosen profession, but the thirty years I've been doing this work has. Among other things, it taught me to read. You should read this."

Paddy put the subpoena in front of Millicent and waited for her to read it. Instead, she demanded to know what it said.

"That is a *subpoena duces tecum*. It's a court order. What it says is, you, Millicent Wainwright, are to produce and surrender to me, Detective Padraig Durr, all documents, notes, and records pertaining to the displaced tenants of 407 Wilson Avenue. If you do not immediately produce and hand over these items, the court authorizes me to drag your bony, elitist ass to jail. Then I take the paperwork anyway. So how do you wanna play it, Princess?"

"I am not a princess, and I'm not an elitist!" she screeched. "I lived in Harlem in college, and I live in Brooklyn now. I help people. What would you know about that? You cops just want to shoot and arrest minorities."

"That's an awful lot of bullshit you're selling, sister. You know I'm a detective, right? I investigated you before I came down here. It wasn't difficult. You've put your entire pampered and pathetic life on the internet. I Googled you, and my computer almost burst into flames."

Paddy shook his head before continuing.

"First of all, Morningside Heights is not Harlem," he continued. "Harlem doesn't overlook Riverside Park. Real Harlem was all burnt-out cars and dumpster fires. I know. When I went to Columbia, I lived on 128th Street and Frederick Douglas Boulevard. My neighbors were all junkies, thieves, and prostitutes. Yours were just other rich people. And the Promenade in Brooklyn Heights isn't *really* Brooklyn. It's a more expensive version of the upper east side, with a better view. So, you're not from the hood, sweetheart. But *I* am. I was born and raised in Bushwick when it was a place you wouldn't have stepped foot in, even with an armed escort. I'm still in the same neighborhood, helping and protecting the people who live there. You, on the other hand, are a tourist. You're only doing this to establish your liberal, shithead cred. Then you'll quit to move back to Connecticut, where you'll marry some other douche-bag one-percenter. You'll squeeze out a few brats, who their nannies will raise, before you send them off to boarding schools to learn to be self-indulgent assholes like yourselves. Meanwhile, you'll graciously accept a seat on the board of some charitable organization—for seven figures, of course. You'll be a big hit at the cocktail parties, relating your adventures helping the great unwashed. Well, I happen to be a card-carrying member, and we recognize you for what you are. We laugh at you because you're not important enough for us to despise. But you are despicable, the way you use us to lie to yourselves about how your pathetic avaricious lives have meaning. They don't, and you won't be missed when you're gone. Now, gimme my fucking stuff!"

Wainwright looked like she had been slapped. She could feel the weight of every disapproving eye looking at her. She knew her co-workers didn't like her, but this was the first time she had an inkling of what a joke they thought she was. Still, she felt the need to retain some semblance of dignity. So, as she gathered up her papers and notes from the fire scene, she mustered her last bit of defiance.

"I'm afraid you're out of luck. The copier isn't working."

"That's okay," Paddy assured her. "I'm taking the originals," he said, pulling them from her hands.

"My address is on the subpoena. When I'm done, you can come to my office to pick them up. Don't bother sending someone else. I won't give them back to anyone but you. I won't be holding my breath waiting for your call, though. I don't believe you have the courage to venture out of this building beyond getting into your Prius for the ride home. It's been real, Millicent," Paddy said as he turned to leave with his documents.

Burnt to a Crisp

Back at the front desk, he thanked Allison for her assistance. She was clearly in a buoyant state, excited and bouncing on her feet.

"That was awesome!" she said. "It must have been very satisfying for you."

"Satisfying is not the word I would use," Paddy frowned.

***

When he got down to Schermerhorn Street, he felt a wave of disappointment and shame wash over him. He realized he had expended precious time and energy to punish someone who deserved to be set straight but in no way earned the acrimony and disdain he focused on her. He knew he was just projecting the unresolved anger and resentment he still held for someone else. He was ashamed because despite leaving that someone else in his rearview mirror over thirty years ago, he still let it twist him into a blinding rage when he thought of her mistreatment.

He hadn't intended for it to happen. Still, when he heard Millicent's northeastern accent, coupled with the entitled condescension, he was thrust back to a time when he had let himself be vulnerable enough to love someone who had no intention of ever loving him back. He was still angry about it all these years later—more so for his gullibility and naivete than at the girl for hurting him. What bothered him even more, was it tapped into his carefully suppressed but still prominent sense of worthlessness. He could find himself awash in the same familiar sense of it, brought on by the nagging feeling that even for all of her cruelty, her low opinion of him was still somehow justified.

Michael O'Keefe

CHAPTER EIGHT

November 23, 1984
Washington Heights, New York
21:30 hours

Paddy was in his final year at Columbia, bartending at Coogan's Pub in Washington Heights. His college football career had just ended. He was now free to work on the weekends to go along with the two shifts during the week he used to sustain himself through school. His scholarship, though generous, only paid for his tuition and books. After his first year, his room and board became his own responsibility. He also needed money if he wanted to eat. He had been fortunate to have two friends—really guardian angels—who hooked him up with the bartending gig. He was now getting along well enough not to need to delve into shadier endeavors to keep himself housed and fed.

Coogan's was conveniently located halfway between Columbia University's main campus in Morningside Heights and the athletic facilities by Wein Stadium at the very north of the island. It was also in the shadow of Columbia's Medical School, attached to Presbyterian Hospital on Broadway. Despite being in the middle of the worst drug-infested war-zone the city had ever known, Coogan's still attracted a loyal following from the hospital staff and medical school. It was also a favored watering hole for the cops and detectives from the neighboring police precincts.

Word had spread south to the main campus. Now, the more adventurous students need only take a short subway ride uptown to indulge their sense of adventure yet remain in a relatively safe and homogenous environment. Paddy got a kick out of their pretensions of being cosmopolitan inner-city dwellers. Coogan's was an oasis in an otherwise teeming desert of violence and bedlam. They were safe and protected there—not slumming—as they imagined. He laughed when he thought how they might react if they were to somehow wander accidentally into *his* old neighborhood. He knew it would scare the *liberal* right out of them.

Paddy spotted Blair Pickering Winthrop at the other end of the bar. She seemed to keep popping up in his world lately. Ordinarily, this wouldn't raise much curiosity. They did attend the same school. Social circles, even disparate ones, tend to intersect in a sample size that small. Even still, Paddy wouldn't have expected to see someone of her pedigree in a place like Coogan's—maybe the Oak Room at The Plaza, but not Coogan's. He started to get the feeling she might be stalking him.

He had first seen her in a sociology elective they were both taking. He got the sense she was looking at him from across the lecture hall, but when he would try to meet her gaze, she would quickly look away. This was not a unique experience for him. In the upper-class academic Mecca of Columbia, he was the eight-hundred-pound gorilla. Though clearly a brilliant student, Paddy made no effort to hide his under-class origins. With his long hair, tattoos, earrings, and casual dress, he was a curiosity for his insistence on not fitting in. He was having no part of the preppy style almost mandated at the school. He wore jeans and tee shirts most of the time. He didn't even own any of the khakis, oxfords, and blazers, which served as his well-to-do classmates' de rigueur outfit.

He owned a dress travel uniform issued to him by the football program. It consisted of a navy-blue blazer, beige dress slacks, a white shirt, and a striped power tie. But, Paddy was only wearing that get-up for travel with the team and football events—like the one at the Downtown Athletic Club, when he was selected for the Academic All-American Team.

At this moment, he was wearing his standard bartender uniform; black tee-shirt, blue jeans, and Doc Martens. Blair Winthrop didn't seem to mind. Paddy noticed she was staring at him, and she wasn't averting her eyes when he looked back.

Michael O'Keefe

As he made his way toward her at the end of the bar, he saw she was alone. That she would show up at Coogan's without a coterie of friends, or at least one male escort, suggested to Paddy she might be there for him. He sauntered over to see for sure.

"Can I get you anything?"

"I'll have a glass of chardonnay," she said.

"Of course you will," Paddy said, smiling.

He poured the wine into a crystal goblet and set it gently in front of her.

"Are you meeting someone?"

"Actually, yes," she said, plunking down an American Express Platinum card.

"I'll get back to you for that," he said, moving off to help another customer.

Paddy considered whether it was worth the effort to break out the credit card imprinter for a two-dollar glass of wine. Discarding it as an option, he decided he was going to buy the rich girl some drinks.

When he returned, Blair smiled at him. Paddy gave her another glass of wine, sliding her credit card back to her.

"You hold on to that," he said. "Your drinks are with me."

"Thank you, but I want to leave you a tip."

"I appreciate it, but the calculus involved in getting a tip from a credit card purchase is beyond even Ivy League math," he said. "Is your date not coming?"

"I don't have a date. I came here to see you," she said.

Paddy was surprised by her candor. He chuckled to himself.

"How do you even know me?"

"We're in Professor Wescott's sociology class together," she reminded him.

"That's a big class in a huge lecture hall. I didn't get the impression you knew I even existed."

"I know you saw me looking at you," she said. "But you never came over to talk to me. I've been noticing you for some time."

"Is that a fact?" Paddy asked, doubtful.

"It is," she insisted. "I must confess, I abhor football, but my girlfriend, Poppy, dragged me to a game last month. I couldn't take my eyes off you. I've never seen intensity like that."

"How did you even know it was me?"

"You had all of that hair and the tattoos. When you came off the field, you took off your helmet to get water. I said to Poppy, 'My God, he's beautiful.' She warned me to stay away, saying you were a savage, but I don't think so. I started watching you in class. You keep quiet. You don't offer your opinion unless

Burnt to a Crisp

Wescott calls on you. Then you're thoughtful—reserved. Dare I say, brilliant? The professor doesn't call on you often because he knows you're smarter than he is. But when you disagree with him, you at least let him keep his dignity. Savages don't act that way. You intrigue me. I was told I could find you here. So here I am."

"I have no idea how to respond," Paddy said with an uneasy smile.

He understood she was seducing him; the flattery slathered on thick. But he had to admit; it was working. Now *he* was intrigued. This incredibly gorgeous, refined, and obscenely wealthy young woman had referred to him as brilliant and beautiful. He certainly didn't think of himself in those terms. He had never been referred to as such before.

What he couldn't figure out was her end-game. He suspected she had one. Prior to this, he didn't regard himself as being of the same species as a girl like Blair. He wasn't prepared to be revered, not by someone like Blair Pickering Winthrop.

Despite not buying in altogether, he still enjoyed the attention. Paddy wasn't about to stop Blair from fawning over him. If it's what she wanted to do, it was okay with him. So, between serving other customers, he kept coming back to her. She was nursing her wine. He only needed to refill her glass twice. She stayed until closing time, not speaking to anyone else at the bar, patiently waiting for him to serve his customers, depending on him to return to her.

At a quarter to four, Paddy mentioned the time.

"It's getting late," he observed. "Do you have a ride home?"

"I was hoping *you* could take me home," she said.

"You're welcome to come with me, but my ride is the *iron horse*."

"The subway?" she said excitedly. "Will you take me?"

Paddy agreed, even though he lived nowhere near her. He surmised she was on the Upper West Side, most likely Morningside Heights. Definitely not in his neighborhood, in the heart of the most crime-infested part of Harlem. He figured he would escort her home and jump back on the train to 125th Street.

After the bar closed and he finished restocking the shelves, he and Blair got on the downtown number one train at 168th Street and Broadway. She held tightly to his arm the whole way. The only other passengers on the train were homeless people. Most of them were sleeping, but a few were awake—staring at her and mumbling to themselves.

"I've never been on the subway before," she admitted. "I'm a little freaked out."

"Relax," Paddy said. "Just keep your hands away from their faces and don't stare directly at them. They'll leave you alone."

A few minutes later, a transit cop entered their car. He walked down to position himself against the door opposite them. Paddy made his act immediately. He saw him repeatedly glimpsing Blair through the corner of his eye, keeping her in his periphery. Blair evidently misunderstood his intent.

"I'm glad the police officer is here to watch over us," she said.

Paddy snorted in laughter.

"What's so funny?" she demanded.

"He's not here to watch over us," Paddy explained. "At least not in the way you mean it."

"I don't understand."

"He's here to check you out."

"That's ridiculous!"

"No, it isn't, and I can't even begrudge him."

"What is *that* supposed to mean?" she asked, her eyes narrowing.

"Don't misunderstand me," he said. "He's not looking to hit on you. To him, you represent a breath of fresh air."

"You've lost me," she said.

"Look at it from his perspective. This poor guy has to ride the trains all night, looking at nothing but dirty, crazy, drunk, and smelly bums. They are the worst-case scenario for what happens when a society decides to empty its mental hospitals as a cost-cutting measure. Where do you think they go? They become *that* man's problem. Not to help them—he's been given no tools or brief to do so. The Transit Authority puts him here to step in if one of them should act out. He spends eight hours a night, for days on end, having to babysit the abandoned dregs of society. How miserable must that be?"

"It's awful," Blair agreed, scrunching her nose.

"But tonight, you come on his train. You're beautiful, behaved, you even smell good. As far as he knows, you're not crazy or likely to attack anyone. So, he's relaxed. He's going to camp out there and stare at you on the sly. It reminds him the world isn't filled exclusively with misery and shit. There's beauty and possibility yet."

"That's sad."

"Yeah," Paddy concurred. "But when the sun comes up, he gets to go home, wash the grime off from his miserable day, and presumably spend time with people he loves. He'll be back on this train at midnight to do it all again. I admire the hell out of him."

"You're sensitive," Blair said as if it just occurred to her.

"Not really," he said. "I just have an appreciation for other people's struggles."

They sat in silence for the rest of the trip. Blair, still with her arm locked securely through his, squeezed and held on a little tighter. Paddy thought it wasn't out of fear anymore and imagined it was genuine affection.

When they got up to exit the train at the Columbia University station at 116th Street and Broadway, he led Blair toward the door their police escort was standing in. He nodded to the cop, who appeared to look disappointed to see them go.

When they got to the street, Blair took Paddy's hand and led him toward Morningside Park. The buildings on their left, overlooking the park and the river, were private residences. They had fancy names and doormen in full livery out front. A New Yorker all his life, Paddy had never been to this section of the city. He felt like he was walking through an alien landscape—one where he didn't belong.

Blair continued to lead him by the hand until they came to an enormous and ornate building. Paddy had to crane his neck back to count all twelve stories. It commanded a presence over everything around it. He was fascinated by the rusticated limestone. The top three stories visually bled into an immense and intimidating capital with intricately carved friezes and cornices. He had seen similar architecture on the older buildings at Columbia, but nothing with this kind of grandeur.

They approached the gilded and glass entrance marquee. The gold lettering announced they were in front of 404 Riverside Drive. Above that, it said *The Strathmore*. Two torches of bronze with crystal globes bracketed the enormous and intricate doors. The doorman was dressed in an ankle-length coat of plush scarlet wool, with gold buttons and brocade everywhere. The enormous shoulder boards and high round-billed officer's hat made Paddy think of a World War II Soviet General. He blanched when the doorman greeted Blair by name and held the door open for them.

He thought he was just walking Blair home, but she kept pulling him forward to the elevator.

"I want you to see my apartment," she said, coming around to face him.

"I would love to, but it's late. I have a class in the morning," Paddy said.

Michael O'Keefe

Blair either didn't hear him or chose not to. When the elevator arrived, she pulled him into the old-fashioned car. An elevator operator in the same elaborate uniform as the doorman also greeted her by name. He manually shut the polished brass gate and door and pushed the lever to send the car lurching upward. Paddy watched as the steel needle above the door tracked the progress of the elevator. It didn't stop until they had reached the top floor.

When they arrived, the operator opened the enclosure and wished them good morning before closing the doors and silently disappearing.

They emerged into an enormous hallway with luxurious rugs over marble floors, numerous French provincial side tables with fresh roses and orchids in elaborate and delicate vases. The walls were decorated with enormous mirrors in gilt frames. Paddy was astounded by the high ceilings—at least fifteen feet tall. Skylights of opaque frosted glass covered two-thirds. The center was commanded by a gold and crystal chandelier. Paddy noticed there were only two doors on the floor. One was listed as 12S and behind him 12N. Blair led him to the second one.

He was astonished when she got to the heavy, formidable-looking apartment door and opened it without the need of a key. This was a phenomenon alien to his understanding of life in New York. Where he grew up and lived, the rule of thumb was you locked up your apartment. If you didn't, someone would be by to relieve you of all your possessions. They would even take a red-hot stove and come back for the smoke. Blair evidently did not live in that reality.

Once inside, she led him through a foyer bigger than his whole apartment. It led to a sunken living room with inlaid parquet floors, area rugs that looked more comfortable than his bed, and stunning white overstuffed couches and loveseats. Just looking at the plush furniture made him feel sleepy—but only briefly. Blair took his pea coat from him and laid it on the sofa. She removed her Burberry plaid coat and placed it next to his, pulling him further into the apartment.

They came to a long hallway that ran away in two directions. Blair yanked him to the right, past a half-dozen rooms, to the last door at the end of the corridor. She opened it to the master bedroom. Though the bed was a huge California king with a canopy in a baroque carved oak frame, it was dwarfed by the room's sheer enormity. Paddy felt like it was the size of a gymnasium. He was surprised when their voices didn't echo back at them.

Blair grabbed him by the back of his neck, coaxing his face down to hers. As their mouths explored each other hungrily, she started tugging at his clothes. Freeing his tee-shirt from his jeans, pulling it up and over his head, and dropping it on the floor at their feet, she caressed the taught muscles of his chest and stomach before taking a step back.

Paddy could see through her sheer blouse and camisole she wasn't wearing a bra, her nipples erect and hard beneath the thin garments. She discarded these, kicked off her pumps, and undid and wiggled out of her skin-tight Calvin Klein jeans. She stood there facing him in just a white lace thong. Drinking in the sight, Paddy found her intoxicating.

Losing all self-control, he picked her up and pushed her back against the door. As he pressed against her, discovering her body with his hands and mouth, Blair reached down and undid his jeans. She slid her hand down the front and got a hold of him.

"You *are* a savage," she growled in his ear, biting his neck.

That did it. Paddy tore away her thong, shed his jeans, and entered her. As he did, she gasped and cried out, wrapping one leg around his hips, using it to guide his furious thrusting. Moments later, they were left gasping for air after exploding together.

As Paddy got his breathing under control, he looked at their clothes in a pile on the floor. He remembered his class in the morning, just a few short hours away.

"I should leave," he said. "I need to get home to shower and change for school."

"Stay with me," she insisted.

"I need clean clothes," he protested meekly.

"I've got you covered," she said as she dismounted him. She collected their clothing and left it in a pile outside the bedroom door.

"The maid will be up in an hour. She'll have everything cleaned and pressed for us by the time we get out of bed—coffee and breakfast too."

"You have a maid?" He was incredulous.

"She has her own studio apartment at the other end of the corridor. Astrid has been with the family for years. My father sent her with me when I came to Columbia, and he bought this apartment for me."

"Twist my arm," Paddy said as he hoisted her into his arms and carried her to the bed.

***

A gentle rap at the door was accompanied by a female voice with a thick Scandinavian accent.

"Miss Blair *dahlink*, it is the nine o'clock."

"Thank you, Astrid," Blair called back from the bed.

She and Paddy hadn't required waking. They had done very little sleeping—none actually. Blair lifted her head off his chest, kissed him, and jumped out of bed to take a shower.

"Join me," she said, heading for the enormous master bathroom attached to her room.

After getting out of the shower, Paddy watched her get dressed. He had nothing to wear, save the bath towel he used to dry himself. He borrowed a comb to straighten out his wet hair, pulling it back into a ponytail. He went with Blair out to the dining room table for breakfast with the towel wrapped around his waist.

Astrid came in from the kitchen with a pot of coffee and a silver tray of fresh scones, clotted cream, and raspberry preserves. The cream and sugar for the coffee were already on the table. As Astrid was pouring coffee for Paddy, she eyed him hungrily. She looked at Blair, smiled, and nodded her approval.

"I *haf* washed and folded your *clothink*, unless you're comfortable like *dat*," Astrid said.

"I think he's fine like that for now," Blair smiled.

"Yah," Astrid agreed, leering at him. "He's fine."

As she went back into the kitchen, Paddy looked at Blair, who was chuckling. He felt like a side of beef that had just gotten a Prime rating from the USDA. He had never minded being objectified, but he had misgivings. Blair kept giving him signals she had a more profound interest in him, but then in the next moment, she seemed to treat him like a big-game trophy.

She had asked for and taken down his phone number and address. She handed him an elaborate calling card, with her name and phone number in neat calligraphy framed in gold leaf on the edges of the buff card. Clearly, she wanted to see him again. Then when they came out to the dining table, she made him sit in a towel to show him off to her maid—the two of them ogling his half-naked form through breakfast. He decided to withhold judgment and not press the issue for a while. He figured her true intentions would reveal themselves soon enough.

***

Blair continued her seduction. She knew Paddy's schedule and arranged to have him spend his free time with her. Then the presents started. She bought him new furniture for his apartment. She wanted to hire an interior decorator, but he vetoed it.

"Blair, this building is on the verge of being condemned. Decorating it now is akin to putting makeup on a pig; it serves no purpose and annoys the pig."

She relented on the decorator, but the gifts kept coming.

She took him shopping to buy new clothes and expensive Italian shoes. Not to change his style; they were just new and better-quality examples of the jeans and tee-shirt motif he had already been sporting. She had him fitted for a suit at her father's tailor on Madison Avenue, but as yet, they hadn't been anywhere he needed to wear it. She incrementally improved his wardrobe to include some sweaters and collared shirts, so he could be more presentable if required. As she kept him primarily to herself, the need hadn't arisen.

They spent the majority of their time together in bed. Blair would have Paddy relate stories about his past in the post-coital interludes between them tearing into each other. She was fascinated with his rough-and-tumble upbringing. He didn't mind sharing with her, but when she would pry the more brutal and salacious aspects out of him, she would get a devious and enthralled look—like a voyeur soaking up someone else's misery for their own sick amusement. It gave him pause, but not enough.

She balanced it by stroking his ego, telling him how heroic his rise from the street was. She was proud of him, she said. She puffed him up every chance she got, telling him how beautiful, brilliant, and talented he was. She predicted greatness and wealth in his future. When she told him she loved him, he set aside all trepidation and bought in.

He had been guarded about allowing himself to be vulnerable. The only time he had done it was with Inez Vasconcellos. When she was murdered in front of him by her husband Hector, Paddy had locked away that kind of emotion out of self-defense. It didn't erase the need. Other than Inez, Paddy had known nothing but neglect and abuse. His family didn't love him; he was resented. He found validation where he could, through school, sports, and meaningless sexual encounters, always keeping everyone at a safe distance, where he thought they couldn't hurt him.

Blair recognized this. She sensed the core of insecurity and self-loathing hidden deep within him and the corresponding need for validation to relieve it. Blair built her seduction upon it. In the space of a month, she managed to crumble his defenses and get him to do the one thing he was most afraid of. *Fuck it*, he thought. *It might never get this good again.* So, he let himself fall. But, there was still a quiet voice in the back of his mind that warned him; *there isn't a safety net at the end of this, just an abrupt stop, and it's going to hurt.* Paddy quieted the voice and dove headlong into what he thought was love.

He should have realized something was amiss when she introduced him to her friends. They were of the American royalty clique, all money and privilege, and mean-spirited disdain for everyone else. More intrigued than pleased to meet him, they seemed curious to know about him—but not to know him. Their general condescension became grating. So, he kept quiet, not speaking unless spoken to and then answering in as few syllables as possible. The debutantes didn't seem to notice. They complimented Blair on her *find* right in front of him, as if he were a pet and had no understanding of the language. He tuned them out. So, he didn't even hear her friend Sydney.

"He's quite a specimen," she said, eyeing him greedily. "He's going to rock your father's world."

Before Christmas, Blair told Paddy he didn't need to keep slogging uptown to Coogan's. Bartending was beneath him, she said. She had plenty of money and didn't mind supporting him until he graduated. It was perhaps the quiet voice inside that prevented him from accepting. Maybe it was pride. More than likely, it was his fierce loyalty to friends who stood by him when he needed them.

"I can't just quit, Blair," he said. "Pete and Dave have been good to me. It's the holiday season. They can't afford to replace a bartender right now. They'd never find a new one in time. Maybe after the New Year."

She seemed to accept that. Looking back, Paddy thought maybe it was because it didn't conflict with her ultimate purpose. She already knew she would be done with him by then.

"I want you to come with me to Massachusetts for Christmas with my family," Blair said.

"I don't know. I don't think I'll fit in with your folks."

"Don't be ridiculous," she said. "They'll love you, just like I do."

"Fathers generally don't love me," he cautioned.

"My father will. He's very sweet."

"All right," he relented. "How should I dress?"

"Your usual is fine. We're very casual for Christmas—very laid back."

CHAPTER NINE

December 25, 1984
Weston, Massachusetts
14:00 hours

Christmas morning, Blair picked Paddy up at his apartment. She was in her metallic-green Aston Martin V8 Vantage. He had heard about the car, but this was the first time he had seen it. She kept it in a commercial garage in Morningside Heights, where it was lovingly maintained for her. It was the most powerful car he had ever been in, and he couldn't believe the opulence. As he sunk into the passenger seat, he found the sensation like being encased and massaged by a soft and warm leather glove—already custom formed.

He had brought gifts for her parents. One of the owners from Coogan's, Pete Walsh, had helped him pick out a bottle of good scotch for her father and an expensive bottle of Merlot for her mother. He climbed in, and they made their way north to her home in Weston.

Paddy felt slightly uncomfortable as they headed up the Henry Hudson Parkway to I-95. He noticed Blair—contrary to what she had told him—was not casually dressed. She looked as if she had come off the pages of a Ralph Lauren catalog. He had followed her instructions about what to wear, except for the Irish cable knit sweater thrown on over his tee-shirt, he was in his customary attire.

He looked presentable until compared with Blair, who was dressed like a preppy goddess. Paddy thought he looked like one of her gardeners. He also noticed she wasn't making much conversation and used clipped one-word answers when she did. Her attitude seemed peremptory and diffident as she pushed the Vantage way too fast. She appeared to be racing to their destination, anxious to get there—or perhaps just to get it over with. He decided to sit quietly and try to ignore the knot of apprehension growing in his stomach.

As they hit the interchange for I-91, Blair accelerated onto the cloverleaf exit ramp. The powerful British sports car bit down on the curved road and cornered like it was on rails. A minute later, she indicated the sign for the Weston exit. As they got off the highway and drove west, away from the bay, the houses and properties became grander. Up in the foothills, Paddy could barely see the homes behind their stone walls and wrought iron fences. The properties were larger, more wooded, and more set back from the road than the ones before.

Blair finally slowed down and turned in at a gated entry. The massive structure was made of decorative black iron and had to be twenty feet high. It was so elaborate it looked like Auguste Rodin could have sculpted it. The stone walls stretching out from both sides disappeared into the surrounding forest. Paddy couldn't see far enough into the property to see a house. *Perhaps,* he thought, *it was just beyond the screen of trees.*

Blair came to the electronic sentry box next to the road. She leaned out her window and depressed the intercom button. A male voice with a slight southern lilt responded.

"Merry Christmas, Miss. Blair."

"You can open it *now*, Maurice," she said, looking impatiently at the video monitor to the left of the big gate.

It slowly creaked open in front of them. Paddy detected a further change in Blair's demeanor. She seemed somehow stiff, even cold, and her voice took on a more pronounced New England nasal quality. The knot in his belly ratcheted a bit tighter.

As they drove, the road meandered into the treeline. It slalomed back and forth through this forest until they came to a clearing. There was an enormous house ahead on the right. Behind it was a large private lake, the surface frozen over.

"Holy shit," Paddy said under his breath.

"That's the servant's quarters," Blair said absently. *"That's* the house," she added, pointing up the hill behind the next line of trees in front of them.

Peaking over the forest, Paddy could see the top floors and gabled roof of the biggest home he had ever seen. His knotted stomach turned to ice, and he could feel his sphincter pucker. The effect only worsened as they came around the trees. This was not a house, Paddy realized. It was a baronial palace.

Blair pulled up in the Belgian block circular driveway, near the marble stairs and grand entrance. She was out of the car in an instant and marching toward the door. Paddy had to hurry to keep up with her.

The door was opened by a distinguished-looking black man in a tuxedo. His rigid posture and austere attitude defied putting an age on him. Paddy guessed he was in his sixties based upon the snow-white hair at his temples. He had never seen a butler before, other than in the movies and on TV. He surmised this was Maurice. The butler held the door open with his left hand, holding out his right. Blair shrugged out of her coat and draped it over Maurice's outstretched arm. He nodded toward Paddy.

"And your coat, Sir?"

Paddy put his gift bag on the floor and took off his pea coat, handing it to Maurice, who closed the door.

"Your parents are waiting for you in the great room," Maurice said.

Blair hurried off through the double doors fronting the first room on the right. Paddy wasn't sure if he was expected to follow her, but he did. He came into a room with an enormous roaring fireplace. Blair's parents were seated in plush leather chairs in front of the fire. They both had cocktails, and there was a full-service bar against the right wall. Blair marched into their vicinity. Her father placed his drink on the end table next to him. With a sour expression, he rose to his feet. Her mother remained on the couch with a numb, far-away look.

"Father, Mother, Merry Christmas. This is my *fiancé*, Paddy Durr," Blair announced, staring at her father as if challenging him.

Paddy was flummoxed. They had never discussed marriage, even as a concept. He noticed the large diamond engagement ring on her left hand for the first time as she held it under her father's nose. He had never seen it before and certainly hadn't given it to her. She wasn't wearing it during the drive north, and he hadn't noticed when she put it on. Her father arched an eyebrow in response, narrowing his eyes and clenching his jaw muscles. Paddy wasn't sure what his role was in this game yet, but he soldiered ahead anyway. He would be courteous until events directed otherwise.

Michael O'Keefe

"It's a pleasure to meet you, sir," Paddy said, extending his right hand.

Mr. Winthrop looked at his hand as if there was a scorpion in it. He finally offered a limp, dead-fish handshake, mumbling something unintelligible. Paddy presented him with the scotch. Winthrop regarded the Pinch single malt with distaste.

"I usually drink McCallan's," he said. Then added distractedly, "Thank you, I guess."

Not enjoying that exchange at all, Paddy decided to have a crack at her mother. This would prove to be a pointless endeavor. When he tried to give her the wine, she smiled crookedly and seemed to look past him.

"Just put it on the bar," she said before disappearing down her rabbit hole again.

At this point, Paddy realized he wasn't likely to be treated like a human being by this family. But, he came here with Blair. Not having another conveyance home, he figured he would buckle up for now and just ride it out. He sat quietly on the sofa, listening to Blair and her father make small talk. He found the exchange forced and joyless.

Maurice called everyone to the dining room for dinner. The butler pulled out the chair to the immediate left of the head of the table. He directed Paddy there. Blair sat opposite him, and Mrs. Winthrop sat to her right. Mr. Winthrop assumed his position at the head of the table.

The seating arrangements had been prearranged. Paddy was alone on his side of the table. Paddy looked down to his left and saw an additional twelve feet of table not being used. Wretched excess was the thought which came to mind. He sat there, remaining quiet, his discomfort growing. No one else moved or made a sound.

Finally, a servant emerged from the kitchen with a tureen. She looked to Paddy to be in her early twenties. She was blonde with large blue eyes and a perfect pale and creamy complexion. Her tight servant's uniform did nothing to hide her lithe and curvaceous body. Paddy thought she looked like a younger, hotter version of Astrid. The way Mr. Winthrop leered at her, he had an idea why he sent Astrid to New York with Blair. He had already hired her replacement. Paddy recognized her thick Scandinavian accent when she asked him if he wanted soup.

She served Mr. Winthrop last. As she ladled the thin broth into his bowl, Paddy saw him run his hand under her short skirt. He must have found the sweet spot because she closed her eyes and shuddered before smiling coyly at him. Mr. Winthrop grinned at Paddy as if gloating. Paddy looked over toward Mrs.

Winthrop to see what she made of this. She was staring into space, oblivious to everything going on around her.

"Thank you, Gerda," Mr. Winthrop said.

As she made her way back to the kitchen with the tureen, Maurice came out to serve the wine. When he left, the Winthrops began eating their soup. Paddy looked in his bowl. Some sort of beef broth; it was thin to the point of anemic and smelled like nothing. He wasn't surprised to find it almost flavorless.

Now that everyone was eating, Mr. Winthrop decided it was time for dinner conversation.

"Durr—what sort of name is that?" he asked.

"It's Irish, sir," Paddy said.

"Northern Irish, to be precise," Winthrop corrected. "Belfast, I believe."

"My grandparents were from there, but I never met them."

"I'm not surprised," Winthrop said. "Alcoholics tend to die young."

Paddy elected to absorb the dig silently, but he could tell more were coming.

"You're a Catholic?" Winthrop asked.

Paddy nodded.

"Hmm," Winthrop said as if it explained something.

"What does your father do?" he asked.

Paddy closed his eyes for a second. He could see where this was headed, and he knew it wouldn't end well. He looked over at Blair. She was paying rapt attention to the interrogation. The cruel grin and expectant look in her eyes told Paddy she was enjoying his discomfort immensely and wasn't about to do anything to diminish it. He now understood his part in this bizarre play. A crushing weight of disappointment descended on him.

"I haven't seen or spoken to my father in four years. I have no idea what he's been up to," Paddy said.

"He frequently gets arrested for drugs and petty theft," Winthrop said smiling. "What about your brothers, Walter, Malachy, and Kevin? What have *they* been up to?"

"Walter was killed robbing a liquor store," Paddy admitted. "I don't know about Malachy and Kevin."

"Malachy and Kevin died of heroin overdoses a year apart. Your mother killed herself soon after. You really didn't know?" Winthrop said, smiling wickedly.

"That was all news to me. Thanks," Paddy spat.

Astonished at such callousness, Paddy couldn't believe someone could take perverse joy at such a thing. He fumed silently. He had to stop himself from overturning the table when he saw Blair trying to stifle her laughter.

"What I want to know is," Winthrop continued. "Did you tell my daughter about your arrest record?"

"I don't have one," Paddy said.

"Oh, sure you do," Winthrop said. "You were questioned as a suspect in a homicide three years ago. Two years ago, you were arrested for extortion and assault when you threw a tavern owner through his own plate glass window. Does any of this sound familiar?"

"I was never charged with a crime either time. The cases were sealed. They're not part of the public record, so you're not supposed to know about them. You just met me today. How do you even know who I am?"

"Do you really think I don't know what my only child is doing?"

"So, you're spying on your daughter?"

Paddy looked to Blair for a reaction. She shrugged matter-of-factly.

"I'm protecting her," Winthrop said. "I can't have some parasite from the gutter latching on to her for my money. I have unlimited resources when it comes to buying information. If a thing happened, I can find out about it. Did you think you could hide your true nature forever?"

Paddy looked over again at Blair. She appeared to be eating this up.

"Really, Blair—nothing?" Paddy asked. "You're going to just leave me here to dangle?"

Blair jutted her chin out defiantly.

"You didn't tell me about the arrests," she snapped.

"Yeah, I did," he reminded her. "In fact, you got off hearing about them."

Blair crossed her arms, huffed, and looked away. But Paddy wasn't done with her.

"You didn't have to drag me up here for this bullshit. If you wanted to go slumming, I was all right with it. You're not the first, you know? I would have still knocked the bottom out of you and walked away graciously. But you had to make me believe it was about more than that. That was unfair. You hooked me. Was it necessary to bring me all the way up here to remind me I'm filthy white Irish trash? I know what I am. I don't need to be confronted with it. Was it your intention to be this cruel, or is it something that just happens naturally with people like you?"

"You had to be a fool to think my daughter could ever have long-term plans for a savage like you," Winthrop said, defending her.

There was that word again.

"Savage, huh?" Paddy said, chuckling. "She didn't seem to mind when I had her on her back, trying to run around the room rolled up on her shoulders."

"God damn your insolence!" Winthrop thundered.

"Which God?" Paddy snapped. "The tight-assed Presbyterian God whose name she kept screaming? You superior elitist piece of shit—you could have ended this a month ago with a phone call. All you had to do was tell me to stop seeing her."

"You would have stopped with a phone call?"

"Probably not. But, it would have been her choice. Most likely, I would have kept fucking her for a while, but I can guarantee I wouldn't have allowed her to drag my ass up here just to get you to pay attention to her. I can't believe I wasted a Christmas getting interrogated by a miscreant like you."

Winthrop slammed his fists on the table in anger. The pathetic weakness of it made Paddy smirk.

"It's time for you to go," Winthrop announced.

"It was time for me to go when you gave me that limp dish-rag of a handshake."

Winthrop called in the butler.

"Maurice, escort this *animal* off the property," he demanded.

Paddy stood up as Maurice approached him.

"You seem like a nice guy, Maurice," he said. "I'm sorry you have to work for soulless douche-bags like these people. As a courtesy, I'm giving you fair warning; if you touch me, I'm knocking you the fuck out. I'll leave. You can show me out. But, nobody is escorting me anywhere."

Maurice smiled and extended his right arm toward the door.

"Please follow me, Mr. Durr," he said pleasantly.

When they had gotten into the hall and the door had closed behind them, Maurice led Paddy toward the foyer.

"You handled that miserable motherfucker quite well, young man," Maurice said over his shoulder.

"I don't know how you can work for a scumbag like that," Paddy said.

"I have my reasons," Maurice assured him. "I live in the big house by the lake you passed on your way up here. My wife is the landscape designer for the property, and she loves it here, even if she can't stand that snobby piece of shit and his pilled-up wife. My kids both go to Harvard. Gonna be doctors. Wouldn't have happened if I didn't work for him. A man has to make sacrifices for his family."

At the closet by the front door, Maurice turned around and winked at Paddy.

"Besides," he said, grinning. "Every time the scumbag gets on my last nerve, I threaten to quit. Then he gives me another ten grand to stay. He knows he won't find anybody else willing to put up with his bullshit. At this point, I'm probably the best-paid butler on the planet. So, as I said, I have my reasons."

Maurice opened the door to the walk-in closet and retrieved Paddy's pea coat. He ran a lint brush over it before helping him on with it.

"I would love to have the chauffeur run you back to New York, but Winthrop would fire me for sure. There are limits to what I can get away with. I can't even call you a taxi. There are none up here. So, you're gonna have to walk."

"Just point me in the direction of the train."

"It's going to be a long walk, about five miles at least. At the gate, make a right toward the bay. You can get the Metro-North there. You got enough money for a train ticket?" Maurice asked, reaching into his pants pocket.

"I got it covered," Paddy assured him.

"I'm sorry you had to get mixed up with that evil child. She's a straight-up witch. You didn't deserve that." Maurice said. "You take care now, Mr. Durr."

"Merry Christmas, Maurice—to you and your family," Paddy said, shaking the butler's hand, leaving.

After hiking to the front gate, it creaked open for him as he approached it. It was either controlled by sensors, or Maurice saw him on the video monitors. Paddy made the right and started walking. There were no sidewalks, and the snow had been piled up by the plows on both sides of the road. So, he had no choice but to walk in the middle of the narrow two-lane road. Fortunately, there was no traffic. He was worried he might be run over. With all the blind curves, it was a distinct possibility.

He was walking no more than five minutes when a police car with its turret lights whirling slowly pulled up next to him. The sign on the door said *Weston Police*. The uniform officer lowered the passenger window and regarded Paddy for a moment with a look of benign curiosity. Paddy bent down to make eye contact.

"Merry Christmas, Officer," he offered, smiling.

The cop grinned back at him and scratched his head.

Burnt to a Crisp

"Merry Christmas to you," he said. "Now, who are you, where are you going, and where the hell did you come from?"

"My name is Paddy Durr. I just left the Winthrop Estate. I'm on my way to catch the next train to New York from the Metro-North station."

"It's five miles, kid. They didn't offer you a ride?"

"I *kinda* got kicked out."

"*Kinda?*" the cop asked. "You didn't steal anything, did you?"

"No, sir. In fact, I left an expensive bottle of scotch. I gave it to the old man as a gift. He acted as if I handed him a bottle of horse piss."

"Sounds like him, all right."

"So, you know him?"

"Unfortunately, I do," he said. "What were you doing up there anyway?"

"Until about an hour ago, I was engaged to Blair Winthrop, but I guess that's over," Paddy said.

"This I have to hear," the cop said. "Get in the car. I'll give you a ride to the train."

"Thanks, Officer...Conner," Paddy said, reading the cop's name tag. "But you don't have to do that."

Connor swung the passenger door open and waved him in.

"It's not a request."

"Well, in that case, thanks," Paddy said, climbing in.

"I'm not doing it for you. I already got five calls for a suspicious male. Who do you imagine that might be? If I don't get you off the road, I'm going to be getting calls until you get to the train. That's not exactly how I want to spend my Christmas."

Connor wanted to hear how he got mixed up with the likes of Blair Pickering Winthrop. Paddy told him about how she had hunted him at Columbia, identifying him as prey, before nailing him down at Coogan's. He related how she completed the seduction, sucking him in, making him believe she loved him.

"She stuffed you full of shit like a Christmas goose. Then she brought you home for the kill," Connor observed. "How did you end up engaged? It's only been a couple of months."

"We really weren't. I didn't find out about it until Blair introduced me to her parents as her fiancé. Next thing I know, she's got this giant rock on her left hand. Between that and the way she stuck me in her father's face, I knew I was only there to jerk the old man's chain. I guess I served my purpose. But I feel like an

59

idiot. I don't know what made me think I belonged in their world. Serves me right for trying to rise above my station."

"Give yourself a break, kid. You got played. That's what those people do. They use folks like us, then they kick us to the curb, like so much trash. I'm sure it hurts. You probably think you loved her. But, you should count yourself as fortunate. You dodged a bullet. She's bad news."

"I know that now, but how do you?" Paddy asked.

"She's always tearing around in that Aston Martin of hers. On these roads, it's just a matter of time before she wraps herself around a tree. I pulled her over once—just a caution stop—to tell her to slow it down a little. She told me she would have my badge. Almost got it too. It will be the last time I'm ever going to try and protect that *squacker* from herself. When she finally flies through her windshield and faceplants on a tree, trust me when I tell you, it won't be the worst day of my career."

Paddy pictured the scene in his mind. He had to admit the idea didn't trouble him either.

"So, now you're free of that mistake. What's next for you?" Connor asked.

"I graduate in May with an English degree. I'm about to be offered a Rhodes Scholarship, but I'm pretty sure I'm gonna turn it down."

"Why the hell would you do that?"

"I don't see a good reason to go to England just to get fucked over by *real* old money," Paddy pointed out. "It was bad enough getting used by people who *think* they're royalty. I can't even imagine what it would be like with people who *are*. I'm done with them. My English degree won't be good for much in the private sector, and I don't want to teach."

"So, what's your fallback plan?"

"I've got two friends who look out for me. They're detectives in Brooklyn. They made me take the test for the NYPD a few years ago. I think I'm gonna take the job."

"That's honorable, but you'll never get rich doing this," Connor cautioned.

"I've never been rich. So, I don't think I'll miss it. Besides, it's not about making money. It's about the work. I don't want to exploit people. I want to help them. I figure being a cop would be my best opportunity to do that."

Connor pulled up to the ticket kiosk of the Metro-North station. He turned to Paddy and extended his hand.

Burnt to a Crisp

"You're a good kid, Paddy, and your heart's in the right place. Stay away from shitty people like the Winthrops, and I think you'll make a fine cop. Merry Christmas," he said, shaking Paddy's hand.

"You too, Officer Connor," Paddy said as he turned to buy a ticket.

CHAPTER TEN

March 13, 2017
Downtown, Brooklyn
15:30 hours

It had been thirty-three years since Paddy had let a woman make him feel this worthless. Blair Winthrop and Millicent Wainright's faces were melding into each other in his mind, becoming indistinguishable. Back in the here and now, Paddy shook it off, having too much important work to do to allow himself to get lost in a class struggle that only existed in his head.

When he got to his squad car down the block on Schermerhorn Street, he was exhausted and feeling foolish. He was kicking himself for expending so much emotional energy trying to convince someone they were bigoted and selfish when that person didn't care in the slightest. He was also angry at himself because he knew he was just lashing out at someone who hurt him years ago, who probably hadn't given him a second thought.

Feeling like a perfect idiot, Paddy needed to speak with Mairead. She was the only person ever able to get him to pull his head out of his own ass and focus on the present instead of dwelling on old hurts and slights as if they were fresh wounds—or in any way significant.

Burnt to a Crisp

He worried that Mairead would be sleeping or incapacitated from the pain meds. As she got sicker, more of her day was spent sleeping from the drain of her illness or zonked out on the morphine for the pain. Her condition had so deteriorated at this point; she now had a Patient Controlled Analgesia pump hooked up over her bed. The morphine could be injected intravenously directly into her bloodstream by the press of a button. The wracking pain she suffered ensured the button was never far from her hand. The days had been so bad recently, Mairead was spending nearly all of her waking hours in a narcotic-induced dream state. Paddy hoped to catch her in one of her brief lucid moments.

He called the home phone from his cell. Mairead's palliative nurse picked up on the second ring.

"Hello, Julissa," Paddy said.

"Hello, Mr. Paddy," she said in her sweet, soothing Jamaican accent.

Her quiet, kind, and resonant voice had become a comfort to Paddy and Mairead since she was assigned to the Durr house. A perfect optimist with infinite faith, she could pray mightily and insisted everyone in the house pray with her when she was so moved—which was often. Even though a cynic, Paddy would reluctantly assent. The prayer sessions never failed to calm Mairead, giving her a brief reprieve from the ravages of her cancer. But they also had a profound spiritual effect on Paddy. Julissa's absolute faith stoked some latent form of his own, buried and beaten but still alive. The experience imbued Paddy with a hope he didn't think he had. In the throes of her strident belief, he thought he could grasp enough of it to accept the possibility of a miracle. He knew he needed one. He wasn't reluctant anymore.

"How is Mairead?" Paddy asked.

"She *havin* a good day. The pain not so bad."

"Is she awake? Can she talk?"

The next sound he heard over the phone was the voice of Mairead—uncommonly relaxed and dreamy—at least there was no hint of pain.

"Is this my man?" Mairead asked.

"It better be," he answered.

"Remind me; which one are you?"

"Not funny, Mairead," Paddy said, laughing, delighted she felt well enough to joke with him.

"How's *your* day going?" she asked.

"It's been a weird one so far. It looks like I caught my homicide—three, in fact. But they're not dead yet."

He quickly brought her up to speed on his investigation, omitting his difficulties with Millicent Wainwright. Mairead didn't need to know how he regressed emotionally, resurrecting feelings of inferiority he should have dispensed with years ago. She sensed the embarrassment in his voice.

"Somebody's got your shorts in a twist. Tell me what the matter is."

Paddy went on to detail his difficulties with the Red Cross worker. Rather than have Mairead ask all the follow-up questions she would have if Paddy didn't give her the whole story upfront, he just came out with the unabridged version. When he mentioned Millicent's wealthy, entitled, and dismissive attitude, Mairead understood in a breath.

"Blair Winthrop, *again*?" Mairead said, exasperated.

"Yeah," Paddy allowed.

"How come every time you deal with someone rich, who thinks their shit smells like lilacs, you have to relive that episode all over again?"

"I can't seem to let that one go," he admitted.

"Correction, Paddy. You can't let *anything* go. You are the most relentless and unforgiving person in the world. Unless the object of your hatred has somehow atoned, you won't stop grinding your ax. What's worse is how you internalize everything. Then it becomes about you blaming yourself—for being mistreated by others. It's madness."

"I'm sorry, Mairead. I didn't mean to drag you down here with me."

"It'll be all right," she said. "But now you have to shake it off. You have three people who are going to die soon. They have no one to speak for them but you. You can't wallow in self-pity over something that happened over thirty years ago and has already sorted itself out."

Mairead was referring to what ultimately happened to Blair Winthrop and her father. When she first heard the story and realized how deeply they had scarred Paddy, she took it upon herself to investigate. This was early in their marriage. At first, it involved a lot of phone calls and trips to the library. She found it amazing the information people will provide if you tell them you're a journalist writing an article for a social register. As the years went by, Mairead was able to follow up in the comfort of their living room. Thanks to the internet, you could track people with a simple name entered in any of the innumerable search engines available.

Mairead was convinced if there was *any* justice in the universe, the karma train would be coming back around for these people. Her diligence was rewarded. In early 2009, she found their names on a registry of victims of the most notorious

Ponzi scheme in history. Following the thread, she discovered that Thomas Pickering Winthrop had been left destitute and took his own life in a Boston hotel room.

Blair's comeuppance took longer, but not by much. She had married a financier who was far wealthier than her father. So, despite losing almost a billion dollars to the scheme, he still had a few million to fall back on. Apparently, they had grown too accustomed to their lavish lifestyles. Blair's husband engaged in a vast money-laundering conspiracy with the Sinaloa drug cartel in Mexico to recoup his losses. The DEA became aware of the scheme. Blair's husband was indicted. The cartel is famous for eliminating witnesses they believe can hurt them. Blair and her husband went on the run from the cartel and the US Government, leaving their children in the care of their nannies. The kids ended up wards of the state when Blair and her husband were found gunned down in a mountain-side bungalow in Monterrey.

"You can bury the hatchet now," Mairead said, laying the copies of the New York Times and the Wall Street Journal detailing the story in front of him.

"That's a rough end," Paddy observed.

"It might not be an atonement," she observed. "But it's certainly an example of sins paid for."

Paddy shrugged. The gesture infuriated Mairead because she knew this still wasn't enough to let him lay his anger aside. Nothing ever was. By now, she knew it was pointless to argue. Rather than trying to get Paddy to do something he wasn't constructed to do, she redirected his attention.

"What's the next step?" she asked.

"I've got to check on my victims' conditions at Cornell. Then it's back to the office to reach out to the tenants from the building. If nothing breaks, I'll be home."

"Don't hurry for me, Paddy. I feel okay now, but the pain will be back. I'll probably hit the morphine button and go to sleep for the night."

"I'll try not to wake you when I get in," he said.

Mairead knew that whenever he got home before he even took off his coat, he would be by her side, gently kissing her on the forehead. She had been pretending to sleep through these greetings, but she was aware every time and looked forward to them.

"Be careful, baby. I love you," she said before hanging up and drifting off to sleep, the morphine already kicking in from the press of the button a moment before.

Michael O'Keefe

CHAPTER ELEVEN

March 13, 2017
Manhattan
16:15 hours

Paddy parked the squad car in Cornell Weill Medical Center's entry circle on 68th Street and York Avenue. He made his way to the E-bank elevators, to the 10th floor. At the nurses' station inside the burn unit, Paddy spoke to the nurse on duty. He identified himself and told her he was there regarding the Santapadre family. She paged the attending physician.

While he waited for the doctor, Paddy looked through the sliding glass doors into the ward. Each room was hermetically sealed with its own sliding door. There was a dressing table containing paper gowns, foot cover booties, face masks, hats, and latex surgical gloves outside every room. No one could enter a room without first donning a fresh set. Paddy understood this was because burn victims were susceptible to infection and had their immune systems compromised.

He saw someone come out of the room directly in front of him. This person removed his protective covering and disposed of everything in the trash receptacle outside the room. Paddy saw he was a doctor from the embroidered name on his white medical coat. Under this, he wore khaki green scrubs.

Doctor Avery Menkovich came out to the reception area and introduced himself.

"I'm Detective Durr," Paddy said. "I'm checking on the Santapadres."

"It's nice to meet you, Detective. Forgive me for not shaking your hand. We're a little maniacal in our effort to avoid infection up here."

Paddy nodded. Married to a nurse, he had a better understanding of medical procedures than most detectives. Still, over the last two years, his education in that regard had expanded while dealing with Mairead's illness. He now felt like he knew more about medicine than he ever cared to.

"Can you tell me how they're doing, Doc?" Paddy asked.

"They're extremely critical."

"Would you characterize them as likely to die from their injuries?"

"Barring a miracle, the three of them will be dead by the end of the week, probably sooner," the doctor admitted.

"I don't need to go into their room, but I would like to see them through the glass if it's all right," Paddy said.

"That would be fine, Detective, but I don't see the point. They're not conscious, and they couldn't speak even if they were. We have them intubated."

"The fire was arson," Paddy explained. "By your estimation, their deaths will be a triple homicide by the end of the week. This is my case. While it isn't necessary, empathy is easier if you can put a face on it. I'm going to be the last person to speak for them—to see they get justice. They deserve every bit of empathy I can give them."

"I thought detectives needed to maintain a professional detachment," the doctor said.

"Homicides are different," Paddy said. "The victims can't tell their own story. We have to tell it for them. It won't work unless I get to know them intimately. I need to care about them as people. I don't know how to do that without making it personal."

Doctor Menkovich seemed to accept this, nodding. He waved for Paddy to follow him through the outer door onto the ward. They came to the sealed room at the end of the corridor. It looked larger than the ones before it, which made sense to Paddy. All three family members were together inside.

Paddy looked in on them for a moment. He noted the fact they didn't outwardly appear to be burned. They weren't wearing bandages. Unconscious, they were breathing rhythmically with the aid of respirators. The tubes inserted in their mouths he knew stretched down their throats and into their lungs. As uncomfortable as this looked, he thought they probably felt nothing at this point.

"Other than the cherry-red skin color, they don't appear to have suffered burns," Paddy observed.

"Externally, they didn't," the doctor said. "But they were trapped in the building, breathing super-heated air. Their lungs and throats are essentially roasted. The red complexions are from carbon monoxide. It should have dissipated by now, but they're not utilizing oxygen efficiently anymore. All we can do for them at this point is to treat their pain while we wait for them to expire."

"Why are they still in the burn unit?" Paddy wondered.

"We would have transferred them if the move to the hospice floor wouldn't have killed them. We're keeping them here. It won't be much longer."

Paddy took another moment to pray silently. *Hey, God,* Durr said to himself. *We need a little help here. Please allow these poor people to have a quick and painless end to their suffering. While you're at it, let their family find peace and closure if such a thing exists. Finally, if it's not too much trouble, grant me the wisdom and strength to give them justice.* When he finished, Paddy looked at the doctor and nodded.

They returned to the nurses' station outside. Paddy produced his business card.

"If you would, Doc, attach my card to the file," he requested. "Let everyone know; when each of them expires, I need an immediate notification. Right now, I'm working this case alone. The minute it becomes a homicide, the protocol changes. Then I get a platoon of help. So, it's kind of important."

"I'll take care of it, Detective," Menkovich assured him. "But you don't look so well yourself. Are you all right?"

"Not really," Paddy admitted. "I've spent the better part of the last two years shuttling my wife back and forth to Sloan Kettering."

"Oh my God, that's awful. Is she responding to treatment?"

"No, it's grade four lymphoma. She's home with hospice care now. So, the Santapadres aren't the only ones I have on death watch. I can't seem to help my wife any more than I can help them. I know there will be no comfort for me, but maybe I can help *their* family find some. That would at least be something, wouldn't it?" Paddy asked.

"I thought I had a shitty deal," Menkovich said. "Dealing with all this suffering and death, but you've got me beat by a mile. With everything you have on your plate right now, you're going to need the patience and fortitude of a saint."

Paddy smiled, even though he felt no humor.

Burnt to a Crisp

"That's unfortunate, Doc," he grinned. "No one will ever confuse me with a saint.

Michael O'Keefe

CHAPTER TWELVE

March 13, 2017
Bushwick, Brooklyn
18:00 hours

When Paddy got back to the 83 Squad, he found it was still buzzing with activity. Fortunately, the bosses from the Hate Crimes Task Force had decamped. Unfortunately, they left their detectives behind. They were now making themselves at home, though as far as Paddy could see, they weren't doing much other than drinking the squad's coffee and texting on their department i-phones. Joe Furio had a look on his face suggesting he might murder one of them. Recognizing this, Paddy told him to calm down, take a deep breath, and think pleasant thoughts.

Just as he finished talking Joe off the ledge, Paddy looked over to his desk. A Hate Crimes detective was lounging in his chair with his feet up. When he saw what picture, taped under the lucite cover on his desk, the young detective had his feet on, Paddy snapped. It was his favorite photo of Mairead and the kids. The idea of this interloper disrespecting the sanctity of his family was the capper on an already infuriating day. The vein in his forehead throbbed and appeared to be ready to burst as he marched over to the reclining detective.

Paddy slapped the unaware detective's feet off his desk, grabbed him by the tie, cinching it tightly around his throat.

Burnt to a Crisp

"That's my family you're smearing dog shit on, cocksucker," Paddy growled, pushing him back until the chair was about to tip.

"I'm sorry, bud. I was just trying to relax," he offered meekly.

"Relax from what? You haven't done anything *but* sit around in my office, scuffing your filthy shoes on my wife's face."

"Take it easy, bro," the young detective said, sounding frightened.

Paddy had heard enough. He picked him out of the chair by his tie and pulled him forward until their noses touched.

"I'm not your bud, and I'm not your bro," Paddy said with quiet fury. "If I catch another of you worthless pieces of shit in fancy suits at my desk again, I'm holding *you* responsible. I will drag your ass out to the parking lot, beat you half to death, and shove what's left in the dumpster. Your welcome here is rescinded. We don't need your help. So, fuck off!"

The Hate Crimes detective looked into the bosses' office. He saw Lieutenant Martino watching impassively. The detective knew he was here under his inspector's orders, so he thought he could throw a little of his boss's rank around.

"Inspector Hardesty wants me involved in this case," he said with defiance. "You can take it up with him."

Mariano Martino's ears perked up when he heard the challenge. He came out to Paddy's desk and addressed the Hate Crimes detective.

"What's your name, Detective?" he asked, smiling.

"Smith," he said.

"Smith? Really? You gotta be fucking with me—first name, please," Mariano said, dialing the phone on Paddy's desk.

"Richard Smith and I don't appreciate being spoken to like this."

"Excuse me a second," Mariano said, reaching to put the phone on speaker. It was answered on the other end.

"Chief Ross, what can I do for you," the voice of the Chief of Detectives answered.

"It's Mariano Martino, in the 83 Squad, Chief. Sorry to bother you."

"How are you making out with the bias case, Mariano?"

"Fine, boss. We're getting ready to break it, but I'm having some trouble with the Hate Crimes Taskforce again."

"What have those assholes gotten up to now?" the chief asked.

"I have a Detective Richard Smith here who thinks he can disrespect my detectives and my office and then throw his inspector's name around like a shield. His squad has done nothing but fuck things up on this case since they got here this morning. I would like them to go away now, so the adults can be in charge for a while."

"Who did he piss off?" the Chief asked, chuckling.

"Pretty much everybody, but most recently, Paddy Durr had his hands around his throat," Mariano said.

"He must have a death wish to fuck with Paddy," the chief observed.

"If he doesn't kill him, Joe Furio will," said Mariano.

"Put the little dipshit on the phone," he ordered.

"We're on speaker. He can hear you."

"Detective Smith," the chief began. "Do you know who this is?"

"Ye-yes, sir," Smith stammered.

"Okay, terrific! Now get the other losers from your office and go back to headquarters. When you get there, have your numbskull inspector call me forthwith. Are we clear?"

"Yes, sir."

"And for future reference," the chief continued. "Stay out of the eight-three. If you should have to go there, stay far away from Durr and Furio. They're way out of your league, and they're homicidal maniacs. They'll murder you and eat the evidence."

Smith rapidly collected his partners and headed for the door. He made the mistake of looking back. Being a last word kind of guy, Joe Furio had hoped he would.

"Don't let the door hit you in the ass on your way out, fuck-nuts!" Furio called after them.

Durr watched the five Hate Crimes detectives head down the stairs to the parking lot. Lieutenant Martino continued his conversation with the chief.

"Where are we on the murder, Mariano?"

"We have the perp identified. We're saddling up now to hit a few addresses," Martino informed him.

"You need any help?"

"No, between my guys and the Homicide Squad, I've got plenty of manpower."

"Great work. I'll be here late briefing the PC. So, keep me posted."

"Will do, Chief."

After hanging up, Mariano turned his attention to Paddy.

Burnt to a Crisp

"That was good advice you gave Joe earlier. So, does strangling another detective qualify as calming down, taking a deep breath, and thinking pleasant thoughts?"

"The thought of making a canoe out of that asshole's head was very pleasant to me. I bet Joe agrees," Paddy said.

"You two worry me," Mariano said.

Martino elected to have Paddy remain in the office for the manhunt. Apart from the fact they already had enough detectives, Paddy still needed to locate and speak with his displaced tenants. While he was doing that, he could man the phones and perform computer assistance for the teams in the field.

He was horrified to discover Millicent Wainwright had temporarily placed the tenants of 407 Wilson Avenue in the Red Carpet Inn on Halsey Street and Wyckoff Avenue. Paddy and every other cop in Brooklyn knew this place. They called it the *Body Rolled up in a Carpet Inn*. One was more likely to find a dead hooker under the bed as get a good night's rest. A notorious *hot-sheets* prostitution spot and shooting gallery, he doubted any of the tenants from Wilson Avenue elected to take the charity of the Red Cross and stay there.

At least Wainwright had bothered to record the cellphone numbers for each tenant. This would obviate the need for Paddy to call the hotel. He knew from experience, the drug-addled clerks who worked there would tell him nothing over the phone. Requiring a visit, he would have to break one of them in half only to find out none of the tenants had elected to stay. He was grateful for small comforts.

He found each of the twenty-two displaced tenants, all residing temporarily with family or friends around Bushwick. As he had predicted, each of them had taken one look at the Red Carpet and made other arrangements. The interviews were straightforward. The mostly middle-aged and elderly tenants woke to intense heat and thick smoke in the building. When they came out into the hallway, they were ushered into the third-floor apartment by Jessica Santiago.

Jessica was the eighteen-year-old daughter of Madeline Santiago. Their apartment was the only one with a window escape to an adjoining garage roof in the rear of the building. Jessica shepherded everyone out this way. It was only after everyone else had managed to escape when they realized the Santapadres were still in the building. By this time, it was engulfed in flame. The firemen ultimately removed the unconscious family from their fourth-floor apartment.

None of the tenants had any insight as to who might have set the fire. They couldn't recall anyone in the building having a problem with anyone. But several of the older tenants seemed to think Jessica Santiago might know more. When Paddy inquired why they thought so, he got the same vague answer. Because she was younger and knew everyone in the neighborhood, she might have a better idea. This was a pretty thin supposition, Durr knew. But he was saving Jessica's interview for last for another reason.

She was the only tenant who had been the subject of any police reports from within the building. She had her (presumably old) boyfriend, Sergio Palmiero, arrested for assaulting her. She had a current Order of Protection against him. As he did not see Sergio among the list of the displaced, he wanted to know the state of their relationship. Palmiero wasn't a suspect yet, but he was definitely a person of interest.

Paddy found Madeline Santiago at her sister's house on Halsey Street. She and her two daughters and the youngest daughter's boyfriend had decamped there immediately after the fire. The kids were out at the moment, she said. Madeline had no more information for him than the other tenants. She never suggested Jessica might have any ideas. Paddy thought this odd.

"Your neighbors seemed to think Jessica might know something," he said.

"Those old hens say that just because she's young," Madeline said.

"How old is your other daughter?"

"Melanie is seventeen."

"And yet, none of the neighbors suggested I talk to her," Paddy pointed out. "You see why I might be concerned?"

"They think she's trouble because of her old boyfriend, *Cucko*," she admitted.

"Who is that?" Paddy thought he already knew.

"Sergio Palmiero, everybody calls him Cucko. Jess had him arrested for beating her up, but that was months ago."

"He hasn't been around since?"

"No. We heard he went back to Puerto Rico," Madeline said.

"Well, I still need to speak with Jessica and Melanie's boyfriend. I don't have his name on anything. He's just listed as Melanie's boyfriend on the Red Cross paperwork. Why is that?" Paddy asked.

"His name is Peter, but everyone calls him *Blanco*. He doesn't live with us; he just stays over sometimes."

"Is Blanco his last name?"

"It's a nickname cause he's a white boy."

"You don't know his last name?"

Burnt to a Crisp

"I don't," she said.

Paddy thought *he* did. If he were the Blanco Paddy knew, then he would want no part of the police. Peter Cammaratta was a twenty-year-old parolee who worked as a steerer and runner for Sammy Bando, also known as *Bungee*. Bungee ran all of the drug spots on Wilson Avenue from Putnam Street to Jefferson Avenue. This case was starting to take on the flavor of a drug beef, but until Paddy could interview these people, all he had was smoke. Usually, where there was smoke, there was fire, but experience had taught him sometimes it was just smoke. He couldn't afford to jump to any conclusions yet. He left his numbers with Madeline Santiago, asking her to have her daughters call him. He didn't bother leaving a message for Blanco. Paddy would just pick him up at his parole visit later in the week. But even that was no guarantee the little felon would divulge anything.

While Paddy waited for his partners and the Homicide Squad to get back from their manhunt, he was struck with the sneaking suspicion he was being stonewalled. All of the building tenants seemed like they had more to say but punted to Jessica Santiago rather than tell him. When he returned to this investigation tomorrow, it would be as much a priority to find out *why* the fire was set as it was *who* set it.

Michael O'Keefe

CHAPTER THIRTEEN

March 13, 2017
Plainedge, Long Island
20:00 hours

Paddy got home and sat down next to Mairead's bed. He had intended to stay there for the night until Mairead reminded him he had an Honor Legion meeting to attend.

"I was going to blow it off," he said.

"You can't. Joe was adamant. He said you had to be there."

"Joe will forgive me. I want to spend time with my wife."

"Your wife wants to medicate and go to sleep. Go to the meeting, Paddy," she insisted.

"What's the big deal? I've been an Honor Legion member since 1986. Suddenly they can't have a meeting without me?"

"I'm not supposed to tell you, but Joe wanted me to make sure you came to this meeting. They're announcing the winners of the Honor Legion Scholarship tonight. Casey is one of them. Someone from this family needs to be there, and you're it, Paddy."

"I guess there's no point in arguing," he observed.

"None whatsoever. Now get ready and get out of here."

"I'll see you when I get home."

Burnt to a Crisp

"I'll be asleep."

"Then I'll just kiss you on the forehead."

***

Paddy Durr stirred his drink. He did this for no other reason than habit. It was just water. He had his last drink twenty-six years ago. Looking in the mirror behind the bar at himself, he decided he didn't care for his reflection. *You look tired, boyo*, he thought. *No*, he corrected himself. *You look beaten*. Having had enough of the image, Paddy threw back his drink—ice and all—finishing it in a swallow before ordering another.

He was at the monthly meeting of the Honor Legion of the NYPD at the Rex Manor in Brooklyn. The Honor Legion is the oldest fraternal organization in the department and the only one you have to earn your way into. You needed to be awarded a Commendation or better just to apply. Paddy knew the majority of the members, like himself, had numerous such decorations. He looked around and identified with the severe faces he saw there—hard-bitten with hyper-alert eyes. He knew the look. It was the same look that peered back at him from the mirror. They were killers. He knew because he was one.

Death in its many forms usually didn't bother him. Even his own death was of little concern to him. He wasn't trying to get killed. He just didn't care, and he made no effort at all to prevent it—other than shooting the bad guy first. At that, he was quite proficient. But only one death was weighing on his mind tonight. It was the impending death of his wife, Mairead, from cancer. She was hanging on, but barely.

He was joined at the bar by an attractive blonde in a blue business suit with a form-fitting skirt. She was appealing to most men. If Paddy didn't know her, she would have been attractive to him. But he did know her and thought she was a meddling, cloying pain in the ass. Her name was Dr. Deborah Levine. She was a psychiatrist at the NYPD's Psychological Services and the unit's new commanding officer. Her specialty was post-traumatic stress, and she and Paddy had a history.

"Hello, Paddy. How are you holding up?" she asked.

"I'm holding up fine, Dr. Levine. What brings you to an Honor Legion Meeting, professional curiosity?"

"I'm actually an honorary member."

"That doesn't seem fair."

"Why is that?"

"Because I had to shoot my way in here. You just have to show up and plunk down some dues. Our respective sacrifices for the privilege of membership seem inequitable."

"Oh, I don't know about that. I deal almost exclusively with the aftermath and repercussions of shootings. It's PTSD all day, every day for me. I'd say I know a little bit about it."

"Like a tourist knows Paris," Paddy said sourly. "Until you make somebody dead, you're nothing but a spectator. It doesn't give you sufficient insight to comment on the horror of my psyche, or anyone else's, for that matter. But that doesn't stop you, does it?"

"I don't act capriciously, Paddy. My primary concern is always for the well-being of the Member of the Service."

"And yet, guns are taken, and careers get drydocked—all on your say-so."

"Would you prefer I leave a depressed cop with the means to destroy himself?"

"I would prefer when you make that determination, there be an apparatus in place to dispute the finding, or at least make it less permanent. As it is, some cops are stuck on the *Rubber-Gun Squad* for years. If you want to know why they're depressed, that might be a place to start looking. Take a cop's gun, and he doesn't feel like a cop anymore. *That* is psychologically devastating."

"I don't want to have to justify the efficacy of what I sometimes have to do. We've had this discussion before, Paddy. Can we just agree to disagree?"

"I don't give a rat's ass about the efficacy, Deborah. Just don't do it to me," Paddy said, throwing back his drink, gesturing to the bartender for another.

Dr. Levine noticed. A look of false concern came over her face. It wasn't missed by Paddy.

"Is there a problem, Doctor Levine?"

"Are you drinking vodka like that?"

"No," he dead-panned. "I have a reverse-messiah syndrome. Christ turned water into wine at the wedding in Cana. I turn vodka into water. That's what it is. I don't drink. You know that."

"I just thought with what's been going on at home; you might have reverted to alcohol to cope."

Durr glared at her with scorn.

"First of all, you never knew me when I drank. And how do you know anything about my situation at home? Did somebody post it in Spring 3100?" Paddy asked, referring to the police department magazine.

"No," she said. "You know I'm friends with Sergeant Nolan. She told me about your wife. I'm very sorry, Paddy."

"No, you're not. What else did Janice tell you?"

"She was concerned you were losing faith—that you were turning in on yourself. You know that's a classic symptom of PTSD."

"Deborah, Please. I'm not losing faith. I'm losing my wife. I *know* God exists."

"Doesn't that give you comfort?"

"Just because I know God exists doesn't mean he doesn't hate me. Or that I don't hate him right back."

"That doesn't sound like faith to me."

"I don't need faith. I have empirical evidence. Whatever he, she, or it turns out to be, I just know there is a greater power in the universe pulling strings."

She gave him a skeptical look, reminding Paddy that this woman of science did not believe in God. She was a humanist, the most deluded of God's forsaken children. He knew if she had his perspective of the human race, she would be looking desperately for something else in which to believe. *Humans were disappointing pieces of excrement*, Paddy thought, and he was about to tell her so when she interrupted him.

"What sort of empirical evidence?" she demanded.

"Ever watch someone die?" he asked. "Did you notice at the moment they do, as soon as whatever is present in us—call it a soul, a divine spark, whatever—at that moment, the human husk is diminished, noticeably so. The body seems smaller in death than it was only seconds before. That's from something leaving—something profound and important."

Paddy first noticed this phenomenon when his friend and mentor, Police Officer Jimmy Crowe, was murdered. He was with him in the emergency room when he expired from the gunshot wound perforating his heart. Paddy attributed what he was sensing at the time to his crushing grief. But since then, he had taken more than a dozen dying declarations from victims, noting the same effect every time. Then there were the hundreds of autopsies he attended. Every single corpse was something less in death than they were when alive.

Reflecting on this, he became even sadder, if that was possible. It wouldn't be long before he had to watch Mairead diminish in this way and right in front of his eyes. He thought it would break his heart if it weren't already shattered in a million pieces—like beams of light through a prism.

"Is that all you've got?" she scoffed. "The perceived shrinking of human beings in death has a whole host of medical explanations."

"Not when it occurs in the instant. But I have other evidence. You like humanity so much; my experience is altogether different. People are often self-centered, avaricious animals who are more prone to fucking each other over for the crumbs left to them rather than helping someone—even family. But I'll grant you; there is balance in the universe. Amid all of this senseless carnage, thievery, and death, some nobility surfaces from time to time. Using ourselves as an example, did you ever notice how doing the right thing—even if no one else knows—just feels good? It is its *own* reward. That brief ability to sacrifice one's self-interest is all that redeems this fucked up human race. It makes something fine seem possible."

"So, there's redemption," she noted. "Surely that can help you do something other than hate God."

"I tried, Deborah. I truly did," he said wearily. "But ultimately, I came to understand that God is a six-year-old with a magnifying glass, and we are nothing more than his ant farm. You can pray all you want, but God isn't leaving us alone till he burns us all."

At this, the doctor eyed him critically. She seemed to be mulling something over. Paddy knew what was coming. She had been trying to get his guns for three years—since she first met him for a trauma debriefing after a shooting. He hadn't actually shot anyone that time. In fact, he hadn't even discharged his weapon. He was able to talk the gun out of the perp's hand and arrest him without anyone getting hurt. But in today's NYPD—where they were so concerned about their civil liability with regards to PTSD—getting shot at was enough to mandate a trauma debriefing.

New to the unit and categorically no friend of cops, she got one look at Paddy's personnel jacket and almost had an orgasm. This was the target she had been looking for. Dr. Levine went after his guns with gusto. But first, Paddy knew she wanted to have sex with him. Levine had seen the videos with the soccer coach when she Googled him. The animal intensity of it all excited her. She wanted to be taken like that. When Paddy flatly refused her offer to take him back to her apartment for lunch, she was embarrassed. His scoffing refusal of what she thought were her irresistible charms enraged her. She decided to make him pay for it. She didn't succeed then, and Paddy didn't want her to think she would now.

"Before you open that scheming cake-hole of yours, I am not a danger to myself or anyone else. Those are the only criteria for an IO-9 proceeding. I'm not depressed. I'm just sad, what with the dying wife and all. If I weren't, I'd be delusional. Then you might have a case. As it stands, the last time you tried to get

Burnt to a Crisp

my guns, the Commissioner almost fired you for overstepping your bounds. I happen to know the new Commissioner doesn't like you either. But he likes me. You'll be fucking with me at your own peril. And just so we're clear, my dick isn't getting within a mile of that rancid stink-hole you sit on—ever."

"You'll pay for that," she said, the smugness oozing out of her. "There is a new power structure in play. I happen to be *very* friendly with the Mayor and his wife. They both outrank the Commissioner in this administration."

Paddy seethed, glaring at Dr. Levine with the malignant stare for which he was famous. It was the precursor for nothing good. Joe Furio saw it and came right over.

"Easy, Paddy. We're all friends here," Joe said.

"She's no friend of mine," Paddy spat.

"He's evincing aggressive and irrational behavior," the doctor offered.

Joe recognized the language and understood its intent. All gunfighters knew the phrase. They were indicators of being a danger to oneself or someone else—a *prima facia* case for the removal of an MOS's firearms. Joe wheeled on her.

"What are you even doing here?"

"I'm an honorary member," she protested.

"No, you're not. I'm the Vice President, in charge of all the members. You're not one of them. You're here on a crusade to screw my partner over. You're disinvited. Fuck off, you imperious cooze. Or I'll have you arrested."

Deborah knew better than to argue with Joe Furio. Especially in light of the fact that he was correct. She was not a member and was here without brief for the express purpose of lodging an IO-9 order against Paddy Durr. She used her friendship with Janice Nolan to insinuate herself into Paddy's life again. This was a vendetta she had been nurturing for years. Because he refused to have sex with her, she was determined to get his guns. Though she was confident she now had the juice to do it, she was out of her breadth and authority to be here. As she headed for the door, she felt like she needed the last word.

"When I'm done with him, you're next, Furio."

She was gone before Joe could get the *fuck you* out of his mouth.

"What are we going to do about her?" Joe asked.

"I thought I saw Jimmy Maselli here," Paddy said, referring to the attorney who was the head of the DEA's law firm. "We tell him. Then we get the union to file a show cause order, hire our own private psychiatrist, and thwart whatever bullshit she has in her bag of tricks. But this will only buy me some extra time. If

Michael O'Keefe

she's really that tight with the Mayor and his wife, it's a lead-pipe-cinch I'll be a *rubber gunner* before long."

CHAPTER FOURTEEN

March 15, 2017
Manhattan
13:00 hours

Mairead was shivering, despite the unseasonably warm March weather. She was bundled in her fleece Plainedge Football blanket, but the warm cover did nothing to counter the draft attacking her emaciated lower body through the thin fabric cover of the wheelchair's seat. She and Paddy were waiting to confer with Dr. Stephen Cheng in his office at Memorial Sloan Kettering. Dr. Cheng was recognized as the hospital's preeminent oncologist. Given Sloan Kettering's reputation as the leading practitioner of cancer research and treatment, Cheng's status expanded until he was regarded as the world's foremost cancer expert.

The Durrs were here with two very different agendas. Paddy was seeking a measure of hope. Mairead had enough and wanted an end to her suffering. She intended to decline all further treatment. The last round of chemotherapy and radiation had not worked and very nearly killed her—along with the cancer already ravaging her. She would have no more of that, viewing it as a lost cause. She wanted to be allowed to die with a measure of dignity, with her family around her and her wits intact. Dr. Cheng disappointed her when he held out the possibility of a *Hail Mary*.

"I'm encouraged by the last blood work and cell cultures we took, Mairead," he said.

"The tumors are shrinking?" Paddy asked, his heart jumping.

"No," Cheng corrected. "But her protein levels are still strong. We were able to isolate Mairead's cancer cells from her blood and lymph samples. We think we can genetically engineer her white blood cells with a sort of kill-switch. We redesign them at the genetic level to only attack cancer cells. Once we perfect the model, we replicate it. After we have enough of them, we introduce them into her circulatory and lymphatic systems, as well as directly into the tumors wrapped around her spine. The new cells not only get to work, but they reproduce themselves. If it works, it becomes akin to a cancer vaccine."

Mairead's shoulders slumped. Paddy watched as her gaunt face, blue shivering lower lip and all, took on a crestfallen and skeptical look. She rolled her eyes and sighed.

"How are these so-called 'kill-switch genes' introduced?" she asked.

"That's the tricky part," the doctor admitted. "We engineer a virus which delivers the genetic material into the cells."

"What are the side effects?" Mairead asked, already suspecting.

"Because we make the virus in a lab, it's very benign—very tame."

"Doctor Cheng," Mairead interrupted him. "I've been fighting this disease for the better part of two years. Cancer hasn't done half the job of killing me the treatments have. Don't bullshit a dying woman. What are the side effects?"

"Most people experience mild flu-like symptoms," Cheng admitted.

"Mild flu-like symptoms?" Mairead laughed bitterly. "The shape I'm in, why don't you just pitch me in front of an uptown bus—same difference."

Paddy had listened carefully. This was the thread of hope to which he had been clinging, but now he saw it evaporating. After the last round of chemo and radiation, he had promised Mairead that he would allow her to decide what more if anything, she would do. So, he couched his pitch in support of the treatment with great care. He decided to rely on Dr. Cheng's expertise to make his argument and to make it seem like it was not *his* argument at all.

"Won't she still be receiving the palliative care and morphine drip?" he asked the doctor.

"Of course."

"Won't that mitigate the side effects of the virus? I mean, this can be administered through an IV, right? It can happen at home, can't it?"

Burnt to a Crisp

"Theoretically," Cheng said. "But it's going to take us a week to produce enough of the genes, and we do it here—in a laboratory setting. We introduce it to her circulatory system and lymph nodes through her existing pic lines. Because we have to also introduce it directly into the tumors intertwined around her lower spine, we would prefer to do it here, under x-ray. It's just safer. Pending your approval, Mairead, I can schedule you for next week."

Paddy switched his attention back to Mairead. He didn't want to use guilt to manipulate her, but he was out of other ideas.

"I think we owe it to the kids to take one last shot, Mairead. I believe they'd be hurt if you didn't try this. They'd feel like you gave up on them. Please think it over. I'll be there with you. The side effects don't sound any worse than how you feel now. I just think you'll be disappointed with yourself if you quit now. You're not a quitter."

Mairead looked at Paddy with withering annoyance. Her glare was on a par with his own. He realized she had seen right through him, and he was ashamed. He waited for her rebuke, but it never came. Instead, she relented.

"You know, Paddy," she said. "Everybody is right. You should have been a lawyer. You're full of enough shit to be a great one. I'll take the damned treatment."

***

In the truck on the way home, Paddy was chatty. Buoyant at Mairead's decision, he was acting as if the treatment was already a success. He went so far as to discuss events in the future, something neither of them had done for at least the last six months. She let him go on like that until they reached the Fifty-Ninth Street Bridge. Half the way to the Queens side, she burst his bubble of optimism.

"It's not going to work, Paddy," she said. "It won't work any more than the surgeries, the infusions, the chemo, and the radiation did. This is it. I've tried every holistic, bullshit Mother Earth remedy that waltzed down the pike. None of it was worth it. This cancer was meant to kill me. Promise me; when the gene therapy fails, you'll let me die."

This was a promise he couldn't make. Not that he didn't want to, but Mairead was the one thing in his life he couldn't part with. He was unable even to agree to do so. Instead, he changed the subject.

"If you're so sure it won't work, why do it?"

Michael O'Keefe

"Because if I don't, you'll blame yourself. I will die, and you'll spend the rest of your life beating yourself up for not convincing me to try this. I'm doing this for you, Paddy—only you. I'm dying anyway. When I'm gone, at least you'll know we did everything we could."

CHAPTER FIFTEEN

March 17, 2017
Bushwick, Brooklyn
11:00 hours

That Friday was St. Patrick's Day. Paddy's only acknowledgment of the occasion were the green stripes in his tie, worn at Mairead's insistence. He no longer marched in the parade or took part in any of the festivities. For one reason, he didn't drink anymore, so that part of it was lost on him. But, his lack of participation had a deeper root.

He started boycotting the parade in 1994. The Cardinal and the Archdiocese were already on shaky ground with him after His Eminence decided to join the mayor's circus and throw him under the bus during the riots in Washington Heights. While Paddy understood the mayor and the drug cartel were just exploiting the old man, he was still pissed off the Prince of *his* church would side against him in favor of a criminal who had tried to kill him.

One of Mairead's cousins worked for the Archdiocese at the time. She was so offended by the Cardinal's actions, she confronted him on it. Chagrined, the Cardinal called Paddy at Mairead's house to explain himself. He politely listened as the Cardinal tried to justify his actions. Paddy then explained why those actions were misplaced and offensive. He realized when the old priest repeated himself with what must have been a prepared speech, he wasn't getting an apology. What he got was a promise.

"If ever there is ever anything I can do for you in the future," His Eminence began. "I will bring all the power and prestige of this office to bear to see you have it."

Paddy put that card away for use at a later time.

When Pete O'Malley had been indicted in 1994, Paddy remembered the Cardinal's promise. He called him and related the disgraceful injustice being perpetrated by the US Attorney. The Cardinal said he would look into it and see what he could do. A week later, he heard back from Mairead's cousin.

"You're not getting a favor from that old, lying bastard," she told him.

"Okay," Paddy suspected as much. "Why not?"

"He called the US Attorney. She told him you and your team are under investigation for being members of the IRA. She told the Cardinal the investigation was called *Operation Bagpipes,* and indictments were forthcoming."

"And he bought it?" Paddy asked.

"He ate it up like cake."

"So, I guess I'm back to his former offer; I should just go fuck myself?"

"It seems so," she said. "He even fired off a memo. No one is to have any further dealings with you. I'm violating that order right now, but I think I've had it with this hypocrisy. The Archdiocese is nothing but a house of lies. So, I guess we're both *personae non gratae* now."

Paddy wrote the Cardinal and the whole Catholic Church off. They were on his shit list, and that's a list no one *ever* came off. So, he started boycotting the parade, as the Archdiocese sponsored it. Paddy had no problem with the Ancient Order of Hibernians, who ran it for the church. But he vowed he would never again march past St. Patrick's Cathedral and salute whatever ass-clown happened to be in residence there. With that history and Paddy's conflicted feelings about God, March 17th was just another day of work.

He finally tracked down Jessica Santiago at her aunt's house on Halsey Street. After he identified himself through the closed front door, he heard some crashing from inside the first-floor apartment, along with the unmistakable whine of an old wooden window being forced open. He chuckled, knowing what he was hearing. Someone beat a hasty retreat out the back window and into the rear yard.

If he had been there to arrest someone, he would have brought help to cover that window. But he just wanted to speak with Jessica. He had a pretty good idea who went out the window anyway. When Jessica opened the door, after giving the fleeing window crasher time to make good his escape, Paddy asked her to step out onto the stoop to speak with him.

"Next time, tell Blanco he doesn't have to leap out the window. I'm not looking for him," Paddy said.

Jessica gave him an embarrassed smile, confirming for Paddy it was Peter Cammaratta. What clinched it was when he observed Blanco at the corner of Broadway trying to hide in the shadows.

"After I leave, you should mention to him he's not invisible. He's going to have to talk to me eventually," Paddy said, handing Jessica his business card. "I'm sure he would rather do that without Parole or anyone else knowing about it. Let him know if he doesn't come in to see me; I'm just going to grab him at Parole or snatch him up on the street. He doesn't want that, and frankly, neither do I."

"I'll give him this and tell him to call you," Jessica promised.

Paddy nodded his thanks and regarded the young lady in front of him. She was a little slip of a thing, just five feet tall and skinny. Paddy noticed she was wearing baggy clothing. Her Denim shorts were cinched up by a leather belt, or they might have fallen off of her. Her baggy tee-shirt hid her upper body but not well enough to conceal the loose skin of her stomach beneath it.

"Did you give birth recently?" Paddy asked.

"No," she said, looking away. "I had an abortion. Some stuff showed up on the last sonogram."

"You don't have to explain yourself to me," Paddy assured her. "I'm just trying to evaluate if it had anything to do with the fire. Was it Sergio Palmiero's?"

"How do you know about him?" she asked, eyes narrowing.

"Because the only police report from the building in the last five years was when you had him locked up for assault," Paddy explained.

"He was the father, but I'm sure it had nothing to do with it," she said.

Paddy was unconvinced. For one reason, Jessica was being evasive, unwilling to make eye contact with him. For another, she had grown restless, shifting her weight from foot to foot. Paddy held his glare until her eyes met his. She looked doleful, he thought—almost embarrassed. Jessica was pretty, but with a hard, world-weary edge about her, making her seem far older than her nineteen years. Her light hazel eyes belied a regret—like she was lying to him but felt bad about doing so. She reminded him a little of his daughter, Casey. She was not as pretty as his daughter, but she had the same long brown hair and regarded Paddy with the same sympathetic, patronizing look. It was seriously pissing him off.

"When did you see Sergio last?"

"When I had him locked up."

"Did he know you were pregnant?"

"Yes."

"How did he feel about it?"

"He wanted me to keep it."

"Did he know about the abortion?"

"I don't think so."

That's a yes, Paddy thought. Why she would lie about it was still a mystery. Something or someone was working on her to suppress the truth, or at least hide it from the police. Paddy got the sense Jessica wanted to tell him more, but somebody told her not to. *What possible motive existed to protect a fire-bug from the law? Who would try to obstruct justice for an elderly couple and their special needs son?*

"Why are you withholding from me?" Paddy asked.

Jessica met his gaze and held it with that same sorrowful expression.

"Do you know who owns the building?" she asked.

"Bernardo Santapadre," Paddy said.

"That may be whose name is on the paper, but Bernardo is an eighty-year-old man with dementia. When you find out who really owns the building, you'll understand why nobody is talking about this."

CHAPTER SIXTEEN

March 17, 2017
Plainedge, Long Island
21:00 hours

That night, Paddy let himself into the house, careful not to wake Mairead. He slipped off his shoes and suit jacket and took off his gun and shield. After gently kissing her on the forehead, he sat in his recliner next to her hospital bed—content to watch her sleep. She was resting, murmuring into her pillow. He was happy to see it. Recently, Mairead had been given to restlessness, tossing, and turning, only to wake in excruciating pain. He hoped this peacefulness would continue.

He used the quiet time for reflection. Since Mairead had gotten sick, he had been excoriating himself for not preventing her exposure to the toxins from 9/11. Paddy knew this was ridiculous. When Mairead wanted to do something, she did it. No amount of arguing would have kept her away from Ground Zero after the attacks.

She was working at Long Island Jewish at the time. Since they were affiliated with Beth Israel and Downtown Beekman, they were looking for volunteers to staff the medical tents for the rescue and recovery. While everyone from LIJ pitched in, Mairead took it to the extreme. Several nights a week, she would work the site, tending to the rescue workers' injuries and discomforts. In the first two weeks after the attacks, Paddy and Mairead saw more of each other at Ground Zero than they did at home.

They were breathing the same poison air. But after seven days, when the mission changed from a rescue to a recovery, Paddy was looking to do more. This admission of hopelessness that there were no survivors depressed him, but it also made him angry. It's why he jumped at the opportunity to go into the Terrorist Taskforce when it presented itself. If he couldn't save the victims, he was determined at least to exact some payback.

Being a nurse, no one was asking Mairead to hunt terrorists. She continued to man the medical tents, giving aid and comfort to the first responders who were down there every day digging their fallen comrades out of the rubble. She was there at least twice a week for the next year. At no time was she provided with a means to avoid the foul, toxic air. She just breathed it in.

Over two thousand first responders had succumbed to various ailments since 9/11. This was more than were killed in the attacks themselves. Despite that, Paddy knew no one would have abandoned their post, even knowing what they all knew now. This tidal wave of rare cancers killing his peers, and now his wife did not sneak up on him. He predicted it the first night he was down on the pile.

***

On September 12, after his twelve-hour extended tour in the 83 Squad, Paddy and the whole platoon headed down to Ground Zero to dig for survivors. They were prevented from entering the rubble pile. It was still too dangerous. There were pocket fires flashing up from the ground as latent gasses would ignite from the sparks from the live wiring buried underground. The site itself emanated a wave of blistering heat, a remnant from the incredible friction generated when a pair of one-hundred-and-eleven-story buildings are knocked from their moorings to disintegrate into a massive pile of ruin and murder. So, the first responders stood by, frustrated witnesses to the deadliest attack on US soil in history, unable to do anything but look at it, burning it forever into their collective consciousness.

"This is surreal, Paddy," Sergeant Steve Krauss observed.

"It looks like the pictures of Hiroshima after the bombing," he agreed.

"What's that smell?" Steve wondered.

Burnt to a Crisp

"That is the smell of two skyscrapers after terrorists fly planes into them."

The odors of human decomposition wouldn't begin to emanate from the ground for another day, but Paddy anticipated it.

"In another day or two, it's going to smell like an open-air morgue down here," he said.

"At least the air is safe to breathe. The EPA tested it this morning. They said it wasn't harmful."

"Really, Steve?" Paddy said with disbelief in his voice. "The air is almost opaque. It's so full of micro-particles, I can barely see my hand through all the shit. This can't be safe. In fact, it's probably deadly."

"You don't trust the government?"

"The only reason the EPA gave the air a thumbs-up is because if they admitted it was toxic, they'd have to evacuate all of lower Manhattan. The only people allowed in would have to wear hazmat suits. The site would never get cleaned. The economy would collapse. Given the consequences, if the air was comprised of flaming asbestos, the EPA would still call it *good to go*."

"That's depressing," Steve said.

"It's nothing," Paddy said. "In the years to come, illness is going to cut through the people here like a scythe. We'll be dying in droves. This shit is poison. Mark my words, Steve. When all is said and done, we'll consider this our Chernobyl."

This was Paddy's prophecy. When he made it, he never imagined Mairead would be one of the afflicted.

***

Mairead's illness didn't sneak up on Paddy, but he thought if anyone in the family were affected, it would be him. So he wasn't prepared when 9/11 gave him a miss and struck Mairead.

Two years earlier, she had been feeling fatigued but attributed it to sleeping poorly. She thought she had strained something in her lower back at the gym. The tightness at night prevented her from getting comfortable in bed. After the ice, anti-inflammatories, and stretching failed to alleviate her discomfort; she hit upon the solution of all fitness obsessives: she would work out until exhaustion, thus forcing herself to sleep.

Paddy and Mairead went for an early evening run at their favorite spot, the Nature Preserve in Massapequa. They started at their usual brisk pace. About a mile into the run, Mairead kept falling behind. Concerned, Paddy slowed to keep pace with her. Most often, he had to struggle to keep up with his athletic wife. He couldn't help noticing her stride was clumsy, plodding even. She seemed to be exerting great effort with every step. He was about to ask her if she was okay when she pulled up, grabbed the small of her back, and cried out in pain.

As her legs gave out beneath her, he caught her just before she hit the ground.

"What's the matter, Mairead?" he asked, frightened.

"My legs have been going numb for the last week. I can't feel them at all right now."

"You grabbed your back. Does it hurt?"

"It feels like my spine is caught in a vise. Paddy, I'm scared."

So was he, but he didn't want her to know that. He shifted into problem-solving mode.

"Can you walk?" he asked.

"I don't think so. How are we going to get out of here?"

"If your back can take it, piggy-back. If not, I'll carry you. It's not like I haven't done it before."

"Not for a mile!" she said.

"I don't think we have another choice. Uber isn't allowed in the preserve, and there's no way an ambulance would make it down the path."

So, he hoisted her up over his back and started walking out the way they had come. About halfway, the cinching pain became too much for her to bear. He took her in his arms and carried her the rest of the way to the truck.

***

The next morning, they had an appointment with their orthopedic surgeon. Doctor Goldstein had been treating them both for a variety of sports-related injuries over the years. That will happen when aging athletes still think they are in their twenties. He was curious about Mairead's back. With her devotion to yoga and stretching, it would be odd for her to have a back ailment—unless there was some recent traumatic event. When that was ruled out, he performed an examination. Paddy noticed the concern on Goldstein's face as he felt around the bottom of Mairead's back.

"What's the matter, Doc?" Paddy asked.

"There is some inflammation, but it feels irregular," he said. "I want to get an x-ray."

Burnt to a Crisp

When the x-ray came back, Goldstein's concern appeared to turn grave. He summoned them into the hallway to view the high-resolution monitor. He had two images side by side.

"One of those is a normal, healthy spine and pelvis. The other one is yours," he said to Mairead.

"The one on the right is cloudy," Paddy observed. "There's no discernable space between the vertebrae."

"That's Mairead's. There is a mass making the image appear cloudy. I'm going to draw some blood and confer with your primary physician," Goldstein said.

Mairead lowered her head. Paddy didn't understand the look of resignation on her face, but she seemed to know what it was, even if Doctor Goldstein wouldn't say it.

"Don't jump to conclusions yet, Mairead," he cautioned her. "It might only be a cyst or something else benign and harmless."

"I'm sure that's what it is," she said, smiling weakly.

Goldstein explained the prescriptions for the MRI and the pain medications he was giving her when the nurse rolled up Mairead's sleeve to draw the blood. The inside of her arm, from wrist to shoulder, was covered with deep blue and purple bruising. Paddy noticed Dr. Goldstein blanch at the sight of it.

"When did this show up?" he demanded.

"This is the first time I'm seeing it," Mairead said.

"Let me see the other one."

Mairead bared her left arm; it was mottled the same way.

"You're going right to LIJ," he told them. "Tell them I'm admitting you. I will let your primary know what's going on, and I'll meet you there."

"Is that necessary?" Paddy asked, trying to quash the growing panic coursing through him.

Mairead took his hand and gazed at him with a look of gentle patience as if he were a six-year-old who had to be told there was no Santa Clause.

"It's necessary, Paddy," she said as she brought his hand to her lips to kiss him.

***

It was not a cyst—pilonidal, sebaceous, or otherwise. It was not benign. The mass was a malignant bone tumor—osteogenic sarcoma. With the prevalence of rare cancers popping up and killing so many of the first responders from 9/11, Paddy had learned the term. This medical jargon had become all too common.

Mairead's blood work revealed she was suffering from leukemia and lymphoma, probably the cause of the tumors—a deadly trifecta of cancer. The tumors were already stage three when they were discovered.

Mairead had been battling it for the last two years only to see it progress to stage four. All of the treatment to this point had done more harm than good. She was at the end of her endurance. Sure she would die; she was giving the gene therapy a chance only for her husband. She had her first infusion two days earlier. It was too soon to know if it would have any effect.

***

Back in their living room, Paddy started to nod off in his chair. When he awoke with a start, he saw Mairead smiling at him.

"How long have you been home?" she asked.

"About an hour."

"And you've just been sitting there watching me sleep?"

"I kissed you when I came in."

Mairead breathed deeply, seeming to savor the air.

"Yes, you did," she sighed. "I can smell your cologne."

"I didn't want to wake you," Paddy said. "You looked so comfortable."

"I was," she said. "But I had a dream about us, and I woke up."

"About us?"

"Mmmm, remember the day-bed on the beach in Punta Cana?"

"How can I forget? We slept all day in that thing."

"We weren't sleeping, Paddy."

"Maybe a little," he laughed.

"C'mere," she said, reaching for him.

Paddy got up and came to her side. Mairead pulled his head down and kissed him. He was surprised, but he met her ardor with his own. It had been months since her illness allowed them to be even this intimate. He wasn't going to let the chance escape. When Mairead reached out and grabbed hold of him through his trousers, he realized it wasn't chance, and Mairead was calling the shots.

He reached under her nightgown to find the sweet spot between her thighs. She rolled her hips, opening herself to his touch. Mairead was wet and warm, as she always was for him. She held on tight to his crotch with her right hand and latched onto his wrist with the other, adding pressure to his gentle stroking. She gasped and shuddered, pressing down to ride it out.

"Oh, God, I needed that," she sighed, pulling him down by his tie to kiss him again.

Paddy continued to run his hands all over her body, beginning with her hips and working his way up past her taut stomach, finding her breasts. The touch of her was like little charges of electricity coursing through him. Even though she was so thin, her body responded to his hands. Her gentle moaning encouraged him. Paddy didn't see the gauntness—not really. Even through her illness—the wretched pain, the weight loss, her hair thinning and falling out in tufts—she was still the most beautiful thing he had ever seen, and he wanted her. He was only concerned about hurting her. So, he was gentle, more so than he had ever been. He just couldn't figure out how to accomplish the act without shattering her pelvis. Mairead had ideas about that.

"Are you sure about this?" he asked. "I don't want to hurt you."

"Get over here," she insisted.

She gently pushed his head down from her face. Paddy took her cue and worked his mouth down over her breasts and stomach, her nightgown bunched up above her chest. Mairead spread her legs to receive him. As he devoured her, she worked to free him from his pants. She was just cascading over the top of another climax as she took Paddy into her mouth. That lasted about three seconds when he stopped her.

"Did I hurt you?" Mairead asked.

"No, of course not."

"Then why did you make me stop?"

"Mairead, for months, I've done nothing but pass water through this thing. If I let you continue for another second, I would've exploded and probably blown the back of your head out."

Mairead giggled at the picture of it.

"Then I'm glad you stopped me," she said. "I want you inside me."

"I want that, too," Paddy said. "But how am I going to do it without hurting you?"

"Remember Punta Cana?" was all she had to say.

Paddy tore his shirt and tie off over his head and kicked his suit pants and underwear off. He was in too much of a hurry to bother with his socks. Mairead turned over on her left side, and Paddy spooned himself behind her. She lifted her leg and guided him into her.

"Baby, I'm worried," he said. "I don't want to hurt you."

"Just relax," she said. "I'll do the work."

She pressed her hips back, grinding herself against him. Their movement was almost imperceptible—so languid, and deep, and fraught with their pent-up desire. They both had to fight to avoid giving in to frenzy. As Mairead moved back against him, he could feel her shudder and moan as he pressed his lips against her cheek. She kept at it, Paddy losing count of her orgasms until he could take it no more.

"I can't hold it," he whispered hoarsely.

Mairead reached back with her right hand to cradle his face to her own.

"It's okay, baby. Come with me," she said.

Paddy could feel the two of them shuddering together, locked at the hips as they were. It was probably only seconds, but it felt like an eternity—one he never wanted to end. A wave of contented ecstasy washed over him as they lay there, Mairead cooing "I love you" in his ear.

A short while later, she could feel his tears, hot and wet, on her cheek.

"What's the matter, Paddy?"

"I can't get the idea out of my mind that this was the last time we'll ever be together like this," he admitted.

"We won't let that happen," Mairead said. "But this was wonderful. If it had to be the last time, I'd be okay with it."

Mairead pressed back against him again. Feeling himself stiffen inside her, he pulled her hips back toward him.

"You're right," he said. "It couldn't be the last time."

***

That morning, Casey came downstairs to leave for school only to behold her father pressed against her mother in her hospital bed. They were naked except for her father's black socks and her mother's nightgown bunched up above her breasts.

"Gross!" she said.

She covered them both with the bedsheet crumpled at the foot of the bed. Slamming the door behind her, Casey headed off to school at Hofstra University. At the Starbucks on Hempstead Turnpike, she had to compose herself before going in to order coffee. As much as the picture of her parents in bed like that repulsed her, she knew it was only because they were her parents. Like all twenty-year-olds, the idea of them having sex was almost unimaginable. But, looking at it through a prism of detachment, what she saw were two people deeply in love, sleeping contentedly in each other's arms. She found the aura of devotion they projected so profound it scared her. No two people ever needed each other more, she knew, and she didn't think her dad could survive without her mother. So, while Casey ached for Mairead's suffering, she prayed it wouldn't kill them both.

CHAPTER SEVENTEEN

March 18, 2017
Bushwick, Brooklyn
16:00 hours

Paddy got into the squad that afternoon. He was about to call the Cornell Burn Center to check on his victims' status when his phone rang.

"Eight-three Squad, Durr," he answered.

"Hello, Detective," Dr. Menkovich said. "I wanted to let you know. Giorgio Santapadre expired a few minutes ago."

"Thanks for the heads-up, Doc. I'm surprised he went first. He was only thirty-five. I would have thought Lucinda or Bernardo would have preceded him."

"It's not surprising. People with Down Syndrome generally have shorter life spans. They tend to suffer from an assortment of immuno and respiratory issues, as was the case with Giorgio. But it didn't really matter. The lung damage was so severe; I was astonished any of them survived long enough even to get here."

"I should be there within the hour," Paddy said.

"Better hurry. Lucinda and Bernardo are hanging by a thread. I doubt if they will make it that long."

"I just have to notify the family, and I'll be on my way."

"The daughter, Cassie, is here already," he said.

I don't know who Cassie is, Paddy thought. He had minimal contact with the Santapadre's surviving family—none, in fact. Thus far, all he had was the name of the eldest son, Miguel. That and his cell number had been on the EMS report the morning of the fire. Paddy's messages had gone unanswered. He needed a family member to verify the Santapadres were not the target of the arson. *Perhaps this Cassie could do that for me.*

"I'll see you as soon as I can," Paddy said.

By the time he got to the hospital, Lucinda and Bernardo had expired. Paddy saw Dr. Menkovich speaking with a stunning and very expensively dressed woman who could have been anywhere between twenty and forty years old. He thought she might be a hospital administrator. Based upon her clothing, he assumed they were either paying them better these days, or this one was living far beyond her means.

She had shoulder-length frosted blonde hair with silvery gold highlights. Rather than suggesting an age, the color variation caught your eye and held it. She looked like one of those people who remained perpetually tan but not from an artificial source. *This woman's skin had been sun-kissed, and recently. I wonder what exotic tropical resort she spends the winters getting her bronze on.*

Chanel, from head to toe, she was arrayed in what looked to Paddy to be a year's mortgage worth of platinum and diamonds. Only her facial expression—sad and serious—gave him the impression she had an emotional tie to anyone on the floor. As he got closer, he could see she had been crying, her eyes puffy and moist with tears.

Dr. Menkovich saw him approach and introduced them.

"Detective Durr," he said. "This is Cassandra Rothman, Lucinda, and Bernardo's daughter."

Paddy extended his right hand for a polite shake and was surprised at the firmness with which she returned it. The intensity of her gaze as she met his was almost unnerving. She seemed to regard him with a sort of pity. Her piercing eyes scrutinizing him in full, a tinge of new sadness seemed to appear that he was sure had nothing to do with her deceased family. Nothing about this woman suggested a Bushwick upbringing.

"I'm Detective Durr, from the 83rd Precinct, Mrs. Rothman," he said. "This is my case. I'm very sorry for your loss."

"Thank you, Detective. Please call me Cassie."

"I'm sorry I wasn't in touch before now," Paddy said. "But I had very little information to go on, so I didn't know about you. I have several messages into your brother, Miguel, but he hasn't gotten back to me."

"Miguel?" she smiled, causing Paddy to be unsure of himself.

"Yeah, Miguel Santapadre. Isn't he your brother?"

"He is, but I haven't heard him called that in a long time."

"Is there another name I should know him by?"

"Definitely," she said. "But he can tell you that. I just spoke with him. He was away on business. He's on his way home now."

"Could I have his address and phone number?" Paddy asked.

"He wouldn't appreciate me giving it out. You'll have to get it from him."

Paddy was a little taken aback by her secrecy but sensed it wasn't her idea. She was protecting her brother's identity, no doubt at his request—probably a demand.

"You don't live in Bushwick," Paddy said. "Or I would have known about you."

"I left Bushwick when I graduated high school and never went back."

"Where do you live now?"

"I'm in East Hampton," she said, handing Paddy her business card.

It was a refined and simple thing, except for her photo in the upper left corner. It was a raised image protruding from the delicately textured cream-colored stock. Without words, it said, *Buy something exclusive and very expensive from me.* The rest of the card consisted of her name, Cassie Rothman, and the business name, Rothman Luxury Real Estate. Then there were her phone numbers, office and cell, in the lower right-hand corner.

Paddy noticed the diamond engagement ring on her left hand's fourth finger fronted by her wedding band, also encrusted with diamonds. From her suit sleeve, he could spy a gem-covered Bulgari Serpenti wristwatch bracelet just peeking out. Paddy no longer wore wristwatches, not since he started carrying a cell phone. *One less thing to break*, he thought. But he had an enduring affection for and a fascination with high-end watches—particularly for women. He loved to buy them for Mairead, enjoying the delight they afforded her and how they looked on her delicate wrist. But the Bulgari Serpenti was a fiscal impossibility for them, as was Cassie's engagement ring—the diamond big enough to choke a horse.

"Rothman," Paddy said. "I know this company."

"Do you?" Cassie seemed surprised.

"Yeah; vintage wines, high-end restaurants, and real estate."

Paddy knew the Rothman Group owned or had sold every exclusive piece of property on Long Island's Gold Coast, and the Hamptons, north and south fork, for about the last hundred years.

"Very good, Detective. You've done your homework."

"Nah," Paddy said. "I just pay attention. And I like steakhouses. The Rothman Group has some excellent ones on Long Island."

"I'm still impressed," she said.

"I went to college with a Lawrence Rothman. Any relation?"

"You went to Columbia?" she asked incredulously.

"Oh no," Paddy dead-panned. "Have I lost my Ivy League luster? So, you know Larry?"

"He's my husband, and *no one* calls him Larry."

"I do," Paddy said.

He's a schlub and an upper-class twit. Even if the Queen of England liked his wines so much, she saw fit to bestow a knighthood upon him. I'm not impressed by old money. He's just Larry to me.

"What in God's name are you doing working for the police department?" she asked.

"I grew up in Bushwick," Paddy said. "And I never really left. When I graduated from Columbia, I had some opportunities to do other things. But I wanted to help people. So, I didn't chase the money. I have a lot of regrets, but not about my career choice. Right now, I want to get justice for your parents and your brother. They deserve it. So, what do you say, Cassie? Will you help me?"

Cassie had that sad, pitying look again, pissing Paddy off to no end. He endured it only because he understood it wasn't her choice to stonewall him. He was sure it was her brother's.

"As I said, Detective. I'm not in Bushwick anymore. My brother, Miguel—as you know him—still has his hooks into the neighborhood. You'll have to deal with him."

"When and where is the wake?"

"This Friday at Raimundo and Sons, on Cypress Avenue."

"I will see you there."

***

Back at the squad, Paddy's first order of business was to change his arson's classification to homicide. This involved preparing an Unusual Occurrence Report, a Homicide Bullet, and notifying everyone and his mother within the police department. Having done that, he had to tell Lieutenant Martino, who had already gone home for the day. So Paddy called his cellphone.

"Sorry to bother you, Lou," Paddy said. "But homicides 4, 5, and 6 just dropped."

"Please tell me this was your fire victims and not three fresh ones," the Lieutenant asked.

"Yeah," Paddy assured him. "It's the Santapadres. They all died within an hour of each other."

"Forgive my elation. But you know where I'm coming from," Martino said.

Paddy laughed. He knew his boss wasn't celebrating anyone's death. He just wanted to be sure there weren't three more fresh bodies he would have to run interference for, so his detectives could do their jobs.

"Remind me," he said. "What have you got on this again?"

"I've got bupkis, Lou."

"Nothing? That doesn't sound like you. I thought you had a guy you liked for it."

"I do, but I have nothing to hang my hat on. I've got motive and opportunity but no witnesses or evidence to tie him to it. It's just supposition at this point."

"How has the canvassing gone?"

"I've only done a couple. Now that it's a homicide, I'll have some help. I'll hit it again, but something is going on in the street. No one will talk to me. They seem like they want to, but someone with influence is shutting them down."

"Who would want to do that?" the lieutenant wondered.

"I don't know yet, but you can be sure I'll find out."

"I know you will, Paddy. Who's got it from Homicide?"

"That's my next call. I think Georgie Fahrbach is up."

"Good, keep me posted on any progress."

Paddy called the Brooklyn North Homicide Squad. George Fahrbach picked up the phone. Anticipating this call, he said he and Sergeant Boland would be right over. The news was comforting. In Fahrbach and Boland, Paddy had two veteran homicide investigators to whom he wouldn't have to explain things twice. He had been working with them for the last dozen years or so and solved whatever they had been working on every time. In addition, they were friends. George and Jimmy both lived near Paddy on Long Island. They knew Mairead and her condition. So, Paddy wouldn't need to waste valuable time trying to bring them up to speed on a situation that was authoring itself and changing frequently—seldom for the better.

George, in particular, had gotten very close to the Durr family. He was the Boro Director for the Detectives' Endowment Association. He was the one to see

Burnt to a Crisp

that Mairead had everything she needed in the house, like the hospital bed and home care. He wouldn't need to ask about her. He was already on top of the crisis.

The next call was to ADA Dan Bibb, and Paddy found it less enjoyable. Dan had been waiting for this call so that he could jump into the case with both feet. The innocence of the victims had struck a chord in him. He was anxious to get started on bringing them justice. The problem was, Paddy didn't have anything for him to do yet.

"I'll be there as soon as I can get a videographer to come with me," Bibb said.

"Take it easy, Dan," Paddy told the rangy prosecutor. "I've got no one for you to interview."

"You don't have any witnesses yet?" Bibb was incredulous, yelling. "What the hell have you been doing for the past week?"

Paddy rolled his eyes and held the phone away from his ear to mitigate the pain from Dan's roaring frustration on the other end. He could relate but was exhausted and in no mood for anyone's bullshit—even from a friend like Dan Bibb. He tried to be calm, as he explained, but he was out of patience. So, it didn't come out the way he had hoped.

"For the past week, I have been working on my own, waiting for the victims to die so I could get a little help. I had no real access to my office, what with the Hate Crimes Task Force hogging all the desks and computers so they could look at their Instagram accounts. I also had a personal matter to deal with, but you know all about that. So, if I have failed to deliver this case in the manner you expected, wrapped in a box with a neat bow around it, please understand, it is with all *due* respect when I tell you to go fuck yourself," Paddy growled.

Bibb had regretted his crack as soon as he made it. He realized he had pushed his weary friend too far.

"I'm sorry, Paddy," Bibb said. "I was out of line. I know how invested you are in this case. I'm just frustrated because I want to do something."

"That makes two of us," Paddy said, calming down.

"Well—what *do* you have?" he asked.

"I've got a potential motive and a guy I like for it, but I can't prove any of it yet."

"Who's on it with you from Homicide?"

"Georgie Fahrbach. We're going to do another canvass as soon as he gets here, maybe shake a witness loose."

"*Hansi!*" Dan said. "Excellent! I'll be on the cell if you need anything."

Michael O'Keefe

"Thank you," Paddy said before hanging up.

***

George *Hansi* Fahrbach had been a detective for a few years longer than Paddy. He got his gold shield while in Manhattan North Narcotics after his undercover had been killed making a drug buy the same night Police Officer Jimmy Crowe had been murdered. George and his team were instrumental in identifying the perpetrators of that murder and uncovered a link to the killers of Jimmy Crowe as well. It was at the funeral for the two cops he and George were introduced, and they had been friends since.

George got his nickname in the usual way cops get them; from another smart-ass cop. When George left narcotics and was transferred to the 79 Squad, an old-timer thought he bore a striking resemblance to a TV character of recent memory. This was before the days of the internet. There was no PhotoShop, and cut-and-paste was done with scissors, glue, magazines, and polaroid photos. When the *hair-bag,* as salty old cops are called, insisted on taking George's polaroid for the coffee club, George thought it a little strange, but as the new guy, he went with the flow.

Until a week later, when he came into the squad to find it festooned with pictures of Sergeant Hans Schultz from the sitcom *Hogan's Heroes*. The pic came from an old TV Guide. Shultz's face was replaced with the polaroid cut-out of George's. This mini-poster, with the words *I know nothing!* Scribbled across the bottom had been photo-copied and hung up around the squad by the hundreds. Everyone started calling George *Hansi*. Even though the likeness was slight, the old-timer had put a lot of thought and effort into it. While George didn't like it, he knew it would be a pointless fight. The name would only become more entrenched. So, he embraced it. He had been known by his friends and colleagues as Hansi ever since.

***

George and Paddy began their canvass for witnesses in 402 Wilson, the three-story, low-rise housing project directly across from the crime scene. The first thing they noticed was a video camera with a cracked lens facing away from the front door and pointing at the entrance to 407 Wilson.

"Think it works?" George asked.

Burnt to a Crisp

"Let's find the super and ask him."

Paddy pressed the doorbell for apartment 1A, listed on the directory as Superintendent. A few seconds later, the voice of an impatient man came through the intercom.

"Wadda ya want?"

"Police," George said. "We got some questions."

"What the hell did I do now?" the man asked, though you could detect the humor in his voice.

"This guy is funny," George said.

"I know, right?" Paddy said, laughing into the intercom, "Nothing that we're aware of. It's about the fire the other night."

"Oh, okay," he said. "I'll be right out."

The super came outside and greeted the detectives with a wry smile. He looked to be in his late fifties, very thin, his arms covered in biker tattoos. Paddy thought he recognized one of them.

"They call me *Jibaro*," the super said by way of introduction.

"No offense," Paddy said. "But you don't look like much of a farmer."

"That's cause I ain't. I came here from Bayamon when I was eight. Because I spoke proper Spanish, and not that *Spanglish* shit the *Boricuas* all speak, they thought I was a hillbilly. It stuck."

"It's a good one," Paddy said.

"I grew up in this neighborhood and never left."

"I think I remember you," Paddy told him. "You used to ride with the Savage Skulls."

"How would you know about the Savage Skulls? We got disbanded years ago."

"I grew up on Hart and Irving. I'm Paddy Durr."

At the mention of his name, Jibaro's eyes went wide.

"Oh, fuck! I remember you!"

"Why does everybody have this reaction to you?" George asked, grinning.

He never tired of these old Paddy Durr stories and sensed he was about to hear another one.

"How do you remember him, Jibaro?" George asked.

"I was there when he gave *Gordo* Melendez the beating of his life and threw him through our clubhouse window."

"So?" George shrugged.

Michael O'Keefe

"He was *seventeen,*" Jibaro said, pointing at Paddy. "Then he climbed through the window and started choking out Gordo with his own wallet chain. He would have killed him if those cops, Bucciogrosso and Curran, weren't there to stop him."

"Butchie and Eddie, again?" George said. "How many times did those guys have to rescue you?"

"They weren't rescuing *him*. They were saving *us*," Jibaro said. "After they pulled him off Gordo, he marched right out and lifted our club president, Pepino, out of his chair by his beard. He said, 'If any of you ink-stained motherfuckers ever gets in my way or try to put your hands on me again, I'll kill every last one of you.' Then he went over to the curb and pushed our bikes down like they were dominoes before he stormed off the block."

"What brought all of that on?" George wondered.

"We used to close the block when we hung out at the club," Jibaro said. "We made everybody cross the street so that you couldn't walk on the sidewalk in front of our clubhouse. Durr wouldn't listen. So, Gordo grabbed him."

"How did my partner react to that, I wonder?" George asked, grinning.

"He went *Diablo-Gringo* on Gordo's ass. I never seen anybody get hit so many times so fast."

"Diablo Gringo, what the hell is that?" George asked.

"It means *devil white-boy,*" Jibaro said. "It's what we used to call him."

"You're exaggerating, Jibaro," Paddy said, trying to short circuit the conversation.

"No, I'm not," Jibaro said. "Pepino called a general meeting of the club to decide what to do about you. He ordered us to leave you alone. He said your mother was a *bruja* and your father was a contract killer. Because of that, you were the deadliest motherfucker ever spawned. He said everyone around you dies, so you were not to be touched. Gordo spent three months in the hospital getting put back together. When he came out, even *he* wanted no part of you."

Paddy remembered his dealings with the Savage Skulls. It was a few weeks after the murder/suicide of Inez and Hector Vasconcellos. He was walking around in an emotional fugue state. All he could feel was guilt for Inez and repugnance for himself. He didn't care whether he lived or died at that point. This emotional void could tip into a destructive rage. Paddy understood now that Gordo Melendez just had the misfortune of being the one who tipped it.

Burnt to a Crisp

The rest of Jibaro's account was as Paddy remembered it. He hadn't known anything about the bruja and hitman stuff, but that was no doubt just neighborhood lore and bullshit Latin superstition. So, he discounted it out of hand.

"I can't believe you became a cop," Jibaro said, calling Paddy back to the present. "We heard you were working for the Bonannos. They said you were the hammer for Fat Archie—making all of his loan shark and gambling collections."

"Oh, fuck! I don't want to hear anymore," George said.

"There is no more," said Jibaro. "He just disappeared one day. No one saw him in the neighborhood anymore."

"Jibaro," Paddy said, focusing him. "Were you home the night of the fire?"

"Yeah. I came out when I heard the fire trucks."

"Who else was out?" George asked.

"Everyone. The whole neighborhood was on the street."

"I'm looking for who might have been on the street before the fire trucks got there," Paddy told him.

"Did you talk to Erika in apartment 2B?"

"Not yet," George said. "Why do we need to talk to her?"

"She's friends with Weird Harold." He said as if it meant something.

"Who is Weird Harold?" Paddy asked.

"He's the retarded kid who lives on Gates up toward Knickerbocker."

"Retarded how?" George asked.

"I'm sorry, retarded is not the right word," Jibaro said. "He's autistic, I guess. He only talks to Erika. Most nights, he can be found right on the corner over there," he said, pointing to the corner of Gates and Wilson. "He hangs out and waits until Erika comes out. You want to talk to him; Erika is the only one who can help you do that."

"Erika in 2B?" Paddy confirmed.

"Yeah," Jibaro said. "She's just a kid, but she's smart. Nice too; she looks out for everybody."

"Then we'll talk to her," Paddy said. "By the way, does that video camera work?"

"Nah, it's a dummy. It's just there for show."

"I was afraid of that," Paddy said, handing Jibaro a business card. "If you ever need anything, *compadre*, give me a call."

"So, we're on the same side now?"

"You better hope so," Paddy said, grinning.

109

"You know, Detective Durr, I like you a lot better now that you've developed a sense of humor."

"That makes two of us," George agreed.

"One other thing," Jibaro said. "I don't think you're going to get anyone from the neighborhood to tell you anything."

"Why is that?" Paddy asked.

"I hear things in this job. The story going around is the guy who runs everything on Wilson Avenue told everyone not to talk to the cops. He said he was going to take care of it himself."

"Who is he?" George asked.

"I don't know," Jibaro admitted. "I haven't been here that long. He's supposed to be an *Original G*, and he runs *everything*. If I hear a name, I'll call you."

They thanked him as they headed up to apartment 2B.

Inez Gomez answered the apartment door. When she saw the two detectives, she became obviously concerned. She clutched at the small carved wooden crucifix she wore around her neck on a leather lanyard.

"Is my daughter okay?" she asked. They could hear the fear in her voice.

"Erika is fine," Paddy assured her. "We were hoping to speak with her about the fire the other morning."

"*Oh, Dios mio! Gracias a Christo*!" Inez exclaimed, blessing herself.

Then she remembered her manners and asked the detectives to come in. She led them to the kitchen table and offered them coffee. Paddy took one look around the immaculate apartment with all the religious iconography hanging on the walls and understood Senora Gomez was a very proper and traditional woman. To refuse her hospitality would have been an insult. He graciously accepted the coffee for him and George.

"We just had coffee," George whispered.

"I know," Paddy said. "But we *need* to have her coffee and don't forget to tell her how good it is. I'll explain why later."

When Senora Gomez returned with their *café con leche*, with two heaping tablespoons of sugar in each, she sat down with her own.

"Is my Erika in trouble?" she asked, but the unconcerned tone of her voice told Paddy she never honestly considered it a possibility. She only asked because she would have found asking *what is this all about?* to be too abrupt—bordering on rude.

"No, of course not," Paddy assured her. "We were told she might know something about the fire from the other morning."

"*Si*, she does. Her boyfriend Harold saw something. She didn't tell me what it was. She was worried about him. He's different, you know?"

"We heard that," George said.

"That's why we wanted to speak to Erika first," Paddy said. "We were told he only speaks to her. We're hoping she can convince him to confide in us."

"If anyone can, it would be my Erika," she said. "But I don't know. He shuts down around other people."

"We have to try," George said. "Three people died in that fire."

Senora Gomez blessed herself again and whispered a prayer in Spanish.

"Erika is not home; I take it?" Paddy asked.

"No, she's at school."

"Does she have a cell phone?" George asked.

"Yes," she said, handing George a slip of paper with the number on it. "But she turns it off in school, and she never has it on around Harold. The phones make him nervous. After class, she's headed over there. She might call me in between."

Paddy handed her his business card, one of the ones with his cell phone number on it. He knew instinctively she could be trusted with it.

"Please have Erika call us as soon as you hear from her," Paddy asked.

"I will give her the message."

George made a big production of thanking Senora Gomez for the delicious coffee and her wonderful hospitality, shaking her hand with both of his. She seemed delighted with the gesture.

After leaving the apartment, they finished canvassing the building for any additional witnesses; Paddy put the needle to George.

"You poured it on a little thick with the thank you," he said. "I thought you were gonna kiss her hand."

"Well, you did say to thank her, and I felt bad about scaring her. So, what do you want to do now, Diablo Gringo?"

Paddy rolled his eyes at the long-forgotten sobriquet. He had hoped it would have stayed forgotten. George would only share the story of his confrontation with the Savage Skulls with their mutual friends, so Paddy would be spared having the nickname resurrected.

"We could probably find Harold ourselves," Paddy said. "I think I already know him. But if we do and he shuts down on us, we'll lose him as a witness. We'd better just wait until we can talk to Erika."

"Makes sense," George agreed.

"Nothing to do now but head back to the barn and type," said Paddy.

Michael O'Keefe

CHAPTER EIGHTEEN

March 19, 2018
Plainedge, Long Island
11:00 hours

Paddy was just climbing out of the shower as his brunch guests were arriving. It was his birthday, and Mairead was feeling well enough to have a small celebration on his behalf. Francine Bender and her wife, Jocelyn, showed up with their toddler daughter, Erin. They had brought an armful of goodies from the bagel store near their home in Forest Hills.

Mairead's nurse, Julissa, had just finished preparing the coffee after helping Mairead get dressed. She had her out of the hospital bed and seated in Paddy's recliner. She looked much better, the color returning to her face. Since ending the chemo in favor of the gene therapy, her hair had made a dramatic comeback. She was able to dispense with the hated headscarf. It was still very short, but Paddy thought she looked beautiful. Mairead was of the opinion she looked like a twelve-year-old boy.

The ladies brought with them an aura of optimism and joy the Durrs had been missing. Their daughter, Erin, was a particular delight for Mairead. She was an adorable, affectionate child with an inquisitive and engaging manner. Her dark brown curls and piercing blue eyes mirrored Paddy's. Mairead's delight came tinged with sadness, realizing this might be the closest she ever would come to having a grandchild. She shook off the thought and continued to play an animated game of peekaboo with the cackling child in her lap.

Paddy's uncanny resemblance to Erin was not a coincidence. In fact, it was by design. After Chief Pasquale was forced to retire, as Paddy had predicted, his replacement was a young and dynamic up-and-comer. For all of his intelligence and exuberance, he did not know how to command a detective boro. Fortunately, his senior adjutant did.

The chief came to rely on Fran for everything. So much so that when he was promoted to Chief of Detectives, he took her with him. The rumors about a romantic involvement between them were already being whispered.

***

They ended abruptly in 2006. Fran had called Mairead and asked if she could come to the house. She was a bit cryptic in saying she was bringing a *friend*. She showed up holding hands with a young woman Paddy already knew from the job. Jocelyn Jacobs was an undercover in Brooklyn North Narcotics. Three years earlier, Paddy had been the catching detective on a spectacular line-of-duty shooting in which she was involved inside a drug spot on Jefferson Street.

Jocelyn, or Joss as everyone called her, had been making a large heroin buy with her *ghost* waiting outside the locked apartment door. This unforeseen complication (an undercover is never supposed to be out of sight from their ghost) should have precipitated an immediate abort to the buy-op. It didn't happen in this case; Paddy discovered, because Joss was committed to the mission, young enough not to know better, and batshit crazy brave—bordering on reckless.

Once inside, she was informed by the dealers the seven thousand dollars of buy money she brought for the *G-pack* of heroin (1,000 glassines) wasn't going to be enough.

"Bad news, pretty lady," the dealer said. "All we serve here is cake and cock, and we're all out of cake."

He put a nine-millimeter pistol to her head and forced her to her knees in front of him.

"You can have your dope," he said. "But the price went up. Along with the money, you're going to have to suck every dick in the room."

Joss did not panic. She surveyed the apartment to see the other four drug dealers, some of whom were already pulling out their penises. She observed they were all armed with nine millimeters like their leader. Noting where everyone in the room was standing and weighing which threat was nearest, she became defiant.

"I ain't sucking anything. You might as well shoot me now. Or, you can take your money and let me leave with my dope. Your choice, but nobody is getting a blow job today."

When the boss made the mistake of racking the action of his gun for dramatic effect, Joss used the distraction to reach into her purse. She removed her .32 caliber Barretta pistol from where it was secreted in a Velcro pouch behind the buy-money.

"Police, drop the guns!" she yelled before shooting the leader through the groin, severing his penis.

From between the shocked and bleeding dealer's legs, she fired six more times, striking the other four miscreants in or near their groins as well. Her support team had overheard the entire episode over her Kell transmitter.

They were already on their way once the ghost lost sight of her. They started running when they heard the dealers try to renegotiate the price. Even if they had run from the start, they wouldn't have been in time.

By the time they got the door down, they entered a living room filled with the smell of expended gun powder, blood, and evacuated rectums. The five-shot and soiled drug dealers were screaming and writhing on the ground. The leader, by now, realizing his penis was lying on the floor four feet away from the rest of his body, saw the heavily armed support team and begged them to kill him. Instead, they kicked him onto his belly and hand-cuffed him. They left his penis right where it was. The EMTs later recovered it to transport it to the hospital along with its owner. Sadly—for him—it couldn't be reattached.

While the EMTs were preparing to transport the shot suspects, and the team was safeguarding the perps' weapons, Joss was calmly reloading a fresh magazine into her Barretta. Sergeant Simmons, her team leader, asked if she was all right.

"Yeah, Sarge, fine," she said. "I would have cuffed them, but I don't have any—being undercover and all."

Paddy's case was a breeze; not usually the situation in a police-involved shooting. The tape from the Kell, the pre-recorded buy-money, the drugs, and the perpetrators' statements told the story and obviated the need for Joss to testify in the grand jury. Paddy, having much experience with these things, advised her not to without a subpoena and immunity. Her lawyer concurred.

The DA's office rarely offers immunity to police officers involved in a shooting. With the tape and physical evidence available, they didn't need to. So,

Joss didn't have to tell her story until the G.O. 15 hearing for the Firearms Discharge Review Board—months after being cleared by the DA. Paddy served as her union representation.

When Joss told Paddy her version of events before the hearing, he was concerned.

"You know, Joss," he said, "you shot five guys. Even if you have no reason to be remorseful, a little less ambivalence will project better. Other than me, no one in that room is your friend. You don't want them getting the idea you enjoyed shooting those guys."

"I know," she said," but I can't seem to give a shit. They were all scumbag rapists. No one died, and the guy who lost his penis only had bad intentions for it. So, sorry—not sorry."

Paddy regarded the diminutive and striking detective with her icy blue eyes, lush blonde hair, and perfect tanned complexion. She was a far cry from the ratty junkie she portrayed the night of the shooting. He knew her shot-out look was the product of makeup, tooth wax, and baggy clothing. But viewing her now, stylishly dressed, coifed, and accessorized to perfection, she looked like a banker in her understated and conservative business suit. Paddy thought she would break her interviewers' hearts if she didn't scare them to death first.

"Think you can fake a little regret for just an hour?" Paddy asked.

"Sure," she said. "I've been faking it all my life."

She did more than fake it a little. She projected a somber remorse Paddy knew she did not feel. When she was asked how she had been since the shooting, she launched into a tear-filled, sobbing lamentation. She told them she couldn't sleep, was overtaken with anxiety and a sense of impending dread. She claimed to be consumed by a latent fear of men since the incident, affecting her relationships. She couldn't concentrate or relax. She desperately wished she had never become an undercover and would do anything to take back that fateful day.

Paddy didn't buy a word of it but was blown away nonetheless. He looked around the table and saw even the douche-bags from Internal Affairs misting up. The usual hard questions never came. The men in the room all sought to comfort and reassure this seemingly delicate lady-detective. It would all be okay, they promised her. The hearing ended, and the department found the shooting justified.

When they left the hearing room, Joss winked and smiled at Paddy.

"How was that, Detective?" she asked.

"It would have been the most impressive thing I ever saw if it didn't frighten me so much. I don't even want to know what goes on in that crazy, scary head of yours," he said, laughing. "So, keep it to yourself."

"No worries," she said. "I'm good at keeping secrets."

***

Paddy had no idea what she meant by that cryptic statement at the time, but as she was walking up to his door that first time, holding the hand of Francine Bender, he had a clue.

After getting settled in the living room and introducing Joss to Mairead, Fran said she needed to tell them something. Paddy already knew, and Mairead suspected, but they let Fran tell it her own way.

"We have been together for more than a year," Fran said, still holding Joss's hand. "We're in love and have decided to come out together."

"That's wonderful!" Mairead said, getting up to hug and kiss them both. Paddy sat there with a dumbfounded look on his face. Fran noticed.

"You don't approve, Paddy?"

"You know better than that, Fran," Paddy said. "I'm just confused how I missed the clues. I know you both and had no idea either of you were lesbians until you told me. I'm starting to think I need to recalibrate my *gaydar*."

"That's because you don't pay attention unless there's a dead body involved," Joss said, laughing. "I practically told you as much at the G.O. 15."

"Yeah, but when you said you were good at keeping secrets, I thought you meant where you had the bodies buried. I wanted no part of that information," Paddy said.

After getting over his initial surprise, Paddy was thrilled. Fran and Joss were two of his favorite people, and they made a cute couple. Mairead was like a sister to Fran and was already warming up to Joss. The two of them had joined forces to poke fun at him for his selective attentiveness. After making him feel foolish for a while, Fran got down to business.

"You are my dearest friends," Fran said. "And Joss trusts you after what you did for her with the shooting. We're here for your advice."

"About what?" Paddy asked.

"How do we do this with the job?" Joss clarified.

"It's not the big deal it used to be," Paddy said. "Even GOAL is out of the shadows now. They marched in uniform behind their banner in the Gay Pride parade last summer," Paddy pointed out, referring to the Gay Officers' Action League, the department's fraternal association for gay cops.

"It may not be a big deal for you," Joss argued. "But I still have to work in the squad. There are a lot of homophobic, ignorant detectives out there."

"Not as many as you think," Paddy said. "Most of the old-school guys are inappropriate because they don't know any better. Educate them. They already know you're a great detective and someone not to be fucked with. Establish boundaries. The old-timers will respect them. The ones who don't are just exposing themselves. Shame them and cut them off."

"What about the bosses?" Joss asked.

"That's easy," Paddy said. "Does Chief Ross know yet?"

"No, but I think he suspects. He's too much of a gentleman to ask," Fran said.

"Then he's the first one you tell, like you're giving him a heads up. Ross is a good guy, and you're his right arm. You know he'll protect you both," Paddy said.

"What about everyone else?" Joss asked.

"That depends on you," Paddy said. "Do you want to make a big announcement and get it over with? Or, you can mention it when you get hit on. I know you both get propositioned on a regular basis. Guys are still guys, and attractive women are still attractive even if they swing from the other side of the plate. Just tell them about the new reality. It'll work itself out."

"What if there's a problem? I don't want to go running to EEO every time some lunk can't take no for an answer," Joss said, referring to the department's Equal Employment Opportunity Board.

"If it's a boss, take it to the chief," Paddy said. "If it's just another detective, straighten him out. Most of the guys in the bureau are already scared shit of you anyway. If that doesn't work, as your union rep, I'll make it uncomfortable for him until he gets the message. But I have faith you can handle this on your own. If all else fails, you know I don't mind being the hammer."

"Wait a minute!" Mairead said. "That sounds ominous."

"Relax, baby," Paddy said. "It only involves the threat of violence. It's the promise of forced, inconvenient transfer that will do the trick."

"Oh, that's okay then," Mairead said. "I don't want to have to bail you out of jail again."

"As I remember it, you left me in there to rot for the weekend last time," Paddy said, laughing, pretending to wince when Mairead punched him in the arm.

"Are you doing the whole domestic partner deal?" Paddy asked them.

They nodded.

"Then that's how you introduce each other. Unless there's another term I'm not aware of."

"Until they let us get married, that's pretty much it," Fran said.

"Is there a ceremony for that?" Mairead asked. "We can have it here. We'll cater it in the backyard. We'll have flowers, a cake, and a deejay. It'll be amazing!"

After Fran and Joss had left, Mairead was excited about planning the coming party. She stopped only long enough to make an observation.

"I'm really crazy about those two."

"It's easy to love them," Paddy observed. "They're extraordinary people."

So, they had their civil union ceremony and party at the Durr house. As Paddy expected, there were few problems for Joss in coming out. The NYPD had a sort of epiphany as it related to sexual orientation in the squad at that time, and those who failed to get the memo were dealt with.

Sometimes a word to the wise is sufficient. Sometimes it takes a word and the threat of a biblical ass beating. Sometimes it just takes a punch in the face. Paddy heard from the delegate in the 79 Squad that Joss had been getting harassed by the lunk-head sergeant there. He kept hitting on her even after she firmly turned him down and explained she was a lesbian. This only encouraged him. He made the mistake of grabbing her behind.

"She laid him out," he said. "That little lady hits like a mule kicks."

"What did the sergeant do?" Paddy asked.

"The idiot took it to the lieutenant to hit Joss with charges."

"What did the lou say?"

"He had the sergeant launched immediately. He's still in the Detective Bureau but in the Lab, and he was warned if there were any other complaints, he could expect a trip to the Trial Room—and termination. The job ain't fooling around with this stuff anymore."

Paddy called Joss to commend her.

"A punch in the face is exactly the elegant solution I had in mind," he said.

"He shouldn't have put his hands on me," Joss said.

"I think he knows that now," Paddy observed. "And so does everyone else. Do you know what they're calling you?"

"No," she said, trepidation creeping into her voice.

"Tiny Mike Tyson," he said.

"Oh, cool!"

Burnt to a Crisp

After the Marriage Equality Act was passed in New York in 2011, the Durrs were honored to stand in as best man and woman for Fran and Joss's wedding that fall.

***

In early 2014, Joss retired on disability after shattering her hand on a resisting criminal's skull. Ten years younger than Fran, she was still in her prime child birthing years. They decided to go the artificial insemination route but were unsure how to find an acceptable donor. They didn't want to leave it to chance. They came over to discuss it with Mairead.

"What qualities are you looking for in a donor?" Mairead asked.

"Intelligence, obviously," Fran said.

"And he can't have an ass for a face," Joss added.

"But mostly, we're looking for someone with a strong moral character," Fran said. "How do you interview a potential donor for something like that?"

"Basically, we're looking for a smart guy who is tall, dark, and handsome and not a sociopath. I don't think they're featured on Craig's List," Joss said.

"Except for the morality thing," Mairead joked. "it sounds like you're describing my husband."

Joss and Fran looked at each other. Joss nodded and gripped Fran's hand a little tighter.

"Neither of us has any other family," Fran said. "You guys are as close as we get. We've thought long and hard about it. We don't want to risk it to chance. We kind of had Paddy in mind all along but were afraid to ask."

"Afraid? Don't be ridiculous," Mairead said. "I'm all for it, and Paddy adores you both. He'd do anything for you and anything I ask him to."

At that moment, Paddy came in the door from work. He entered the living room to find the three women with knowing smiles staring at him.

"What mischief have you witches been brewing up?" he asked.

"I just volunteered you to be Fran and Joss' sperm donor," Mairead said.

Joss and Fran looked at him, hopefully.

"I'm honored," Paddy said. "But I can think of at least two problems with that scenario."

"Like what?" Mairead demanded.

"For one thing, I don't think either one of them is into guys."

"They're going to use artificial insemination, you dope," Mairead said. "And I thought I made it clear no one else gets to see that troublemaker of yours but me."

"That takes care of one problem," Paddy said. "But I had a vasectomy after Casey was born; nineteen years ago. I doubt I have any viable *swimmers* left."

"You still produce sperm," Mairead assured him. "They just have nowhere to go since you cut the vas-deferens."

"So, what happens to them, they just collect in there? I haven't noticed any swelling."

"They get reabsorbed into your body," Mairead told him. "The good news is, we can still get them. The bad news is it involves a big needle and a lot of pain."

"How much pain?" Paddy asked, narrowing his eyes.

"Remember when you got shot?"

"Yeah."

"Worse than that."

"Oh, fuck me!" Paddy exclaimed.

Paddy looked at Fran and Joss seated together on the couch. They seemed disappointed by his response. He wasn't refusing them. He was just thinking about how bad it hurt to be shot. It was twenty-seven years ago, and the memory was still excruciating.

"If it's what you really want, I'll do it," he said. "But I may have a better idea that won't involve so much pain."

The three women were curious, turning their eyes to him, listening.

"What you really want is my DNA," he said. "I know a twenty-two-year-old rookie cop who can give you that, and Mairead's as well."

"Oh!" Mairead said. "I didn't think of Patrick."

"I don't know," Fran said.

"If we decide to go that way, how are you going to get Patrick to agree?" Joss asked.

"It won't be a request."

"We'll think about it," Fran said.

"Yeah, do that. But whichever way you decide is fine. You know I'd take a dozen needles in the groin for you two."

For two weeks, Fran and Joss considered it. Fran had known Patrick since he was little. She knew he was a sweet kid who looked like a combination of Paddy and Mairead and was intelligent and had the same English degree as his father.

Burnt to a Crisp

That he was a cop probably helped matters. In the end, they agreed to use Patrick as a donor, sparing Paddy the agony of the long needle.

Two days later, Patrick came home with his dirty clothes. Like most twenty-two-year-olds who lived alone, their last vestige of dependence was laundry, and there would be no urgency to cut the cord as long as Mairead was still willing to do it for him.

Paddy caught him as he was climbing the stairs to his old bedroom.

"Patrick. Catch," Paddy said, tossing the small plastic container to his son, who bobbled it twice before grabbing it.

"Still can't catch, I see," Paddy observed.

"What is this?" Patrick asked.

"It's a specimen jar. I need you to fill it with sperm."

Patrick looked at him as if he had lost his mind.

"You're gonna need to explain," he said.

"It's for Aunt Fran and Joss. They want a baby. The plan was for me to donate, but since the vasectomy, I'm not qualified. You're the next best option. You are a combination of your mother and me; so, it's sort of a family project."

"You know I'll do anything for them," Patrick said. "But I don't want a baby right now."

Paddy rolled his eyes and sighed.

"Oh, the ego on this kid. Relax. It won't be yours."

"Whose will it be then?"

"Fran and Joss'."

"With my sperm."

"I'll make it easy for you, Patrick. Hypothetically, let's say the neighbor comes over to borrow a cup of sugar. She started making cupcakes for her daughter to take to school for her birthday the next day when she realized she didn't have enough. You're a nice guy. So, you give her the sugar. But you haven't contributed more than that. You're not emotionally or financially invested in the cupcakes. You just lent the mom one necessary ingredient. Now your work is done. The next day, when the little girl brings her cupcakes to school, she won't be giving you credit. All you did was lend her mom some sugar. You didn't make the cupcakes. Now, go get the fucking sugar."

Patrick shrugged his assent. He loved his father's analogies and metaphors. Sometimes he asked questions just to elicit them.

"Oh, one other thing," Paddy said, smiling. "After you put the goodies in the jar and seal it, clean the outside of the cup. If I have to put my hand in your mess, you're gonna find out what the old man has left in the tank. You won't like it."

"Okay, Pop," Patrick said laughing, before disappearing into his room.

**

This all transpired before Mairead had gotten sick. Through her illness, Joss and Fran were in contact every day, offering to help with anything. There wasn't much for them to do other than being a support mechanism for Mairead. At this, they were invaluable. Paddy realized, not for the first time; they were not just his and Mairead's dearest friends; they were family. Baby Erin's genealogy just put the period on the end of that sentence.

After everyone got their bagels and coffee, they made a big deal of presenting Paddy with a little square birthday cake. It was a carrot cake, Paddy's favorite, with one big fat candle in the middle. Scrolled across the top in red icing were the words *Retire Already!* Paddy laughed and blew out the candle. After allowing himself a forkful of cake, he was summoned into the kitchen by Fran, who had gone there under the guise of helping Julissa clean up.

"Chief Ross got a communication from the PC's Office yesterday," Fran said, concern in her voice. "It was an order to convene an I.O. 9 hearing for you. The mayor's wife was cc'd on it. So was that twat psychiatrist from Psyche Services who likes you so much. They want to take your guns, Paddy."

"Has Ross seen it yet?" Paddy asked.

"Yeah. He told me to tell you, so you can get your ducks in a row. He's gonna sit on it for two days, but that's as long as he can stall it."

"Doctor Levine works fast," Paddy said. "Fortunately, she tipped her hand at the Honor Legion. I've already sat down with Jimmy Maselli to draft an Article 75. I've been examined and cleared by our independent psychiatrist, who makes Levine look like the incompetent neophyte she is."

"Will the department listen to him?"

"They don't have to. I just have to convince the administrative judge. Along with being the department chair of Psyche at Bellevue, he's a she. I don't know why it should matter. Still, if the judge has to pick one psychiatric opinion over another, I'm gambling he will like the old lady who wrote a dozen textbooks about PTSD and runs the most renowned psyche center in the world over the strident, insolent child whose only credential is being friends with the mayor's wife. What do you think?"

"Well, you better work fast, Paddy. You've only got two days."

"I need to be notified first," Paddy said. "Then I can call Jimmy, and he'll be in front of a judge within the hour."

"I hope it works."

"It will for a while, but if they want me bad enough, eventually they'll get me."

CHAPTER NINETEEN

March 19, 2018
Ridgewood
17:00 hours

Paddy and George Fahrbach pulled into the parking lot of Raimundo and Sons Funeral Home only to discover every spot had been taken. They put the squad car in the bus stop across the street, throwing their department plaque in the window, and took a moment to survey the scene.

"It's only five o'clock, and the place is already mobbed," George said, noting the throng of people gathered outside the front doors, waiting to enter.

"I would attribute it to the fact that it's a triple funeral, but the mourners seem to suggest something else is at work," Paddy said.

"What do you mean?"

"The dynamic of the mob waiting to get in tells its own story." Paddy pointed out. "Most of them are high-level drug dealers from the neighborhood. There's probably a narcotics connection to this case. I just don't know what it is yet."

They crossed the street and parted the crowd on the sidewalk. The majority were veteran criminals, and they all knew Paddy. They grew quiet at the detective's approach, avoiding eye contact. He made a point of looking as many of them in the face as possible, making a mental note of who they were if it became important later in the investigation. It wouldn't be the first time a murderer attended his victim's wake to assess the damage he caused.

Burnt to a Crisp

    As he and George entered, they waded through the mass of humanity in the lobby. There were stanchions and pedestals of floral arrangements stretching out to the door. The funeral home had been dedicated exclusively to the Santapadres; the partitions pulled back to open the six viewing parlors into one massive room. People and flowers were spilling out of every door and into the hallways. Paddy let the antiseptic smell of the home wash over him. The most potent aroma were the flowers, and there were so many here, they rivaled the arrangements at Jimmy Crowe's Inspectors Funeral.
    Camouflaged behind it was the embalming fluid's chemical smell, and under that, the slight hint of putrefaction. Paddy knew no amount of chemical intervention could entirely hide this post-mortem effect. We died and began rotting immediately. Preserving dead flesh doesn't prevent decomposition. It only delays it. Paddy could sense its presence even through the riot of competing aromas. When he thought about it, he realized he and death were interwoven. He wasn't sure if it was following him around as much as popping up wherever he went. Given his chosen profession, he shouldn't have been surprised, but death had seemed to be stalking him far beyond the bounds of their professional relationship. It had always been so, and he had begun to wonder if death was his affliction—or perhaps he was just a carrier.
    As they entered the viewing room, Paddy was struck by the dichotomy of the mourners present. Outside were all the neighborhood people, including the drug dealers and criminals. In here, Paddy saw the higher echelon of Bushwick criminality, sharing the room, but not intermingling with the people he understood with just a glance were *The 1%*; billionaires with a capital B. These he knew were the friends and business associates of Larry and Cassie Rothman. He saw the Rothmans at the front of the room, receiving greetings and expressions of sympathy from these people, who were fewer in number to the criminal element, but still commanded half of the room. It was as if each understood they were not part of the other's world.
    On the other side of the three closed caskets stood a man Paddy hadn't met but had become intimately aware of over the last dozen years or so. He was receiving the criminals his sister had not. While the people fawning over him were recognizable as drug dealers, this man was not. He looked to be in his late forties, tan and fit, his fine suit crisp, stylish, and well-tailored. But for the company he was keeping and the alert animal cunning hidden just under the surface, Paddy thought he could have passed for one of the other group.

"That's *Bless*," Paddy whispered to George, nodding at the man in the charcoal grey suit.

"Bless?" George asked. "You mean the John Gotti of Bushwick?"

"A dozen years ago, he might have been Gotti," Paddy said. "Since then, he's insulated himself to the point where he gets nowhere near the work product. He touches nothing, not even the money. But he still gets paid for every grain of narcotics sold in Brooklyn. And every drug-related murder is either ordered or okayed by him. He's more Michael Corleone than John Gotti."

"You want to talk to him?" George asked.

"We'll get to him," Paddy said. "First, we need to be condescended to by the very wealthy for a while."

"Do they have anything to offer that can help us?"

"No, but while they waste our time and treat us like indentured servants, Mr. Bless will be wondering what we're waiting for. I want him a little on edge when we speak."

"He'll just lawyer up and tell us to go fuck ourselves if we go at him hard," George predicted.

"That's why I'm going at him easy," Paddy said. "We'll appeal to the better angels of his nature—if he has any."

"You lost me," George admitted. "You don't think he was the target?"

"No, I don't. He doesn't live in the building and hasn't for years. He has a big house on a hill in Jamaica Estates. There's no one big enough to go after him, and there's no one crazy enough to try. Bless is feared because he makes people disappear. Whoever did this probably didn't even realize his connection."

"So, why are we talking to him?"

"Because he's the reason the neighborhood won't talk to us," Paddy said. "He knows who did this, and he's going to take care of it himself. We're going to convince him to let us in on the resolution. We just have to get him to lift the gag order."

They approached Cassie and Lawrence Rothman. Paddy saw Cassie whisper in her husband's ear when she noticed him. Rothman looked up and smiled. It seemed to Paddy like he was struggling to convey a friendship and fondness that never really existed between them. He thought it looked forced, cloying, and obsequious and returned a tight smile and a nod in response.

"I'm very sorry for your loss, Mrs. Rothman," Paddy said, shaking Cassie's hand. "This is my partner, Detective Fahrbach. He'll be helping me with the investigation."

Burnt to a Crisp

Cassie shook George's hand and thanked them both for coming. She introduced her husband, stating she thought he and Paddy were already acquainted.

"Actually, I tried to recruit Detective Durr for my fraternity in college," Rothman said. "For four years, I just couldn't seem to entice him to join us. He would have been a great addition to our membership. Alpha Phi was the poorer for his absence."

Paddy remembered Larry's attempt to pledge him differently. Alpha Phi was dominated by old-money trust fund babies like Rothman. Their membership had become somewhat stultified. An athlete with genuine New York street cred would have helped them with that, but mostly, they wanted him for the fact that he was a bartender at Coogan's, their favorite spot to drink when slumming. By this point, Paddy had quite enough of being exploited by the elite. So, he turned them down—again, and again, and again.

"Don't take it personally, Larry," Paddy said. "I would never belong to any club that would have me as a member."

Rothman winced at being called Larry.

"I haven't been Larry for a long time," he said.

"Sure you have," Paddy corrected. "We are always what we were, even when we become something else."

Rothman blanched at the intimation of his past. He knew Paddy remembered his college days being fraught with cocaine, booze, high-priced hookers, and a very near miss with a widespread cheating scandal. Only his father's money and influence kept that whopper from the light of day. Paddy put him at ease.

"Don't sweat it, Larry. That's just rhetoric from an English major. It doesn't mean anything."

Relieved, Rothman decided to catch up on what his classmate had been up to these past thirty years. Paddy realized, despite his having periodically emerged from anonymity every few years—alternately celebrated or vilified in the newspapers and local television newscasts—Larry Rothman had not been aware. As Durr's exploits weren't reported in the financial pages of the Wall Street Journal, Rothman had been none the wiser. Durr conceded his existence to people like the Rothmans was inconsequential—unless they needed something. Then they made you feel you were the most vital person on the planet—until they had what they wanted from you. Then you were a non-entity again.

Not looking to get sucked into that vortex, he politely declined Rothman's offer of employment he suspected was coming.

"I could use a man with your skillset."

And, there it is.

"Thank you, Larry, but I like my job," Paddy said. "I think I'm going to do it for a while longer."

"The city won't pay you as well as I will," Rothman pointed out. "And you wouldn't have to get down in the muck and grime anymore if you worked for me."

"That might be true, but you're forgetting I came from the muck and grime. I'm in it because I like it."

"Well, if you ever change your mind, you know you only need call."

Paddy understood Rothman wanted him because he needed a fixer. Presently, he was under investigation by the SEC for a stock fraud allegation. He needed someone who could cut through the lawyers' hyperbole and speak to the federal investigators to see what real evidence they had. But, the idea of investigating financial crimes bored Paddy to tears. Investigating financial crimes on behalf of the financial criminal was nauseating and beyond the realm of possibility.

"I'll stick with my murder gig," Paddy smiled. "But good luck in all of *your* endeavors."

After extending their condolences again to Cassie, Paddy and George stood to the side, opposite where Bless was receiving mourners. They waited for a while, staying where they could see him and where Bless could see them. Durr caught him glancing over a few times, clocking them. He was starting to look uncomfortable.

Paddy was about to head over to him when he was confronted by one of Cassie and Lawrence Rothman's associates. She was a haphazardly preserved specimen with a ton of makeup to cover her over-indulgence in plastic surgery. Not all of it had gone well. Paddy thought the collagen injections in her lips looked like she had spent the night getting punched in the face by Connor McGregor. This effect had to battle for primacy with her eyebrows, one of which was raised askew as if she sensed something amiss. While her forehead had no signs of a wrinkle, that question mark of an eyebrow was disconcerting. Paddy was still unsure what Botox was meant to do. He had only seen it make people look ridiculous.

"So, you're the detective for this fiasco?" she asked Paddy without preamble.

"Yes. I'm Detective Durr. And you are?"

"I'm Judith Hardesty-Flintlock," she said, handing Paddy a buff-colored business card.

Burnt to a Crisp

He looked at it briefly and realized there was no business information on it. It merely bore her name in a delicate script and an email address, along with the Hardesty family crest in the upper left corner. He realized who she was. There was no business listed because Ms. Hardesty-Flintlock's business was her family name. She was a billionaire socialite, a descendant of the railroad magnate Edmund Hardesty. Her husband was the scion of the shipbuilding Flintlocks of Connecticut. Neither were involved in the ancestral sources of their prodigious wealth anymore, other than to own massive stock holdings. Paddy knew their function in life was to go to cocktail parties, and evidently, wakes.

"Have you spoken to Cassie's brother?" she asked.

"Is there a reason *you* need to know?"

"Well, it's just that Cassie has always been so secretive about her past, and her brother looks like a criminal," she said.

"Is that so?" Paddy asked.

"It explains a lot," Hardesty-Flintlock sniffed. "I knew she was hiding something. Up from nothing, coming out of nowhere, now she is suddenly the doyenne of the social register. It appears the Rothman's are receiving their comeuppance. It's back to the gutter where she came from."

Paddy smiled obsequiously at her, a wicked gleam in his eye. George saw the look and knew Ms. Hardesty-Flintlock was about to get both barrels of Durr's indignation—right in her plastic face.

"That's an interesting assessment coming from someone like you," Paddy began. "Considering the fact your grandfather and his father before him were robber barons—land thieves, I believe. Your father was just a stock cheat. Then there's your husband's money to consider, made by gouging the government for rebuilding the navy during, not one, but two World Wars."

Hardesty-Flintlock was briefly stunned to silence. Paddy thought the question mark eyebrow looked like it was trying to scurry off her head. He knew her face would have been one of horror and confusion if she hadn't Botoxed it to the point of being expressionless.

"Now you want to cast aspersions at Cassie's family. Why, are you envious?"

This awakened something in her. She responded by scoffing.

"Why would I ever envy *them*?"

"Because her brother over there—who you so charitably identified as a criminal—is actually a self-made millionaire. He's an entrepreneur who builds and invests in local businesses and residential properties. He creates jobs in poorer neighborhoods and gives the residents somewhere affordable to live. Look at the turnout here. He's beloved by his community. And Cassie is the most sought-after realtor in New York. Neither of them inherited anything but a work ethic. You, on the other hand, never did anything *but* inherit. The only thing you've ever created is misery. Your stock-in-trade is snotty, imperious, backstabbing. I bet you've never had a real friend. Meanwhile, Cassie and her brother are surrounded by them. That sounds like a cause for envy if ever there was one."

"How dare you speak to me in that way!" she hissed.

"I didn't want to speak to you at all, you vengeful crone," Paddy laughed. "Now, before I tell you to fuck off, here's some free advice; knock it off with the plastic surgery. It can't fix ugly. It only makes it look silly."

Paddy watched her hobble off. She grabbed her husband—equally desiccated—and dragged him out of the funeral home.

"Was that really necessary?" George asked.

"Yeah. I hate the idle rich. They don't *do* anything, and they're fucking mean."

"Can we talk to Bless now?"

"Since I just defended him, I guess we should."

They walked over to the other side of the parlor after pausing at the caskets to say a prayer. Paddy made eye contact with the people speaking with Bless. He gave them a respectful nod, which seemed to catch them off-guard. They returned the gesture before bleeding away, leaving Bless by himself. Paddy stepped up to offer his hand.

"I'm very sorry for your loss, Mr. Santapadre," he said, shaking his hand. "I'm Detective Durr. This is my partner, Detective Fahrbach. We will be investigating the murders. With all you're dealing with right now, we don't want to pressure you with a bunch of questions, but we will need to speak in the coming days."

Bless rolled his eyes and smiled wanly. He regarded Paddy through narrowed eyes.

"You know who I am?"

"Of course," Paddy nodded.

"And you can't wait to start asking me questions about my business."

"Actually, I have no interest whatsoever in your business," Paddy said. "I have no reason to believe it had anything to do with this crime. Your family were unintended victims. But they were victims. You are the surviving family. So, I work for you. I'm just looking for a little help."

"I can't imagine what help I could provide. I wasn't even in the country when this occurred."

Burnt to a Crisp

"True, but now that you're back, everyone is waiting to see what you're going to do about it," Paddy said. "I know what you're going to do about it. I don't blame you. If it were my family, I would do the same. I'm not looking to get in the way of *your* justice. I just want you to understand; we want the same thing."

Bless peered at him suspiciously. He couldn't believe this detective just implied he would murder whoever did this—even though that's exactly what he was going to do—and he did it with a straight face. He had heard a great many things about Durr over the years. He was described as tough and relentless, never letting go of a case once he got his teeth into it. Despite that, even the criminals in Bushwick conceded he was fair. He wouldn't do anyone unless they deserved to get done, but everyone agreed on one thing; Paddy Durr had no patience for bullshit. So, he didn't truck with it. He said what was on his mind, letting the chips fall where they may. Bless was as impressed with his fearlessness as he was with his candor, but this kind of honesty was a little dangerous. Out of respect, he would speak with Durr in the future, but he was determined to be very careful with his words.

"I'm not coming into the precinct to talk to you," he said.

"I wouldn't expect you to," Paddy said. "I'll meet you wherever you want."

Bless seemed to consider this for a second, nodding his assent.

"Let me bury my family, Detective. I'll call you after the funerals."

Paddy tried to give him his business card. Bless politely waved it away.

"I already have it. You've flooded Wilson Avenue with them," he said, grinning.

CHAPTER TWENTY

March 19, 2018
Bushwick, Brooklyn
22:15 hours

Paddy and George got back to the squad a little after ten. The brooding detective, Aramis Maldonado, was waiting for them. Paddy felt bad for Maldonado. He had no business being in a detective squad, looking like he had just walked off the pages of GQ, which he had. Before becoming a cop, Aramis was a male model. Between his exquisite wardrobe and delicate bearing, he looked out of place. He was trying, but Paddy suspected he was never going to cut it in Brooklyn North.

Arriving under a cloud, he had been launched unceremoniously from the mayor's protection detail. More accurately, he had been assigned to the mayor's wife's detail and served more as her personal man-servant than her bodyguard. Along the way, something happened, and he landed with a thud in the 83 Squad. He was a First Grade Detective, but everyone knew he held the rank only because of his previous assignment. In truth, he had never done a day's police work in his ten-year career—let alone any detective work.

Lieutenant Martino asked Paddy and Joe Furio to take him under their wings, show him the ropes, and try to mold him into a functional member of the squad. Aramis gave it his best effort, but he really wasn't suited to being a cop. He must have realized this because other than keeping his cases up to date, his chief talent and primary tactic was to sulk. Paddy thought he sulked mightily. Given what

Durr already had on his plate, he had no desire to expend precious time trying to soothe Aramis's bruised sensibilities. So, he was pleasantly surprised to find Maldonado had some help for him.

"Erika Gomez called a few minutes ago," Aramis said. "She is at her mother's house with Harold. She'd like you to come over to talk to them."

"Thank you, Aramis."

"I just took the message," Maldonado shrugged. "Is there anything else I can do to help with your case?"

"Not really," Paddy said. "Right now, the information is coming in very slowly. I only have one thread to pull at a time. But, when it heats up, and there's more to do, I'll be glad to have your help."

Aramis appeared skeptical but must have decided Paddy was genuine. He nodded.

"I appreciate the way you and Joe have been looking out for me. I know I suck at this. Everyone else makes fun of me, sometimes to my face. But you guys never do. I have no idea how I can help, but all you have to do is ask."

"Hang in there, kid," Paddy said, patting him on the shoulder. "You've only been at this for a few weeks. When I have something for you to do, I won't hesitate to ask."

On the ride to Erika's apartment, George wanted to know how Aramis was coming along. As the Boro Director of the DEA, he was somewhat responsible for his welfare.

"He's not a bad guy, George. He's just clueless."

"The fact he's a *First Grader* can't be helping."

"No, but it's just par for the course. We've had first grade long enough to know everyone without grade, resents everyone with it. Envy is human nature. Aramis's issues run deeper. It's his personality. He just doesn't fit in."

"Coming from the mayor's detail, he probably thinks his shit don't stink. Brooklyn North is no place to have that kind of an attitude."

"Yeah, except he doesn't. If anything, this has been a humbling experience for him—bordering on humiliating. He's discovered he's a beta fish in a sea of sharks. If he doesn't grow some teeth soon, he's gonna get eaten. What he needs is a little bit of success, so he can start believing in himself. But there's something else bothering him. I just haven't put my finger on it yet."

"No doubt, you'll help him," George said. "Let me know if there's anything the union can do."

Paddy's eyebrows went up.

"You could have him transferred out of the squad, for starters."

"Not gonna happen, Paddy. He was put here. The mayor's wife wants him punished. He's not going anywhere."

"I figured as much," Paddy said, getting out of the car in front of 402 Wilson. "Let's go talk to Erika and Harold."

CHAPTER TWENTY-ONE

March 19, 2018
Bushwick, Brooklyn
22:30 hours

After Senora Gomez ushered them to the kitchen table and served them coffee, Paddy and George introduced themselves. Erika kept a calming hand on Harold's, speaking softly for both of them.

"This is my boyfriend, Harold Berrios," she said. "He wants to talk to you, but for him, it's difficult. He suffers from a lot of anxiety around strangers."

Paddy knew Harold's anxiety was caused by more than just meeting strangers. He had met this young man a couple of years before.

***

Three years earlier

Harold was big for his age. When Paddy first met him, he was seventeen, six feet tall, and sturdy, standing on the corner of Wilson and Gates, staring at the building across the street. Erika's building, but Paddy didn't know that then. As he watched Harold shifting from foot to foot, chain-smoking cigarettes, and glaring across the street like he had bad business in mind, Paddy was conflicted. The behavior he was witnessing should have spiked his *perp fever,* but for some reason, it just didn't register.

"What are you thinking?" Gio Fernandez asked him from the driver's seat.

"Well, it's midnight. That big kid is raised up about something, but strangely, I'm not getting a bad feeling about him."

"Wanna give him a toss?" Gio asked.

"Nah, he ain't holding nothing. He's wearing shorts and a tee-shirt. If he's packing, it would have to be up his ass."

Gio cast a concerned look.

"You're not gonna make me look in his ass, are you, Paddy?"

"No," he laughed. "There's nothing up there. Something is bothering him, though. So, let's just ask him."

The kid didn't seem to notice their approach, still staring at the entrance to the building across the street. So Paddy cleared his throat and flashed his shield. The kid froze as if he were an animal caught in a spotlight. He looked at Paddy and then quickly averted his eyes. He said nothing, seeming not even to breathe. Even though his eyes were cast down and to the side, Paddy saw real fear there. Gio saw it too.

"The police are talking to you, pal. Look at us when we speak to you," Gio barked.

"That's all right, Gio," Paddy said. "Our friend here is just a little shy around new people. Isn't that right?"

The kid looked into Paddy's face and looked away again, nodding.

"I'm Detective Durr. This is Detective Fernandez," Paddy said. "What's your name?"

"Harold," he croaked, looking up and then away again.

Paddy understood this would be his pattern throughout any ensuing conversation. He forced himself to adjust to it.

"Where do you live, Harold?"

"Gates Avenue," he said, pointing up the block.

"What are you doing *here*?"

"Waiting for my friend."

"Does he live there?" Paddy asked, pointing across the street.

"Not he!" Her name is Erika."

"Oh, that explains it." Paddy chuckled. "It's a date. That's why you seem so nervous."

Harold let out a guffaw, looking at Paddy with a bashful grin. He started to blush as he averted his eyes.

Burnt to a Crisp

"Okay, Harold," Paddy said. "C'mon, Gio. Let's leave the man to his mission. Good night and good luck, son."

Harold looked up and smiled, a wave of relief seeming to wash over his face as the detectives got back in their car.

"What the fuck was up with that kid?" Gio asked.

"Besides being in love? He's autistic."

"I just thought he was an idiot."

"Far from it. He's probably brilliant. His autism makes communicating with others difficult. So you get what you get."

"How do you know so much about it?"

"I coached a few autistic kids at the high school."

"They let retards play football in Plainedge?"

"Not retarded." Paddy laughed. "High functioning autism. Plainedge is a small community. If you want to play, we have room for you. I never had to cut a kid except for a discipline problem, and I only ever had to do that once. So, if you show up to work, you're one of us. I might not be able to get you in the games, but you're on the team. A couple of them turned out to be real ballplayers. But they were all great teammates, and they made us better because of it."

"Like mascots?"

"No. Players. Once you open up communication, there's no limit to what these kids can accomplish."

"How do you do that?"

"First, be their friend. After they trust you, the rest happens organically."

"So, you want to be Harold's friend?"

"Yeah, I do. I got a feeling we're going to need each other one day."

So Paddy made an effort after that day to stop and say hello to Harold whenever he found him on the corner, which was often. In time, he seemed to grow comfortable with their meetings, even if their conversations didn't advance beyond Paddy inquiring after Harold's welfare and the young man assuring the detective he was fine.

Durr made a point of making sure Harold had his business card. He was instructed to show it to any police officers with whom he might have dealings. He was told to tell the cops he was Durr's friend. More importantly, he was reminded that he was to call Paddy immediately if he was ever bothered by anyone from the street. They would straighten out any problems together.

***

Back at Senora Gomez's table, Paddy waited for Harold to look up at him. When he did, Harold smiled before looking down at his and Erika's hands.

"Harold and I are already acquainted," Paddy said.

"He told me," Erika acknowledged. "He said you were nice to him. It's the only reason he will speak to you."

"I'm grateful he trusts me."

"How do you want to begin?" Erika asked.

"I have an idea of what he told you. I'll begin with that. If I'm incorrect, stop me. If I need something clarified, I'll ask. It'll be just a couple of old friends telling each other a story. You good with that, Harold?"

Harold looked up and nodded. He seemed to be growing more at ease as the minutes passed. So, Paddy jumped right into it.

"The day of the fire were you on the corner of Gates and Wilson?" he asked.

"Yes."

"What time was that about?"

"After two."

"How do you know it was after two?"

"It was 1:45 when I left my house to smoke. I was on the corner for about a half-hour when I saw it."

"Saw what?" Paddy asked.

"Cucko burn the house down," Harold said as if it told the whole story. In his mind, it did.

After Harold blurted out the nickname, Paddy stopped him. He produced a photo array with Sergio Palmiero as the subject.

"Is Cucko in here?" he asked, laying the array in front of him.

"That's him," Harold said, pointing to photo number four.

Paddy now had an ID for his suspect. But he would have to go into greater detail with Harold to nail down precisely what he saw Cucko do.

Harold didn't think in terms of sensory perceptions, minutia, and not drawing conclusions, which were the ground rules of witness testimony. He absorbed the things he saw and heard, considered them with the things he already knew, and made suppositions—usually sound ones. This is how everyone thought, but Harold processed the information much faster. His brain was a veritable whirling dervish. He arrived at what he understood was the truth more rapidly than the average mind, and he grew impatient when others didn't see what he did as quickly.

Burnt to a Crisp

Paddy had to explain that testimony had to be restricted to what he saw. The jurors would have to decide what it meant. To provide them with a clear picture, Harold would have to answer all the little questions: like where he was standing, how far away, and for how long. These were the brushstrokes that created the broader painting of truth. His autism, coupled with his preference for one-word answers, made this a time-consuming and frustrating process. Because of his experience dealing with people like Harold, what would have been a maddening impossibility for most detectives, was merely an aggravating and challenging task for Durr.

What emerged was a clear picture, drawn from Harold's observations. He said he knew Cucko for several years when he lived with Jessica Santiago in the apartment house that burned down. Harold saw him on the morning of the fire when Cucko turned onto Wilson Avenue from Woodbine Street. He was carrying a blue and white rectangular can of some sort. He said he saw him rush into the building. A minute later, Cucko came running out, sprinting down Wilson, across Palmetto to Gates, where he ran up toward Knickerbocker Avenue.

Harold said Cucko didn't even look at him. He seemed in a panic and was still carrying the blue and white can. From this distance, Harold could see it was made of metal. He watched him run up Gates, stopping only to throw the can on a low garage roof, before making the right on Knickerbocker and disappearing.

When Harold looked back toward 407 Wilson, he already saw smoke and flame billowing out the front door. He ran to the corner across the street, in front of the public school. There, he used one of the last payphones in Brooklyn to call 9-1-1.

Paddy already had a printout of the brief phone call, made at 02:19 hours. It was the first of forty-seven 9-1-1 calls reporting the fire. He had already interviewed every other caller, but none of them were witnesses. They lived in the vicinity and were awakened by the smoke. Their calls came in after Harold's and long after the perpetrator had fled the scene.

Harold was sure he and Cucko were the only two people on the street at the time, but he noticed a beige Lexus parked at the corner of Woodbine and Wilson. It started up and pulled away minutes after Cucko ran past him. The car made the right on Palmetto, toward Knickerbocker. He thought he had seen the car before but didn't know who owned it.

It took some convincing to get Harold and Erika to accompany them down to the DA's office to be audio-taped. When Paddy assured Harold, ADA Dan Bibb was a good guy with everyone's best interests at heart; he finally agreed to go.

Michael O'Keefe

***

At the Homicide Bureau, Paddy had George sit with Harold and Erika in the conference room while he briefed Bibb in his office. Given the big man had been awakened from a sound sleep and dragged into work in the middle of the night for this interview, he was less than thrilled at what he discovered when he got there.

"Are you fucking kidding me, Paddy?" Bibb roared. "One witness, and he's autistic with communication issues. Any defense attorney worth his ass is going to be licking his chops to cross-examine this kid. With his anxiety, they'll twist him into knots. You didn't bring me *nothing*, Paddy. You brought me less than nothing."

Paddy pointed out Harold was the first 9-1-1 caller, locking down their time of occurrence.

"We already have the call, and you can't cross-examine a recording and a printout. So, he's not less than nothing," Durr pointed out.

"Well, there's that," Bibb conceded.

"And Harold's autism is a very high functioning one. He's too smart, if that's even possible. His mind works way too fast, so it sounds confused because he's only verbalizing every third thought. We need to slow him down, make him answer all the questions one at a time. He knows what he knows. Nobody is going to shake him on the facts. He might get anxious and angry during cross, but he won't get confused. If anything, it might be to our advantage if they try to beat him up on the stand."

"How's that?"

"I'm telling you, Dan, you're going to love this kid, and so will everyone else in the courtroom. When the defense tries to fuck with him, they run the risk of pissing off the jury. They'll hate the defendant and his lawyer for putting Harold through the wringer."

After recording Harold's statement, painstaking as it was, Bibb had to agree Paddy was correct—to a point.

"You're right, Paddy; I love him. But he's not enough to make a murder case by himself. You're going to have to get me more. You can start by finding the blue can the perp was carrying."

"I wouldn't hang my hat on that," Durr said. "It's been exposed to the elements for a week, and we've had rain. Any prints are probably long gone. Other than Harold's testimony, I don't know if we'll ever be able to put it in Cucko's hands."

"But if you recover the can, we'll know what the accelerant was," Bibb pointed out.

"We already have a pretty good idea; it was kerosene, and I'm going to get the can. I'm just saying, don't expect the mutt's prints to be on it."

"I'll take what I can get at this point," Bibb said.

Michael O'Keefe

CHAPTER TWENTY-TWO

March 20, 2018
Bushwick, Brooklyn
02:00 hours

After dropping Harold and Erika home, it didn't take long for Paddy and George to locate the garage roof on Gates. There was only one on the block. The homeowner was less than pleased to have to wake up to the police at his door. His humor didn't improve, but he allowed the detectives access to his garage roof.

Sitting right there in the middle of the roof was an empty one-gallon aluminum can, blue and white, just as Harold had described it. The only words Paddy could read plainly in the early morning darkness were the brand, *Esparza*, and the word *queroseño*. Without touching the can, he used his cell phone to illuminate the rest of the label. There wasn't an English word on it.

"Shit," Paddy muttered.

"What's wrong?" George asked.

"It's all in Spanish."

"So?"

"There's no English label for the chemical contents or any warning stickers."

"You've lost me, Paddy."

"It means this kerosene came from Puerto Rico."

"Again—so?"

"It's a petroleum product. The EPA would never allow foreign petroleum products to be sold in the states unless it was labeled in English, had all the warning stickers, and had the chemical contents listed. This kerosene is probably loaded with lead, so it would never have cleared customs. It's in Brooklyn illegally. It was smuggled here."

"Why is that important?"

"If the importation is undocumented, so is its distribution. Short of finding where it was sold by going door to door, we'll never find out where Cucko bought it; needle in a fucking haystack."

"Shit."

"Yeah, I already said that."

He swallowed his frustration and called Crime Scene. Maybe there was a readable print still on the can after all.

"Crime Scene, Leoniak," a gruff voice on the other end of the phone answered.

"Is that you, *Handsome Avenger*?" Paddy asked, instantly brightening.

"Well, if it isn't Paddy Durr," Leoniak beamed. "What can I do for you, old pal?"

"I need an *A-run* on my arson triple, Andy. I got an aluminum kerosene can on a rooftop that needs printing and processing. Are you up?"

"Give me the address. I'll be there in twenty minutes."

After hanging up with Andy, Paddy nodded to George.

"Was that your old partner," George asked.

"The one and only, Andy Leoniak."

"Handsome Avengers; What's that all about?"

While they waited for Detective Leoniak to arrive, Paddy told George the genesis of their ironic nickname.

***

While working together for a year on late tours in the old three-four, they had a particularly tough time of it one night. Just as the sun was coming up, they responded to a shooting. They were the third car to arrive. So, they left the first two sectors to deal with the victim and the crime scene while they took the description of the perp and began canvassing. They found him on 184th Street and Wadsworth Avenue, and the chase was on.

The perp ducked into a building and ran up to the roof. What ensued was a twenty-minute foot-pursuit over rooftops, down alleys, and through backyards. They had already recovered the perp's gun when he ditched it in the first stairwell, so this wasn't ending in a gunfight at least. But it didn't make the obstacle course they had to traverse any easier.

At one point, they had to fight their way through a pack of feral pit bulls, but not without getting mauled a little. They finally caught their man when he got himself entangled in razor wire trying to go over a wall. They delivered their quarry and the gun to the sector assigned, who would process the collar. Then they went end-of-tour.

As they arrived at the stationhouse, the day-tour was waiting in the parking lot to take possession of the incoming cars. When Paddy and Andy climbed out of their radio car, they were disheveled, tattered, and a bloody mess.

"Ooh, look," one of the day-tour wags said, pointing at them. "It's the Handsome Avengers."

The name stuck until Andy got transferred to Crime Scene, and Paddy hooked up with Tommy McPhee.

***

After being directed to the roof of the garage by the cranky homeowner, who realized he wasn't getting back to sleep any time soon, Detective Leoniak let Paddy brief him about the nature of the evidence he was there to process. He scratched his chin, thinking on the matter.

"Okay, here's what I can do for you," Andy said. "I'm not gonna print the can. The elements have washed the visible ones away for sure. I'll bag it and send it to the lab. They may be able to raise a print if they fumigate it."

"What about the residue in the can, to compare against the residue at the scene?" Paddy asked.

"That will be its second stop. But you know, Paddy, in fire cases, it's unusual to get a satisfactory match between accelerants and the scene."

"Why is that?" George asked.

"Two reasons. One, the fire burns much of the chemical signature away; two, accelerants are so similar in ingredients you can't differentiate one from the thousands of others of the same type unless it's gasoline. That shit has so many impurities added during the refining process they don't ever completely burn off. And each oil company uses different stuff. You can tell what brand of gas was used by what's left. No such luck with kerosene. By the way, why is it spelled like that?" Andy asked, indicating the label on the can.

"It's from Puerto Rico," Paddy said.

"That might be a lucky break. Who processed the original scene?"

"Two fire marshals from SID, Capparzo, and Kennealy."

Burnt to a Crisp

"I know them—good guys. Ask them to resubmit the debris for a lead analysis. Foreign petroleum products are loaded with lead; if the content from this can matches the scene, bingo! They're connected. Now, all we gotta do is link the can to the perp."

"I knew about the lead," Paddy said. "I didn't know it could be used as a chemical link."

"Sure. The compound is called tetraethyl lead, and its signature is pronounced."

"That's good," George said. "Maybe we're finally catching a break."

"Oh shit! I just thought of something," Andy said, snapping his fingers. "If the asshole used this can to spread the accelerant and he stayed long enough for the fire to get rolling, he might have burned off enough skin cells from his hand to adhere to the handle. Before anything, we'll swab it for DNA. It tends to hold up in the elements better than fingerprints."

"That's brilliant." George marveled.

"Nah," Andy laughed. "I'm a Polack. Polish and brilliant aren't allowed in the same sentence."

"I'm calling bullshit on that," Paddy said. "I've known you for more than thirty years. Brilliant is *exactly* the word."

"Thanks, partner. On another matter, I'm sure you're tired of being asked, but how is Mairead?"

"Better, actually," Paddy said. "The gene therapy seems to be helping. Her hair is growing, and she's put on a few pounds. Fingers crossed—she's got another infusion later this week. Hopefully, she keeps improving."

"Let her know Christine, and I are praying for her."

"Will do. Now, do your magic, *Polska*."

Michael O'Keefe

CHAPTER TWENTY-THREE

March 21, 2017
Bushwick, Brooklyn
09:00 hours

Paddy was at his desk early that morning researching the chemistry of tetraethyl lead and kerosene. *Thank God for Google*, he thought, when his phone rang.

"Eight-three Squad, Durr."

"Just who I was looking for. This is Parole Officer Dottie Nesbitt. I got a message from you about Peter Cammaratta. What's up?"

"I need to question him about a homicide—three homicides, actually."

"Holy shit! Is he a suspect?"

"Nah, but he has information, and he's been hiding from me."

"Is this about the fire?" Nesbitt asked.

"How did you know about that?"

"He called me the day after to let me know he was staying somewhere else."

"You knew he was cribbing at 407 Wilson?"

"I authorized it. It was a serious upgrade. His mother is a junkie prostitute and hangs out exclusively with criminals. The Santiagos are good people. Honest, hardworking, I thought he had a much better shot at staying out of trouble with them."

"So, you like him?"

"I kinda do. He's been a model parolee—punctual, polite, and his urines have been clean as a whistle. I've been doing this long enough not to buy into anyone's bullshit, but he's only seventeen. If he wants to get straight, I wanna help him."

"I know he's got a visit today. When he gets there, will you call me?"

"No need, Detective. The kid is like clockwork. He'll be here at 10:00 hours. Why don't you show up at 10:15?"

***

Paddy arrived at the ramshackle and very dirty offices of Brooklyn Parole on DeKalb Avenue and Fulton Street. The interior looked like an off-track betting parlor, with filthy scraps of paper almost ankle-deep on the floor. The hard plastic seats were bolted in rows into the ground, and they were full of nervous, hard-eyed parolees waiting to be let upstairs to see their parole officers. He could tell by the look in some of their eyes that a few wouldn't be leaving except to Rikers Island—in handcuffs. Visit day is often violation day as well.

Paddy had to wait behind one of the denizens, checking in and nodding off at the same time in front of the receptionist's window, encased behind bulletproof glass. When she figured out who he was and which P.O. would no doubt be violating him that day, the receptionist told him—not politely—to sit down. Paddy knew this guy's urine would be so full of heroin; the test kit might explode.

He checked in with the receptionist, was buzzed into the inner doors, and directed to the second floor. He popped his head into room 218. A rear-cuffed Peter Cammaratta looked up at him and dropped his head to his chest in dejection. A tough-looking woman in her early thirties was scowling into the computer at her desk. She sensed Paddy's presence, looked up, and smiled.

"Detective Durr, right on time," she said, standing to shake his hand.

Paddy felt the firmness of her grip, almost crushing his hand, and saw faint bruising and swelling on her knuckles. He took a better look at her.

Her blonde hair was packed in a tight bun at the top of her head. Paddy could see she was thickly constructed, about a hundred and forty pounds, packed firmly on her five-foot three-inch frame. Making eye contact, he noticed the hint of a latent bruise around her right eye, deftly covered—but not hidden—by makeup. With her blue eyes, high cheekbones, and upturned nose, Paddy thought she was cute if a little on the deadly side.

"How did you know it was me?" he asked.

"When I got your message, I asked around about you. Your name is golden in this office. Jamal Witherspoon suggested I Google you. So, I did. You're quite the shit-stirrer. That's a compliment, by the way."

"Graciously accepted. Call me Paddy," he said, handing her his card.

"I'm Dottie, but not to you, Peter," she said to Cammaratta. "I'm still P.O. Nesbitt as far as you're concerned."

To Paddy, she said, "Do you want a private room, or is my office okay?"

"This will do fine. That way, you can listen in and participate where needed. Are the cuffs necessary?"

"It's office protocol when a detective asks us to detain a parolee. The cuffs stay on until you tell us they're not needed."

"They're not," Paddy said.

As Dottie bent over at the waist to uncuff Cammaratta, he couldn't help noticing her thick, muscular legs and glutes, straining against the tight denim of her faded Levis. He knew girls like this from the gym. Her nickname could very well be *Quadzilla*. He wondered how much weight she could squat and thought she looked like Rhonda Rousey's tougher sister.

Cammaratta looked up at Paddy with a glimmer of hope in his eyes. He thought maybe he might be leaving here without the cuffs and a free ride to Rikers. Paddy recognized the look and grinned.

Dottie yelled at Cammaratta when she saw him smile back.

"Do you think this is a joke, Peter?" she thundered. "Your parole is predicated on you cooperating with law enforcement in any and all matters. It doesn't look like you've been doing that. You're a hair away from spending the next three years finishing your bit."

Cammaratta lowered his head and mumbled, "Yes, ma'am."

Paddy felt a little bad for him. He wasn't here to scare the kid, just get some information. So, he went at him gently.

"You should have just come in to see me, Blanco."

"Detective Durr, I wanted to, but I just couldn't."

"Why not?"

"Bless doesn't want anyone talking to you. He says he's gonna take care of it himself."

"I already know who set the fire. I need the why. You've been living with Melanie and her family. I know you know something."

"I can't," Blanco said, his eyes pleading.

"This does not qualify as cooperation, Peter," Dottie said.

Burnt to a Crisp

"I know, Officer Nesbitt, but I can't do this. I understand you have to violate me if I don't cooperate, but my choices are to do the three years or talk to the police and get disappeared by Bless. There's no guarantee that he won't hurt Melanie and her family when he comes for me. I'll do the three years standing on my head before I'll put them in danger."

Paddy considered Blanco's commitment. He decided it was genuine. He was starting to like this kid, finding a new respect for his loyalty to the Santiago family.

"Blanco," Paddy said. "What can I do to get you to talk to me?"

"Get Bless to okay it, and I'm all yours."

"I'm going to do that," he said. "When I do—hypothetically—what can I expect to hear?"

"You're gonna hear that Cucko knew Jessica was carrying his baby. He came over to the house to beg her to keep it. She was already downtown having the abortion. You're gonna hear that he told Melanie and me, '*Ya'mo* burn that fuckin house to the ground and cook that murdering *puttana*.' You might also hear that I knocked his ugly ass out—but not from me."

"I'd really like to hear *that*," Paddy said.

"What would you like me to do, Detective?" Dottie asked.

"Do what you have to, but I wouldn't violate him. What he says about Bless is true. He's a scary killer, and his word is bond. If he tells you to do something, and you do something else, bad shit of the permanent kind will start to happen. I'm going to get him to lift the embargo. When I do, I'll call on Peter again."

"You caught a break, kid," Dottie said. "You should be very grateful Detective Durr is such a nice guy. You're free to go. I'll see you next week, same time."

As Cammaratta jumped up to leave, Paddy stopped him.

"One more thing, Blanco. I'm not that nice. I won't call you until Bless gives everybody the nod to talk to me, but when I call, if I have to call a second time, I'll hunt you down in the street. I won't leave Officer Nesbitt anything left *to* violate. Are we understood?"

"Yes, sir," he said as he headed for the door.

After Cammaratta left, Dottie said, "If this guy Bless is as scary and dangerous as you say, how are you going to get him to turn around his gag order?"

Grinning, he said, "I have a bit of a reputation of being a little scary and dangerous myself."

"I don't doubt it."

"Never mind that. I'm curious. Just a guess, but MMA?"

"Very good. How'd you know?"

"I'm a detective, remember? I notice things. I see the scuffed knuckles, the hint of an eye jammie there, coupled with the fact you look like you could knock out a horse and kick down a brick wall, and I see a fighter. Are you any good?"

"I'm getting there." She smiled. "I've had two professional fights and won them both—one by knockout, the other by submission."

"I'll tell you right now, Dottie. I wouldn't fight you. I'm pretty sure you'd give me a proper ass-kicking."

"I doubt that." She laughed. "You look like you've been in more than a few scrapes yourself."

"Yeah, but I'm old as dirt now. I got no fight left."

"Now you're sandbagging me, Paddy. I bet you got plenty of fight left."

***

Back at the squad that afternoon, Paddy briefed Lieutenant Martino on his progress. He liked what he heard but was curious.

"How are you going to flip Bless?"

"If I can convince him I'm not coming after *him*, and I'm not looking to get in his way when he finally takes care of Cucko, he might come around. After all, the little murderer will be easier to find and get to in jail than he has been on the street."

"Just so long as Bless doesn't drop the body in the confines of the eight-three. Then we gotta go after *him*."

"I think he realizes that. It's probably why he hasn't found and killed the little fucker yet. I hope he understands once I arrest Cucko, I don't give fuck number one what happens to him in jail."

"Well, get to it, Paddy."

Back at his desk, he left a voicemail and a text on Bless's phone, asking for him to call back to set an appointment for a sit-down. He was about to go back into his research on Google when he heard Lieutenant Martino yell from his office.

"What!? Are you fucking kidding me?" he thundered. "Wait a second; I need a pad and a pen. I gotta make a telephone message and a command log entry."

Paddy looked in at the lieutenant behind his desk, and Martino waved him in. He sat down in one of the chairs in front of the desk and waited until the lou got off the phone.

"This just came down from the Chief of D's; A *must appear* for tomorrow at IAB for an IO-9 hearing. Where is this coming from, Paddy?"

"Dr. Levine in Psych Services."

"She's after you again?"

"Yeah. But now she thinks she has the juice to get me. She just might."

"You better call your lawyer," Martino said. "Christ! Tomorrow? They didn't give you much notice."

"I saw this coming. Jimmy Maselli already has an Article 75 ready to go to Administrative Court."

Paddy took the notification from the lieutenant and photographed it with his iPhone. He sent that to Maselli's phone and called him.

"I just saw the text," Jimmy said. "I'm heading over to administrative court now. Stay put. I'll get back to you as soon as I know."

"Thanks, Jim," he said, clicking off.

"What's up?" Martino asked.

"He's on his way to court for a temporary injunction. If you don't mind, I'm gonna stick around on overtime till we get an answer."

"Absolutely, Paddy, I was going to head home myself, but I think I'll hang out with you for a while."

While they waited for Jimmy's call, Paddy made a fresh pot of coffee, and they sat in Martino's office drinking it and shooting the shit. Paddy brought him up to speed on Mairead. He explained the gene therapy, the infusions, and the science behind it. Martino was pleased to see that even if Paddy wasn't quite confident in the treatment, he at least was hopeful. This was a far cry from the blizzard of despair he seemed to be walking around in and trying to hide these past few months.

After talking some football and considering what the Giants might look like this coming fall, Martino was curious about something else.

"With everything you've been through, how do you stay on point? If anyone else had to endure the hardships you've fought through, they would have been shot-out cynics—if they survived at all. But you keep on fighting the good fight. You don't lose your sense of justice. You don't lose your commitment. You make sacrifices, choosing to do what's best for everyone else—even if it's not what's best for you. Doing the right thing seems like a religious calling for you."

"That's an overstatement." Paddy laughed. "You make me sound like Gandhi, for fuck's sake."

"Maybe if Gandhi had been a gunslinger. My point is, you seem to operate from a philosophical dogma, and it's inviolate and sacrosanct. My question is, where does that come from?"

"That's pretty deep, boss," Paddy said, scratching his chin. "I sometimes wonder myself. I figure it breaks down this way: I grew up in shit, and I hated it. My family were amoral imbeciles. Except for a certain criminal cunning, the only indication they had any brains at all was when they were trying to separate some poor sap from his hard-earned cash—or drugs—they loved taking drugs. Thank God, or I'd still be stuck with them."

"That doesn't explain it. Kids born into those types of environments usually end up becoming the same sort of shitheads as their parents. Why did you zig when you coulda zagged?"

"I guess because they hated me, and I hated them right back. I was determined to be different. I also noticed at a young age, being kind and generous just felt good. It felt right, and it was its own reward. So, I tried to do that whenever I had the chance."

"What about the justice thing? I notice you are not generous and kind to criminals."

"No, definitely not." Paddy laughed. "I think it's because as a kid, I detested bullies. I had grown up being abused by my father and brothers, who were the miserable, back-stabbing, relentless kind. So, when the smaller of my classmates got picked on, I deputized myself. I learned at a young age the cure for bullying was a punch in the face. For me, it was fun. It was like beating up my father and brothers by proxy, and I found out I like protecting people."

"So, everything you know about morality you learned in grade school?"

"No, of course not." Paddy chuckled. "But the original lessons kept repeating and developing. Some things happened which demonstrated how shitty it felt when I acted selfishly. If that didn't reinforce things, there were Bucciogrosso and Curran."

"Ah," Martino smiled. "Yoda and Obi-Wan."

"Don't call them that." Paddy laughed. "Butchie *hates* when Furio calls them that."

"Yeah, but it's who they are. They're the Jedi Masters to your Luke Skywalker."

Burnt to a Crisp

"I can't believe that just came out of your mouth," Paddy said. "Do you have any idea how lame it sounded? What they were was my first positive example of how to behave like a man. They also bailed me out of a lot of stupid shit I got involved with as a kid. And talk about doing the right thing; they went to war with the Bonannos and crushed them, even after there was a price on their heads and an attempt made on the lives of their families. These guys didn't just look out for me; they're my fucking heroes. It's because of them I decided to become a cop."

"And squandered an Ivy League education."

"I wouldn't quite say I squandered it," Paddy said. "It was at Columbia when I was able to categorize and quantify my moral code. I had already known or suspected much of it, but I never discussed it with anyone. At Columbia, liberal arts students have to take philosophy 101 and 102. Suddenly, I'm reading John Locke and learning about things like free will, the God-given rights of men, and their corresponding responsibilities. Then there was Immanuel Kant, who discussed things like revealed divinity in nature, proof of the existence of God, and the possibility of goodness in man evidenced by the gift of reason. If that weren't enough, John Henry Newman theorized that human conscience was proof of the existence of God and his existence within us."

Durr paused, as much to catch his breath as to let it sink in.

"Now these were religious men, so their message was tempered by the understanding that God-like perfect morality was a goal and not really attainable by guilty, sinful man. This explained some of my more—let's say unchristian tendencies—like distemper and an inclination towards violence—and lust; yay, I have been lustful. Now I had a codex that informed me of the validity of those things that I had always suspected but now knew. You follow?"

Martino looked at him silently for a long moment.

"You know, Paddy, I'm an educated man—not one, but two degrees. But sometimes, when we talk like this, you leave me wondering if I know anything at all."

"Don't be ridiculous," Paddy said. "You're one of the smartest guys I know. Did you take philosophy in college?"

"No, it was all criminal justice and governmental administration."

"There you go. You can't be expected to know about stuff outside your field of study or area of expertise. You should read some philosophy, though."

"Why is that?"

"Because it's a fucking hoot when you discover yourself in the texts, and it deconstructs and explains you."

"No thanks." Martino laughed. "I don't need my mind blown like that."

Just then, Paddy's cell phone rang. The caller ID said it was Jimmy Maselli. Durr and the lieutenant had been talking for three and a half hours. He didn't know where the time went and wasn't ready for this call. He was reluctant to take it, afraid of the outcome. Martino broke the spell.

"Answer the fucking thing!" he yelled.

Paddy Put it on speaker so the lieutenant could hear, then swiped the screen to answer the call.

"Yeah, Jimmy?"

"We got a reprieve," he said. "Administrative Judge Alan Kapperstein ruled the department didn't sufficiently prove its case. There is not enough cause to warrant an IO-9."

"That's good news," Paddy said, all the tension draining out of his body.

He slumped in his chair and grinned.

"So, It's over?" Paddy asked.

"I wouldn't go that far," Jimmy said. "They're going to rewrite their presentation and go judge shopping. Kapperstein was a Bloomberg appointee, so he's a real judge. They're going to look for a recent appointee by the present mayor—meaning a political hack who will give them whatever they want. But it should take them about three weeks, so we have time to prepare for the next round. You sound beat, Paddy. Why don't you go home and rest for a few days?"

"That's exactly what I'm going to do," he said.

"You like to dance between the raindrops," Martino observed when Paddy hung up.

"Yeah," Paddy agreed. "But I would prefer an umbrella. This shit is getting exhausting."

CHAPTER TWENTY-FOUR

March 22, 2017
Plainedge, Long Island
08:00 hours

Jimmy was wrong. They didn't have three weeks. Paddy woke to the sound of loud knocking at his front door. He bounded out of his recliner next to Mairead.

"Who is it, baby?" she asked.

"I don't know," he said.

Paddy opened the front door and was confronted with a two-star chief in uniform. His name tag said Hammond. Behind him were two guys Paddy thought looked like twerps in cheap suits. Behind them were two other guys with detective shields hooked on their belts. Aside from the chief, who looked uncomfortable to be there, the guys in plain clothes reeked of Internal Affairs. At least Paddy thought so. There wasn't a cop vibe emanating from any of them.

Paddy opened the storm door a crack and addressed the chief.

"What's this about, boss?"

"Detective Durr, I'm sorry to be the one to have to do this. I'm Deputy Chief Hammond, from Queens South. I have the duty this morning."

"In Queens," Paddy interrupted. "This is Nassau County."

"Nearest Boro has to respond to an emergency duty modification. That's what this is, I'm afraid."

"Oh," Paddy grinned. "Whose duty is getting modified?"

Paddy knew the procedure and the protocol. He also had a good idea of why they were here. Dr. Levine and her coterie had found a judge last night to issue an overriding injunction. But he wasn't about to do anyone's job for them this morning. The chief got it. He smiled. The four IAB officers in plainclothes appeared to become indignant. So, Paddy decided to ratchet up their tension level.

"You two in the K-Mart suits; you better show me some creds, or I might confuse you for a home invasion team. You won't like that. It'll be messy."

"I'm Lieutenant Donald..." the first one started to say when Paddy interrupted him.

"I don't want to hear your fucking name," Paddy said. "Just show me the shield and ID card. I'll learn your name from the receipt you're going to give me when I surrender my guns and shield. That *is* why you're here, right?"

Lieutenant Donald *Something* reluctantly showed his shield and ID. Paddy nodded at the other one, who flashed a sergeant's credentials. When the two gold shields in the rear tried to show their IDs, Paddy cut them off.

"You don't have to do that," he said. "I don't give a rat's ass who you are. IAB detectives are volunteers; true-believers—worth less than a bucket of warm spit."

The chief had to suppress a laugh. He coughed and said, "Judge Efraim Zayas, Bronx Administrative Court, filed an injunction late last night giving the city authorization to hold your IO-9 hearing. In addition, he sanctioned the immediate removal of your firearms pending the outcome of the hearing. Here's your copy of the order," he said, handing it through the open door.

Paddy read the order, already knowing what it would say. When he finished, he looked up at the chief.

"I'll go get them."

"Can't we come in?" the IAB lieutenant asked as if he were entitled.

"Sure," Paddy said. "Go get a search warrant."

"If we don't come in, how can we verify you're giving us all your firearms?" the lieutenant whined.

"Because you have my *ten-card*," Paddy said, referring to the NYPD's Force Record card, listing all his guns. "I only have three: the two revolvers and a Glock."

"How do we know you don't have any unauthorized weapons?" the lieutenant asked.

"You don't." Paddy grinned and bored his eyes through him until he took a step back. "But unless you have probable cause and a search warrant issued in

Nassau County, you ain't getting in this house. I mean, you could try. But I'm prepared to defend it with my life. Not your life though. Yours will be forfeited. But if it's what you want, go for it. I fucking dare you."

The chief didn't like the lieutenant any more than Paddy did. But he didn't want him killed in front of him either. So, he jumped in.

"Knock it off, Lieutenant!" he thundered. "I'm sick of your bullshit. I've been dealing with your smug attitude all morning—enough!" To Paddy, he said, "Go ahead and get your guns, Detective. We'll wait here."

Paddy nodded his thanks and closed and locked the door. He turned to go downstairs to get the revolvers out of his gun safe when Mairead asked.

"Who is it, baby?"

"It's Internal Affairs," he said. "I'll tell you all about it when I get rid of them."

After collecting his three firearms and deciding not to unload them, he removed his detective shield from its holder. Paddy opened the door and handed all of it to the lieutenant in a haphazard pile.

"Are the guns safe?" he asked.

"No, of course not," Paddy said. "They're guns. They're inherently dangerous, particularly to the ineperienced. So, try not to shoot yourself in the foot. Now, where's my fucking receipt?"

The lieutenant handed Paddy a typed voucher with the three guns and his shield listed as confiscated. Paddy scanned the document for the cheese-eating lieutenant's name. There it was at the bottom; Lieutenant Donald Wormwood.

"Hah!" he laughed. "Your name is Wormwood? That's fantastic! And not at all ironic. Now, get the fuck off my porch and go play in traffic."

Paddy watched as the IAB personnel slinked toward their car. *Look at the rats scurrying away,* he thought. *I wish I had laid out some glue traps.* He turned and spoke to the chief, who had come in his own car, the young cop who was his chauffer inside, idling in the driveway.

"None of that was for you, Chief Hammond," Paddy said. "You've been nothing but a gentleman. Sorry you had to watch me jerk the *Rat Squad* around, but I never miss an opportunity."

"That's all right. I don't like them either, and it was funny as hell. You're good under stress, Detective," the chief said winking.

Paddy extended his hand and the chief took it.

"I hope you crush those cocksuckers," Hammond said.

After they left, Paddy sat down dejectedly in the recliner beside Mairead.

Michael O'Keefe

"What happened, Paddy?" she asked.
"I just got transferred to the Rubber-Gun Squad."

CHAPTER TWENTY-FIVE

March 23, 2017
Manhattan
11:00 hours

Mairead was feeling good this morning. The weather had grown mild, the sun shining, and the temperature nearing a balmy sitxy degrees. As good as she felt, she was troubled for Paddy. He explained what happened with IAB, but the source of his troubles was really Dr. Levine. Mairead remembered her from when she tried to harpoon Paddy three years earlier. When she found out Levine was using Paddy's psyche as a pretext to delve into the Roxanne Barcellos fiasco, he had to restrain Mairead from hunting her down to kick the doctor's ass.

"What does that twat want with us now?" Mairead asked.

"Same as before—my guns."

"For what, Paddy? You haven't shot anyone in years."

"It's a vendetta. She never forgave me for shaming her the last time. Now she's got the backing of the mayor's wife. She thinks she can get me. She's using your illness as a ploy to suggest my psyche is crumbling under the strain—given my past *indiscretions*, as she calls them."

"Gunfights are indiscretions now?" she asked. "She's delusional. What make-believe world is she living in?"

Mairead silently fumed as she looked out the truck window on their ride to Sloan Kettering. Her furious foot-tapping told Paddy her anger was about to erupt. He waited for it.

"After my infusion today," she said. "I want you to take me down to Police Plaza. You can wait in the truck. I won't be long."

Paddy laughed. He was happy she felt strong enough to want to fight *anyone*. It had been a long while since she showed that kind of fire. Her eyes were like emerald infernos when her blood was up. He didn't wish to discourage her passion, even when it was expressed as anger, but he had already packed down and shelved his frustration and humiliation at the mistreatment of Dr. Levine. He would deal with it later. Right now, the only thing that mattered to him was Mairead.

"Psyche Services isn't at Police Plaza," Paddy informed her. "It's in Queens, and there's no way I'm going anywhere near that building. She might have me committed."

"She can't keep getting away with this."

"She won't," Paddy said. "The karma train's gotta turn around eventually. But I'm not worried about her right now. Let's take care of you."

After parking the truck, they rode the elevator up to the infusion center on the twenty-seventh floor. Since their last visit, Mairead had improved so much, Dr. Cheng decided to remove the IV portal for the morphine button. She had been using it less and less, and she agreed she didn't need it anymore. To be on the safe side, Cheng sent them home with a box of twelve morphine syrrettes. It had remained unopened on the table next to Mairead's bed.

After her infusion, they met with the doctor in his office. He was greatly encouraged by how well Mairead had responded to the treatment so far. He informed her that for this infusion they had decided to enrich the ratio of stem cells. Her body had been making such efficient use of them, Dr. Cheng was ready to try to expedite the process. He again advised them of the potential side effects, but even he didn't think they were likely.

***

Later that evening at home, Mairead began to feel tired and weak. She was able to climb into the hospital bed in the living room only with Paddy's assistance. She laid there, confused as to what was happening.

"I felt so good today, Paddy. What the hell is going on?"

"I don't know. Maybe with everything that went on this week, you wore down. The infusion has to take something out of you. Maybe this is just your body telling you to rest."

Burnt to a Crisp

"Yeah, maybe," Mairead said, but she didn't believe it.

Her suspicion was validated when the uncontrollable shaking started. She was shivering and could not get warm. After adding two blankets, Paddy covered her body with his own, but it didn't help. She kept trembling even under the additional weight and body heat. Then the soaking sweats began.

Paddy felt it first. She drenched right through her clothes and blankets, leaving her mattress sodden. He went to get some warm washcloths. Mairead neither wanted nor needed anything cold in this shivering state. Paddy was wiping the sweat away from her face and arms when the cramping commenced.

"Oh, shit! Ow!" Mairead cried out as her calf knotted up and would not let go.

Paddy saw her foot snap down and her toes curl. It looked to him like her foot was trying to fold in on itself; hinging where there was no joint. He messaged her calf, trying to get it to release. Having Mairead drink water, Paddy hooked up a bag of saline solution on the IV stanchion and attached it to the picc line in her arm. He went back to work massaging her calf. It seemed to be working.

No sooner did the first cramp abate than her arms snapped across her chest and her fists locked up, balled, and tightly dug in under her chin. She was screaming in agony when Paddy injected her thigh with the first morphine syrette. While he waited for the opiate to take effect, he massaged her biceps trying to get them to release their death grip. Mairead was alternately shrieking and crying, shaking her head from side to side, spraying perspiration and tears all over the room.

Paddy kept massaging and kneading her upper arms. It felt like a futile exercise, but he didn't know what else to do—he had to do something. Mairead cried out in a guttural scream.

"More morphine!" she wailed.

Paddy went into the muscle of her shoulder with the second syrette. He got back to work on her arms. He could feel the knotted muscles start to release. For a moment Mairead stopped screaming. Sobbing now, she sounded exhausted. Paddy was going to suggest they call Dr. Chen, until her thighs and hamstrings locked up as if enclosed in a vise.

The same agony ensued, only worse. Paddy repeated the massaging to no discernible effect. Mairead had her teeth clenched and her eyes pressed shut, the tears streaming down her face. Her screaming had given way to a throaty, agonized growling; emanating from deep within her. Through this, she managed one word.

"More!" she croaked.

Paddy sent the third syrette into her right thigh. The saline bag empty, he hooked up another. He rubbed her legs, front and back. After a while, they released. This time, Paddy had no illusions the storm was over. He was waiting to see where the cramping would attack next when Mairead let out a blood-curdling howl and arched her back so severely the blankets made a tent over her.

He was massaging the muscles in her lower back when Mairead, with pleading eyes, croaked his name.

"Paddy," she said through her sobs. "You have to end this."

"What?" he said, confused and horrified. He knew what she was alluding to but chose denial.

"You promised," she wailed. "You said you wouldn't let me suffer like this. Make the hurt stop. Please, if you love me, you'll end this."

Arrant disjointed thoughts flashed through his mind. *I could snap her neck with a twist, or use my forearm to press across her throat and cut off her air. It wouldn't take but a minute. Or the pillow over her face; I could feel her last breaths as the life slowly ebbed out of her. It would be quick, and it would be over. She would finally be at peace—with no more pain.*

In the next instant, a wave of shame, revulsion, and horror cascaded over him. In anguish, he cried out as if in pain. The thought of hurting her was repugnant. He laid himself over Mairead's, rigid, convulsing, and sweaty body, leaning his face in to press his mouth against her ear.

"I can't, Mairead," he said through his own sobs.

"You promised," she reminded him. "You can't leave me like this."

He just wept, holding the broken and agonized husk of his wife, apologizing for failing her. At that moment he hated God for doing this to her, and for not taking him instead—as he had pleaded he do for so long. Mostly though, he hated himself. He felt like a coward. Then he felt like a villain for having even considered it. He was that conflicted.

He endured her suffering until she started repeatedly screaming, "Kill me now!"

She wasn't pleading. She was demanding it. When he could take no more, he got another syrette of morphine from the box. He knew this much of the drug might kill her anyway, but he had to find her some relief. He plunged the fourth syrette into her neck, right into the carotid artery. Whatever was going to happen, Paddy knew would occur quickly.

Burnt to a Crisp

Seconds later, he watched as her body eased back down onto the mattress, her spine releasing its iron-like grip. Her breathing—still ragged—began to slow. He feared it might be an overdose. He leaned in to whisper, "I love you." If he had killed her with the final syrette, he wanted her to know that much. If these were the last words he would ever say to her, he wanted these to be the words.

"Get the fuck away from me," she growled.

Her words pierced him. Shaken, Paddy pulled himself off her and sat in the recliner next to the bed. He felt such disgust with himself right now; he perfectly understood Mairead's revulsion. He sat there moldering in his self-loathing. Mairead started talking to him, her voice slurred, in a dream-like cadence, but the anger intense—focused.

"You're a coward, Paddy. You failed me when I needed you most. How could you let me suffer like that? You're a selfish prick. It's always been about you, hasn't it? You couldn't bear to let me go because you need me to do every little thing, to wipe your ass for you. You're an emotional cripple, helpless on your own. Wipe your own ass from now on. I'm done with you. You're useless to me now."

He absorbed it wordlessly. When Mairead put her head back on the pillow and was quiet for a minute, he thought she had fallen asleep. He got up to go down into the family room, sensing she wanted him nowhere near her.

"I hate you," she said as he reached the stairs.

"I know," he said, pausing to turn around. *But you'll have to get on line behind me*, he thought.

He went downstairs into the darkened family room, grabbing the afghan throw her mother had knitted for him. Wrapping himself in it, he sat down on the overstuffed sofa and pulled inward, hoping to bury himself so deep into the soft leather, he might never emerge.

CHAPTER TWENTY-SIX

March 24, 2017
Plainedge, Long Island
11:00 hours

The next morning, Mairead, having slept like a log in her opioid-induced fog, stirred awake at 11:00 A.M. Paddy, who hadn't slept at all, was back in the chair by her side. She looked over at him. He read ambivalent distaste in her expression. It was an artifact of the morphine, but he didn't know that. He wasn't forgiving himself anyway, so he had no expectation Mairead would. So distaste it was.

"How do you feel?" he asked warily.

"Like I'm underwater," she said. "But still alive—pity that."

"Are you in pain?"

"No, but that can change in a heartbeat, can't it?"

"Do you want me to call Dr. Cheng to tell him what happened?"

"Fuck him," she said. "And while you're at it, fuck you too. You *both* did this to me. Him with his magic bullets; it's cancer, for Christ's sake! He looks at me and sees a lab rat to experiment on, and you let him. All I wanted was to die with a little dignity, and neither of you would let me. Now I have to deal with you and your hangdog face, moping around here like you lost your teddy bear—even after you were the one who guilted me into this. I'm tired of you both. Just leave me alone."

Paddy nodded and went upstairs to shower and shave. After getting dressed, he came down to leave for work.

"I have to go in early," he told Mairead.
"Why early?"
"I have to get a new ID card."
"What's wrong with the old one?"
"It isn't stamped No Firearms," he said.
"Oh," she said, turning her back to him.
Realizing he had been dismissed, he left for Brooklyn.

***

Joe Furio was waiting for him when he got there. As the DEA Boro Trustee, he would bring Paddy down to headquarters for the indignity of having his ID stamped. From there, they would head over to the DEA Offices on Thomas Street to talk to Jimmy Maselli. Paddy had called Joe after getting modified. Despite it being his day off, Joe burned up the phone lines getting a plan of action in place. At Furio's insistence, everyone in the union was trying to pull strings to overturn the injustice.

Joe was concerned about Paddy's physical and mental state. He looked exhausted. On top of which, he had never seen Paddy with his shoulders so slumped, hanging his head like a whipped dog. He wasn't speaking, except for one-word answers, which were mostly grunts. On the way downtown, Joe broached the subject—and not delicately.

"You look like two hundred pounds of hammered shit," he said. "When I spoke to you after Mairead's infusion, you seemed okay. What the fuck happened?"

Paddy told Joe about Mairead's episode the previous night. He spoke in a slur, distractedly, as if he were merely a witness and not a participant. Then he told him about what she said after and what she said this morning.

"That was just the dope talking, Paddy," Joe tried to encourage him.

Paddy was having none of it, already buying into Mairead's screed and blaming himself. He was despondent. Frightened, Joe thought for a minute, *It's probably a blessing he can't get his hands on a gun right now.* Then he chided himself for thinking such a thing.

Once they got to *The Puzzle Palace*, as police headquarters was derisively known, Paddy eschewed conversation heading to the elevators. He returned silent nods to the several cops who knew him and said hello. Seeing his countenance and no doubt absorbing the negative aura he was projecting, no one pushed the matter further.

At the ID Desk, Paddy let Joe do the talking. When the officer at the desk was going to ask him if he wanted a new photo taken, she took one look at Paddy's lifeless eyes and disconsolate face and decided to make the call herself. She elected to use the pleasant, smiling face in the photo they already had on file.

***

At Thomas Street, they sat down with Jimmy Maselli. The lawyer was furious, raging over Dr. Levine and the city's lawyers backdooring the system. They shouldn't have been permitted to do it. He said that was what he was going to make the basis of his appeal motion.

"That asshole judge in the Bronx overstepped his bounds. He can't overrule a jurist from the same court, who, by the way, has been a judge since this jerkoff was in pre-law. He's not even in the right borough. He's got no business even commenting on a ruling in Manhattan, let alone reversing it. He was on the verge of being disbarred before the mayor made him a judge. He's been on the bench for all of a month, and every single ruling he's made has been overturned on appeal. I read them, Paddy. They're all going to get reversed, and so is this."

"Hmm," Paddy said distractedly, looking out the window.

Jimmy was a little concerned by his lack of a reaction. The Paddy Durr he knew was a fighter. The detective in front of him looked like he had already quit, thrown in the towel, and gone home.

"What am I missing here?" Jimmy asked.

Paddy just stared back at him. So, Joe answered.

"He's been up all night. Mairead had a bad reaction to her treatment yesterday. He just needs a good night's sleep."

"I'm sorry, Paddy," Jimmy said. "I didn't realize. Go home and get yourself right and let me worry about this. Give me a day to write the appeal. We should have a hearing set in State Supreme Court in a couple of days. We're gonna get your guns back."

Paddy stared back blankly. *If I had one now, it would go right in my mouth*, he thought, taking a deep breath through his nose and exhaling in a sigh. It sounded like surrender.

"Don't knock yourself silly over this," Paddy said. "At some point, they're gonna get their IO-9. When they do, they're gonna take my guns. Why keep fighting if it's a foregone conclusion?"

"Because it's wrong," Jimmy said. "The union won't stand for it, and as your lawyer, I can't. I'm gonna fix this. If not for you, then for every other detective, so they can't pull the same sneaky shit on them."

"All right, Jim. If you gotta, go ahead. Let me know if you need anything from me," Paddy said as if he were disinterested. Because he was.

Michael O'Keefe

CHAPTER TWENTY-SEVEN

March 25, 2017
Bushwick, Brooklyn
09:00 hours

Paddy was at his desk early, staring distractedly at his open cases in the computer on his desk. He had just gotten in, and he was already just waiting for the tour to end, so he could take his misery somewhere else. The expressions of concern on his co-workers' faces were becoming annoying. Thinking he was undeserving, he was grateful for the solitude when everyone left the office to either go to court or work on their cases. It was just Paddy and the Police Administrative Aide, Ms. Lena.

A while later, Ms. Lena woke Paddy from his brooding trance.

"Paddy," she called over to him. "I have Carmelo Boreo on hold. He's looking to talk to Joe."

"That's his perp from the bias murder," Paddy informed her.

"I know. That's why I put him on hold."

"Transfer him over. I'll talk to him."

Ms. Lena sent the call over to his desk and turned to face away from him in an effort to seem like she wasn't listening. But Paddy knew she heard every word and understood things far beyond what she was expected to. Despite the fact she was in her early seventies and was an old-school church lady, the woman had some serious street smarts and intuition. She had learned from her friend and

Burnt to a Crisp

predecessor, Ms. Flo, that her job working with detectives was to hear everything, retain little of it, and never, ever repeat any of it. Discretion was her primary responsibility, and she was excellent in this regard.

Paddy was unconcerned about her overhearing anything sensitive. He knew her loyalty to the squad was absolute. The detectives adored her and treated her like a beloved aunt. She, in turn, regarded them as *hers*, referring to the squad in conversation with the other PAAs as "my detectives." Paddy thought so much of her instincts; he would sometimes ask for her opinion on his cases. Her understanding of human nature was so acute; her insights were never far off the mark.

"This is Detective Durr," Paddy said, answering the phone. "I'm Furio's partner. How may I help you, Carmelo?"

"Detective Furio wanted...my mother said if...I have this card, and..."

Paddy could tell he was in a stressed-out lather. He kept tripping on his own words, not able to come near to finishing a sentence. Though he didn't feel like it, Durr knew he had to soothe this kid's anxiety. As jacked up as he was, it was going to take a serious stroke job.

"Calm down, Carmelo," Paddy said. "Joe is a nice guy. From what I know, he just wants to speak with you. A guy died on the steps of your building. He has to talk to everyone who lives there, and you're the only one he hasn't caught up to. He just needs to take your statement to close the case."

"Well, I had nothing to do with it," Boreo said, still in a panic.

"It's my understanding nobody was responsible," Paddy lied. "It looks like the guy was drunk, fell, and hit his head."

Durr could almost hear the decompression over the phone. Boreo bought the lie because he wanted to; because he needed to. Now he was anxious to talk about the case.

"That's what I heard," he said. "But I was inside. They said that..."

"I don't know anything about the case," Paddy interrupted. "Anything you tell me, you're going to have to tell Furio. Just let me know where you are. I'll send someone to pick you up. Joe will ask his questions, and we'll take you home."

"I'm at my girlfriend's aunt's house."

Paddy rolled his eyes.

"I don't know her. Does she have an address?"

"Oh yeah, her name is Consuela Herrera."

"That didn't help," Paddy sighed. "I need you to listen to my questions. Then answer them. Don't anticipate what I want to know. Just tell me what I asked. What is her house number?"

"It's 1423, apartment 3R."

"Close. You almost had it. Now—this is important—is there a street in front of the building?"

"Oh, Saint Nicholas Avenue."

"Very good, Carmelo. You sit tight. I'll have someone pick you up in a few minutes."

After hanging up, Paddy called over to Ms. Lena. He needed the number from which Boreo had called. She had anticipated as much, already copying it from her caller ID. Before he could even ask, she said, "718-386-3245."

"Thanks, Ms. Lena," Paddy said, impressed but not surprised.

He entered the number into a reverse directory on his desktop. Sure enough, the call came from 1423 St. Nicholas Avenue, apartment 3R, registered to Consuela Herrera. Paddy looked around the office. It was unnecessary. He already knew he was the only detective there, and he was unarmed and forbidden to leave the precinct.

He called Joe on his cell phone. It went directly to voicemail. Evidently, Joe was testifying. He left him a message, informing him Carmelo Boreo was looking to talk. Paddy just had to figure out how to get him into the office.

Paddy tried Tommy Crowe on his cell.

"Yeah, Paddy," he answered.

"Want to make a homicide apprehension?"

"Absolutely!" Tommy said. "But I'm already down in Central booking. We grabbed a *burner* off Schaeffer Street earlier in the tour."

"Are your partners around?"

"It was just me and Andy Summers, and he's down here with me. We should be back in a few hours."

"I need you now. Next time, I guess," Paddy said, hanging up.

He called down to the desk, expecting to speak with Lieutenant Dailey. He was surprised to hear the voice of Carmine Demiri.

"Eight three desk, Officer Demiri, how may I help you?"

"Carmine, what are you doing there?"

"I'm the Assistant Desk Officer today."

"Is *Handsome Dan* working?"

"He's off today. Sergeant Feigling has the desk. You want to talk to him?"

Burnt to a Crisp

"I'd rather stick needles in my eyes. If I want something fucked up, I'll fuck it up myself. Stay away from that asshole. He's dangerous."

"So you've told me," Carmine said. "I'm doing my best."

Paddy was left to mull it over. His options were few. In fact, they were nonexistent. He had no one to reach out to and was forbidden to go himself. A conundrum; he would just have to swallow the putrid taste of letting a murderer slip through his fingers. He found it revolting, the imaginary coin flip over before the quarter was even in the air.

He grabbed his coat, a radio, and a set of squad-car keys and headed for the door.

"Where you going, Paddy?" Ms. Lena demanded, glaring at him through narrowed eyes.

"I gotta buy a pack of cigarettes," he said.

"You don't smoke. Please don't go after that man. You don't have a gun or backup. Joe will be back from court in a couple of hours. He can go get him then."

"He won't be there in a couple of hours."

"He's not worth it," she pleaded. "You've given this job enough. They don't deserve your life too. Your family needs you. You just can't do this."

"I couldn't live with myself if I didn't. If I'm not back in fifteen minutes, avenge my death," Paddy said, heading out the door.

When he got to 1423 St. Nicholas, Carmelo Boreo was waiting for him on the stoop. He parked and got out of the squad car.

"Remember me, Carmelo?" he asked, approaching the stoop.

"Sure," Boreo said. "You're Detective Durr. Is Furio with you?"

"He's at the precinct," Paddy lied. "He asked me to give you a ride."

Carmelo came down the steps and put his hands behind his back.

"What are you doing?" Paddy asked.

"You don't have to cuff me?"

"What for? You haven't done anything illegal that I'm aware of. I do have to pat you down, though—department regulations. But if you're clean, you can sit upfront with me."

"Oh, cool!" Boreo said.

Paddy thought so too, inasmuch as it obviated the need to admit he didn't have handcuffs and wasn't authorized to use them if he did. *As a matter of fact, this whole scenario was a gross violation of NYPD rules,* Paddy thought. *But Boreo doesn't need to know that either.*

After giving him a quick but thorough rub for weapons, Boreo hopped into the front passenger seat. Paddy got in and cautioned him.

"I don't know anything about your case, so don't ask me. Save everything for Furio."

"Okay," he said.

But he couldn't help himself.

"I hope Detective Furio doesn't think I killed that *Polack*."

Paddy ignored him, pretending not to hear. But, he flipped on the flashing grill lights and accelerated.

"I know Furio has people who saw me with the baseball bat, but I was just putting it away. I didn't want to get blamed for hitting him."

"I don't know what you're talking about," Paddy said, hitting the siren and further accelerating toward the precinct, now running stop signs and red lights.

"I don't…I mean…I was…oh fuck!" Boreo whimpered.

"Shhh," Paddy said softly, trying to calm him.

Boreo started crying. He was rocking in his seat and moaning to himself. Durr tried to ignore him, but he would not be ignored.

"I'm so sorry I killed that man," he wailed. "I just meant to scare him. I aimed for his shoulder, but he was drunk and got his head in the way."

Paddy slammed on the brakes, screeching to a halt in the middle of the intersection of Bleecker Street and Knickerbocker Avenue. He leaned across the seat and poked Boreo in the forehead.

"Did I not tell you I knew nothing about this case? Didn't I say to save it for Furio?"

"You did."

"So shut the fuck up!" Paddy yelled.

Boreo went silent, cowering in the corner of the front seat the rest of the way into the precinct. Once in the rear lot, Paddy came around the squad car, grabbed Boreo by the ear, and whisked him up the back steps to the squad. He shoved him into the interview room and slid the bolt lock shut.

Ms. Lena came over to his desk to tell him the lieutenant had called looking for him.

"What did you tell him?"

"That you were out getting a pack of cigarettes."

"You lied to him?" Paddy asked.

"It ain't my lie. You said it first."

"You think he bought it?"

Burnt to a Crisp

"Probably not. But he's on the way in. You can tell him whatever you want when he gets here."

"Thanks, Ms. Lena."

"Don't you thank me, Paddy Durr. I'm angry with you right now, making me lie to that man instead of telling him the truth—that you're out there trying to get your stupid ass killed. It's not right, scaring me like that."

"I'm sorry, Ms. Lena," Paddy said. "But you knew what had to happen."

"Just cause I know what has to happen don't mean I have to like it none," she said, walking back to her desk in a huff.

A while later, the lieutenant and Joe Furio got to the office at the same time. Martino viewed Paddy warily. Durr was looking off into space as if he were the only one in the room. The lieutenant coughed to break his trance.

"Where were you when I called?"

"Taking a shit," Paddy lied.

"Who is that staring at me from the interview room?"

"That's Carmelo Boreo."

"How did he get here?"

"That's a funny story," Paddy said.

"Really?" Martino asked.

"No, not really," he admitted.

The lieutenant ordered Joe and Paddy into his office and had them shut the door.

"What the fuck went on here today?" the lou demanded.

"I don't know nothing," Joe said. "I was in court all morning."

"Did you go get Boreo by yourself?" he asked Paddy.

"Yeah."

"Why would you do that?" Martino asked.

"There was no one else around. I called Joe and got his voicemail. Anti-Crime was down in central booking with a gun collar. When I called the desk, Julien Feigling was the boss. Could anything good come from asking that rim job for help? I did what I had to."

"And put yourself and this whole squad in harm's way," Martino said. "I'm fucking pissed at you right now, Paddy."

"If you want to write me up, go ahead. But you're going to have to get in line for your pound of flesh, and I don't think Dr. Levine is going to leave you any," Paddy said, shrugging.

173

"I'm not looking to hurt you, Paddy, but if this had gone bad, I wouldn't be able to protect you either."

"Hell, I know that, boss. I took a calculated risk. This might be the last police work I ever do. I don't want to be remembered as the guy who let a murderer walk because he was afraid to act."

"Nobody would remember you that way, Paddy."

"I would remember me that way," he said, jutting his chin out in defiance.

"I can't talk to you when you're like this," Martino said. "Get out of my office."

Paddy and Joe went to the coffee room to discuss what to do about Boreo.

"Did he give it up?" Joe asked.

"In three sentences," Paddy said. "But you can't use it."

"Why not?"

"Because I'm the disgraced psycho-detective who had his guns and shield taken away. Do you want to rest your case on that? No, Joe, you're gonna have to get him to give it up again. But don't worry. He doesn't know how to shut up. He wants to be forgiven. Go hear his confession, Father Joe."

Joe went into the interview room and had a written confession in minutes. While they waited for the DA to get there with a videographer, Paddy sat at his desk and descended into a deep emotional funk.

A few hours later, back from central booking, Police Officer Tommy Crowe came into the office looking for Paddy. He said he had information on his arson murders. Tommy came over to the desk and was a little surprised to see Paddy just look up at him—distracted. Ordinarily, he would have met Tommy halfway across the floor, embracing him in a hug.

Paddy was Tommy's mentor, just as Tommy's father, Jimmy Crowe, had been Paddy's—before being gunned down by a stick-up team in 1988. Tommy had been a young boy at the time. Paddy remained close to the family.

Since Tommy had come on the job, Paddy had served as his *Dutch Uncle*, guiding him, protecting him, and teaching him what was required to get home safe at the end of his tour. Tommy didn't need much assistance. He was a natural at police work. He had his father's hero blood coursing through his veins and was rapidly developing his father's legendary street smarts. But right now, he was confused.

Paddy looked up at him, took notice of the long hair worn on the top of his head in what was called a *man bun*. The ginger beard he was sporting looked spotty and unkempt, but it went well with the hemp hoody he wore. It covered his

Burnt to a Crisp

vest, gun, and handcuffs. He completed the get-up with torn faded blue jeans and distressed brown work boots. The overall look screamed "hipster shithead," which was a perfect cover for a plainclothes cop in Bushwick in 2017.

Tommy knew any of these sartorial accouterments would have ordinarily drawn Paddy's sarcastic, rapier wit and precipitated a blistering round of ball-breaking. Instead, Paddy just looked up at him vacantly.

"What's up, kid?" he asked.

"The super from 402 Wilson, Jibaro, asked me if I knew you. When I told him we were friends, he gave me information on your homicides. I told him he should talk to you directly, but he said you scared him. He would rather just tell me."

"Yeah, I'm the Boogie Man. Everybody is afraid of me." Paddy laughed. The bitterness dripping off of every word.

"He said your doer is Cucko. He's been hiding out in Flatbush. He gave me the address. He's been staying with his cousin, a woman named Emma Calderon, and her fifteen-year-old son. He didn't know the kid's name, but everybody calls him *Mierdito*."

"Really?" Paddy said. "Mierdito?"

"Yeah, why?"

"It means Little Shit."

"Oh, that's funny." Tommy laughed, trying to give him his notes.

"You know I got modified yesterday, right?" Paddy said, waving him off. "Hold onto that. When they figure out who's going to take over my cases, I'll have them talk to you."

"Uh…okay, Paddy," Tommy said.

"Anything else, kid?"

"Nah, that's it."

"Stay safe out there," Paddy said, dismissing him.

As Tommy left the office, he was troubled. Paddy's ambivalence was so uncharacteristic it frightened him. It would be understandable if he were pissed off about being modified, but Paddy didn't seem angry—more like he just didn't give a shit—about anything. Tommy decided he would stop by his mother's house to discuss it with her that night.

At 18:00 hours, Paddy signed out in the blotter and left the squad without saying goodnight to anyone, slinking down the backstairs to the parking lot. This obviated being seen by anyone before getting in his truck and driving home to Plainedge.

A few minutes later, Joe went looking for him to ask if he needed anything done on his cases since Paddy couldn't leave the station house. He checked the blotter and saw he had signed out.

"Did Paddy just sign out and leave?" he asked Armando Gigante.

"Yeah. I thought he was headed to the can, but then he never came back. I saw in the log that he signed out. That ain't like him. Is everything all right?"

"Oh, what the fuck?" Joe said, rubbing his forehead.

"What's going on?"

"Paddy's in a real bad way, Armando. I'm afraid for him."

"You don't think he'd try and hurt himself, do you?"

"I honestly don't know at this point," Joe admitted.

"What *are* we gonna do?" Armando asked.

***

That night in Massapequa, Tommy Crowe spoke to his mother about Paddy's mental state. He described his listless, emotionless inattention.

"I get being upset about being modified," Tommy said. "But this is something else. Bad as it is, Paddy wouldn't let something beat him down like this. He would fight. Right now, he's given up. He's despondent. I know Mairead is ill, but I thought she was doing better. Something else has to be going on with him. I'm worried."

"He's just decompressing for a day or two after a setback. He'll bounce back," Katelyn said, but the concerned look on her face did not escape her son.

"Mom, we gotta do something. From what you've told me, and from what I've heard from the other detectives, he's faced way worse than this and never even broken stride. He's been in and out of trouble his whole career—as if he likes it—and he brushes it off like it just doesn't matter. Something has changed."

"I'll get to the bottom of it and go see Paddy and Mairead tomorrow morning," she promised.

After Tommy left to go to his apartment, Katelyn called Joe Furio. She had come to know him well through Paddy. She also worked with him through The Honor Legion on behalf of The Survivors of the Shield. She liked and respected Joe for his commitment to his guys and the widows and orphans, but she loved him for his loyalty to Paddy. So much so, she had no problem yelling at him.

"What the hell is going on with Paddy, Joe?" she shouted through the phone.

Burnt to a Crisp

Joe told her everything, describing Paddy's despair in excruciating detail, leaving nothing out. Paddy seemed crushed by Mairead's seeming personality change.

"I can't believe she said those things to him," Joe said.

"It's not surprising," Katelyn said. "Pain can be cleansing, but it can also be a poison. It can make you say and do things you never would otherwise. Don't forget; she was on enough morphine to knock out a horse. She wasn't herself. I'll remind her who she is."

Joe knew Katelyn could get to the core of Paddy much faster than he could. Since he was at a loss for what to do next, he wanted her to know everything. This was her area of expertise. Joe was smart enough to defer to her.

Katelyn considered Paddy's shattered psyche. It seemed worse to her than when he and Mairead almost divorced. At least he retained a sense of hope back then. It sounded like he had abandoned it now.

She thanked Joe for his candor. She was happy Paddy had such a staunch advocate as his partner. She knew Furio would do anything for him.

"What are we going to do, Katelyn?" he asked.

"I'm going to head over there tomorrow morning," Katelyn said. "I'll straighten them both out."

"Thank you," Joe said, relief in his voice.

Then Katelyn's Irish temper kicked in. She needed to vent at someone. To his dismay, Joe Furio was the nearest at hand.

"I seem to remember telling you to take care of him," she seethed. "Letting him get to this point doesn't exactly qualify. Are you going to up your game, Joe, or do I have to come down there and straighten you out too?"

"Katelyn, I'm trying, but I'm out of my element here. I've never seen him like this. I didn't know what to do—short of kicking his ass—and I don't think I can. He's bigger than me, and he might be the only son of a bitch in New York meaner."

"I'm sorry, Joe," Katelyn said. "I'm worried and frustrated. I just needed to blow off a little steam. I know you're doing the best you can. Let me do my thing, and we'll talk."

***

Michael O'Keefe

When Paddy got home, Mairead was in the hospital bed, facing away from him. He thought she might be asleep. At least she was breathing. He could see her blankets rising and falling.

"I'm home," he said softly.

"Good for you," Mairead replied without turning around. She waved the back of her hand at him, dismissing him with indifference.

Paddy slinked downstairs without another word into the dark family room, cocooning himself in the afghan—disappearing into the couch again.

Burnt to a Crisp

CHAPTER TWENTY-EIGHT

March 26, 2017
Plainedge, Long Island
09:00 hours

Paddy was awakened by the sound of pounding at the front door. As he made his way up from the family room, Mairead shouted at him.
"Will you answer the damned door already?!"
"I'm trying to," Paddy said.
"Who the hell is it at nine o'clock in the morning?"
"Maybe Internal Affairs is back with a search warrant," he surmised.
Whoever it is, they sound pissed off, he thought, undoing the locks on the door. Opening it, he was confronted by an agitated Katelyn Crowe. He watched her face change from impatient annoyance to disbelief and fear. Paddy glimpsed himself in the mirror at the side of the door and realized the cause. He looked like the victim of an atrocity. Two days without sleep—all the while punishing

himself—had done a number on him. He opened the door and beckoned Katelyn in.

"What the hell is going on with you, Paddy?" she demanded. "You look like death warmed over."

"I'm all right," he lied. "I just haven't been sleeping well."

"Bullshit! You're depressed. Do you think I don't know what it looks like? You've been moping around the office in a fugue state, feeling sorry for yourself."

"The job took my guns and put me on modified assignment," Paddy said by way of explaining.

"We both know that's not it. And I know about what went on with you two the other night."

Mairead sat up. Until now, she had lain there, not really caring about anything, but that got her attention.

"Who the hell is sticking their noses into my business now?" she slurred from the living room.

Katelyn glared, holding up her hand to silence her.

"Not now, Mairead, I'm angry with you, but I will deal with you when I'm done with him."

Mairead seemed momentarily stunned, but it was probably just an artifact of the latent morphine which hadn't yet cycled out of her system. Whatever the cause, she sat there—remaining quiet.

"You scared the hell out of Tommy yesterday," Katelyn said. "He barely recognized you. I called Joe and found out the rest. I'm sorry you're going through a rough time, but you have to wake up now. There are people who depend on you."

"Their faith in me is misplaced. I'm done—with all of it."

Katelyn's open right hand shot out, lightning-quick, and came down across Paddy's face with a loud crack. This focused his attention, but not enough to see the other hand coming. It got him as squarely as the first. Mairead took all of this in and snickered. Katelyn glared at her again and then got back to Paddy.

"You don't just get to quit, Paddy. You don't get to give up on your partners, or Mairead, and you damn sure don't get to quit on my son. He loves you. You're his hero, and he needs you."

Paddy glanced over in Mairead's direction. She continued to look into space. He realized she wasn't indifferent as much as oblivious. *Perhaps it was the morphine*, he thought. Katelyn misread his mind, thinking he was sulking about the way Mairead had treated him. So, she poked him in the chest—hard.

"Paddy," she said, refocusing his attention. "You can't turtle on the people who love you. You owe them more than that. And not everything wrong in the world is your fault. In fact, none of what's going on right now is. You're not God. You don't have the power to fix everything. But you decided instead of persevering; you would hang upon this cross of your own making, to pay for imaginary sins—because it's easier. You're copping out like a coward. If Jimmy were alive to see what you let yourself become, he would be ashamed."

Paddy took a step back. He got angry, glaring at Katelyn with that thousand-yard stare.

Finally, she thought. *Some sign of emotion; he was still in there somewhere.*

It only lasted for a moment. Realizing she was right, Paddy shrugged. Now that he was forced to think about it, it felt like cowardice.

"All right. You got my attention, Katelyn. What would you like me to do?"

"Go upstairs and take a shower. You stink of sweat and desperation. It doesn't become you. And don't forget to shave. You look homeless. Then you're going to eat something and go to bed. You need at least eight hours of sleep."

"I've gotta go in for a *four-by* today," he protested.

"You're taking an *E-day*," she said, referring to the NYPD shorthand for an emergency excusal. "I'll call Furio and arrange it for you."

"Are you going to hit me anymore?" he asked.

"Not as long as you do what you're told," she said.

"Yes, ma'am."

Paddy headed upstairs to the shower.

After hearing the bathroom door close and the water in the shower running, Katelyn turned her attention to Mairead, but Mairead beat her to the punch.

"You know, he's never going to grow up if you keep coddling him like that," she slurred.

"Coddling? You think that was coddling?" Katelyn scoffed. "I just pulled him out of the abyss. You're the one who put him there."

"I just want to be left alone to die in peace," Mairead said. "All of that pain the other night was his fault. If it had been up to me, I would already be dead."

"But you didn't leave it up to you, did you? You wanted Paddy to do it for you, so you could escape. You would make him a murderer and your children orphans so you could avoid further suffering? That's disgusting."

"You don't know what it's like. You've never had cancer," Mairead said.

"You're right, Mairead. I can only imagine your pain. But I know loss. I know how *that* hurts. And that's what you would be consigning Paddy and the kids to. I lost my Jimmy almost thirty years ago. I found a wonderful man in Ed to love and spend the rest of my life with, but even still, there are days the loss is so overwhelming; it's all I can do to get out of bed. It never goes away. But I carry on because there are people who love me and are counting on me."

Mairead made a sour face, not liking the taste of Katelyn's words at all. Her Irish stubbornness stood in the way of allowing her to see the sense in them.

"He let me suffer. It's not like he hasn't killed anyone before. He wouldn't do it for his own selfish reasons."

"Mairead, there is so much wrong with that statement; I don't know where to begin. First of all, he wasn't letting you suffer. He was doing everything he could to alleviate your pain and beating himself up for failing. And yes, he's killed people, but it was never murder. Look how he still carries guilt from every one of those. They continue to punish him. He still sees their faces in his nightmares. Now you want him to commit premeditated murder on the most important person in his life, the one person with whom you know he can't do without? You can't ask that of him. It would end him so quickly; he'd get to hell before you did. You think he's selfish? He'd do anything to lift this curse from you and put it on himself. He's not a religious man, but for that, he prays. That's not being selfish, you stupid bitch. It's called devotion."

Mairead was stunned to silence. Her mind wasn't working quickly enough to process everything Katelyn had said. When the opioid fog cleared, perhaps she would get it. But it would be another few hours before that would happen. Katelyn wanted to be clear about one other thing.

"I don't care if you want to be mad at him. Knock yourself out. Just stop *blaming* him. He didn't invent cancer, but you would think he did, the way he already feels responsible. You can't let him do that. He's not as strong as you. If he ends up like this again, you better pray it's because you died. Because if you didn't, I'll know it was your fault. I don't care if you're already on your deathbed. I will kick your bony ass."

Katelyn felt bad when Mairead started crying. The tears streaming down her cheeks coupled with her gentle sobs would have been pathetic enough, but the look of guilty shame on her face was breaking Katelyn's heart. She had given her the tough love. Now she knew it was time for some tenderness. She came over to the bed and took Mairead up in her arms.

"It'll be all right," Katelyn said.

"I'm sorry. I should never have done that to him," Mairead blubbered through her sobs.

"It's okay, honey," Katelyn said, rubbing her back. "But you don't need to apologize to me. When Paddy wakes up, tell him."

"I will. I promise."

"Good. While I'm here, do you need me to do anything for you?" Katelyn asked.

"No. I'm okay. Julissa will be here soon, and the girls should be home from Spring Break tonight."

"They both went away?"

Mairead nodded.

"Oh, to be that young again," Katelyn lamented.

"I'd probably screw it up again by meeting a cute cop who would turn my whole world upside down." Mairead laughed.

"Me too." Katelyn grinned. "But you know what? Even after everything, I'd do it all the same."

"I can't imagine doing anything else," Mairead agreed.

After Katelyn left, Mairead broke down and called Dr. Cheng. She still had no idea what caused her episode the other night or if it might recur. When she got Cheng on the phone, she described what happened. He was curious why he was only hearing about it now.

"Why didn't you or Paddy call me when it was happening?"

"We were too busy trying to make it stop. Then it got a little weird around here, but we're better now."

"I wish you had called. We could have taken care of it with one syrette of morphine."

"It took four," Mairead reminded him.

"It didn't have to. I could have talked Paddy through it. One shot into your lower spine, directly into the central nervous system would have ended it."

"Well, what the hell was it?"

"It's very rare, but it happens. You're not going to believe it, but it's good news. Those weren't cramps. They were muscle spasms generated by the dormant nerve tissue springing back to life. Your dead cells are regenerating. In this case, a little too quickly. If it hasn't recurred by now, it probably won't. But if it does, have Paddy call me. I gave you my home and cell numbers for a reason. Use them for Christ's sake."

"So, this happened because I'm getting better?"

"Yeah, Mairead. You're getting better."

Dr. Cheng was confused when he heard Mairead crying through the phone. They didn't sound like tears of joy.

"What's the matter?"

"I'm just a horrible person, is all."

When Paddy came down from the bedroom nine hours later, he looked rested and refreshed but not at all sure of himself. Julissa was checking Mairead's vitals.

"Julissa, would you go into the kitchen and fix me a cup of tea?" Mairead asked.

"*Irie*, Ms. Mairead. Would you like a cup too, Mr. Paddy?"

"Thanks, Julissa. That would be wonderful," he said, smiling.

After she left the room, Paddy asked, "Can I talk to you?"

"Only if you let me apologize first," Mairead said.

"You don't have anything to apologize for," he said. "But if you want, go ahead."

"I need you to forgive me. I was mean to you. It was wrong. But you need to forgive yourself first. None of this is your fault. I'm so sorry I ever let you believe it was."

"That's all right, baby," Durr said. "I was hoping it was just the dope talking."

"Yeah, about that," Mairead said. "I called Dr. Cheng."

"And?"

She related their conversation. The doctor explained the cause of her reaction, their inefficient use of the morphine, and that the pain and muscle spasms were a good thing.

"So, it's progress? You're getting better?"

"I am. But I feel so stupid. If you had done what I asked, it would have killed us both and done God knows what to the kids."

"That's what I wanted to talk to you about," Paddy said. "It couldn't have happened, Mairead. So, it's moot. I'll do anything for you—except that. I can't bring myself to hurt you—not intentionally. I promised to love and protect you—forever. That still goes. But I can't kill you, no matter the circumstances. It's off the table. The decision-making about your health is yours. I'll support whatever you want to do. But I cannot be the agent of your demise."

"I'll never ask it of you again."

"So, we're good?" Paddy asked.

"We're good." She smiled. "And I don't hate you, Paddy. I should never have said that. It was a lie."

"I'm not as concerned about you hating me as you might think," Paddy said.

"Oh?"

"Love and hate aren't necessarily exclusive of each other," he said. "They often run concurrently. The opposite of love isn't hate anyway. They're both hot, intense emotions. You have to be seriously committed to feel them. Your indifference is what I fear. That would be the end of me."

"Well, then you're safe," Mairead said, pulling him in to kiss her. "I love you even when I hate you, Paddy Durr, and I feel very strongly about it either way."

Michael O'Keefe

CHAPTER TWENTY-NINE

March 27, 2017
Bushwick, Brooklyn
08:00 hours

Paddy was at his desk bright and early that morning. He was going over his case with a fine-toothed comb to see if he might have missed something. So far, it looked like the only thing interfering with his progress was Bless's edict and the fact he wasn't allowed to leave the office. He knew there aren't many clues to be found just hanging around in a detective squad, and the best investigations were run on shoe leather.

At 10:30 hours, Jimmy Maselli called. Paddy had left him a voicemail when he first got in. He wondered where he could have been. It turns out he was in New York State Supreme Court all morning.

"Check the FINAST teletype. Your modified assignment has been lifted. While you're picking up your guns at the Property Clerk, you can pop upstairs to get a new ID card and your shield back."

Burnt to a Crisp

"What happened?"

"Judge Killrain from Supreme Court not only overruled Zayas, but he also recommended his censure for gross incompetence. You are at full duty pending the IO-9 hearing. So, you've got a week."

"Good news. Hopefully, I can crack my murder case before that."

"You sound much better since we last talked," Jimmy said.

"Yeah, Jim. I'm back. It's *motherfuckers beware time* again."

***

After Paddy and Joe Furio got back from Police Plaza, Paddy left a series of voicemails and texts for Miguel Santapadre. Despite promising to speak with him, Bless had been ignoring Paddy's calls.

"No answer?" Joe asked.

"He's been ducking me."

"So, what are you going to do?"

"For now, I'm gonna go talk to Butchie and Eddie."

"Tell Obi-Wan and Yoda I said hi."

"If you keep calling them that, Joe, one or both of them are gonna put a bullet in your ass."

***

When Paddy got to the Glendale Diner, Joey Bucciogrosso and Eddie Curran were already seated in their customary booth in the back. Apart from being two of the greatest detectives ever to wear the shield, they were Paddy's mentors. When he was a kid, they were his protectors. A solid argument could be made they were also his saviors.

Since they had retired, they served as extra sets of eyes for his homicide cases. Their fresh perspectives had often been instrumental in helping Paddy find a solution when the cases bogged down—as they often did. He needed their perspectives today.

"How's it going, fellas?" he asked as he slid into the booth opposite them.

"What's the rumpus, Boyo?" Eddie asked in his sing-song Irish brogue.

Paddy proceeded to tell them about his case. Already aware of the drama with Psyche Services and that he had been modified, they were thrilled with the news he got his guns back. They were also delighted with Mairead's progress with the gene therapy. He left out the part about his emotional melt-down. It had already been straightened out. He needed their help with other things.

"So, until I get Bless to lift the information embargo, I'm stuck in neutral."

"He's dirty as fuck," Butchie observed. "Couldn't you leverage him into cooperating?"

"I could. But it would involve crushing everyone underneath him until they flipped. That would take two years and a federal indictment to accomplish. I may only have a week."

"Why only a week?" Eddie asked.

"I got the IO-9 hearing next Friday."

"That miserable whore still gets her hearing?" Butchie asked.

"Yeah," Paddy confirmed. "So, I need to motivate Bless before that."

"Well," Eddie said with a mischievous grin. "*Ye* could throw him through a plate-glass window. *Dat's* always worked so well for *ye* in the past."

Apart from the episode with the Savage Skulls, Eddie referenced another event from Paddy's misspent youth, which had been much more perilous.

***

After finishing his second year at Columbia, Durr was in a bind financially. His scholarship only covered his room and board for the first two years. He was expected to pay for his own housing for the remaining two. There was no room in the dorms for upper-classmen, especially ones who were native New Yorkers. His estrangement from his family did not qualify as a special circumstance.

He had to find more lucrative employment other than the low-paying jobs the university was offering. He would have to work eighty hours a week in the library or cafeteria just to afford a studio apartment the size of a closet in Manhattan. Between football and school, there weren't enough hours in a day. He returned to the old neighborhood to look for a better-paying opportunity.

He found it by working collections for Donato *Fat Archie* Archipolo, a Bonanno loan shark. He had been spending his free time visiting various slow payers in Ridgewood. He hadn't had to put his hands on anyone yet, but it was a job based upon confrontation. A word to the wise sometimes wasn't sufficient. An eventual problem was inevitable.

Antonio Barbero was a degenerate gambler. He was also a shiftless grifter who was as lazy as he was conniving. His many personality flaws dictated that when money got tight—and it always got tight when you couldn't pick your nose,

Burnt to a Crisp

let alone a winning horse—there was bound to be a shortfall. Adding his many gambling losses to the usurious vigorish he had to pay Fat Archie every month became a recipe for disaster.

Paddy visited Barbero's gin mill on Gates Avenue and Fresh Pond Road. He delivered his message on behalf of Fat Archie and left the bar. The deadbeat barman followed him to the street. Barbero remembered Paddy from the neighborhood. Berating Paddy's family evinced no reaction. Why would it? He hated them himself. But then Barbero got personal, suggesting Paddy was no better than his mongrel, thief of a father. That got Barbero thrown through his own window.

Paddy barely had time to enjoy the sound of the breaking glass when two detectives from the 104th Precinct ordered him down on the ground at gunpoint. They had been seated in their unmarked on the corner, surveilling the gambling operation fronted by the Italian coffee shop up the block. They cuffed him up and checked on Barbero, who was still breathing. The throat punch with which Paddy hit him landed squarely, so his vocal cords were still too stunned for him to tell the detectives he didn't want to press charges. Barbero knew if he had Fat Archie's guy arrested, he might well end up in the trunk of his car in the long-term lot at Kennedy Airport.

At the 104 Squad, Paddy was seated in an interview room. One of the detectives asked him questions. He seemed like a nice guy, but Paddy wasn't saying anything. He wouldn't even identify himself.

Detective Gribben went through his wallet. When he discovered Butchie's and Eddie's business cards—with their home phone numbers written on them—he called them. They came down to Ridgewood and convinced Gribben to squash the arrest. By then, they knew Barbero wasn't pressing charges anyway.

Discovering Paddy's financial quandary, Butchie and Eddie hooked him up with the bartending gig at Coogan's, with the understanding he was to stay the hell out of Bushwick and Ridgewood.

***

"You're never gonna let me live that down, are you, Eddie?" Paddy asked, grinning.

"Never," he said, laughing. "Far too funny to ever be forgotten."

"Now, tell us about that triple homicide," Butchie said.

Paddy brought them up to speed, ending with the part about Bless discouraging anyone from talking to him.

"*Ye* don't have enough time to RICO him, *dat's fer* sure," Eddie agreed.

"You know who's running his business?" Butchie asked.

"Yeah."

"Then shut them down. Make em' squeal. They might not give him up but Bless won't like it when the cash flow dries up," Butchie said.

"Do *ye* know where he lives?"

"He's in that huge house on the hill in Jamaica Estates—by St. John's. You can see it from the Grand Central."

"*Dat's* who lives in *dat* house? It's a *fooking* palace," Eddie marveled.

"You been there yet?" Butchie asked.

"Not yet."

"Go there—every day. And make sure all his neighbors know you're the police when you do. Call him and text him every hour till the prick returns your call. Let him know you're not going anywhere until he lifts the gag order," Butchie advised.

"In other words, *ye* got to be the eight hundred pound gorilla. Sit on his *fooking* chest until *ye* have his proper attention."

Paddy nodded, recognizing the advice as sage.

"It's time for you to be Paddy Durr again," Butchie said.

Burnt to a Crisp

CHAPTER THIRTY

March 27, 2017
Bushwick, Brooklyn
07:00 hours

Paddy got back to the office later that morning and got right to work trying to soften up Bless. He left the first of what would be hourly phone messages and texts, the tone of which had changed. He was no longer asking. *Call me right now, motherfucker*, was the gist of it. *Good opening salvo*, he thought.

Next, he called the Chief of Brooklyn Narcotics; Nick Affronti had been a rookie cop in the one-oh-eight when Paddy met him. Nick had been freaking out because he just lost a prisoner during a transport to central booking. It wasn't really his fault. One of the other prisoners had a cardiac episode on the way to the bookings. Nick pulled the guy out of the back and administered CPR. His partner should have been minding the other prisoners. Instead, he stood by with his thumb up his ass while Nick saved the prisoner's life. The junkie in the rear managed to slip out of his cuffs and the rear of the van unnoticed.

Nick covered for his partner, telling the bosses he had helped him administer CPR until the ambulance arrived. Because Nick was listed as the van's operator, it was technically his responsibility to safeguard the prisoners. The partner wasn't stepping up, and Nick wouldn't give him up. So, he was left holding the bag. It looked like he would get suspended and hammered in the trial room—if not fired.

Paddy calmed him down and framed a story for him that would still cost him ten days in the trial room but would allow him to skate on a suspension. Paddy found an independent witness to verify Nick had been the one performing the first-aid. Paddy brow-beat Nick's partner into agreeing they shared the CPR duties. It didn't exonerate them, but it did mitigate the pain they would face. His PBA delegates were going to let Nick fall on the sword alone. It wasn't really their fault; they didn't know any better. One was a summons man, and the other did the roll calls—not much experience to fall back on when defending a cop in harm's way.

Nick never forgot what Paddy did for him. He promised if he could ever return the favor, he would. That favor was coming due now.

"What can I do for you, Paddy," Chief Affronti asked.

"I need every module in Brooklyn Narco to focus on Wilson Avenue, between Gates and Hancock. A week should do it. I want to *buy and bust* them into oblivion."

"Why the urgency?"

"I've got an IO-9 hearing next Friday. I need to shake a homicide witness loose before then."

"I heard about that. It's still on?"

"Yeah, Nick. I'm up to my ass in alligators here, but I still gotta clear the swamp."

"Consider it done, Paddy. I'll have my guys make it so no one can sell so much as a nickel bag out there."

"I knew I could count on you, Chief. I'll let you know when you can call the dogs off."

With that in place, Paddy and George Fahrbach made the first of what they thought would be many visits to Bless's home in Queens.

When they showed up at 09:00 hours in an unmarked auto that was nonetheless unmistakably a police car, the neighbors were all out waiting with their kids at the school bus stop. Everyone stopped and stared at them. To avoid any confusion as to who they were, George left the portable turret light on top of the car.

After meandering up the hilled driveway, they made their way to the huge ornate front doors. Paddy leaned on the buzzer for a full thirty seconds while George continuously pounded the brass door knocker.

"That should get their attention," Paddy said.

A second later, an exasperated woman's voice came out of the intercom.

"Who is it?" she demanded.

"This is Detective Durr, from the eight-three. I want to talk to Bless."

The woman seemed taken aback by his use of Santapadre's street name because she stammered before answering.

"He-he-he's not here," she said.

"Of course, he isn't," Paddy fumed. "Tell that shithead he needs to contact me. He knows what I want. And make sure you tell him I said Wilson Avenue is closed for business until I get it. I'll make it a ghost town. That sound he'll hear in the background will be fucking tumbleweeds."

"I don't know what that means."

Paddy could hear the evasiveness in her voice. He remembered Bless was married to a Bushwick girl from Hancock Street—Esmerelda Villalobos.

"Sure, you don't, Esme," Paddy mocked her. "We'll be back later when your neighbors are getting home from work. Unless I get what I want, your cover of legitimacy is gone. Everyone in Jamaica Estates will know your husband is a narco-trafficker. See you later, Esmerelda."

When they got back in the car to return to Brooklyn, Paddy told George to hit the lights and sirens and drive slowly.

"What for?"

"So even the stupid people will know the cops are hassling their suspicious neighbor."

"You're fucking mean when you want to be, Paddy."

"You don't blame a scorpion for stinging. It's just his nature."

***

Back at the eight-three, Paddy and George were brainstorming, trying to conceive somewhere they might have overlooked a lead. They were at a loss.

"We've canvassed more than a dozen times for video or witnesses. There's nothing out there, Paddy," George said.

"We know who we need to talk to. We just need to keep the pressure on Bless. Sooner or later, he's going to figure out it's better to get out of our way before we decide to get in his on a permanent basis."

"Still, there ought to be more witnesses," George observed. "Everyone was in the street that morning. With all the media there, it was a regular *Movie of the Week*."

Paddy cocked his head at that. *The media—we haven't checked the media*, he realized.

"Brilliant, George," Paddy said, picking up the phone.

"Oh yeah, check out the big brain on George," he said. "How am I brilliant now?"

"DCPI," Paddy said, referring to the Deputy Commissioner of Public Information, the department's liaison with the media. "We need to see if they have any footage from the fire. We'll be able to see who was on the street. Then we work our way backward to see who was there first. We might get lucky and find an eyeball."

"Damn," George marveled. "I am smart."

Paddy spoke to a Lieutenant Pascarella. She was very nice and excited to help, but she turned out to be no help at all. The morning of the fire, it hadn't yet been considered a crime. DCPI only collects reports and footage for things involving or impacting the department. They didn't start gathering information about the fire until it became a homicide, and there was little new material by then.

"That was a great big nothing burger," Paddy said, hanging up.

"So, I'm not smart?"

"No. Not so much. Unless the fire department has an equivalent to DCPI."

"Oh, they gotta," George said. "Those guys are publicity hounds. I think every ladder truck and engine company turns out with its own camera crew. You couldn't get the smoke-eaters off the fucking TV if you had dynamite."

"Well, do they have a DCPI or not?" Paddy asked.

"I don't know. I'm not a fireman. Call Capparzo and Kennealy. They'll know."

"And just like that, you're smart again." Paddy smiled.

He got a hold of Danny Capparzo, who verified the FD had a publicity department that served the same function as DCPI. They were right in his building down at Metro-Tech Plaza. Danny said they would collect whatever they had and bring it over in an hour.

When Danny and his partner Tom Kennealy got to the squad, they brought a manila folder with copies of every newspaper article and photo related to the fire generated by the media. Helpful, for sure, but Paddy was looking for some video.

"It's all right here," Capparzo said, holding up a computer thumb drive.

Paddy inserted the drive into the USB port on his desktop and opened up the file. There were forty-two separate news telecasts arrayed in a spreadsheet. They were chronological, so Paddy worked from the first file backward. Right away, he noticed the same face: sneaky, haggard beyond its years. It showed up in every screenshot. He seemed to be listening to everyone being interviewed before slinking off.

"Fuck," Paddy muttered.

"What's the problem?" Tom Kennealy asked.

"You see that slimy creature right there?" Paddy said, pointing.

Everyone nodded. They had noticed him too.

"That is Sammy Bando, also known as *Bungee*. He's one of the two managers for all of Bless's dope spots."

"That's good. You know him," Danny said.

"*Not* good," Paddy said. "He fucking hates me."

"Why?" George asked, laughing.

"A few years ago, I needed him to give up two of his dealers for an assault 1. Asking didn't work. I had to press him hard."

"What does that mean?" Danny asked.

"I gave him my undivided attention, and he *really* didn't like it."

"Maybe he'll talk to us," Tom Kennealy said.

"It's worth a shot," Paddy agreed. "You can bring him in for questioning. He's on life parole. If you do, though, be careful when you search him. He's back to using his own shit. You don't want to get stuck with a hype or a crack stem; probably get the monster. That piece of shit looks like a carrier."

"We're up for it," Capparzo said.

"Hit me on the cell when you have him."

"Where are we going to be?" George asked.

"We will be in Queens tormenting Mr. Bless," Paddy said. "First, we have to stop at the Task Force to borrow a bullhorn. I don't think *all* of his neighbors know he has a problem with the police yet."

***

Paddy was just finishing telling everyone in southeast Queens that Bless, or Michael Santapadre—as he liked to be known by his neighbors—was obstructing the investigation into the murders of his own family. He promised Bless, and everyone who had gathered in the street in front of his house, they would be back every day until he gave them what they wanted. He was just putting away the bullhorn when his cell phone rang. It was from Danny Capparzo.

"We got Bungee in your office, Paddy," Danny said.
"How's it going?"
"He's talking, but he's high as fuck. None of it's useful. He's all over the place."
"I'll be back in a little while. We'll see if we can't refocus him."

***

When Paddy and George stepped into the interview room, Bungee saw Paddy and looked like he wanted to vomit. He started shaking his head vehemently.
"What's the matter, Sammy? You don't look so happy to see me," Paddy said.
Sammy kept shaking his head and repeating the word *"No"* over and over.
"We've done this dance before," Paddy reminded him. "You give me what I want; your life gets a whole lot less complicated."
"Fuck you, Durr!" Bungee sneered. "The last time I talked to you, you almost ripped my arm out of the socket."
"How else was I going to beat you to death with it?"
"No! Never again. You can suck my dick!" Bungee suggested.
"Look, Bungee," Paddy began reasoning with him. "You're in every camera shot on every video from the fire. You live right on the corner. You were probably the first one out there. You know who did this, and you know who saw him do it. Tell me the names, and I'll pull that army of narcotics cops off your set. Tell me not, then you, your partner, and your boss will starve before you ever sell another grain of narcotics."
"You ain't shit without that badge and gun, Durr," Bungee challenged. "Take 'em off, and we'll see what you're made of."
"You mean *this* badge and gun?" Paddy said, removing them from his belt and handing them to George.
Bungee's eyes went wide. He hadn't expected Durr to take up his challenge, and he hadn't forgotten their last encounter—when Paddy had turned him into a human pretzel.
"There," Paddy said. "Now we can converse as equals. If you work with me on this, I go away."
"I would never work with you," Bungee spat. "Besides, we heard you've got problems with your own job. They finally figured out you're a psycho. We just have to wait it out. The police department will take care of you for us."

Burnt to a Crisp

Paddy's eyebrow went up. Capparzo and Kennealy couldn't have mentioned it. They didn't know. *So, who?* he wondered.

Bungee sensed his apprehension and confusion. Enjoying the sensation of having Durr back on his heels, he couldn't help himself. He just kept twisting the knife.

"That's right, Durr," he laughed. "We got a detective on the inside. He told us *all* about you. Cops talk too!"

"More than they should, it would appear."

"We also heard your wife is sick." He was leering now. "I hope that twat is in pain every day!"

Paddy's right hand shot out so quickly, no one in the room even registered it until Bungee was lying in a heap on the floor. Paddy's big open palm hit the drug dealer in the face so flush; it sounded like a gunshot. Bungee's brain was temporarily scrambled. Everyone else was stunned to silence.

Paddy picked Bungee up by the scruff of his neck and pushed him against the wall, glaring right through him. Bungee thought he was looking into the face of the Angel of Doom. For all intents and purposes, he was.

"Now you've done it, you subhuman piece of excrement," Paddy rasped, almost whispering. "I no longer have anything to do *but* you. Nothing else matters. Fucking you out of the rest of your life will be my only priority. You should have *Property of Paddy Durr* stenciled on your clothes because your ass is fucking mine."

Durr released Bungee and stepped back. Watching him slide down the wall to the floor, Paddy saw he at least had the good sense to realize he had gone too far. The look of abject terror on his face said as much.

"Get this piece of shit out of my building," Paddy told the fire marshals.

They helped Bungee off the floor and led him down the stairs to the front door. Paddy followed to make certain he left. Bungee's wife was waiting for him in the fishbowl. When she saw the big, hand-shaped welt, bright purple and throbbing over the left side of her husband's face, she started screeching.

"What did those animals do to you!?!"

"Shut the fuck up!" Bungee said, grabbing her arm and shaking her. "You want him to come out here and give you one of these?"

He dragged her out of the hallway through the front doors—almost running. They disappeared into the street.

"He thinks you're the devil," Capparzo observed.

"He's not wrong," said Paddy.

Michael O'Keefe

Back upstairs, the fire marshals asked if there was anything else they could do on the case. Paddy realized until he could shake his witnesses loose, there wasn't much left. Then he thought of a few things.

"We recovered what we think is the kerosene can," Paddy said, handing Capparzo a copy of the voucher and request for laboratory analysis. "Could you follow up with the lab to have it compared with the residue at the scene?"

"Sure thing," Kennealy said. "Anything else?"

"Did you interview the firefighters and the first officers on the scene?"

"Done," Capparzo said. "We already brought them down to the DA to be taped."

"Then, that's it for now."

"What about tomorrow?"

"I'm off for the next two days," Paddy said. "Bungee wasn't wrong. My wife *is* ill. I'm gonna spend the swing with her."

"We're sorry to hear that, Paddy," Kennealy said. "Is she gonna be all right?"

"We can pray."

"What are you gonna do when you get back?" Capparzo asked.

"Fall on that motherfucker, Bungee, like a building," said Paddy.

Burnt to a Crisp

CHAPTER THIRTY-ONE

March 29, 2017
Bushwick, Brooklyn
16:00 hours

Paddy and Mairead took full advantage of their two days together. Having an uninterrupted opportunity to enjoy each other without the lingering fear death would impose itself at any minute felt liberating. Neither operated under the illusion Mairead was better—but she wasn't worse, and that was something.

When Paddy returned to the squad that Monday afternoon, George was already waiting at his desk. He had a concerned look. Paddy thought he knew why. He had been chewing over the same thing during the swing.

"What's on your mind, George?" Paddy prompted.

"I been thinking about what Bungee said about Mairead and about them having an inside man."

"Me too. It would seem we have a stranger in our house."

"What bothers me is I can't even guess who it might be," George said.

"Same here," Paddy agreed. "If it's no one obvious, that means the bad guys asked, and someone actively checked me out to give them the information. I don't know if treason is the right word, but it feels like it."

"What do you want to do about it, Paddy?"

"I'm not calling IAB. That's for certain. They couldn't find their own asses with a flashlight, a map, and an ice pick. I'm more inclined to get Bungee dirty. Then wring it out of him. Shouldn't take long. Did you see how bad he looked the other night? He's been getting high on his own supply. Now he's a stone junkie."

"How do you want to do it?"

"I'm going to call Trinnie Alvarez. He'll get us close enough to Bungee so we can count the hairs on his head. We'll just follow him till he goes somewhere to get high."

Paddy called Sergeant Trinidad Alvarez in Major Case Narcotics. He knew Trinnie from when he was a detective in the eight-one Squad. He also knew he was already out on the Wilson Avenue set—part of the narcotics mobilization Chief Affronti had set up.

"What can I do for you, Paddy?"

"You still doing the surveillance van?" Paddy asked, referencing the state-of-the-art surveillance vehicle the department had been gifted from the DEA.

Bought with seized drug proceeds, the van was a non-descript white, rusted-out panel van. Other than the driver's compartment, there weren't even any windows in the thing. But the rust was fake, put there to dissuade the curious. From the outside, Paddy thought it looked like a worthless piece of garbage. In reality, thanks to the new-age surveillance equipment, hi-tech digital monitors, and invisible (to the naked eye) pinhole cameras and scanners, the van cost more than a million dollars. It even boasted night vision and thermal capabilities.

Sergeant Alvarez was disappointed Paddy needed none of those toys. He was looking for an assist to do an old-fashioned gum-shoe type tail.

"I'm delighted to help you, Paddy," Trinnie said. "But you don't need my van for this. You could do it from the back seat of an Uber."

"Maybe, but the subject is an *OG*. Right now, he's a broke-down valise, getting high off his own product. But he knows you guys are out here, and he's still pretty cagey."

"Who is he?"

"Bungee."

"Wow!" Trinnie whistled. "That's a high-value target."

"Yeah, but I'm not looking to arrest him if I don't have to. I just want to catch him dirty, so I can leverage him for information."

"You want a couple of my guys for backup?"

"Thanks, Trinnie, but your young detectives probably shouldn't know how I leverage people. It might cause them a moral dilemma, and I got enough outside intervention as it is."

Burnt to a Crisp

"Okay," Trinnie said. "My guys can be trusted if you want to go old-school, but I understand wanting to fly solo. Just know we're here if you need us."

***

Paddy and George were in the back compartment of the van with two of Trinnie's detectives who were operating the video monitors. It was a tight fit, made all the more uncomfortable by the humming electronic gadgetry, which couldn't be turned off even though they were using nothing but the overhead scope. The reboot time was just too long—an hour and a half—so the gizmos had to stay on. Of course, this added to the already stifling heat.

They were grateful when moments later, they observed Bungee come bounding out of his house on the corner of Wilson Avenue and Madison Street. As they watched him bop down the avenue, Paddy noticed two things: he looked awful, like he hadn't slept in days. And he was raised up, his head on a swivel like he had the sense he was being followed—which he was. They stayed put until they saw him make the right on Putnam and enter the abandoned crack house and shooting gallery off the corner. Paddy gave Trinnie a knock on the partition. When they were certain no one was watching, he and George slipped out the back of the van.

They took a slow walk toward the crack house, giving Bungee a chance to get started on whatever nefarious doings he was about to get up to. Paddy knew he wasn't selling drugs at the moment. Narco had Wilson Avenue on lockdown, and 1302 Putnam was where one went to get high. It was not a drug spot. Three stories tall, the junkies had already trashed the first floor beyond habitation. Paddy knew nothing went on down there anymore unless someone very brave decided to use it to evacuate their bowels. Other than that, everyone was prudent enough to advance directly to the second floor.

When Paddy and George got to the second floor, they peered into the first apartment. All the doors had long since been removed, being used now as makeshift furniture and bed platforms by the denizens. They were able to enter noiselessly. When he got into the living room, Paddy wasn't surprised by what he saw.

A filthy Bungee was seated on a milk crate with his pants around his ankles. He had a syringe sticking out of his right arm; his belt still wrapped tightly around his emaciated biceps. Protruding from his drooling mouth was a smoking glass crack stem—crack and heroin; the poor man's speedball. Paddy noticed Bungee's pupils were the size of dinner plates. On her knees, with her head bobbing up and down in his lap, was a young junkie prostitute Paddy knew.

Suki Hyong was a sometimes informant who had hit bottom hard. Unfortunately for her, there didn't appear to be a rebound in her future. Paddy knew her parents. The Hyongs, Korean emigrants, owned a grocery in Middle Village. After Suki had skipped out of three rehabs, they decided to employ a tough-love strategy. At twenty-two, thrown out of the house and cut off, she made a beeline for Wilson Avenue, doing *anything* to keep the drugs coming her way.

So far, the strategy seemed to be long on the tough, not so much on the love. But Mr. Hyong couldn't completely cut the cord. He would occasionally call Paddy to look in on and deliver money to his wayward daughter. While this was against Paddy's better judgment, it was what Mr. Hyong wanted. Mrs. Hyong, on the other hand, had written Suki off. She would have been cross with her husband if she knew he had been checking on her.

"Wakey, wakey, eggs and bakey," Paddy said, announcing their presence.

Suki lifted her head, looking at Paddy, smiling as if in a dream. She wiped the drool from around her scab-encrusted mouth. Bungee looked quickly to his right, at the loaded nine-millimeter laying on the erstwhile door, propped on cinder blocks, serving as a table. The gun was just out of his reach but still qualified as being in his lungeable area.

"Really, Bungee," Paddy said. "In the state you're in, do you think you can get to it before I can put a window in your chest? Do you want to make it *that* easy for me?"

Bungee's shoulders slumped in surrender. Paddy told Suki to get lost.

"If I were you, Suki, I would go directly to the emergency room and get a blood test."

"Does he have AIDS?"

"That's not something I would leave to chance. Now let's go. We're burning daylight."

Suki grabbed her things and was about to leave when she thought of something else.

"He didn't pay me," she said, thrusting her chin toward Bungee.

"How much did he promise you?"

"Four vials."

"I'm not giving you crack, Suki," Paddy said, reaching into his pocket and holding out a twenty-dollar bill.

Burnt to a Crisp

She seemed briefly disappointed before snatching the bill from his hand and running out of the squalid apartment and down the stairs.

"Now, what to do about you," Paddy said to Bungee. "You don't want me to kill you. We've already established that. Is it prison then? Between the gun and the drugs, I've got enough to put you away for the rest of your miserable short-assed life. But you don't want that either, do you? You won't be getting any drugs or blowjobs at Dannemora unless it's with a hairy-chested, tatted-up lifer—but given the shape you're in, you'll be on the providing side of those. You don't impress me as the sort of guy who enjoys being a giver. So prison isn't on your wish list either. Those are your two choices. What'll it be, Bungee? Or, maybe…Oh, never mind. There is no or. That's pretty much it."

Bungee knew he had no escape. He desperately needed an ally. The only one else in the room was George. So, he took his shot with him.

"You're just gonna stand there and let him do this to me?" he asked.

"Yep," George said.

"You'll let him kill me?"

"I'm not here for *you*, motherfucker," George said. "I'm only here to make sure that *when* he kills you, he gets away with it. So, you better pray there is an option number three cause you're not much good to *me* alive either."

Bungee slumped down on his milk crate just a little lower. The hopelessness of his situation apparent to him.

"Okay," Paddy said. "With all of this chitchat, I may have come up with a third option. You ready?"

Bungee just nodded.

"You answer two questions. Tell me who set the fire and who witnessed him set it. Then I'll just arrest you."

"That's the same as option two," Bungee whined.

"Oh! You're right. It is," Paddy said. "Okay. What if I add a bonus question? If you get that one right, I'll let you walk on the gun and the drugs. Sound good?"

"What's the bonus question?"

"Uh, uh," Paddy said. "Not until you answer the first two. If at any time you lie to me—and I'll know if you do—I will torture the truth out of you. Then I flip a coin to see if I kill you or drag your broken ass to jail. Are you in or out?"

"Cucko set the fire. Tranquillo saw him do it," Bungee said without further prompting.

"How do you know?" George asked.

"Because Tranquillo was sitting in his car in front of my house waiting for me to come downstairs. He called me from his cell phone as it was happening."

"And that cell phone number is?" Paddy asked.

"It's in my contacts under Tranquillo," he said, handing George his phone.

"You're doing well, Sammy. You might actually walk out of here—and in one piece. Just get the bonus question right."

"What is it?"

"Who is the fucking detective talking about me?"

"I don't know his name, I swear," Bungee pleaded. "He's Tranquillo's boy. He's a Dominican kid who used to be a narc, but now he works in Williamsburg. They go on vacation together. On my mother's eyes, that's all I know."

Paddy looked back at George to gauge his reaction. From his stern expression, he could tell George had an idea about whom Bungee was talking.

"Sound like anyone we know?" Paddy asked.

George nodded. "We'll talk about it back at the barn."

"Ladies and gentlemen, we have a winner," Paddy said. "Now pull your pants up and get the fuck out of here, Bungee. I don't want to see that chewed piece of gristle ever again."

"Can I have my gun?" he asked.

"Nice try," Paddy laughed. "We're vouchering that as found property—in case there's a body on it."

***

Back at the squad, George was hesitant to share his suspicions with Paddy. He thought he knew, but he wasn't certain. So, he was loathe to cast aspersions on a fellow detective without hard evidence. Paddy understood all of that, having been a union delegate himself.

"Just say it, George. I'm not going after the guy without proof, but I need to know where my vulnerabilities lie."

"There's a new guy in the nine-oh," George said. "He came from Manhattan North Narco about a year ago. He was considered a shady cat when he was there. Guys thought he was a little too enamored of his subjects. There were whispers but no proof. The job rotated him to Brooklyn North in the hopes he would knock it off. I guess he found a new drug dealer to play with."

"Are you gonna tell me his name, or is this a mystery?"

Burnt to a Crisp

"George Nova, but he insists everybody call him Jorge. It's almost funny. The kid was a Fucking-Long-Island-Dickhead from East Meadow. He works a little while in the barrio, and he thinks he's Pablo fucking Escobar."

"I don't know the asshole," Paddy admitted. "So, if he has information on me, he had to ask around to get it."

"I'll check it out," George said. "Then we'll decide if we have to do something about him."

"That's good," Paddy agreed. "Cause I don't have time to deal with this piece of shit right now. In the interim, I'll put a package together for Tranquillo. Then we'll go see if we can find him."

CHAPTER THIRTY-TWO

March 30, 2017
Bushwick, Brooklyn
11:00 hours

Before heading home the night before, Paddy and George invaded Wilson Avenue for the purpose of finding Patricio Liriano, also known as *Tranquillo*. Paddy already knew him well. Liriano was the other head of the snake, along with Sammy Bando. Together they managed Bless's drug spots in Bushwick. In a previous assault case, wherein Tranquillo was the victim, Paddy had to convince him to testify against two of his workers who had beaten him to a pulp.

The idiot Leon brothers, as they were known by everyone, had delusions of grandeur. They thought they could vanquish their boss and magically be awarded his drug spots. Liriano was that rare drug dealer who didn't need to use force or intimidation to keep his workers in line. He was a brilliant manager and a very generous employer. He had no issues with loyalty because everyone who worked for him made a ton of money. Sammy Bando saw to the day-to-day operation of the business. Tranquillo handled all the money and resupply of the spots. It was a very lucrative and largely peaceful enterprise—until the idiot Leon brothers decided to make their move.

The other reason Tranquillo didn't need force or intimidation was because he had the ghetto equivalent of the Angel of Darkness as his protector. Bless would handle the rough stuff if required. The Leon brothers failed to account for that, which wasn't surprising—they were, after all, idiots.

Burnt to a Crisp

When word went out that Bless and his henchmen were looking for them, they went into hiding. Through an informant, Paddy knew where they were. Durr had independent witnesses to the assault. It went down right on the corner of Putnam and Wilson in broad daylight. All Paddy needed was Tranquillo to testify. Being a drug dealer, Tranquillo was reticent to do so. He went into hiding as well.

Finding him was a difficult proposition. Liriano didn't actually have an address. What he had was a battalion of women who allowed him to crash at their homes for a day or two. The women knew about each other, but since Tranquillo was paying their bills, they seldom complained about his divided attentions. Because he never spent more than one night anywhere, his efforts in avoiding Paddy were effective—at first.

Paddy knew Tranquillo hung around and managed most of the storefront businesses on Wilson Avenue. It's how he laundered his drug money. So, Paddy bombarded those. He would intermittently pop into the barbershop, bodega, dress shop, mechanics, and every other business on the avenue, handing out his business card and asking for his "good friend" Tranquillo. After a few days, he became such a nuisance, Tranquillo finally relented and came forward.

With this history in mind, Paddy and George didn't waste time visiting phantom addresses where they knew Tranquillo didn't reside. They made nuisances of themselves. Last night's efforts hadn't yet born fruit.

This morning, they were preparing to launch a second wave. After first visiting the Santapadre estate and making Bless a little crazier, Paddy was going over the checklist of locations to hit on Wilson when the phone on his desk rang.

"Eight-three Squad, Durr."

"*Jus* who I was looking for," a male voice said in a Spanish accent.

Paddy had heard a lot of Spanish accents in his life. He grew up in Bushwick and was very nearly fluent. But this accent sounded wrong, like an affectation.

"And who is this?"

"Detective Nova, from the nine-oh. I hear *jou* been bothering my informant."

"And who might that be?" Paddy asked.

"Patricio Liriano. He's a good guy and not involved in anything. I want *heem* left alone."

There was so much wrong with that statement; Paddy wasn't sure where to begin. So, he deconstructed it one piece at a time.

"If he's not involved in anything, how can he be your informant? If he's a good guy, why is he on Wilson Avenue all day, every day, running the dope spots? And if he's your informant, why is he listed fourteen times in the NITRO system as a subject in a narcotics investigation, and none of them are *your* cases?"

"I'm not fucking around here, *cabron*," Nova said, trying to sound tough but not carrying it off. "*Jou* know who I am? If *jou* don't leave my guy alone, *jou* gonna have a big fucking problem. Then *jou'll* find out who I am."

Paddy had seen from the caller ID, Nova was calling from the nine-oh. George knew to whom Paddy was talking. He was surprised Paddy hadn't blown his top yet. Actually, his top had blown sky-high. But he wasn't given to exploding. Instead, he seethed. He was seething now.

"Stay right the fuck where you are. Don't go anywhere," Paddy fumed. "I'm coming down to the nine-oh right now. Wait for me."

Paddy slammed the phone down, grabbed the keys to the squad car, and stormed out of the office.

Lieutenant Martino had heard the phone call from his office. He watched as Paddy's expression changed. A pit formed in his stomach. He had seen this before. When he heard Paddy growl at whoever was on the other end, he knew this probably wouldn't end without someone getting hurt.

"Where did Paddy go, George?" the lieutenant asked.

"I think he's on his way to the nine-oh Squad to straighten out a detective."

"Oh no!" Martino said. "Which detective?"

"George Nova."

"Why?"

"Nova's been giving information about him to the drug dealers on Wilson. Now it looks like he's trying to interfere with this case."

"Fuck! I gotta call Kerrigan to warn him," the lou said, heading back into his office.

***

At the Nine-Oh Squad, the commanding officer, Lieutenant John Kerrigan, hung up his desk phone. He had just learned from his counterpart in the eight-three that Paddy Durr was on his way to straighten out Kerrigan's least favorite detective. John had known Paddy since they were rookie cops in the "old" three-four. He also knew when Paddy Durr was going to *straighten someone out*; it portended nothing but trouble—the kind of trouble that would require a hospital stay for someone at the very least.

"Nova!" he bellowed from his office. "Get in here right fucking now!"

Burnt to a Crisp

"*Jou* want to see me, Lou?" Nova asked.

"Yes, and knock off that ridiculous accent. You're from lily-white Island, for fuck's sake."

"What's up, boss?" he answered, sans the accent.

"You're leaving. Don't sign out. Don't fill out a slip. Just get the fuck out of the building—right now!"

"Why?" Nova asked.

"Because Paddy Durr is on his way here. I don't know what you did, but you stirred up a hornet's nest. He is pissed. If you're in the building when he gets here, he's going to kill you. Now, get the fuck outta here, and take the back steps. We might already be too late."

"But, Lou…" Nova stammered.

"Now, goddamnit!"

Nova took off running out of the office and down the stairwell at the rear of the building.

Just then, the front door of the squad flew open, having been kicked in by an enraged Paddy Durr. He stepped into the squad and growled.

"Where is that motherfucker, Nova?"

The detectives at their desks all knew Paddy, if not in person, then by reputation. They seemed to be collectively holding their breath lest he decide to redirect his ire in one of their directions. Lieutenant Kerrigan bailed them out. He waved Durr into his office.

"Sit down, Paddy. You can calm down now. Nova is gone."

"Where did he go?"

"I sent him home."

"Why the fuck did you do that?"

"Because Mariano Martino and I like you and don't want to see you get any more jammed up than you already are. Trust me as an old friend, Paddy; you want nothing to do with George Nova."

"I beg to differ," Paddy said.

"Shut the door, would you?" the lou asked.

Paddy did so and sat back down. He understood the shut door implied they would be speaking confidentially. Kerrigan turned a radio on behind his desk with the volume up loud. Paddy understood they weren't just talking off the record. If someone was attempting to hear their conversation via electronic surveillance, they were thwarted. So, there were ears Kerrigan wanted to keep deaf.

"I'm not supposed to tell you this," Kerrigan said. "Hell, I'm not even supposed to know it, but that piece of shit Nova is already under sealed indictment for working for the drug crew on Wilson Avenue. One of my sergeants is wearing a wire, for Christ's sake. For all I know, Nova is too. You don't want to be anywhere near either of them. The last thing you need is to get roped into this federal clusterfuck."

"Which sergeant?" Paddy asked.

"The fat, stupid one."

"That really doesn't narrow it down," Paddy said.

"True," Kerrigan laughed. "It's that moron, Bob Kerrey."

"I appreciate the heads up, John. But I'm working a triple homicide. I'm *this* close to breaking it," Paddy said, holding his thumb and index finger an inch apart. "And here comes this cocksucker telling me I can't talk to my star witness? He needs to be dealt with."

"I'll take care of it," the lou said.

"You better. Because if Nova's boy, Tranquillo, isn't in my office by the end of business today, I'm gonna get his address off his ten-card and beat the shit out of him on his front lawn."

"I'll tell him, Paddy."

"And one other thing, John. Make sure that crooked fuck understands that if my name ever escapes his lips again, I'll fix it so the FBI will be the least of his problems."

***

At the eight-three, George and Lieutenant Martino were relieved to see Paddy come walking—calmly—back into the squad.

"How'd it go?" George asked.

"Somebody warned Kerrigan I was coming," Paddy said, grinning at Martino. "I hope you're proud of yourself. All you did was save a scumbag, dirty cop from getting the beating of his life."

"What I did," the lou corrected. "Was prevent my detective from shooting himself in the foot, and I'm proud as fuck about that. Don't you have enough problems on your plate already?"

"Nova's not off the hook yet," Paddy said. "Tranquillo better be in here by the end of the day, or I go see Nova again. This time I won't let anyone know I'm coming."

Burnt to a Crisp

Just then, the squad police administrative aid, Ms. Lena, interrupted them.

"Excuse me, Paddy," she said with the phone cocked to her ear. "There's a Patricio Liriano in the fishbowl looking to speak with you."

"Wow!" George said. "Like magic."

"More like black magic," Martino said. "Let me know how you make out with him."

***

In the interview room, Tranquillo tried to smooth things over between Paddy and Nova. Paddy was having none of it.

"Do not speak that piece of shit's name in my presence again. If he ever again utters mine, I hope you're not there when I find him. I don't like anyone's chances of getting out of that room alive."

Tranquillo seemed to realize the subject was closed. He shrugged and waited for Paddy to continue.

"Tell me about the fire," Paddy said.

Tranquillo said he was parked out in front of Bungee's house, waiting for him to come down to talk to him. Paddy had a pretty good idea; the purpose of the meeting involved an exchange of funds to Tranquillo and a resupply of material to Bungee. Still, he wasn't complicating the matter by asking them to incriminate themselves. He needed an eyewitness.

Tranquillo said he was on his cell phone, letting Bungee know he was there when he saw Cucko bopping around the corner onto Wilson with a blue and white tin can in his hand—like the kind in which they sell paint thinner. He watched Cucko dip into 407 Wilson. He thought it odd. Having heard that Jessica threw him out, he didn't think he was welcome there.

About thirty seconds later, he saw Cucko come running out of the hallway, still carrying the can. He ran down Wilson, making a right on Gates toward Knickerbocker. Tranquillo could see the glow from the fire already coming out of the front door of Jessica's apartment house.

"Did you notice anyone else on the street?" Paddy asked.

"Yeah. Weird Harold was in his usual spot on Gates. Cucko ran right past him."

He said Bungee came down to the street. They talked, and he drove off to visit a friend in East New York. He could already hear the sirens from the fire trucks by the time he hit Irving Avenue. Bungee called him as he was driving, giving him a play-by-play of the fire scene.

"I don't need the address," Paddy said. "But where in East New York did you go?"

"She lives in those new condos on Cypress and Jamaica. I stayed the night."

"What car were you in?" George asked.

"My Lexus," Tranquillo said.

"Model and color?" Paddy asked.

"It's the newest sedan, pearl metallic."

"You mean beige?" George asked.

"Yeah, I guess so."

"Let me get your cell number, so I don't have to hunt you down in the future," Paddy said.

He gave a different number than the one Bungee had provided for him. So, Paddy dialed it. Nothing rang. Then Paddy dialed the number from Bungee. A Cardi B song started playing in Tranquillo's pocket.

"Now, why would you lie to us?" Paddy asked. "You were doing so well."

Tranquillo looked embarrassed. He took his phone out of his breast pocket. Paddy told him to put his number in his contacts, as they were definitely going to be in touch.

"I'm sorry," Tranquillo said. "Force of habit; I generally don't want cops to have my number."

"I bet that scumbag, Nova, has it," George said.

"That's different. He's my friend."

"No," Paddy corrected. "He's a sycophant, and you're just using him. Friendship has nothing to do with it."

Tranquillo shrugged. He wasn't going to argue the point. He was a drug dealer. For him, it was a distinction without a difference.

"Make sure you tell your boss I said Wilson Avenue stays closed until he lifts the gag order," Paddy told him.

"Who do you think told me to come see you?" Tranquillo said.

"I assumed it was Nova."

"Well, him too, but I don't take orders from him. Bless told me to cooperate—to give you whatever you needed."

"What did Nova say?" George asked.

"The same thing, but he was scared. What did you do to him?"

"Nothing. I never laid eyes on him," said Paddy.

Burnt to a Crisp

Dan Bibb arrived within the hour. He audiotaped Tranquillo's statement, and Paddy sent him on his way, with the warning that if he valued his freedom, Tranquillo better answer when he called.

After he was gone, Paddy asked Bibb the magic question.

"Can I arrest Cucko now?"

"Not yet," Bibb said.

"Why not, Dan?" George wanted to know.

"Because both witnesses are compromised or have a motive to lie," Paddy answered for him. "Harold is autistic, and Tranquillo is a drug dealer who works for the family of the victims. With the pressure we're putting on the drug spots on Wilson, it gives a defense attorney all the ammunition he needs to suggest Tranquillo would tell us anything just so we would leave him alone. We need to match the tower hits to his cellphone to verify he was even here the night of the fire. We need some physical evidence to tie Cucko to the scene, and we need those other witnesses to come forward."

"Very good, Paddy. Would you like to prosecute the case as well?" Bibb asked.

"No," Paddy said. "I leave that in your capable hands."

Before he left, Bibb wrote the subpoenas for Tranquillo's and Bungee's phones. Paddy would hand these off to Ronnie Kingsbury in TARU in the morning. It being too late to visit Bless's house, Paddy contented himself with a phone call. He was surprised when Bless picked it up.

"Detective Durr, I was disappointed you didn't come see me this afternoon," Bless said.

"Why is that?" Paddy asked.

"I put the word out in Bushwick; everyone is to help you."

"Why the sudden turnaround?"

"Because you're a fucking psychopath, and you'll stop at nothing to break this case. You've become a pain in my ass I don't need right now. I suppose I should be grateful. You're working hard on behalf of my family, but I'm conflicted, given what I do for a living. I decided to trust you. You said you'd keep my business out of this. Everyone says you're a man of your word. I guess we'll see."

CHAPTER THIRTY-THREE

March 31, 2017
Bushwick, Brooklyn
09:00 hours

Paddy started his tour at TARU's telephone unit in Queens. Ronnie Kingsbury was waiting for him. He took the subpoenas and told Paddy he would have the turnaround that afternoon.

"You don't have to burn a contract for me," Paddy said. "I'll wait for them."

"You haven't let me do anything for you since I got second-grade," Ronnie reminded him. "I know that was your doing."

"You got the bump because of your work. I had nothing to do with it."

"Bullshit, Paddy. My chief told me I jumped twelve names on the grade list because of your phone call. Getting your subpoenas expedited is the least I can do."

When Paddy got to the eight-three, Jessica Sanchez, her sister, Melanie, and her boyfriend, Peter Cammaratta, were waiting for him outside his office. *When it rains, it pours,* Paddy thought, leading them into the squad.

"Bless called last night and said we should talk to you," Jessica said.

"Just to be clear," Paddy said. "You want to talk to me, right? You're not just here because Bless said so?"

"No," Peter said. "We wanted to come in from the jump. It was only cause Bless told everybody not to that we stayed away."

Burnt to a Crisp

Paddy and George interviewed each of them separately. Peter reiterated what he had told Paddy hypothetically at his parole visit, careful to leave out the part about knocking Cucko out. So, now they had a threat of arson prior to the event. Melanie told the same story, also leaving out the fact that Blanco laid Cucko out.

Jessica was able to provide a little more. She said she met Cucko about eight months ago. She thought he was cute, so when he kicked it to her, she was receptive. She didn't know where he lived at the time, but a week later, he asked if he could move in with her, as he was losing his apartment. She got a bad feeling about it when he moved in with all of his earthly belongings in a single shopping bag.

Right from the beginning, he was a nuisance. He followed her around like a puppy dog. He'd even follow her to school and wait outside until she got out. She finally forbade him from doing that. So, he spent all day hanging around the apartment. He managed to go to work for Bungee as a steerer, but that lasted only a few days. He started robbing the crackheads in the hallway instead of bringing them up to the spot.

"When Bungee found out, he kicked him in the balls and pistol-whipped him," she said.

After getting fired, he just hung around the apartment all day. But then her neighbors' apartments started getting broken into while they were at work. The only apartment not hit was hers. Cucko argued unconvincingly it was only because he was home that the burglars didn't hit them.

At this point, she had enough. She packed his shopping bag for him and told him he had to leave. She had started experiencing morning sickness. So, Cucko knew she was pregnant. He agreed to go under one condition.

"That's my baby in you," he said. "I'll go, but I want you to keep it. I got nothing else in this world to remember me by when I'm gone."

Jessica agreed to keep the baby just to be rid of him. She said she should have realized he wasn't going away that easily. He started coming by the apartment to check on her pregnancy. When she suggested she might terminate it, he got threatening.

"If you kill my baby," he warned, "it's gonna get real hot around this motherfucker here."

All of his subsequent threats had something to do with fire. Even if it was to just stare at her from the corner, flicking his zippo lighter.

"Where was he living?" Paddy asked.

"I heard he hooked up with some woman who works in Assemblywoman Duran's office on Knickerbocker. I ran into them on the avenue. He introduced her as his cousin, but she isn't. She's a crackhead. She lives somewhere in Flatbush with her son. I saw the son a few times. I pity her."

"Why do you pity her?" George asked.

"Because her son is a hyperactive mess. He bounces around all the time and says stupid, inappropriate things to people he doesn't even know. When they slap him up, he cries and runs away. They call him *Mierdito*. That means 'little shit.' Now she's stuck with two of them."

***

Paddy and George brought the three of them down to the DA's office. Bibb interviewed them and put their statements on audiotape. After escorting them out to the reception area, Paddy and George went back to Bibb's office to get the verdict. Durr suspected he already knew the answer.

"Can we lock up Cucko *now*?" George asked.

"Not yet," Bibb said.

"Why the hell not?" he demanded.

"Want to take a crack at why, Paddy?" the big prosecutor asked.

"Because Blanco is compromised in two ways," Paddy said. "He's on parole, and he works for the same drug organization as Bungee, Tranquillo, and Bless. The defense could argue they conspired to set up Cucko over some drug beef. The girls are great. They're victims of the crime. But they're also third-generation hoodrats. The new Brooklyn jury—yuppies and urban pioneers—won't trust them. They'll be looking for any reason to disbelieve them."

"What more do you want, Bibb?" George asked.

"Get me a witness who heard him bragging about it after the fact," he suggested. "Or, better still, get the lab off their asses and get me some physical evidence that ties the piece of shit to the crime."

"Oh, is that all?" George said, throwing his arms up in frustration.

***

After dropping off their witnesses, they headed back to the eight-three. George was still miffed over Dan Bibb. Paddy let him vent.

"What the fuck, man! What more do we have to do? He wants this case on a silver platter. It's a Brooklyn North murder case—everybody is compromised! We should go lock this fuck up without *His Majesty* Bibb's permission. Then we'll get it out of him in the truth room. Or will that not be enough either?"

"What if we can't get it out of him?" Paddy asked.

"If you and I can't get a confession out of that mutt, no one can. I like our chances."

"But what if we just can't? What if he's such a psychopath, he won't give it up? It's not like he's got anything to lose. He lives out of a shopping bag. Other than throwing his ass in jail, where he'll get *three hots and a cot*, we've got nothing we can take away from him. For him, prison is a better deal."

"Bibb is never gonna let us close this case," George groused.

"He will," Paddy said. "If we were lesser detectives, we would have already gotten the indictments. But he knows we can get what he wants. So, let's get it. Then it won't matter what that miscreant has to tell us."

***

Back at the eight-three, Paddy called Ronnie Kingsbury at TARU. As promised, his phone work was back from the telephone company. The two phones matched, verifying the time and length of the conversation.

"The tower hits verify your witness' statement," Ronnie said. "The conversation begins at 02:17 hours. The crime is first reported at 02:19. Both phones are hitting the tower at Gates and Central until 02:21. Then Tranquillo is on the move. We can follow him all the way to East New York until he's bouncing off the tower in the cemetery at Cypress and Jamaica, right by the condos he described. At 03:00, the conversation ends. Then there's no activity until 09:00 hours."

"That nails down Tranquillo," Paddy said. "He was exactly where he said he was."

"I'll send the reports right to your case file," Ronnie said, hanging up.

Paddy told George about the phone work.

"That firms up Tranquillo's statement, but Bibb is gonna want more. Where are we gonna get it?" George asked.

"I think I know."

Paddy called down to the desk and had Anti-Crime report to the squad. Though there were two Crime teams working that tour, everyone knew a summons to the squad meant Paddy was looking for Tommy Crowe. A few minutes later, Tommy tentatively approached Paddy's desk.

"You wanted to see me, Paddy?"

"Yeah, kid," Paddy said. "Give me that info about Mierdito."

"Sure," Tommy said, handing Paddy his notes, looking relieved.

Paddy noticed. He couldn't allow that.

"You dimed me out to your mother, you little bastard."

"I'm sorry, but I was worried about you," Tommy defended himself. "You looked like shit the last time I saw you. You look better now. So, I'm not sorry."

"Good call on your part. She was exactly what I needed. It looks like mentoring you is paying off." Paddy smiled.

***

Paddy and George were at 1016 Clarendon Road, a two-story private house in the heart of Flatbush. Like much of Brooklyn, Flatbush was experiencing a renaissance. This building must not have gotten the memo. It would have been a ramshackle mess even if it hadn't fallen into disrepair. Now it was an atrocity masquerading as a dwelling. The crumbling cement stoop led up to a front door that had obviously been kicked open at one time and left that way under the theory of why fix what will only be broken again. The blankets and sheets covering the inside of the windows—half of which were cracked or broken—screamed flophouse.

They were there to speak with Emma Calderon and her son, who they only knew as Mierdito. Given the condition of her living quarters, Paddy wondered what she was spending her paycheck on from the councilwoman. When she answered the door, it became apparent.

As Jessica had said, Emma was a crackhead. Her sunken cheeks, vacant eyes, and dirty clothes were a dead giveaway. The toxic chemical smell emanating off of her cemented it.

Paddy introduced himself and George. He told her they were there to talk about Sergio Palmiero. When he said his name, Emma roused from her drug stupor and appeared to become frightened.

"He's not here, is he?" she asked in a panic.

"No," Paddy assured her. "We were told he was living here."

"Not since last week when I threw him out."

"Why'd you throw him out?" George asked.

Burnt to a Crisp

"Because he tried to set my son on fire in his bed."

"Is your son okay?" Paddy asked.

"Yeah. The fire wouldn't take. The blankets were wet. Mierdito is a bedwetter."

"How old is he," Paddy asked.

"Fifteen."

"And he still wets the bed?"

"All the time."

"Why would Cucko try to burn him?" George asked.

"Something about the fire he set in Bushwick. He was afraid Mierdito was going to tell on him."

"How did Mierdito know about it?"

"Cucko told him the day before the fire that if Jessica aborted the baby, he was going to burn the house down. The next day he came back and warned my son, 'If you tell anybody, I'll burn you next.' I guess he didn't trust him to keep a secret. I only found out about it after I threw Cucko out."

"I only know your son as Mierdito," Paddy said. "What's his real name?"

"Juneo."

"Who gave him the nickname?" George asked.

"I did," said Emma.

"I know it means 'Little Shit.' Why would you call him that?"

"You'll see when you meet him," she frowned.

"Is he here?" George asked.

"Sure. I'll get him. Mierdito, *ven aca*!"

Paddy observed a nervous undersized teenage boy in a torn tee-shirt and dirty, yellow-stained underwear, peek tentatively into the hallway. Durr thought he had a frightened, rat-like look about him.

"These detectives want to talk to you about Cucko," Emma said.

The boy wailed, "Oh, no!" and dropped into a crouch, whimpering. He started gnawing on his fingernails, which Paddy could see were already chewed to bloody stumps. He decided he wasn't staying there a minute longer.

"Let's go, Emma," Paddy ordered. "Get him dressed and out to the car. We're going back to the precinct."

For Paddy and George, the ride back to the eight-three was a horror. Mierdito was bouncing around in the backseat, alternately threatening to kick the detectives' asses, crying, and begging for protection from Cucko—when he wasn't claiming he would jump out of the moving car. Paddy finally had to jam

219

on the brakes, lean over the front seat, and threaten to handcuff him. After pissing in his pants, he sat back in the wet car seat, whimpering for the remainder of the drive.

***

Back at the eight-three, Paddy put Emma and Mierdito in one of the interview rooms while he and George waited for Bibb to get there. Dan originally wanted them to bring the witnesses to him, but Paddy flatly refused.

"You come to me. I'm not getting in a car with that fucking kid again. When you're done with him, I'm paying out of my own pocket for the Uber to take them home."

Bibb came out. He liked the kid's testimony, even if it was an ordeal to get it. Paddy had to yell at Mierdito just to get him to behave and focus on the questions. As soon as they were done with Bibb, Paddy whisked them into an Uber as promised.

The three of them were at Paddy's desk when Bibb spoke to George.

"Are you gonna ask me?"

"Oh, sure," George said. "Like this kid is the last piece to put us over the top. He makes Weird Harold look like a super witness. If I want to hear the word 'no,' Dan, I'll ask my ex-wife for a break on the alimony."

Bibb looked like he felt bad for them. He knew they were busting their asses to make this case. But it had to be as strong as possible. Arsons are hard cases to try. Largely circumstantial, he would need all he could get to sell it to a jury. But Bibb wasn't unreasonable.

"Tell you what, George," he offered. "Let's wait to hear back from the lab. We need a chemical match on the accelerant. The mutt's fingerprint would be better. A DNA match would be a slam-dunk. But, hit or miss, I'll greenlight the arrest of Cucko."

"I guess we'll just have to light a fire under some scientists—no pun intended," Paddy said.

"Good luck with that," said Bibb.

CHAPTER THIRTY-FOUR

April 1, 2017
Plainedge, Long Island
07:00 hours

Paddy woke up early that morning with a start. Mairead had spent her first night in their bed in months and slept well beside her husband. Things were looking up for them. She was feeling stronger every day, and Paddy's homicides were finally breaking. She was happy, knowing how important the case was to him. They were feeding off each other's positive waves and riding the crest. But when Paddy sat bolt upright, Mairead sensed his apprehension.

"Are you okay?" she asked.

"I don't know," he admitted. "I was just coming awake, feeling good, when a wave of dread hit me out of nowhere."

"Is it gone?"

"No, and I can't even say what it is. I just have this nagging feeling something is about to go sideways—like someone's getting ready to take a giant shit on my birthday cake."

"Remnants of a bad dream?" Mairead suggested.

"No," Paddy said. "I slept like a log."

"Maybe it's just you, not knowing what to do with good fortune," she surmised.

"Could be," Paddy agreed. "We haven't had much of it lately."

Michael O'Keefe

***

When Paddy got to the eight-three, his anxiety hadn't abated. He was walking around like he was waiting for the other shoe to drop. Joe Furio noticed.

"What's eating you?"

"Something is up," Paddy said. "I've got a bad feeling."

"What could be up?"

"I don't know, but I'm sure we're going to find out."

Just then, his desk phone rang. The caller ID indicated the call was from the federal courthouse building in Brooklyn. Nothing in the detectives' experience suggested anything good ever came from there. Paddy looked at Joe over the tops of his reading glasses as if to say, "See." Joe now shared his apprehension.

"Eight-three Squad, Durr," Paddy answered.

"Hello, Paddy," a high-pitched male voice with a nasally New England accent said. "This is Dennis Pritchard. Do you remember me?"

He did remember him, and not fondly. They were at Columbia together, and Paddy remembered Pritchard as an entitled prick. He was one of those people who had been born on third base and thought he had hit a triple. Paddy could feel the acid churning in the pit of his stomach just from the sound of his voice.

While at Columbia, Pritchard very nearly went down in the same cheating scandal that almost ensnared Larry Rothman. He escaped the same way Rothman did—on Daddy's old money. Despite being very guilty, Pritchard blamed his problems on the cops. In this case, the detectives from the DA's Squad. As a bartender in Coogan's, Paddy had befriended many of the cops and detectives who ate and drank there. Pritchard gave him guff about it.

"Your detective friends have really tried to stitch me up," Pritchard whined.

"If you took some responsibility for your own actions, Dennis, perhaps you wouldn't keep getting your cock caught in your own zipper."

"They're only picking on me because I have money," Pritchard huffed.

"No," Paddy said. "You're guilty as fuck. You're only getting away with it because you have money. Your Boston accent has gotten on my last nerve. Get the fuck out of here and don't come back."

Paddy dumped Pritchard's half-full mug of beer in the drain and nodded toward the door. He had hoped his ass and elbows were the last he would ever see of him.

Burnt to a Crisp

Paddy knew Pritchard became an attorney, working for a short time in the Manhattan DA's Office, before becoming an FBI Agent. The last he heard was he was enjoying his assignment to the Official Corruption Unit in the Eastern District, where he got to hunt cops to his heart's desire. Paddy thought he could hear the sound of the other shoe dropping in the background of Pritchard's snotty, condescending voice.

"Yeah," Paddy said, switching the call to speaker so that Joe could hear. "I remember you. You're a dick. I'm kinda busy. What do you want?"

Pritchard hesitated for a second. He chose to ignore the insult and push on.

"I'd like to talk to you about a Detective Nova," he said.

"Who?"

"Detective George Nova, from the ninetieth precinct."

"Never heard of him."

"That can't be true," Pritchard said. "We heard you had a confrontation with him the other day."

"You heard wrong."

Pritchard seemed to get flustered. Like most FBI agents in Official Corruption, he was used to people just rolling over and giving him whatever he wanted. Most of his subjects and witnesses were a little dirty themselves and were looking to cooperate immediately, lest they become covered in the mud. Failing to get that from Paddy, Pritchard reached for the only other trick in his kit-bag—threats.

"You know it's a crime to lie to an FBI agent, Paddy?"

"Actually," he corrected. "For it to be a crime, I have to *knowingly* lie to an FBI agent. But you're just an unpleasant voice on the other end of the telephone. I don't know who the fuck you are. And don't come around here waving that toy of an FBI shield in my face. The answer is go fuck yourself."

"I'm sorry to hear that," Pritchard said. "Now, I'll be forced to make you a subject of my case."

"Well, then I'm safe," Paddy laughed. "The FBI couldn't investigate a boil on their own asses, and Official Corruption is a special kind of incompetent. You want to talk to me; it's with a subpoena or an arrest warrant. But even then, same answer; go fuck yourself."

Paddy slammed the phone down into the cradle, ending the call. He looked at Joe, who seemed concerned.

"What if they got you on tape?" he asked.

"They don't, or he would have said so."

"How do they know about the other day?"

"It was nobody here," Paddy knew. "It had to be one of the guys in the office in the nine-oh."

"Ah, shit!" Joe said.

"Yeah, but whoever it is, they can't hurt me. They only heard Nova's side of a telephone call. They can't say for certain I was on the other end. Then when I got to the nine-oh, all they can say is I asked where Nova was."

"What about your conversation with Kerrigan?"

"They couldn't have heard it. It was just John and me behind closed doors. They can only speculate what it was about."

"What if Kerrigan tells them?"

"He won't," Paddy assured him. "John would sooner cut out his tongue than give me up."

"How do you know?"

"Because I'd do the same for him," Paddy said. "I need a favor, Joe. Go down and tell Kerrigan he has another rat in the office. Make sure it's just you and him, and no one else can hear."

"Got it," Joe said. "Is this the problem you were anticipating?"

"Nah. The feds are lightweight problems. I've been stiff-arming those losers since 1993."

"What are you going to do about them?"

"I'm gonna refuse to talk to them."

"What if they subpoena you?"

"Then I'll lie to them."

Joe considered that. He didn't think it was such a sound strategy, particularly since the only one it benefitted was a dirty cop who already gave drug dealers personal information about him.

"He's dirty as fuck, Paddy. Wouldn't it be easier to just give them what they want?"

"It's too easy. I know he's a drug dealer. You know it. The feds know it. It's their case. Let them prove it. They want me to give him up for obstructing my investigation, but he didn't really do that. He's a gnat on the ass of a fly—meaningless. And what happens when all they can get him for is obstruction?"

"I don't know. He goes to jail?"

"For three whole years, and they'll shut down the drug case because they've already blown it up. All they want is a cop's scalp for a headline. Granted, he's dirty, but what they're going to charge him with isn't even a crime in state court. It would only be an association case in the Trial Room—thirty days and a year's probation. I am not participating in that kind of shoddy investigative work. I'm not doing their jobs for them. I won't let them make me look like a rat because they're lazy. They're going to have to work for a living for a change. They owe us that much."

"I can see your point, but I don't think they will."

"I'm not worried about them. They're awful investigators, and the only thing they do well is set up perjury traps. Since I won't be talking to them, I won't be perjuring myself."

"All right." Joe nodded. "I'm gonna head down to the nine-oh to talk to Kerrigan. I'll let you know what he says."

After Joe left, Paddy checked with the lab. He was told by one of the technicians that the chemical profiles for the scene and the can of kerosene would take at least a few more days. The good news was they were able to lift a partial print from the handle of the can. The bad news was the fumigation process needed to lift the print had set them back a week on the chemistry work.

The print was presently being cleaned up and enhanced before it was put into the AFIS and SAFIS systems. He was told the DNA analysis would take at least another month—at the earliest. *So much for expediting things*, Paddy thought.

Lieutenant Martino came in. After he signed in and got his coffee, Paddy gave him an update on the case. Martino was pleased with their progress, but he could tell Paddy was not.

"What's the matter, Paddy?"

"I'm having this premonition something is about to go ass over tea kettle," he admitted.

"I can't imagine why. It seems like everything is coming together nicely. The case is moving forward. Mairead's feeling better. You're not worried about her, are you?"

"Well, yeah. Always, but it's not that."

"This doesn't sound rational."

"I didn't say it made sense, Lou. I just said I felt it."

"Then we'll just see what happens, and we'll deal with it."

Paddy went on to tell him about the situation with Nova and the feds, informing him he sent Joe down to the nine-oh to warn John Kerrigan face to face.

"That was good thinking," the lou said. "John will appreciate it."

"We've been friends for more than thirty years. It was the least I could do. My question is, how's he gonna smoke out the rat?"

"That's an easy one," Martino said. "He knows it's someone on Nova's team. I'm sure he has a suspicion about one of them already. He moves him out of the team. If there's outside intervention, like a call from the Boro, or the Chief of D's, telling him he can't, he guessed right. The guy is the rat."

"You see," Paddy laughed. "You are a smart guy."

Joe got back a short time later. As the lou had predicted, Kerrigan already had his suspicions. He had begun to employ the tactic Martino laid out.

"Is Paddy still freaking out about nothing?" Joe asked the lou.

"Yeah, but I've come to trust his instincts. Now I'm worried."

"He told you about the feds?"

"He did, but that isn't it. He's been tying those pricks in knots for years."

"Maybe it's nothing, and it'll just blow over," Joe said hopefully, but he was worried too.

The rest of the team came in, along with George Fahrbach and Jimmy Boland from Homicide. They all noted Paddy's uncharacteristic anxiety, the tension written on his face. When the lieutenant got the call from the Chief of Detectives, *everyone* recognized it as the sound of the other shoe dropping.

It was a must appear notification; *Detective 1st Grade Padraig J. Durr to appear at 09:00 hours the following morning at Internal Affairs, with counsel, for the purposes of an IO-9 hearing.*

"I'll call Jimmy Maselli," George said. "Maybe he can get another stay."

"Probably not," Paddy said, shrugging. "The Second Circuit ruled they could still have their hearing in a reasonable time when they overturned that idiot, Judge Zayas. The time has apparently come."

"Well, we have to try," George said.

George called Jimmy Maselli. He agreed they should try a *Hail Mary*, but even he had no faith they would succeed. Nonetheless, Jimmy filed the article 75 in the Second Circuit Court of Appeals. But asking an appeals court to reverse its own ruling is a bit like pissing into the wind—you'll be pissing on yourself and likely be laughed at. There would be a definitive ruling sometime this evening.

With nothing more to do on his case, Paddy got the fives up to date. If he were modified, another detective would have to take over. All he or she would have to do to get spun up was read the fives.

After that, Paddy sat around the squad waiting to hear the verdict from Jimmy. Martino invited him into his office for coffee and what Paddy imagined would be a pep talk.

"Hang in there, Paddy. It might work out."

"But it won't," he said. "I've had time to run the scenarios again and again. There are only two. The first is the unlikely event Jimmy gets a stay. The other one involves having my guns and shield taken and being put on modified assignment."

"If that happens, I'll take care of you."

"You won't be able to, Lou," Paddy said. "I won't be here. The moment I get put on modified, Dr. Levine will have the mayor's wife transfer me to the most demeaning and inconvenient assignment available. I'm thinking central booking, or *The Boy in the Bubble* at Motor Transport."

"What the hell is that?" the lou asked.

"He's the idiot in the booth outside vehicle services who raises and shuts the gate. Either way, it'll be back in the bag with a bad commute for steady day-tours, no overtime."

"You could appeal the finding."

"That would take a year, and there is no guarantee I'd win. Besides, she knows I won't stand for the indignity of being in the Rubber-Gun Squad. She'll get what she wants; I retire and have to sue to get my guns back."

"That sucks," Martino said.

"I had a good run," Paddy said, shrugging. "It had to end eventually. My only real regret right now is not getting to close this case. I would have liked to be the one to throw bracelets on that sick fuck."

"You've closed hundreds of homicides," the lou noted. "Why is this one special?"

"Because of the innocence of the victims. I had the rare chance to provide real justice instead of the perp-on-perp debacles most murders are. To get short-sheeted when I was so close is disappointing beyond words."

Later that night, Jimmy called. As expected, the court shot down their Hail Mary. The hearing would go on as scheduled in the morning.

As Paddy was preparing to sign out, Aramis Maldonado asked to speak with him. Paddy thought he had been behaving strangely since coming in for the *four-to-one* tour, listening intently to what was going on, staring at Paddy like he was waiting for the perfect opportunity to talk. *He whiffed on that one*, Paddy thought. At this point, Durr had no desire to speak with anyone.

"Whatever your problem is, Aramis, you'll have to bounce it off of Joe or George. I'm about to become a civilian, in case you hadn't heard. So, I won't be able to referee your little tiffs and squabbles anymore."

Aramis was taken aback and a little hurt by his remark. He had been doing much better the last two weeks, thanks to Paddy and Joe showing him the ropes. He was starting to feel like he belonged and was even getting along better with his squadmates. He was trying to keep what he had to say to himself, but he really couldn't in good conscience. Paddy had been his biggest advocate since the transfer. He chalked up his uncharacteristic rudeness as frustration with the mistreatment he was receiving. So, he forged ahead.

"It's not about me, Paddy."

"I don't have the time right now, Aramis."

"I think I can help you with that twat, Levine," he blurted out.

Paddy snapped his head around. He had never heard Aramis speak that way. At least now he knew they had a common enemy. The heat delivered with the profanity was genuine.

"I'm listening," Paddy said.

"Better you just watch," Aramis said, handing Paddy his phone.

***

Back home, Paddy told Mairead everything that had transpired throughout his insane day and what he would do tomorrow.

"If this goes bad, I'll be arrested," he said.

"Yeah, but so will they," Mairead pointed out.

"I don't care if they have a lawyer. Just so long as I do. I can't use Jimmy. It would be a conflict of interest and cast suspicion on him. If I get pinched, you've got to call Steve Losquadro to tell him what's going on."

"Your friend we used for the closing?"

"And the wills, and the DNRs and every other thing we've needed a lawyer for."

"Good, I like him," Mairead said.

"Well, I love him. Steve used to write up my gun cases in Manhattan. When the feds were trying to lock the team up, he testified in the grand jury on our behalf."

"Then he's our guy," she said.

Paddy nodded.

"And maybe our last line of defense."

Burnt to a Crisp

CHAPTER THIRTY-FIVE

April 2, 2017
Manhattan
09:00 hours

Internal Affairs had relocated from their decrepit headquarters on Poplar Street in Brooklyn in the early 1990s when they were converted from merely a *Division* to a *Bureau*. Early in his career, Paddy had been called down there to be interrogated for a nonsensical allegation lodged by a disgruntled criminal. He found the building the most unpleasant and forbidding one in the NYPD. If One Police Plaza was the Kremlin, as it was often called, then Poplar Street was Lefortovo Prison. The building had been constructed shortly after the Civil War, and Paddy thought it hadn't been painted or cleaned since. Everything about the place reeked of mistrust and fear. The old wood railings and paneling were neglected—rubbed raw by countless sweaty hands. The color scheme on the walls could only be described as vomit-green. If despair were a place, Poplar Street was it. Paddy felt like there should have been a sign above the front door that read, *Abandon hope, all ye who enter here.*

In contrast, 315 Hudson Street was a beautiful and stately old building in lower Manhattan. Built in the early 1930s as the headquarters for New York Telephone, the art deco design and high-vaulted and gilded ceilings of the lobby were a warm and inviting change of pace—until one got upstairs to the offices. The same sneaky suspicion and mean-spiritedness which had poisoned the old building were still flourishing. *It wasn't the bricks and mortar that sucked*, Paddy thought. *It was the people who worked here.*

George and Joe elected to accompany Paddy and Jimmy—a welcome show of support from the DEA. Strangely, everyone but Paddy was on edge. In contrast, he was the picture of quiet serenity. To protect his friends, he hadn't told them what he planned to do. They assumed his carefree attitude was a product of being under stress from this issue for so long; he was relieved to just be getting it over with.

They rode the elevator to the 16th floor, to the offices of *Group Zero*. Internal Affairs had always been broken up into investigative groups, along the federal model. Each group had traditionally been in charge of their own particular zone or area of the city. Group Zero had been created shortly after the present mayor was elected. They were answerable only to him, bypassing the Police Commissioner and the rest of the NYPD's chain of command. Their sole purpose was to execute the desires and schemes of City Hall. They were a political hit squad who targeted people, not allegations of wrongdoing. They had no interest in rooting out corruption, the stated intention, and purpose of IAB. Rather, they were tasked with crushing whomever His Honor wanted crushed. Paddy was now squarely in their crosshairs.

After being subjected to the usual IAB tactic of being made to wait in the reception area to stew in one's own juices, Joe became frustrated with the eye-fucking they were getting from the scurrilous staff.

"These fucking scumbags," he muttered. "They should all die of demeaning ass cancer."

"Relax, Joe," Paddy chuckled. "You'll be out of here in a few minutes."

"What about you?"

"I might be leaving in cuffs."

"What the fuck are you talking about?"

"I have a plan."

"Oh, no! As your delegate, would you care to enlighten me?"

"I'm afraid that's none of your business, Joe."

"What's none of my fucking business?" he demanded.

"Relax. It's for your own protection. Even Jimmy doesn't know. If it goes right, I'll tell you all about it on the ride home. If it goes tits up, you can read all about it in the papers tomorrow."

"Oh, Jesus!"

"Let's hope He's on our side today," said Paddy.

A detective finally beckoned them inside, leading them down the corridor to a conference room. Waiting in there were Dr. Levine and an inspector who Paddy had never seen before.

"I am Inspector Bernard Crawley," he said, extending his right hand. "I'll be the ranking officer for this hearing."

Paddy looked down at the inspector's hand as if he had been offered a turd.

"I've heard of you," he said. "Did you know the rank and file call you *Creepy Crawley*? They fucking hate you."

"I'm glad dirty cops hate me," Crawley said, puffing out his narrow chest.

"The dirty ones don't. You don't bother *them*. You're the mayor's hatchet man. Not surprising you're the CO of this group."

Crawley looked like he was about to explode when they were interrupted. Lieutenant Donald Wormwood entered wearing his trademark cheap and ill-fitting suit and an obsequious smile that could rot teeth.

"I see he still couldn't find a Men's Wearhouse," Paddy said to Joe. "Is that suit made of paper mache or a horse blanket?"

This caused Joe to cackle out loud, chasing the smile off Wormwood's face.

"I'm glad to see you're in such high spirits," Wormwood sneered. "Are you having a good day?"

"Let's dispense with the niceties, Lieutenant," Paddy said. "I don't like you, and I don't trust you as far as I could spit a rat."

Jimmy Maselli had been grabbing Paddy by the sleeve, trying to get him to stop taunting his adversaries. With the last comment, he grabbed and tugged.

"Stop pulling at me, Jimmy," Durr ordered. "I'm going to say whatever the fuck I want, to whomever the fuck I want. So, knock that tugging shit off. I'm paying for you to be my lawyer, not my filter."

"I think we should just get down to business," Wormwood said.

"Before we do," Paddy interrupted. "I would like a word with Dr. Levine in private."

Jimmy slapped his forehead and looked like he would throw up. Joe was anxious to see what would happen next. George, who knew nothing of his plan, knew Paddy well enough to know something was afoot. He just looked curious. Dr. Levine, who had been squirming in her chair all this time, was now bouncing around in her seat, delicious anticipation etched on her face. Paddy thought she looked like she was on the verge of an orgasm and was trying desperately to delay it. This was her chance to finally fuck Paddy Durr, and she wanted to get to it. It was Durr's intention to throw cold water on her.

"That would be highly irregular," she said.

"No more irregular than trying to yank the guns from a decorated first-grade detective with over thirty years in service," Paddy observed. "You are technically *my* psychiatrist, Dr. Levine. Indulge me. It won't take a minute."

"Well, since this is your last day of full duty," she sneered. "I'll play along."

She walked out and down the hallway to join Paddy, who had his cellphone in his hand.

"What do you want, Durr?"

He handed her his phone and said, "Just press play."

She did. A few seconds later, her face became a mask of horror.

She observed a naked Aramis Maldonado fill the screen. The cameraman panned away to show Aramis performing fellatio on what appeared to be a fourteen-year-old boy. Levine gasped, looking horrified.

"That young man would be Assemblyman McCallister's son, Ricky," Paddy said. "When his mom found out what you all were doing to her little boy, she wanted everybody's head on a stick. The assemblyman had another arrangement in mind. Just keep watching. It gets better."

The next screenshot showed two women engaged in oral sex on a couch in what looked like a government office. The cameraman zoomed in on the women to reveal they were the doctor and the mayor's wife.

Levine looked ill, but she continued to watch, noticing for the first time the mahogany desk in the background, bracketed by two standing flags. One was the American flag, the other the official flag of The City of New York. The nameplate on the desk was the First Lady's. It would be obvious to the casual observer where this was taking place. Because she was a co-star, Levine already knew they were in the First Lady's office. Within the next few minutes, everyone in the video had some form of sex with everyone else.

"I notice you really like wearing that strap-on," Paddy said. "Does it make you feel powerful? It didn't look like Aramis shared your enthusiasm."

"Where did you get this?" she shrieked.

"This? I have twenty-nine more where that came from," Paddy cautioned. "But if I were you, I would be more concerned with what I was going to do with them. Aren't you curious?"

"What *are* you going to do with them?"

"I'm going to cut an even sweeter deal than the Assemblyman. It all depends on you, though. Unless *all* of my conditions are met, those videos are going out to every media outlet in the country. I'm also going to send them to the District

Burnt to a Crisp

Attorney and the American Medical Association. For starters, you're looking at losing your medical license. But that will be the least of your problems. The narcotics distribution raps ought to get you a minimum of ten years. Didn't you realize when you were prescribing pills for that imbecile cameraman Barry and the First Lady you were committing a crime? It was only a matter of time before you got exposed. Bernard is a junkie, and you got the First Lady so pilled-up she rattles. How much Xanax can that woman eat in a day?"

"They were my patients," she moaned.

"With whom you made sex videos? Fucking your patients is an automatic license revocation. Did that strike you as being somehow prudent, ethical behavior? You're not much good at the decision-making thing, are you? Now you, the First Lady, and Barry are looking at child pornography charges."

"But Ricky was seventeen," she said, her whole body shaking.

"The federal statute specifies eighteen as the age of consent for the purposes of recording a sex act. Lucky for you, Assemblyman McCallister is an even bigger whore. I understand he sold his son for political clout. Disgraceful, but that's between him and the Mayor. Now all you have left to worry about is me. That's not good news. You're looking at ten years," Paddy said, smiling.

"I have money! I can pay you!" she rasped, grabbing his sleeve.

"I don't want your money, you depraved twat."

"Then I'll have sex with you—whenever you want!"

"Please! I turned you down the first time you offered yourself. It's of no value to me."

"Then what?!"

"To begin with, you're going in there to announce that Health Services is not ready to proceed. Then you're going to close this matter forever, giving me a pristine bill of mental health."

"Consider it done!" she wailed.

"But, *I'm* not done. When you leave, you're going straight to the Police Commissioner's Office to resign from the department. When I see your resignation on the teletype, I'll sit on the videos."

"For how long?"

"Oh, I'm keeping these forever," Paddy said. "Also, tell the First Lady and the Mayor, I want Group Zero disbanded. The First Lady is to disassociate herself from the police department, leaving the commissioner to run it as he sees fit. Lastly, me, Maldonado, and everyone else in the eight-three Squad are heretofore untouchable. As time goes by, let them know I'll be popping by if I need anything else. Impress upon the Mayor, if he thinks he's compromised by Assemblyman McCallister, he better understand, I own his bony ass. I'll call first before I come over to burn my brand on it."

Dr. Levine continued to shake. Tears welled up in her eyes and began to roll down her face. She started biting her manicured fingernails. The ones on her left hand were now chewed down to stubs. She was staring off, seemingly distracted. Paddy brought her back on point.

"You're going to need to get cracking on this, Dr. Levine, or you, the Mayor, his wife, and Assemblyman McCallister are going to get real famous—and not in a good Las Vegas way."

She wobbled down the hall on rubbery legs, entering the conference room. She approached the table and spoke in a shaky and far away voice as if she weren't completely there.

"The Health Services Division isn't ready to proceed at this time. I am postponing this hearing indefinitely."

"Wait a second!" Wormwood yelled. "What the hell is going on here?"

"I'll tell you what's going on," Inspector Crawley said. "He's got dirt on her."

"Right out of your playbook, right, Crawley?" Paddy said, smirking.

"You motherfucker," Crawley said. "I'll get you for this!"

"No. You won't," Paddy assured him.

"Dr. Levine," Paddy said. "Before you go, please let the Mayor and the First Lady know; I want the inspector and Lieutenant Wormwood back in uniform and on patrol, in the precincts furthest from their homes. That's not negotiable and needs to be on the same teletype as your resignation. You may go now."

"I don't have the authority for all of this," Levine whined.

"No, you don't," Paddy agreed. "But the mayor does. Just tell him what I have and what I'll do with it if my demands aren't immediately met."

After Levine had wobbled out of the room, Crawley glared at Paddy.

"Easy with the 'fuck you' eyes, Crawley," Paddy said. "You're a paper tiger now."

"That must be some leverage you have, Durr," Crawley spat.

"Oh, it's fucking huge," Paddy assured him.

***

In the car on the way back to the eight-three, after ensuring their conversation was protected under attorney-client privilege, Paddy told them what he had done.

"You got balls of titanium," said George, shaking his head.

"You do like to walk the razor's edge," Jimmy observed.

"Only when circumstances put me there," Paddy said.

"And only when he's not juggling chainsaws—you fucking lunatic," Joe added.

"So, Aramis is gay?" George asked.

"Is that all you took away from this?" Paddy laughed.

"No, of course not," George said. "But it might explain why he was so awkward when he first got to the squad."

"I think it was more anxiety over what to do with the videos," Paddy reasoned.

"Speaking of, where did he get them? It's not like he filmed them. He was the star of the show," Joe said.

"The First Lady has her own videographer," Paddy said. "He's a junkie. Levine has been giving him all the oxys and Fentanyl he could take. On Aramis' last day, the cameraman was nodded out at his desk. He had all the videos on his phone. Aramis just texted the files to himself."

"He wasn't worried about getting charged as a participant?" Jimmy asked.

"He was. But he said he didn't care. He knew Levine and the First Lady would never be done fucking with him. They were coming after him again either way. He figured helping me was worth the risk."

"That kid is flying high on my good guy list right now," Joe said.

"Why do Levine and the mayor's wife have such a hard-on for him?" George asked.

"When the First Lady informed him she had found another boy toy for an intern, he dropped the bomb that he was gay. They tried to convince him he was just bisexual, and they could continue the same as before. But he told them no. Then Levine had the balls to try and give him an order. He got hot. He punched his transfer ticket when he told them, 'I am never having sex with you nasty *putas sucias* again!' He was in the eight-three the next day."

"Well, he's ours now," Joe said. "An official member in good standing of our little zoo crew."

"Cheers to that," said George.

Michael O'Keefe

CHAPTER THIRTY-SIX

April 3, 2017
Plainedge, Long Island
09:15 hours

Paddy woke up with the early spring sunshine peeking through the curtains. He leaned over to check the time on the bedside alarm clock. Mairead was already up. He could smell the coffee brewing. The clock read 09:15 A.M., late for him. But, it was his RDO—regular day off—as opposed to the first day of his retirement—a very near thing. After the stress of the previous two days, Paddy thought he deserved to sleep late. What he wanted now was to make breakfast. The kids were home, finally, everyone under one roof. Paddy wanted to get them all at the table before his active children flew out the door to pursue their hectic lives.

Yesterday, he had hung around the squad to await the teletype messages he insisted upon seeing. He was rewarded for his patience. The first message to come in was the announcement Inspector Bernard Crawley had filed for service retirement from the NYPD, effective immediately. That meant he had gotten the heads up from someone his transfer to Patrol Services was imminent. A few minutes later, the resignation from the Police Department of Honorary Inspector-Police Surgeon Deborah Levine was followed by Lieutenant Donald

Burnt to a Crisp

Wormwood's transfer from the Internal Affairs Bureau to the 123rd Precinct in Staten Island.

Paddy laughed. He hoped Wormwood enjoyed his commute from Kings Park. He knew he would appreciate paying the exorbitant toll every day. *This was the price you had to pay if you wanted to be a hatchet man*, Paddy thought. *Sometimes, you're the one who gets chopped.*

Coming into the kitchen, he kissed his wife, who had just poured coffee for him.

"Good morning, Detective," she smiled.

"We're lucky you can still call me that," Paddy said, hugging her.

"Better to be lucky than good, but good and lucky is better still."

"Aye, *tis'*. Now out of my kitchen, woman," he said, swatting her on the backside.

Mairead had begun to put on some mass and muscle tone after wasting away for so many months. Paddy liked the feel of her round firmness in his hand, almost becoming distracted with other ideas until getting back on point for his intended purpose.

"I'm making us a traditional Irish breakfast."

"Thank God for the internet and the microwave," she said. "It will be nice to have some freezer space again."

Paddy had a craving for black and white pudding several months earlier. He found an Irish gourmet provider online. By the time the tubes of sausage arrived, Mairead's illness had advanced. He no longer had a craving for anything—save a miracle. The sausage went into the freezer until this morning.

He proceeded to whip up enough eggs, bacon, sausage, fried tomato, and black and white pudding to feed a battalion. Mairead called the kids down to the table.

This was the first time in a long time the entire family was present under one roof, with Mairead feeling well enough for them to gather like this. Paddy had forgotten the simple joy of the easy camaraderie and good-natured kidding that always occurred around the table with his brood. He realized he missed it dearly.

As was the case when they were together like this, they discussed family news—keeping each other abreast of what they were up to. Mairead began by telling the children about their father's ordeal over the last few weeks, ending with the good news of how he once again vanquished his enemies. They were vaguely aware of the tumult as they came and went. Now that all of that was settled, Mairead started to go into detail when Paddy had to stop her.

"That's enough, Mairead," He cut her off. "They can't be questioned about crimes they know nothing about."

"You had to commit a crime?" Casey asked.

"Of course he did," Patrick joked. "He's an arch-criminal. He commits them every day."

"This is New York," Paddy said. "Everything is a crime in New York."

About that, Paddy wasn't really joking. Between city ordinances, state law, and the byzantine federal statutes, almost every imaginable behavior violated some law. He had long since given up trying to make sense of them or conform. The only law by which he conducted himself was his conscience. He decided in every event what the right thing was and acted accordingly.

"Never mind me," Paddy said. "What's going on with you. How's school going, Casey?"

"I thought biochemistry was difficult," she said. "But anatomy is insane."

"Is Dr. Tollefsen's book any help?" Paddy asked, referencing the textbook authored by his friend, the Medical Examiner.

Dr. Bjorn Tollefsen was the Chief Medical Examiner in Brooklyn. He had taken a paternal shine to Paddy over the years, considering him his prized pupil and practitioner of homicide investigation. Paddy thought the world of him. When Dr. Tollefsen heard Casey was in pre-med, he gave Paddy a well-read and richly annotated copy of the anatomy textbook he had written. It was presently in use by most medical examiner's offices in the country as their primary anatomy reference source.

"If it weren't for Doc's book, I'd be totally lost," she said. "I don't even look at the textbook for the course anymore. It sucks by comparison."

"Well, that's four hundred bucks wasted," Mairead said. "Maybe we can use it as a doorstop."

"And what about you, my love?" Paddy asked Katelyn.

She made a face and stuck her tongue out at her father, pretending annoyance at the endearment. A few short years ago, she wouldn't have been pretending. Paddy's infidelity had hit Katelyn harder than any of the other Durr children. One reason was that it had been with her soccer coach. But the real cause of her devastation at the time was that her illusions about her father had been shattered.

She had been closer to him than her brother and sister. Katelyn regarded Paddy as a superhero—her superhero. When that was taken from her, she was hurt and angry. She felt she had been betrayed. Because she was so like her father, her anger burned hot. Her ability to hold a grudge was every bit the equal of his own—and Paddy was a famous grudge holder. Over time she came to understand, with the help of Mairead's insight, that her father was only human. A kind, caring, protective, and above all, loving man—but in the end, just a man—with all of humanity's flaws and imperfections.

She also saw how her father never tried to rationalize or excuse his actions, no matter how reprehensible they were. He owned his sins and tried to atone for them with a religious-like zeal. She could see no one was more disappointed in him than himself. He carried his guilt like a lodestone. She began to feel bad for him before she could forgive him. When she realized her mother, the most aggrieved party in all of this, was prepared to do so, she thought she had better start, especially in light of the fact she knew he would never forgive himself.

They slowly grew close again, but the experience had changed her. She developed a fierce independent streak. She would never again be daddy's little girl, but she knew he adored her, and she adored him right back. She just became more realistic in her expectations, holding him accountable, even correcting him when she saw fit. Paddy loved her all the more for it.

"I graduate next month," Katelyn said. "Same degree as you, Daddy. English lit."

"Then what, grad school?" Paddy asked.

"Something like that."

"What is *like that*?" Mairead demanded.

"I'm going into the police academy in July," she smiled sheepishly.

"Oh, good Lord! Another one," Mairead said. "Well, that settles it. No sleep for me—ever again."

"Relax, baby," Paddy said. "She can handle it. In a house full of people hard as coffin nails, that's the toughest one right there."

"Yo, Pop," Patrick said. "I'm sitting right here."

"Easy, boyo. You're still behind me and your mom on that line."

"Kinda makes what I've got to say anti-climactic," he said.

"What is it, Patrick?" Mairead asked.

"I'm going into Anti-Crime next week."

"That was fast," Paddy observed.

"Yeah, it was," Patrick said. "Did you have anything to do with it?"

"I think maybe the two robberies and eleven gun collars you made last month had *everything* to do with it. You're a gifted young cop. You deserve it."

"I just hope the guys in the seven-five agree."

Michael O'Keefe

"We discussed this," Paddy reminded him. "There are two kinds of people on the job. The absolute best human beings you will ever meet; dedicated, generous, loyal, and honorable—they would take a bullet for you. Then there are the other kind; miserable, backstabbing, jealous pieces of shit who would walk over your bleeding body to get your spot in a detail. The problem is you might not know who's who until it's too late. I'm sorry to tell you this, but you're going to discover some people you thought were your friends are in the second category. Identify them and cut them out of your life."

"How will I know who they are?" Patrick asked.

"They're usually the empty suits. The people who least deserve to be in plain clothes have the biggest mouths. They'll expose themselves. Starting Monday, you'll hear the shit-talkers whispering in the background, getting dead silent when you get near their conversations. Your true friends will straighten them out and let you know they did."

"That's just disappointing," Patrick said.

"It's the nature of a bureaucracy. You have to learn how to wade through the bullshitters and their bullshit so you can do your job—because *they* won't be doing it."

"Are you sure you still want this job, Kate?" Patrick said, smiling at his sister.

"Most def," she said.

"Where do you want to go when you graduate from the academy?" Paddy asked.

"Oh, no!" Katelyn said. "I'm not letting you do any contracts or favors for me. I'll go where I'm sent to make my own way on the job."

"It's just a phone call and a precinct assignment," Paddy laughed.

"Except it's not," she argued. "Everybody knows you. It's already going to be hard enough just being the daughter of *The Legend* without you smoothing the way over for me. No one will ever take me seriously. I want to be judged for what I do, not who my daddy is."

"Yeah!" Casey said, high-fiving her big sister. "Talking truth to power!"

Paddy grinned broadly. He was so proud of Katelyn he thought he might burst. This was just like her. She was determined to make her way, certain she would succeed without anyone's help. Paddy was a believer.

"I have no doubt you will make your mark, and it'll be indelible. Just be aware, I'm here if you need me."

"Well, that's settled," Mairead said, turning her attention to her youngest daughter. "Casey, please promise me you're not going on that lunatic asylum of a job. I won't be able to swing a dead cat in here without hitting a cop."

Michael O'Keefe

CHAPTER THIRTY-SEVEN

April 4, 2017
Manhattan
11:00 hours

Paddy and Mairead were both nervous this morning. Heading into Memorial Sloan Kettering for another infusion and examination, they both remembered Mairead's reaction to the last one. Dr. Cheng assured them those kinds of side effects were very rare. He showed Paddy where on Mairead's lower spine to inject the morphine syrette if the muscle spasms should recur. He gave them another twelve-pack of morphine but assured them they would not need it, despite the fact he had further enriched the infusion.

They were seated with Dr. Cheng in his office, waiting for Mairead's blood work and the results of her CT scan. Cheng became a little apprehensive at one point while going over Mairead's symptoms.

"How has the pain been since your last treatment?"

"Overall, much less," Mairead said. "But my lower back is the same. It feels very tight, and it still feels like it's bulging around my spine."

"Does it hurt?"

"Only when I move too quickly," she said. "Then it's like a tugging sensation."

"Is that bad?" Paddy asked.

"I had hoped those symptoms would have lessened by now."

Burnt to a Crisp

When the CT scan came back, Cheng looked at the imagery on his high-definition screen on his desktop computer. The look of worry on his face was troubling.

"What is it, Doc?" Paddy asked, actually demanded.

"The tumor entwined throughout her lower spine has not diminished in size."

"Not even a little?" Paddy asked.

"No," Cheng said. "The good news is the lymph nodes we haven't removed look encouraging. The tumors there have all noticeably shrunk. The one under your right armpit looks to be gone completely. I'm not sure why the spinal tumors haven't responded the same way."

Dr. Cheng put the image on a split screen and signed into the lab portal on the other half of his monitor. He brought up Mairead's blood work. He saw something in her white blood cell count that might be of concern, or it might be indicative they were on the right track enriching the genetic material in her infusions.

"Your white blood cell count is low considering we're doing an intense immunoglobulin regimen. It's possible they were so effective fighting the cancer, the extra cells have been expended at this point. Rather than indicating the treatment isn't working, I would rather hope the genetic infusions might just need to be richer still."

"So more will be better?" Paddy asked.

"It stands to reason," Cheng said. "We already enriched her treatment since the last one. We won't know anything until the next examination when we'll be able to see for sure."

"So long as the tumor isn't growing, will Mairead be all right?"

"Malignant tumors don't just stagnate, Paddy. They either grow, or they diminish. A pause is exactly that—only a pause. It's temporary. We'll have to see if this infusion kicks it in the right direction."

On the way home from the hospital, Paddy was quiet. Mairead knew he was going over the information from Dr. Cheng, furiously trying to find a silver lining in his words. The fact he was at it for this long told Mairead he wasn't finding any.

"We can't overthink this, Paddy. It's going to be what it's going to be. Agonizing over it helps no one. Let's just stay positive and wait and see."

Paddy nodded, but Mairead knew his overactive brain would not rest until he had a definitive answer. Unfortunately, the answer would have to wait a week. She would do her best to distract him as much as she could until then.

Michael O'Keefe

***

After getting settled at home, Mairead slipped into his arms in the kitchen. Paddy thought it was just a hug until Mairead ran her hands over his body and reached up with her mouth to find his. She kissed him long and deeply, ending with her hand gripped tightly at his crotch, already bulging.

"C'mon," she said. "Take me to bed. We'll burn off some stress for a while. Then we can figure out what to do about dinner."

***

That night, they were in the family room watching TV when Mairead felt the first cramps beginning in her calves. Paddy went upstairs for a syrette of morphine. He injected Mairead right where Dr. Cheng had shown him. Instantly, the tugging sensation in her calf abated. A warm relaxing sense of wellbeing washed over her. She laid down on the couch with her head in Paddy's lap. Soon after, she was asleep, softly purring.

Paddy carried her up the stairs without waking her, gently putting her to bed. He shed his sweatpants and tee-shirt, climbing under the covers next to her. They were both fast asleep within minutes, Mairead safely cocooned in his arms.

CHAPTER THIRTY-EIGHT

April 5, 2017
Bushwick, Brooklyn
09:00 hours

Paddy jolted upright at the sound of the ringing phone. He didn't know where he was at first until his eyes focused, and he saw the prone form of his wife, Mairead, sleeping in their bed next to him. He looked over at the phone in its cradle on the nightstand. He couldn't read the caller ID without his glasses, so he just picked it up.

"Hello?" he answered.

"Paddy," he heard the excited voice of his former partner say. "It's Andy Leoniak. I've got some good news I didn't think you'd want to wait to hear."

"What the hell time is it, Andy?"

"It's 09:00 hours. Too early?"

"You got my attention, *Polska*. What have you got for me?"

"I took it upon myself to call the lab to try and expedite things. I hope you don't mind."

"No, of course not," Paddy said. "You did the B-run on the garage roof. It's your case too. What did they say?"

"We got a partial thumbprint from the handle of the kerosene can. It was only fourteen readable points of comparison, so it's small. I had them run it against Sergio Palmiero's prints. Twelve similar points, the tech is calling it a match."

"Wow!" Paddy said. "Talk about waking up to good news."

"It gets better," Andy said. "The chemical signature of the kerosene is a match for the residue in the hallway."

"Damn, boyo!"

"But wait, there's more. We also got usable DNA off the handle—skin cells. The lab isolated the DNA, and we have a definite profile of the doer. The problem is, we don't have a DNA sample for Palmiero on file. His previous collars were misdemeanors, so no one took a sample."

"The print ought to put me over the top for an arrest. We can take a sample from him then."

"If it's post-arrest, let's do it right—with a search warrant," Andy said. "I'll handle that if you want."

"That would be awesome, Andy. I'm heading into the office now. I'll let you know what Bibb says."

Paddy woke Mairead to tell her the new development on his case and that he was going to head in early. But he wanted to make sure she felt well enough to be on her own until Julissa got there.

"Go," she said. "I feel fine. I might even drag Julissa to the movies with me. Break this case. You've worked so hard on it."

***

When Paddy got into the eight-three, he called Dan Bibb to inform the prosecutor of his progress. Bibb was thrilled and couldn't help saying, "I told you so."

"With enough time and determination," Bibb said. "There's *nothing* NYPD detectives can't do."

Paddy had heard Bibb say this to other prosecutors before. He appreciated the confidence he had in them, but Paddy felt luck played a greater part in investigations than the DA was acknowledging.

"So, are you gonna ask me or not?" Bibb teased.

"May I please arrest Sergio Palmiero for the murders of the Santapadres?"

Burnt to a Crisp

"Tell Georgie I said, 'Go get that motherfucker,' and call me when you do, so that I can get started on the search warrant for the DNA."

Paddy called George Fahrbach and the rest of his team to see if they wanted to come in early. It was unanimous. They all wanted a piece of this case. Out of respect and as a way of thanking them for their hard work on the case so far, he notified his favorite fire marshals, Carpazzo and Kenneally. They were stuck in the Bronx on a commercial fire but thanked Paddy for thinking of them.

When everyone was assembled, Paddy had to admit he didn't have anything for them to do at the moment. He had no idea where Cucko was hanging his hat. They knew his last address, but that was with Emma Calderon and Mierdito. After trying to set the kid on fire, Cucko wasn't going back there. So, Paddy suggested they all get coffee while he worked the phone.

He called Tranquillo on his cell. For a change, the drug dealer picked it up on the first ring. He asked him to put the word out he wanted Cucko, and he wanted the whole neighborhood ready to call him if he poked his head up. Tranquillo promised to get his people on board. Next, he called Bungee and made the same request, but Bungee understood it was a duty, not a favor.

"If I find this motherfucker for you, will you leave me alone?"

"If *anyone* finds him for me, I will leave you alone. Just put the word out," Paddy said.

Lastly, Paddy reached out to the Santiagos. Jessica, her sister, and even her mom promised to keep an eye out for him. Peter Cammaratta deputized himself and wanted to head up his own one-man posse. Paddy advised against it.

"Just keep your eyes open and my number handy, Blanco. I don't want you to get in trouble when you have to bust him up. That's my job, and I can do it much better than you. Besides, I'm down by law. So, just make the call and let everyone know there's a pot of gold at the end of this rainbow. There's a ten thousand dollar reward on his head."

"I'm on it, Detective," Peter said.

Lieutenant Martino had been listening. The ten grand offer of reward got his attention. It was the first he heard of it, and he didn't remember reading about anyone else approving it in the case folder.

"Is that reward coming out of your own pocket?" he asked. "Because it ain't coming out of mine."

"I probably put the cart before the horse on that one, Lou. I'll call Crime Stoppers now to get it up and running."

"First, we need a *Wanted Card*," the lieutenant reminded him. "Have Georgie do that. Have Joe make a *BOLO* and run it through NCIC. I'll knock out a flyer and the unusual and call the CO of Crime Stoppers myself. We might be able to make it in time for the evening news."

Detective Maldonado, just returning from court, walked into this storm of activity. He saw Paddy and the whole C Team working the phones and the computers, and his curiosity was piqued. *The team wasn't even due in for another hour, and here they were,* he thought.

"What's going on, Paddy?" he asked.

"My arson triple just broke. If you're feeling froggy, go get ready to jump. I'm just waiting for a tip."

"You want me to help?" Aramis asked.

His voice said he was dubious.

"Are you serious?"

"I don't talk just to hear the sound of my own voice. If you want in, get your vest. You can ride with George and me when it's go time. You ever assist on a homicide collar?"

"No," Aramis admitted.

"Good. Maybe you can pop your cherry today."

Paddy's desk phone rang. The caller ID indicated it was a payphone. *This is the call*, he thought. His fingers were tingling with what felt like tiny electric charges as he picked up the phone.

"Eight-three Squad, Durr."

"Hello, Detective Durr," a nervous-sounding man said. "I don't know if you remember me. I own the bodega at Hancock and Knickerbocker."

"Sure, sure," Paddy said. "Juan Candelaria, right?"

"Yes. Bless said I should call you if Cucko popped up. Well, he's in my bodega right now making a sandwich for himself."

"How the hell did that happen?" Paddy asked, circling the index finger of his right hand above his head, the universal signal for *mount up*.

"I used to feel bad for him. I would let him work in my store for a meal and some walk-around money. He showed up today, saying he hadn't eaten. I told him to help himself."

"How did you get out of there without raising him up?" Paddy asked.

"I told him to watch the store for me while I went to the bank."

"Good thinking, Juan. Sit tight. Don't go back in the store till we come out."

Burnt to a Crisp

"Okay, Detective, but if you can manage it, please don't shoot up my bodega."

"If I don't have to, Juan, I promise I won't."

Paddy hung up and addressed his squadmates.

"Our mutt is behind the counter in the bodega on Hancock and Knickerbocker. We'll go in two cars. Joe, Armando, and Gio take the squad auto. George, Aramis, and I will take the homicide car. I know this store. There's only one way in or out. We'll come in the front and fan out. We'll shoo the customers out if there are any, and we'll just take Cucko down. Any questions?"

When he was met with resolute stares, he announced, "All right, let's cowboy the fuck up!"

***

The two unmarked cars arrived at the front of the bodega simultaneously. The detectives jumped out and advanced on the front door. Paddy was relieved to see the store empty except for Sergio Palmiero, who was at the cutting board at the end of the counter. He had a large knife in his hand, having just cut his hero sandwich in half.

Paddy advanced to within ten feet of the counter and drew his service nine-millimeter. Assuming a modified Weaver stance, he pointed the gun two-handed at Cucko.

"You're going to want to drop that knife," Paddy said calmly.

Palmiero looked up with recognition. He knew who Paddy was and why he was here. He reversed the knife in his right hand, like an experienced knife fighter. Paddy saw the insane glint in his eyes and realized he was entertaining the notion of trying to slash and dash his way through the armed detectives between him and the door.

"Really, Cucko?" Paddy said. "Are you going to make it that easy for me? I can close this case with a double-tap right now. If your heels even leave the floor, I'll make a ghost of you. Lose the fucking knife."

Evidently, Palmiero believed him. He threw the knife on the ground in front of the counter. Before it could even bounce, Aramis Maldonado, who was next to Paddy on his left, closed the ten feet between them in two long strides. He grabbed Cucko by the front of his tee-shirt and yanked him off his feet and over the low counter. Flipping him onto his belly, he rear cuffed him in one fluid motion.

Michael O'Keefe

He caught his partners by surprise. Decisive, expert, and lightning-fast were words none of them expected to be used to describe Aramis Maldonado. Finally, Joe Furio made the sound of an explosion, breaking the stunned silence.

"You know what that was?" he asked Aramis.

Aramis just shook his head.

"You didn't just bust your cherry. You nuked the motherfucker."

Burnt to a Crisp

CHAPTER THIRTY-NINE

April 5, 2017
Bushwick, Brooklyn
14:00 hours

After securing Sergio Palmiero in the interview room, Paddy notified Dan Bibb, telling him he was sending Andy Leoniak down to swear out the search warrant for Palmiero's DNA. He called Andy to tell him to get his ass down there—forthwith. The DA already had all the paperwork he would need to write the warrant application. Paddy sent Joe and Gio out to get some fillers for the line-ups he and George would conduct. Only after the IDs would they begin the all-important interrogation.

While waiting, Paddy went into the lieutenant's office to bring him up to speed on the case and sing the praises of Aramis Maldonado.

"You know, Paddy, I was a little offended you didn't ask me to come out for the apprehension," Martino said, pretending to be wounded.

"No, you're not," Paddy scoffed. "Besides, I needed your seat for Aramis—a little confidence builder, as it were."

"How'd he do?"

"Awesome! The kid is really showing some promise."

"I'm glad to hear it. I was a little concerned he might be a plant from the mayor's wife to try and get some dirt on you."

"No, quite the opposite; he hates them as much as I do."

"Wow! That's a lot of hate."

"Well, it's easy with them."

"Speaking of *them*," the lieutenant said. "Do you want to tell me how you managed to dance through the raindrops again. I thought they had you this time."

"All due respect, but as your friend, I'm not going to tell you. It's for your own protection. We'll just leave it that Health Services decided their case wasn't strong enough."

"And simultaneously, Dr. Levine decides she doesn't want to work for the police department anymore. Quite a coincidence. Then there was Inspector Crawley's unexpected retirement and the transfer of Lieutenant Wormwood from IAB to patrol in Staten Island. It all smells a little fishy."

"You don't want to know," Paddy assured him. "All I'll say is these fortunate coincidences have *everything* to do with Aramis. He's been a real warrior and put himself in harm's way to help me."

"That's good to hear," Martino said. "But an observant man like myself might conclude you have the mayor's nuts in a vise. How tight, I wonder?"

"Put it this way, boss. If you didn't already have *the money*, you would have it today."

"That tight?" Martino let out a low whistle, clearly impressed.

"You might also see the entire squad getting grade promotions in the very near future."

He looked at the lieutenant and saw the genuine wonder expressed on his face. Martino was curious, but Paddy didn't want to put him in the uncomfortable position of having to deny knowledge of a crime committed by several of his subordinates. He had worked for Martino for five years now. In that time, he had come to respect him to the point where he regarded him as the best boss he ever had. For that, Paddy was loyal and knew his loyalty was reciprocated. His impulse was to protect him. But Martino was a grown man and an experienced and savvy investigator. Knowing the lieutenant would never betray his trust, Paddy realized it wasn't his place to decide what Martino wanted to know and didn't.

"Do you really want to know?" Paddy asked.

"I do," Mariano admitted. "But I trust your instincts. If you're hesitant to tell me, maybe you shouldn't. Just promise me, when we're both retired, and the statute of limitations has expired, I want every detail."

"That's a deal."

The witnesses arrived at the precinct and were brought to the muster room and asked not to discuss the line-up until they all had looked at it and had been dismissed. Joe and Gio returned with the fillers and set the room up. The identifications were a mere formality. They all knew Cucko. Legally speaking, a line-up wasn't required. A simple confirmatory identification would have sufficed. But in a homicide case, no one wanted to leave the opportunity for the defense to suggest the IDs were suggestive, or worse—coerced. So they ran the line-ups, and video recorded them as well.

Paddy and George huddled up in the coffee room to plan their interrogation. With this defendant, there were a number of ways they could play it.

"I think we should just ambush him with the truth," George suggested. "He's an amateur, no felonies on record. He doesn't know the difference between circumstantial and red-handed."

"For an amateur, he doesn't look very nervous," Paddy said. "He's sitting there with a cat-ate-the-canary look—like he can't wait to talk to us. But I don't think ambushing him will work. If he doesn't think he can twist us or direct the narrative, he might shut down."

"What do you suggest?"

"We go in like boobs. Pretend he's here only on the strength of the two witnesses—Harold and Tranquillo. He ran by them both. So, he knows they saw him."

"What about Mierdito and Jessica's family?"

"He doesn't know we know about them. Let's lock him into a statement and let the other witnesses and evidence slip out a little at a time."

"Good thing I had a big breakfast," George said. "Sounds like we're gonna be at it for a while."

The detectives went into the room with nothing but a Miranda warnings sheet and their notepads. The idea was to let the suspect think they had very little on him. If he thought he could talk his way out, he might be more effusive. After the warnings, Cucko asked if he was under arrest.

"We haven't charged you yet," Paddy said—the truth. "The case is still under investigation. But you are not free to leave."

"What's this about?" Cucko asked.

"The fire on Wilson Avenue where those three people died," George said.

"I wasn't around that night. I haven't been to Bushwick for weeks. So, I don't know anything about it," Cucko said. "Can I go now?"

"No," said Paddy.

"Why not?"

"Because we have two witnesses who saw you go into the building and run out after it was in flames," George allowed.

"Good luck with those two," Cucko laughed. "A drug dealer and a retard—I won't even need a lawyer for this one."

"We never told you who the witnesses were," George said.

"The whole neighborhood's talking," Cucko said quickly, looking away.

"How would you hear anything from the street if you weren't around for weeks?" Paddy asked.

Cucko appeared to become nervous. He fidgeted in his chair and went after an imaginary hangnail on his thumb while he racked his brain for a way to cover his mistake. He finally looked back up to meet Paddy's impassive eyes. Durr was making an extreme effort not to bore down on the suspect with his famous glare. He wanted to keep him talking. So far, it was working.

"I spoke to Bungee on his cell," Cucko said. "He told me Weird Harold and Tranquillo were talking shit about me."

"Oh, good," Paddy said. "I have Bungee's cell phone number. What number did you call him from?"

"I don't have a cell phone. I called him from a payphone."

Paddy and George had carefully gone over Bungee's cell phone records since the incident. They both knew he didn't receive any calls from a payphone—an endangered species in today's New York. They exchanged a knowing glance and got back to work on Cucko.

"Where was this payphone?" George asked.

"In Flatbush."

"What were you doing there?"

"I was staying with a friend. Her son is fifteen and has problems. She asked me to stay awhile and see if I could help him out. Like a good influence and shit."

"Let's change the subject," Paddy said. "Tell me about the building at 407 Wilson. You used to live there. Who with?"

"Jessica Sanchez and her family. I lost touch with them. Do you know where they're living now?"

He's fishing, Paddy realized.

"We don't know," he lied.

"Why did you leave?" George asked.

"It was getting too crowded in there. Melanie's boyfriend, Blanco, moved in. He don't like me for some reason, even punched me in the face once."

Cucko snapped his fingers as if something important had just occurred to him.

"You should take a look at Blanco," he said. "He sells drugs for Bungee, and he's on Parole."

"Why would he burn the building?" George asked.

"I don't know. Maybe some drug shit?"

Paddy was ready to pause the questioning. He had listened to enough lies for now. He planned to change the tenor of the conversation when they resumed.

"We're going to take a break now," Paddy said. "Are you hungry?"

"I could eat," Cucko said.

"Italian food okay?" George asked.

"Yeah, sure."

"Okay, Cucko," Paddy said. "When I come back with your meal, I want you to consider that we know more than we're letting on. Think about how long it took to do the line-ups. We've got more than two witnesses. See you when the food comes in."

When Paddy came out of the room, he told Joe Furio to keep the videos and mikes rolling. Cucko might be one of those rare imbeciles who talked to himself, thinking he had a modicum of privacy in a police facility. The other advantage was, they could monitor how nervous he was in their absence. If he was fidgety and anxious, it might be time to ratchet up his stress level by making the questioning more confrontational. One thing had already been accomplished. They had Cucko locked into several provable lies. They would build off of that.

While they waited for the food to be delivered, Andy Leoniak came into the squad with the signed and sworn search warrant for Sergio's DNA and a kit to retrieve it. Paddy brought Andy up to speed on the interrogation so far. This was so he didn't tip anything off, which hadn't yet been discussed. Paddy had an idea.

"When we go into the room to get the DNA, don't be nice to him. He's a curious fucker. When he asks you why we need his DNA, ask him if he touched anything the morning of the fire he might have left DNA on. Let him chew on that for a while."

"So we're going to start showing him our cards?" George asked.

"Yeah," Paddy said. "He thinks we've got a small pair. In the next hour, he's gonna find out it's a straight flush."

After Cucko devoured his spaghetti and meatballs, washing it down with a Tropical Fantasy pineapple soda, the detectives entered the room.

"This is Detective Leoniak from the Crime Scene Unit, and this is a search warrant for your DNA," Paddy said, placing a copy of the warrant on the table in front of Cucko.

"What if I refuse?" Cucko said.

"You see that warrant?" Andy said. "It authorizes me to use force. If I want to, I can use a Hurst Tool to open your mouth."

"What's a Hurst Tool?" Cucko asked.

"The *Jaws of Life*," Andy said. "We use them to tear the tops off of cars. They'll have no trouble prying open your weak little pie-hole."

"I don't think I like him," Cucko said.

"Well, that's a *you* problem, Fucko," Andy answered. "Now, are you gonna say "ah" for me, or am I gonna get creative?"

Cucko took one look at the burly detective with the rubber gloves and the menacing scowl and elected to open wide. Leoniak inserted a swab into the suspect's mouth, rubbing the inside of his cheeks, collecting saliva and skin cells. He slid the swab into a test tube, taping the stopper shut and initialing it.

"Why do you need my DNA?" Cucko asked.

"Because you left something at the crime with some of you on it. Now we'll have the proof it was yours. You're gonna fry for this, motherfucker," Andy said.

Paddy enjoyed the concerned look on Cucko's face. He could almost smell the wood burning in his head while the suspect was thinking hard for an innocuous reason his DNA might be part of a crime scene. He was still puzzling it out when Paddy interrupted him.

"Don't go anywhere," he said, with all the sarcasm he could muster, before leading the other detectives out of the room.

"That felt great," Andy said.

"It had the intended effect. He's shitting his pants right now," said George.

"You know," Leoniak went on. "I've been in Crime Scene for the last twenty years. I forgot how satisfying it was to look in the eyes of a murderer and call him a motherfucker to his face. I got an idea now why you haven't retired yet, Paddy."

"Oh, we're just getting started putting this miscreant through his changes," Paddy said. "By the time we're finished, he'll beg to confess."

"How long is that gonna take?" Andy asked.

"As long as it does." George smiled.

This time, when they returned to the room, Paddy brought the homicide box. Stenciled on all four sides were the words *People of the State of New York Vs. Sergio Palmiero* and *Homicides # 4, 5, 6*. In smaller letters underneath were the victims' names in the order they had expired. This was purely for Cucko's benefit. Paddy stenciled it there after Bibb greenlighted the arrest. The gloves were off, and now Palmiero knew it.

Burnt to a Crisp

Paddy had him move away from the table and sit in one of the hard-backed line-up chairs, taking another for himself. He sat close to Cucko, leaving only inches between them. Now he broke out the famous Durr stare.

"Let's go over a few things," Paddy began. "Partly to refresh, and partly to ensure we don't have to keep going over the same bullshit we already know is bullshit. We have seven witnesses. Two of them saw you go into the hallway with a can of kerosene. Then they saw you run out, still with the kerosene can, the hallway already in flames. You ran right past Harold on the corner, and he watched you throw the can on the roof of a garage on Gates."

Paddy paused for a minute to let that sink in.

"George," he began again. "Hand me the crime scene photos from Andy's B-run."

George went into the box and retrieved the photos, handing them to Paddy. He dropped them in Cucko's lap.

"Go ahead. Look at em'," Paddy said. "That's the can. We know you had it because we have your thumbprint on the handle. In addition, the kerosene used to light the building up is a chemical match to the residue found in the can. We also have your DNA. Skin cells left by you have already been isolated. With the sample taken out of your mouth just this evening, it'll take a little time, but the lab will match the two. I'm telling you this, so you understand, stone-walling me won't help. Every lie you tell just makes you look guiltier."

"You said you have seven witnesses," Cucko said. "That's only two."

"Good, you're paying attention," Paddy said. "Melanie and Blanco will testify you came to the apartment to threaten Jessica. She wasn't around, so you told them, '*Ya'mo* burn that house to the fucking ground!' Those were your words. Then the next day, the place goes up like tinder. I don't believe in coincidences. Neither will a jury."

"That's still only four witnesses," he said, a look of supreme smugness on his face.

How many witnesses does this asshole think I need? Paddy wondered.

"Okay, you want more?" Paddy asked. "Mierdito tells us the day before the fire; you told him you were going to do it. Then after you did it, you warned him if he told anyone, you would burn him next. I guess you didn't trust him because you tried to set him on fire in his bed. He was fortunate for two reasons; he wets the bed—a lot, and you were out of kerosene."

"Who is the other witness?"

"You know who she is," Paddy said. "We'll get to her in a while."

"Why not now?"

"Because I want you to think about the case I already have against you. I got you lock, stock, and barrel. You did it. The fact you set the fire is already proven beyond a reasonable doubt."

"If you already got me," Cucko said. "Why should I talk to you?"

"Good question," Paddy said. "Maybe you have some justification we don't know about. Because as it stands now, you look like a callous firebug who torched a building in the middle of the night where three people died. You haven't said why. Doesn't it bother you that an old couple and their disabled son perished in a fire you set?"

Cucko looked directly back into Paddy's eyes. The two of them keeping eye contact, neither blinking. Paddy considered what he saw there—or rather, what he didn't. Nothing was staring back at him. He realized Cucko's sense of guilt could not be appealed to. Paddy wouldn't be bringing this suspect's conscience into the conversation—because he didn't have one. The staring contest ended when Cucko sat back and shrugged, those flat soulless eyes laughing at Paddy as if to say, *Who gives a fuck?*

Paddy got up and collected the case box. He knew now what he needed to know.

"You think about what we've got on you. Then we'll come back in to address the Jessica Santiago situation," Paddy said as he and George left the room.

Back in the coffee room, they discussed their next tactic.

"He didn't even blink when you brought up the victims," George said.

"That's because he doesn't care."

"How do we appeal to his empathy when he doesn't have any?" George asked.

"I'm not wasting my time with that. He's a psychopath. It's a futile endeavor. I saw it when I looked into his eyes. He's dead inside."

"So, what do we do?"

"I'm going to strip him of his dignity. You see how smug he is; all he has is his pride. We'll crush that, make him question his worth as a human being. Deep down, he believes he was justified. He wants us to believe it too. Hell, he wants to brag about it. If we can touch his tender spot, he just might crumble."

"I'll follow your lead, Paddy. Just tell me what you want me to do."

"When I start deconstructing him, laugh when I make a point. Let him know how despicable and weak you think he is. There will be no 'good cops' in the

Burnt to a Crisp

room from here on out. It's 'bad cop, bad cop' now. Let's give him a half-hour to stew. Then we'll have at him again."

This time when they went back into the room, they were empty-handed. Paddy had everything he needed in his head. He resumed his position, invading Cucko's personal space. *If I wanted*, Paddy thought, *I could lean forward and kiss him. Or bite the nose right off his smug little face.* This is what cascaded through Paddy's mind before he shook it off and got down to business.

"You had a good run living with the Santiagos before you fucked it up," Paddy said. "Jessica was a major upgrade for you, based upon what I could see of Emma. You must have a vendetta on your prick to lay down with her. She's a walking public service announcement. 'Crack is whack,' is what Keith Herring said. But I guess a gutter-snife like you figures the only bad sex is the sex you're not getting. But enough about where you stick your dick. It's meaningless.

"At heart, you're just a petty thief. You couldn't resist breaking into your neighbors' apartments while they were at work. Do you even know them? Or were they just nameless potential victims? They had stuff you wanted. So you took it. Of course, they knew you did it. The only job you ever had before was when you were steering for Bungee. But you couldn't even cut it as a doorman for junkies. You had to start robbing the customers. Your natural inclination to be a fuck-up is otherworldly in scope. You are a Grand Master. Do I have that about right?"

Cucko didn't answer, but Paddy could see he was getting angry. His gaze boring through Durr, his flat brown eyes finally showing a spark of human emotion. *Getting there*, Paddy thought.

"Let's talk about Jessica. You knocked her up with your demon seed. She had already thrown you out when she found out. That had to be a kick in the ass for her. She thought she was rid of you only to discover you left an infection in her womb. But to the curb, you went anyway, with everything you own in a plastic Stop and Shop bag—how fucking pathetic is that?"

George cackled, drawing a glare from Cucko, who sucked his teeth. Paddy could feel the fury growing inside him.

"You are truly alone in this world, and it's your own fault," Paddy continued. "You take advantage of everyone you meet. You have no friends. You alienate them all. Even Juan Candelaria, who once pitied you, called me when you showed up at his bodega. He couldn't wait to give you up. You have no family…"

"That's not true!" Cucko spat, interrupting him. "I have a mother in Puerto Rico."

"Oh, yeah? Where exactly?" Paddy challenged him.

"I don't know," he admitted, trying to look at the floor, but Durr was too close, forcing Cucko to look in his face.

"You don't know," Paddy laughed, "because you are such a scum-bucket, your own mother, your flesh, and blood, wants *nothing* to do with you. She won't even tell you where she lives, afraid you might come back around to further ruin her life. Nah, you've got nobody. You ingratiate yourself to people just long enough to be invited to crash at their place—until they figure out what you are; a parasite. You latch on to a host and suck them dry. Then you're back on the street again. That's what happened with Jessica, isn't it?"

"Why do you care?" Cucko asked.

"Because it fascinates me. But to her, you were worse than a parasite. You managed to infect her with your sickness. You were a virus, leaving your disease behind. I don't blame her."

"Don't blame her for what?" Cucko demanded.

"You know what," Paddy baited him. "You thought that as worthless as you were, you could still leave something endurable behind—something to prove to the world that you were ever here. It's why you came back to the apartment, to beg her to keep the baby—your baby. When you found out she was going to have an abortion, you started threatening her. You told everyone what you were going to do if she killed your child. But aborting your offspring was a public service. Nobody wants your inferior shit in their gene pool, making it more shallow. When you found out she terminated the pregnancy; you did what you promised—but not well. Like everything else in your life, you fucked it up. Jessica and her family escaped, and you killed three innocent people. God, you're pathetic."

"Pathetic? No!" Cucko yelled. "I told that *asesina puta* if she killed my baby I would burn her house down. So, I fucking burned it!"

"Yes, you did," Paddy said. "And now I know why."

"Fuck you, Durr! You fucked up, and you don't even know it."

"How's that?" Paddy asked, grinning.

"You told me who the witnesses are. The first thing I'm gonna do when I get outta here is kill every one of them!"

"You think you're getting out of here?" George laughed. "You committed a triple homicide. That's three consecutive life sentences. You'd have to be reincarnated three times to even see the sun again. You're dying in jail, Cucko."

"I'll make bail," he said, defiance in his voice.

"Not after threatening to kill the witnesses," George reminded him. "No, you're done. On the bright side, you won't have to serve much of that sentence."

"Why not?" Cucko asked.

He seemed to sense an out for himself, real hope flashing in his eyes. Paddy was quick to slam the door shut on that.

"Your victims were the parents and the little brother of a deadly—and now motivated—drug lord. Bless has plans for you. I would expect your incarceration to be a short one."

A look of abject shock appeared on Cucko's face. He hadn't known who the victims were. To him, they were just *the old fucks and their retard on the fourth floor*. He never bothered to even learn their names. A wave of realization washed over him. It was quickly replaced by panic, finally morphing into resolute despair.

"Oh, fuck me! Fuck me!" he wailed, grabbing his temples, burying his head between his knees.

"Why would anyone bother?" Paddy asked. "You seem so determined to fuck yourself."

Michael O'Keefe

CHAPTER FORTY

April 5, 2017
Bushwick, Brooklyn
18:00 hours

After briefing the lieutenant on the successful interrogation, Paddy went back into the interview room to see if Cucko wanted to be interviewed by the DA.

"Fuck you, *cabron*," Cucko said. "I want a lawyer."

"Now?" Paddy asked. "You should have asked for one of those this morning."

Paddy called Dan Bibb to tell him what happened, informing him Cucko had lawyered-up and wouldn't be talking to him. Dan was disappointed only because he wouldn't get the opportunity to confront him across the table. He knew from experience working with Paddy and George, the video from the interrogation would be sufficient to nail down the coffin. But he insisted on watching it anyway.

When Dan got there, he sat down at Lieutenant Martino's desk to watch the feed already uploaded on Martino's computer. When he came out, he was impressed.

"You got him," Dan said. "Though I could have done without the name-calling."

"No, you couldn't have," Paddy said. "If we didn't shame him, he never would have given it up. He would still be sitting in that chair with that stupid, smug expression—instead of tearing his hair out and crying because he knows he's finished."

"I guess. But, you and Leoniak are probably going to get your balls broken on cross-examination."

"Not for long," Paddy said.

"Why not?"

"Because when defense counsel asks if I called the defendant a motherfucker, I am going to smile at the jury and say, 'Yes.' If counsel is stupid enough to ask me why, I'm going to smile even wider and say, 'Because the defendant is a murdering motherfucker.' Any further questioning along those lines and you will object, as the question has already been asked and answered."

"Are you *sure* you don't want to try this case, Paddy?" Bibb laughed.

"You can take it from here, Dan-o."

Bibb seemed to be mulling something over; he wanted to say something but was unsure if he was pushing his luck. Paddy knew it was coming no matter.

"You know what I would like?" Bibb asked.

"Oh, Christ. Here we go," George said, rolling his eyes.

"I would love to know where he got the kerosene."

"What's the matter, Dan?" Paddy asked. "The ribbon on this gift-wrapped case isn't decorative enough for you?"

After the complaint was written, Paddy and George took Cucko to Central Booking. Lieutenant Martino had made all the notifications downtown. He called the commanding officer of DCPI to see if there was any media interest in a *walk-out*; the classic staged event where the defendant is led out of the precinct in handcuffs, cameras flashing, and is placed into a squad car to be whisked to jail. There was none. Evidently, the arrest of a depraved arsonist who murdered three innocents in the poorer part of Bushwick was not newsworthy.

Paddy found the disinterest depressing but not unexpected. If the victims had been hipsters from the other end of the precinct, or if the fire had occurred in Manhattan, the case would have been front-page news. Paddy knew the mass media in this city were the arbiters of which lives mattered and which ones didn't. To the press, the Santapadres were of the wrong social strata to be of any importance. So, they walked Cucko down the back stairs, into the rear parking lot, and drove him unceremoniously to jail.

"This is bullshit," George said. "It seems nobody cared about these people but us."

"Then we were the right guys to catch this case," Paddy said. "We don't do this job for fame and fortune. There is none. We do it because if we don't, no one else will."

***

After dumping Cucko at Central Booking, Paddy and George returned to the eight-three to go end-of-tour. They'd be back at it early the next morning, getting the case ready for the grand jury. After signing out, Paddy headed for home.

On his way up Cooper Street, at the corner of Irving Avenue, something blue and white flashed in his peripheral vision. The color and shape of the kerosene can; he thought he saw it in the window of the bodega on the corner. Paddy swung a couple of u-turns and pulled in front of the store. Sure enough, in the front window were four cans of *Esparza queroseño,* identical to the one recovered on the garage roof on Gates Avenue.

Paddy went into the bodega to speak with the clerk. He identified himself and asked directly about the kerosene in the window.

"Why do you want to know?" the clerk asked.

"Look," Paddy said. "I'm not Customs Enforcement, and I'm not the EPA. I've had a long day. Please just answer my questions."

The clerk laughed. He could see the fatigue in Paddy's face. From the detective's plaintive eyes, he gathered he meant him no harm.

"I'm Pedro Ruiz," he said, offering his hand. Paddy shook it. "My brother Nestor and I own the store. About eight months ago, a guy in a beat-up pick-up truck with a bed full of this Puerto Rican kerosene going for cheap wants to sell us some. Nestor takes five cans off him. That was a mistake. It's been sitting in our window ever since. *Nobody* in this neighborhood uses kerosene."

"There are only four cans left," Paddy observed. "Somebody bought one."

"Yeah, that fucking asshole, Cucko. Do you know him?"

"I know him a little," Paddy laughed. "When did he buy it?"

"It was a weekend night…actually morning. A couple of weeks ago, in the middle of the month. I was open late cause the *skells* were still hanging around buying Heinekens and loosies."

"About what time?"

"It was around 1:30 in the morning."

"Monday, March 13[th,] maybe?" Paddy asked.

"Yeah, that sounds about right."

Burnt to a Crisp

"How do you know Cucko?"

"He's a pain in my ass," Pedro said. "I sell loosies; seventy-five cents for one, two for a buck. He's always trying to get me down to fifty cents a smoke. Sometimes I cave in just to get rid of him. That morning he comes in and wants a can of kerosene. I told him 'five bucks.' The fucking asshole wants to negotiate. I ask him, 'What the fuck do you need kerosene for?' He tells me he's got a hot date. I tell him, 'You couldn't get laid in a ten-cent whorehouse with a seabag full of dimes.' I went down to three bucks and sent him on his way with the kerosene. Come to think of it; I haven't seen him since."

"Are you willing to identify him?"

"Sure. Why?"

"I'll tell you after you ID him."

Paddy called the squad and got Aramis Maldonado on the phone. He asked him to bring a photo pack with Cucko up to the bodega. A few minutes later, Pedro identified Cucko and asked what he did.

"He took the can of kerosene and burned down an apartment house on Wilson," Paddy said.

"Oh, fuck! Not the one where that family died?"

"That's the one."

"I'm dumping the rest of that kerosene."

"I'll be taking a can off your hands," Paddy said. "I'll need to send it to the lab to compare it to the one we recovered."

Paddy took a five-dollar bill out of his pocket and tried to hand it over the counter to Pedro. He waved Paddy off.

"Just take it," he said. "That shit is cursed."

"Thanks," Paddy said. "I need you to do one more thing for me. A district attorney needs to come here to record your statement."

"Whatever I can do to help, Detective."

Paddy called Dan Bibb on his cell phone.

"What's up, Paddy?" Bibb asked.

"Meet me at the bodega on Cooper and Irving and bring a tape recorder. I found your fucking kerosene."

Michael O'Keefe

CHAPTER FORTY-ONE

Spring 2017-Winter 2018
Brooklyn

Sergio Palmiero was indicted for the three murders of the Santapadres and remanded to Rikers Island pending trial. Much to his chagrin, he did not make bail, contrary to his prediction. None was offered. His attorney laughed at him when he mentioned it.

"Are you out of your mind?" the attorney asked. "This is a triple homicide. You're a predicate felon. The Son of Sam had a better shot at bail than you."

***

Aramis Maldonado continued to work hard to assimilate into the detective squad. He demonstrated a natural inquisitiveness and a talent for investigation once given a chance and a little direction from Paddy Durr and Joe Furio. Finally deciding to come out publicly—beginning with his squadmates, he was surprised when no one seemed to care one way or the other. Only one of his fellow detectives had a question.

"So, what do you want to do for dinner?" Gio Fernandez asked.

Burnt to a Crisp

***

Before the hearings and trial, Sergio Palmiero was attacked on a stairwell inside the Anna M. Kross Center, the dormitory for pretrial detainees on Rikers Island. Another inmate, a former drug associate of Sammy Bando, was awaiting trial himself for a triple murder. He had killed his wife, her mother, and his stepdaughter in a drug-induced, paranoid rage. He jumped Cucko without provocation and stabbed him more than thirty times in the right shoulder with a homemade shiv, fashioned from a metal serving spoon smuggled out of the cafeteria. He was overheard by guards telling Cucko, "Bless sends his regards."

Palmiero didn't die, but he nearly lost his right arm. In any event, he would never again be able to use it. It would dangle for the rest of his life like a dead mackerel from his wrecked shoulder.

Paddy got word of the assault from Dan Bibb. He went over to see Bless at his home in Queens. For once, he was welcome, invited in, and served coffee. They spoke at the kitchen table.

"I know I told you I didn't care what happened to Cucko after the arrest," Paddy said, absently stirring his coffee. "But I put a lot of work into this case. It might be the tightest homicide I've ever handled. As a matter of personal pride, I'd like to see the scumbag convicted and sentenced to spend the rest of his miserable life in prison. After that, when or how his life ends is of no consequence to me."

"I want what you want," Bless said, holding his hands out as if in supplication.

"What happened this week at Rikers seems like someone else has their own plan."

"Not so much," Bless said, pointedly making eye contact. "I don't think the assailant intended to kill him. Or, he would have stabbed him somewhere other than the shoulder."

Paddy decided not to point out that Bless knew many of the details about the event, which Paddy hadn't divulged. The silence hung between them as the two men understood their respective roles in the conversation.

"Do you think someone was just sending a message?" Paddy asked.

"So it would seem," Bless said. His face took on a more serious edge when he asked, "What happens if he beats the case, gets off on some technicality, and walks away scot-free?"

"The world would have to slide off its axis for him to beat this case," Paddy said.

"Yeah, but what if it does?"

Paddy slammed his open right hand on the table, knocking the teaspoon from his coffee cup. He brought the hand up and crossed his heart.

"On my life," he swore. "If the universe turns upside down and that miscreant somehow beats this air-tight case, I will murder the son-of-a-bitch myself."

"That's good enough for me," Bless said, smiling. "I'm sure he'll be fine at least until he gets upstate. Then, all bets are off."

"Not my jurisdiction," Durr said.

Bless looked off into the distance as if he had something to say and was trying to frame the proper words with which to say it. Paddy sipped his coffee and waited for him to continue.

"On behalf of my sister and I, we want to thank you for all you did for our family," Bless began. "No one usually cares about people like us. At least the cops and the city never have. But you put all of yourself into this case. Even when I was being an asshole to you, you never gave up. I wanted to do something for you, to show our appreciation, but Cassie said you wouldn't take it."

"She was right," Paddy nodded. "Besides, doing the right thing for your parents and brother is reward enough."

Bless nodded, silently acknowledging his sincerity.

"With all I'm into, I took a chance trusting you," Bless said. "I'm glad I did. You did everything you said you would, and you kept my business out of it."

"That's only because your business wasn't part of it."

Bless laughed. "If it had been, we wouldn't be having this conversation; I take it?"

"Nah," Paddy chuckled. "You would have been waiting for trial on Rikers with Cucko."

"That's a given," Bless acknowledged. "I'm thinking of divesting myself from Bushwick anyway. I've got enough legitimate interests now. I figure, why not leave the risk and aggravation of playing cat and mouse with the law to someone else."

"Now would be a good time," Paddy agreed. "Your managers are compromised. You should sell your interests now and take what you can get before one of them steps on their dicks and tries to trade you for a plea deal."

"Do you know something I don't, Detective?"

"I probably know a lot of things you don't," Paddy said, smiling. "But that's all I can say about it."

As the two finished their coffee and got up from the table, Bless reached out to shake Paddy's hand.

"Thank you again," he said. Evidently, the gesture didn't fully convey his appreciation. He reached out and enclosed Paddy in an embrace.

**

A few months later, the FBI dropped the hammer on Detective George Nova. As Paddy had anticipated, they botched their case, exposing themselves before they were able to prove Nova sold or benefitted from selling drugs. The only one who could testify that he did was Tranquillo, who flipped on Nova at the first opportunity. But he was a co-conspirator. Without other corroboration, they couldn't charge him with the drugs. They were left with a worthless criminal association case—not even a crime in state court.

The feds had spent an exorbitant amount of money trying to get Nova. They pulled out all the stops, from round-the-clock surveillance to Title III wiretaps and throwing wads of cash at informants to turn on him. It all turned up nothing. They jumped him prematurely. Because of that, Paddy knew they were left holding a stinking bag of shit. The FBI came looking for Durr to rescue them from their own incompetence.

Agent Dennis Pritchard had the gall to visit him at his own home—to beg Paddy to help them substantiate an obstruction of justice charge against Nova. Durr physically shoved Pritchard off his porch and kept pushing until the agent was standing in the street.

"I told you assholes I wasn't doing your jobs for you," Paddy seethed. "Now you've fucked up your case and want me to rescue it by testifying against Nova. It's not going to happen. For the last time, George Nova did not obstruct my homicide case. He doesn't make a pimple on my ass as far as I'm concerned. Now, stay off my fucking property."

Paddy knew he was forestalling the inevitable. Eventually, they would subpoena him, and he would have to deal with the problem of Detective George Nova. But he wasn't about to make it easy for the FBI. For his entire career, they had done nothing but complicate his life. He would return the favor for as long as possible.

Michael O'Keefe

***

Early the next winter, Sergio Palmiero went on trial for the murders of Bernardo, Lucinda, and Giorgio Santapadre in New York State Supreme Court in Brooklyn. The case for his guilt was overwhelming. Between the compelling witness testimony, physical evidence, and the confession, Cucko's attorney had few options in the way of a defense. He went with the old standbys; *the cops were lying, the evidence was manufactured, the confession coerced, and the government had framed his client.* How or why anyone would want to frame Palmiero was never discussed, let alone proven. All this tactic served to do was further annoy and alienate the jury, who had already begun to detest the defendant and his strident, condescending lawyer.

They were out for deliberation for only an hour, and that was just so they could finish their lunch. They came back and found the defendant guilty of all counts, the foreman even asking if they could tack on some of the lesser, included charges. They were informed they would have to satisfy themselves with the three counts of murder and the arson.

A week later, they were back in court for the sentencing. Paddy wasn't sure if Cucko had developed an uncommon level of composure, or he didn't comprehend he had breathed his last gulp of air as a free man, but he seemed calm and resolute as he listened to his fate. The judge began by saying his only disappointment was that he couldn't sentence the defendant to death, the option no longer available in New York State. He did the next best thing, giving Palmiero three consecutive life sentences for the murders and an additional forty years more for the arson—basically death by a lifetime of incarceration. Cucko shrugged when asked if he understood the sentence. But then he made the mistake of making eye contact with Bless. He regarded Cucko with a knowing smile that was so sinister and diabolical; it gave Paddy chills.

Cucko fell apart completely. He had to be carried out of the courtroom by the court officers—a handcuffed, weeping, blubbering mess of pure misery. It was as if he finally comprehended that his life sentence would last only long enough for him to get his cell block assignment at Dannemora.

The murderer who had assaulted Cucko at Rikers—crippling him—had pled guilty and was serving his own triple-life sentence. He was waiting for Cucko in general population. Palmiero's first day in the exercise yard would be his last one on earth. Stabbing him numerous times in both lungs with another homemade shiv—this one carved out of the handle of a toothbrush—Palmiero died slowly and in pain, suffocating and drowning simultaneously from the blood pooling in his useless, shredded lungs.

That the killer was even at Dannemora and had access to Palmiero after having seriously assaulted him in jail was chalked up to an oversight and bad luck. Paddy remembered the look Bless gave Cucko at the sentencing and thought influence and bribery probably had more to do with it. But there was no escaping the pristine justice of it. So, he kept his reservations to himself.

***

During this time frame, Mairead had continued with her gene therapy. Two weeks after Cucko's arrest, she and Paddy went back to Memorial Sloan Kettering for her third infusion of stem cells. After this, her blood work was encouraging. Her cell counts were at optimum levels. The results of her CT scan were even better. The tumors on her lymph nodes were gone as if they had never been there. The tumor entwined in her lower spine was finally shrinking. Dr. Cheng was ecstatic. He had never seen such a positive response. But gene therapy was in its infancy, so there wasn't that large a body of evidence with which to compare it. He was very pleased, nonetheless. The tumor wasn't small enough yet to plan a surgery, but he was confident it was in Mairead's near future.

As pain-free movement was out of the question as long as the tumor was resting on her spine, Mairead wanted it out of her body as soon as possible. She accepted the doctor's advice and would remain patient. But as soon as the tumor was small enough to mitigate the danger, she expected to be on the operating table.

"As soon as I can get at the mass and be sure I won't damage your spine, we'll go and get it," Dr. Cheng promised.

"Is she in remission?" Paddy asked.

"I won't call it that yet," Cheng said. "But I expect to. I'm hoping one day soon to call her *cancer-free*."

Mairead continued her treatment and continued to improve. After three more infusions and positive examinations, Paddy suggested sending the hospital gurney back to the DEA. It was presently sitting in their garage—swapped out with the furniture that was back in the living room where it belonged.

"I don't want to jinx it, Paddy. We're not out of the woods yet. Cancer is insidious. It has a nasty way of coming back. For now, let's leave the bed right where it is.

Michael O'Keefe

ACKNOWLEDGMENTS

Burnt to a Crisp is the third installment in the Detective Paddy Durr Series, based on another of my old homicide cases while working as a Detective in the 83 Squad. It has been said that the truth is stranger than fiction. While this is true, I made factual changes wherever I felt like, to improve upon what was already—in my humble opinion—a thoroughly gripping story of love, loss, devotion, and justice. I have many people to thank.

My friend and classmate from Saint Francis Prep, Lynn Mitchell Connolly, has worked for many years in the field of oncology. She is also a fan of my novels, particularly my heroine, Mairead Durr. She was kind enough to give my plotline involving experimental cancer therapies the thumbs-up for plausibility. It turns out I didn't have too much to worry about. The fields of gene and immunotherapies are expanding so rapidly that nothing is implausible anymore. This is good news for my wife and me and the thousands of other surviving 9/11 first responders who would like very much not to die of a rare cancer stemming from our service then.

As this story unfolds in the 83 Squad in Bushwick, my characters are based on my old partners and supervisors. While I changed their names because many of them are still active, their characters will be readily recognizable to anyone who ever met them. I could not have become the detective I did without their help. As such, I would have no stories to tell without them. So this book is as much theirs as it is mine. I am not sharing the royalties, though. Thanks nonetheless to Detectives Joe Tallarine, Artie Barragan, Geoff Hernandez, and the best squad boss I ever worked for, Marc Marino.

As the murder in the story was an arson, in the actual case, two senior fire marshals were instrumental in the investigation. I couldn't have solved the case without their expertise and hard work. Appearing in the novel as Fire Marshals

Burnt to a Crisp

Dan Capparzo and Tom Keneally, Dan Caruso and Tom Kane were essential to the successful conclusion of the case, working tirelessly in the pursuit of justice. And I never had so much fun hanging out with firemen.

Appearing in the book as himself is Retired 2nd grade Detective Andrew Leoniak, my former late tour partner in the "old" 34 Precinct. An accomplished crime scene investigator, he was a fun addition to the story for me. I also got to tell the old war story that gave birth to an ironic and ridiculous nickname that was thrust upon us. We still call each other Handsome Avengers and get a good laugh when we do.

Paddy Durr's partner for this case, and my partner for the actual murder investigation, retired 1st Grade Detective George Fahrbach, from Brooklyn North Homicide, is a dear friend. I was fortunate to be able to work with him on several murders in my career. Brilliant isn't a strong enough word. Unfortunately, I was forced to roughen George's dialogue so as to differentiate his speaking style from Paddy Durr's. Any grammatical errors found in his lines were put there by me. George is every bit as well-spoken as Durr, but I had to make them sound different as a service to the reader. I think his brilliance surfaced unscathed despite my butchery. Genius emerges. It's just what it does.

Dan Bibb is a legendary homicide prosecutor from Manhattan. He is an old friend dating back to the mid-1980s when I was a young pup in the Anti-Crime Unit in the three-four. His integrity, professionalism, and status as an all-around great guy made him easy to write into the story. I know he is none too happy about being portrayed as working in Brooklyn, but I think I did his larger-than-life personality justice. So, hopefully, he'll get over it.

Also getting a mention was retired 2nd Grade Detective Sam Gribben. Sam was my training detective when I was a rookie. He is the one who talked me into heading uptown to the three-four, where all the trouble started. He remains a great friend and a wonderful source for NYPD lore in the '70s and '80s.

When I needed another attorney for Paddy Durr during his confrontation with the evil psychiatrist, another prosecutor from Manhattan, who has provided me with legal services and tons of free advice over the years, was my friend Steve Losquadro. A brilliant and principled attorney, he graciously allowed me to use his name. And I continue to forward it to any friends in need of a good lawyer.

A special thank you and shout-out goes to Pete Walsh and Dave Hunt. My dear friends since my days in the Heights, they are the owners of the legendary Coogan's Bar and Restaurant in Washington Heights. They graciously hosted the launch parties for my previous books. Tragically, they were forced to close the bar because of the pandemic. A Manhattan institution is no more. But it lives on in the hearts and minds of its loyal patrons, and it will live on in the pages of my novels. I featured Dave, Pete, and Coogan's in *Burnt to a Crisp* and will do so in my future books. Thank you guys for all you've done for me. Slainte.

A very gracious thank you to all my beta readers from the Farmingdale Creative Writers Group, the Long Island Literary Guild, Mystery Writers of America, The International Thriller Writers, and the Future Best-Selling Novelists of Long Island. Their attention to detail, advice, and feedback was essential in crafting this novel.

Since undertaking this writing journey, I have been fortunate to develop a following. It's nice to know that people care as deeply about my characters and their stories as I do. But two followers stand out above the many others. My dear friend Patricia Pasqua has become such a fan of my writing that she asks me every day she sees me in the gym when the next book is coming out. She's so loyal; she started re-reading my first novels. As a result, I let her have a first look at the manuscript for *Burnt to a Crisp*. Pat is a discerning reader, and she loved it. I hope you agree.

Inestimable credit goes to my lovely wife, Janet. She is my first and primary reader. No one gets to see my work unless Janet has given it her seal of approval. She has been instrumental in suggesting plot threads and character developments that are always on point and invariably end up in my novels. So, they are as much her's as mine. Ever my muse, I doubt I would be writing without her firm and unwavering support. Yeah, she inspires me like that.

Thanks to my children Ryan and Kelly. They tolerate me monopolizing the kitchen table to write and endure my voice when I read aloud. Ryan also serves as an ego check, occasionally whispering in my ear, "Remember Caesar, you are mortal," when he suspects my head is getting too big. Kelly is my primary helper at my launches and author events, setting up my table and selling my books. I know she won't cheat me, and she knows I won't skimp with the profit-sharing.

A big thank you goes out to my friend and neighbor, Patty Buckheit, who assists me with my cover designs. She brings a professionalism and expertise to my wild ass creativity that wouldn't be there without her. Patty and her wife, Michelle Antinucci, also assisted me by reading the manuscript and making key suggestions to help the narrative.

Most importantly, I need to thank my editor, my mentor, and my dear friend, Judy Turek. Known professionally as J R Turek, she is a celebrated award-winning poet who has written at least a poem a day for 15 years. I trust her editing and advice absolutely. None of my writing will see the light of day until it is well marked by her purple pen—yes, purple. And she has never steered me wrong.

Lastly, to my readers, thank you for continuing to appreciate my work. These books are for you. I hope you like reading them as much as I enjoy writing them.

Michael O'Keefe

What they're saying about *Burnt to a Crisp*, By Michael O'Keefe.

"Nobody writes New York cops—or police work—better than Michael O'Keefe. With *Burnt to a Crisp*, he re-introduces Paddy Durr, a stellar detective and flawed human being, and sends him on an investigation involving arson and murder. You want mindless action and cardboard cliches, watch a TV cop show. You want to experience the granular detail of detective work through the experiences of fully realized characters who happen to be police officers and public servants, read *Burnt to a Crisp*. Do yourself a favor, get this book -- NOW."

T.J. English, Best Selling author of the true-crime classics, *The Westies, Paddy Whacked, The Corporation, Havana Nocturne,* and *Where the Bodies are Buried.*

"*Burnt To A Crisp* grabs you by the collar and won't let go. The novel holds nothing back; revealing a heartfelt and brutal reality. Having witnessed the worst of human nature as a New York City detective, O'Keefe knows firsthand the ravages poverty, drugs, and alcohol can cause. His Irish roots add to the authenticity of his prose, as he obviously has up close and personal experience with the social ills he describes. Reading *Burnt To A Crisp* made me feel like I was riding right alongside Paddy Durr cruising the streets of Brooklyn, canvassing the neighborhood in search of the evidence to bring closure to some poor victim's family. You can't get more authentic than that!"

Bill Cannon, Sergeant of Detectives, NYPD, Manhattan North Homicide Squad-Retired, host of the hit Podcast, *Police Off the Cuff-Real Crime Stories.*

"Burnt to a Crisp takes the reader for an intimate and up-close ride through the bitter recesses of life as a New York City detective, with all the grit and chaos—treating them to all the authentic dialogue, action, and emotion only a former Detective can accurately convey. After reading this outstanding procedural the only question the reader will have is, when will Paddy Durr catch his next case? Another tremendous novel by an extraordinary Author."

Steve Aberle, Edelweiss & Net Galley reviewer, Book blogger @ Greatmysteriesandthrillers.weebly.com

---

"Detective Paddy Durr and his heroic wife, Mairead, are back in the long-awaited follow-up to *Shot to Pieces*. But the road isn't any smoother for them in *Burnt to a Crisp*. Mairead's 9/11 related cancer, an NYPD psychiatrist out to get Paddy's job, and a triple-homicide no one wants solved compete to wreck their worlds. It'll take a miracle and some old-school detective work to get them through it. Another must-read from Author Michael O'Keefe."

Dr. Gabriella Rosetti, PHD, Amazon-top-Rated Reviewer

Michael O'Keefe

"O'Keefe writes of the city streets he used to police with the veracity of a New York City Joseph Wambaugh. The world of *Burnt to a Crisp* is frequently an ugly one, steeped in suffering and loss. But O'Keefe's writing never lacks for urgency and thrills. You are in the hands of a talented and knowledgeable author whose life bleeds through the pages."

Tom Wickersham
The Mysterious Bookshop, New York City

Want more Michael O'Keefe?

Check him out @

WWW.MichaelOkeefeAuthor.com

Sign up for his newsletter to get free stuff, like original poetry and samples of upcoming books!

Michael O'Keefe

Previous books by the author

Shot to Pieces, a Detective Paddy Durr novel—2016

Not Buried Deep Enough, a novella—2017

13 Stories-Fractured, Twisted & Put Away Wet-short fiction—2018

A Reckoning in Brooklyn-a Prequel in the Detective Paddy Durr Series—2019

Available on Amazon.com and wherever fine books are sold.